About the Authors

Lynne Marshall has been a Registered Nurse in a large California hospital for over twenty-five years. She has now taken the leap to writing full-time, but still volunteers at her local community hospital. After writing the book of her heart in 2000, she discovered the wonderful world of Mills & Boon Medical Romance, where she feels the freedom to write the stories she loves. She is happily married, has two fantastic grown children, and a socially challenged rescued dog. Besides her passi... loves to travel and rea... long walks every day...

To find out more ab... www.lynnemarshallw...

Alison Roberts lives in Christchurch, New Zealand, and has written over sixty Mills & Boon Medical Romances. As a qualified paramedic, she has personal experience of the drama and emotion to be found in the world of medical professionals, and loves to weave stories with this rich background—especially when they can have a happy ending. When Alison is not writing, you'll find her indulging her passion for dancing or spending time with her friends (including Molly the dog) and her daughter Becky, who has grown up to become a brilliant artist. She also loves to travel, hates housework, and considers it a triumph when the flowers outnumber the weeds in her garden.

Caroline Anderson is a matriarch, writer, armchair gardener, unofficial tearoom researcher and eater of lovely cakes. Not necessarily in that order! *What Caroline loves:* her family. Her friends. Reading. Writing contemporary love stories. Hearing from readers. Walks by the sea with coffee/ice cream/cake thrown in! Torrential rain. Sunshine in spring/autumn. *What Caroline hates:* losing her pets. Fighting with her family. Cold weather. Hot weather. Computers. Clothes shopping. *Caroline's plans:* keep smiling and writing!

Hot Single Docs

COLLECTION

July 2018

August 2018

September 2018

October 2018

November 2018

December 2018

January 2019

February 2019

Hot Single Docs: Giving in to Temptation

LYNNE MARSHALL

ALISON ROBERTS

CAROLINE ANDERSON

MILLS & BOON

Published in Great Britain 2018
by Mills & Boon, an imprint of HarperCollins*Publishers*
1 London Bridge Street, London, SE1 9GF

HOT SINGLE DOCS: GIVING IN TO TEMPTATION © 2018 Harlequin Books S.A.

NYC Angels: Making the Surgeon Smile © 2013 Harlequin Books S.A
Special thanks and acknowledgement are given to Lynne Marshall for her contribution to the *NYC Angels* series.

NYC Angels: An Explosive Reunion © 2013 Harlequin Books S.A
Special thanks and acknowledgement are given to Alison Roberts for her contribution to the *NYC Angels* series.

St. Piran's: The Wedding of the Year © 2010 Harlequin Books S.A
Special thanks and acknowledgement are given to Caroline Anderson for her contribution to the *St Piran's Hospital* series

ISBN: 978-0-263-26814-0

09-0918

NYC ANGELS: MAKING THE SURGEON SMILE

LYNNE MARSHALL

Many thanks to Mills & Boon for the opportunity to participate in this wonderful Medical continuity. Special thanks to Flo Nicoll for creating Polly and John, two characters I grew to think of as friends by the end of this book.

CHAPTER ONE

MONDAY MORNING POLLY SEYMOUR dashed into the sparkling marble-tiled lobby of New York's finest pediatric hospital, Angel's. The subway from the lower East Side to Central Park had taken longer today, and the last thing she wanted to do was be late on her first day as a staff RN on the orthopedic ward.

Opting to take the six flights of stairs instead of fight for a spot in one of the overcrowded elevators, she took two steps at a time until she reached her floor. As she climbed, she thought through everything she'd learned the prior week during general hospital orientation. Main factoid: Angel Mendez Children's Hospital never turned a child away.

That was a philosophy she could believe in.

Heck, they'd even accepted her, the girl whose aunts and uncles used to refer to as "Poor Polly". It used to make her feel like that homely vintage doll, Pitiful Pearl. But Angel's had welcomed her to their nursing staff with open arms.

Blasting through the door, completely out of breath, she barreled onwards, practically running down a man in a white doctor's coat. Built like a football player, the rugged man with close-cropped more-silver-than-brown hair hardly flinched. He caught her by the shoulders and helped her regain her balance.

"Careful, dumpling," he said, sounding like a Clint-Eastwood-style grizzled cowboy.

Mortified, her eyes shot wide open. Sucking in air, she could hardly speak. "Sorry, Dr.…" Her gaze shifted from his stern brown eyes to his name badge. "Dr. John Griffin." Oh, man, did that badge also say Orthopedic Department Director? He was her boss.

She knew the routine—first impressions were lasting impressions, and this one would be a doozy. Without giving him another chance to call her "dumpling"—did he think she was thirteen?—she pointed toward the hospital ward and took off, leaving one last "Sorry" floating in her wake.

At the nurses' station, she unwrapped her tightly wound sweater, removed her shoulder bag and plopped them both on the counter. "I'm Polly Seymour. This is my first day. Is Brooke Hawkins here?"

The nonchalant ward clerk with an abundance of tiny braids all pulled back into a ponytail lifted his huge chocolate-colored eyes, gave a forced smile and pointed across the ward. "The tall redhead," he said, barely breaking stride from the lab orders he was entering in the computer.

Gathering her stuff, and still out of breath, Polly made a beeline for the nursing supervisor. Brooke's welcome was warm and friendly, and included a wide smile, which helped settle the mass of butterflies winging through Polly's stomach.

Brooke glanced at her watch. "You must be Polly and you're early. I wasn't expecting you until seven."

"I didn't want to miss the change-of-shift report, and

I don't have a clue where to put my stuff or which phone to clock in on." Would she ever breathe normally again?

"Follow me," Brooke said, heading toward another door, closer to the doctor. "I see you already ran into our department director, Dr. Griffin. Literally," Brooke said, with playful eyes and a wink.

Polly put her hand to the side of her face, shielding her profile from the man several feet away and still watching her. "I think he thought I was a patient."

"Did he smile at you?"

"Yes."

"Then he definitely thought you were one of our patients. He doesn't smile for staff."

An hour later, completely engrossed in taking vital signs in a four-bed ward of squirming children wearing various-sized casts, splints and slings, Polly heard inconsolable crying. She glanced over her shoulder. "What is it, Karen?" The little girl had undergone femoral anteversion to relieve her toeing-in when walking, and was in a big and bulky double-leg cast with a metal bar between them keeping her feet in the exact position in which they needed to be to heal.

Polly rushed to the toddler's crib and lowered one of the side rails. "What is it, honey?"

With her face screwed up so tight her source of tears couldn't be seen, Karen wailed. Polly could have easily done a tonsil check while the child's mouth was wide open, but knew that wasn't the origin of Karen's frustration. She lifted the little one, who weighed a good ten pounds more than she normally would have because of the cast, from the bed and cooed at her then patted her back. "What is it, honey, hmm?"

Perhaps the change in position would be enough to

help settle down the tiny patient. No such luck. Karen's cries increased in volume as she swatted at Polly, who sang a nursery rhyme to her to calm her down. *"Oh, the grand old Duke of York..."* Maybe distraction would work?

"Oh, look! Look!" Polly moved over to the window to gaze out over beautiful Central Park. "Pretty. See?" Praying she could distract Karen for a moment's reprieve, Polly pointed at the lush green trees, many with colorful white and pink blooms still hanging on though late June.

"No!" Karen shook her head and kept crying.

Polly bounced Karen on her hip, as best she could with the toddler's cast, and jaunted around the room with her. "Let's take a horsey ride. Come on. Bumpity, bumpity, bumpity, boom!"

"No boom!" Karen would have nothing to do with Polly's antics.

"I'm going to eat you!" Polly said, digging into Karen's shoulder and playfully nibbling away. "Rror rror rrr."

"No! No eat me."

Felicia, the five-year-old in the corner bed with a full arm cast began to fuss. "I want a horsey ride."

Polly danced over towards Felicia's crib-sized bed, which looked more like a cage for safety's sake. Factoid number two from orientation: hospital policy for anyone five or under. "See, Karen, Felicia wants a horsey ride."

Now both girls were crying, and all the goofy faces and silly songs Polly performed couldn't change the tide of sadness sweeping across the four-bed ward. Erin, in bed C, with her arm in a sling added to the three-part harmony. The only one sleeping was the little patient in bed D, who would surely be awakened by the fuss. What the heck should she do now?

"Hold on," a deep raspy voice said over her shoulder. "This calls for emergency measures."

Polly turned to find Dr. Griffin filling the doorway. He dug in his pocket and fished out a handful of colorful rubber and waved it around. Making a silly face at Karen, he crossed his eyes, stretching his lips and blowing out air that sounded like a distant elephant. Polly tried not to laugh. Quicker than a flash of rainbow he diverted the children's attention by inflating long yellow and green balloons and twisting them into a swan shape. Factoid number three: all balloons must be latex-free. How did he get them to stretch like that?

"Here you go, Karen. Now go and play with your new friend," Dr. Griffin said.

To Polly's amazement, Karen accepted the proffered gift with a smile, albeit a soggy smile in dire need of a tissue.

"Me next!" Felicia reached out her good arm, her fingers making a gimme-gimme gesture.

Dr. Griffin strolled over to her bedside and patted her hand. "What color do you want?"

"Red," she said, practically jumping up and down inside the caged crib while she held onto the safety bars.

"Do you want a fairy crown or a monkey?"

"Both!"

In another few seconds Felicia wore a red crown with a halo hovering above, and gave a squeaky balloon kiss to her new purple monkey friend.

Dr. Griffin glanced at Polly, with victory sparkling in his dark eyes. The charming glance sent a jet of surprise through her chest. Blowing up two more balloons and twisting them into playful objects, he handed one to the remaining child and left another on the sleeping girl's bed, then sauntered toward the door. *Was he confident or what?* He stopped beside Polly, who had just finished putting Karen back into her crib, and blew up one last balloon. It was a blue sword, and he handed it to her. "Use this the next time you need to save the day." He glanced around the room at the quietly contented children. "That's how it's done," he said.

Polly could have sworn he'd stopped just short of calling her dumpling again.

He left just as quickly as he'd entered and she paused in her tracks, feeling a bit silly holding her blue balloon sword. Outside she heard a child complaining to the nurse. "I'm sick of practicing walking."

Dr. Griffin joined right in. "I double-dog dare you to take ten more steps, Richie," he said. "In fact, I'll race you to that wall."

Was this really the man the staff said never smiled?

Humbled by the gruff doctor's gift with children, Polly went about her duties giving morning medications and giving bed baths to three of her four patients. At midmorning the play therapist made a visit, relieving her of both Karen and Felicia for an hour. Erin's mother had also arrived, which gave Polly one-on-one time with her sleeping princess, Angelica, the most challenging patient of all. She had type I osteogenesis imperfecta and had been admitted for pain control of her hypermobile joints. Her condition also caused partial hearing loss, which was probably why the three-year-old had slept through the ruckus earlier.

Thinking twice about waking the peacefully sleeping toddler, Polly gazed affectionately at her then drifted to the desk and computer outside the four-bed ward to catch up on her morning charting.

"How are things going?" Darren, a middle-aged nurse with prematurely white hair pulled back into a ponytail, asked. By the faded tattoo on his forearm, she knew he had once been in the navy.

"Pretty good. How about you?"

"Same as always. Work hard, help kids, make decent money, look forward to my days off."

So far Polly wasn't impressed with the general morale of the ward. Everyone seemed efficient enough, skilled in their orthopedic specialties, but, glancing around, there didn't seem to be any excess energy. Or joy. She found it hard to live around gloom, and had learned early on how to create her own joy, for survival's sake. Some way, somehow she'd think of something to lift the ward's spirit, or she wouldn't be able to keep her hard-earned title of professional people pleaser.

A physical therapist came by, assisting one of the teen patients who did battle with a walker. Polly gave a cheerful wave to both of them. The P.T. merely nodded, but the boy was concentrating so hard on his task that he didn't even notice.

Orientation factoid number four: Angel's is the friendliest place in town!

Really?

Polly turned back to Darren. "Can you show me how to work that Hoyer lift? I've got a special patient to be weighed, and I need to change her sheets, too."

"Sure."

"Sweet. Thanks!"

"Now?"

"There's no time like the present, I always say." Polly finished her charting and escorted Darren into her assigned room. Together they gently repositioned and lifted Angelica from the bed. The child stared list-lessly at them, her pretty gray eyes accented by blue-tinged, instead of white, sclera. "Are you from New York, Darren?"

"Yeah, born and raised. Where're you from?"

"Dover, Pennsylvania." She smiled, thinking of her tiny home town. "Our biggest claim to fame was being occupied overnight by the Confederates during the civil war."

Darren smiled, and she saw a new, more relaxed side to his usual military style.

"Don't blink if you ever drive down Main Street, you might miss it." Self-deprecating humor had always paid off, in her experience.

He laughed along with her, and she felt she'd made progress as they finished their task. She could do this. She could whip this ward into shape. Hadn't that al-ways been her specialty? Just give her enough time and maybe the staff would actually talk and joke with each other. She accompanied Darren to the door and sat at the small counter where the laptop was, and prepared for more charting.

"Yo. Whatever your name is." Rafael the ward clerk said, peering over his computer screen. "I've got some new labs for you."

After looking both ways for foot traffic, Polly scooted across the floor on the wheels of her chair in-stead of getting up. "Special delivery for me? Sweet. I love to get mail."

He cast an odd gaze at Polly, as if she were from an-other planet. When he found her lifting her brows and smiling widely, he quit resisting and, though it was half-hearted, offered a suspicious smile back. "Just for you," he said, handing her the pile of reports. "Don't lose 'em."

Brooke came by as Polly perused her patients' labs. "How're things going so far?"

"Great! I really like it here. Of course, it's ten times bigger than the community hospital where I worked the last four years."

"We call it controlled chaos, on good days. I won't tell you what we call it on bad days." The tall woman smiled.

Orientation factoid number five: Teamwork is the key to success at Angel's Hospital.

Hmm. Maybe the staff needed to go through orientation again?

"As long as we all help each other, we should survive, right? Teamwork."

Brooke glanced around the ward, with everyone busily working by themselves, and her mouth twisted. "Sometimes I think we've forgotten that word."

Which put a thought in Polly's mind. As soon as Brooke strolled away, she checked to make sure everything was okay in her assigned room, then went across the ward to a nurse who looked busy and flustered. "Can I help you with anything?"

The woman glanced up from calculating blood glucose on the monitor. "Um." Caught off guard, she had to think, as if no one had ever asked to help her before.

"Anyone need a bedpan or help to the bathroom? I've got some free time."

The woman's honey-colored eyes brightened. She pushed a few strands of black hair away from her face. "As a matter of fact, why don't you ask my broken-pelvis patient in 604 if he needs a bedpan?"

"Sweet," Polly said, noticing a surprised and perplexed expression in the nurse's eyes before she dashed toward 604.

Polly took her lunch-break with two other nurses and a respiratory therapist in the employee lounge. They'd all brought food from home like she had. She'd have to count her pennies to survive living in New York City.

"Is your hair naturally curly?" One of the other young nurses asked, as they ate.

Polly slumped her shoulders. "Yes. Drives me nuts most days."

"Are you kidding? People pay big money to get waves like that."

"And people pay big money to have their hair straightened, too," the other nurse chimed in.

"Well, I can't pay big money for anything but rent," Polly said. The two nurses and R.T. all grinned and nodded in agreement. "That's why I stick to my hairband and hope for the best." She thought about her most uncooperative hair on the planet, and as if that wasn't curse enough, it was dull blonde. Dishwater blonde as her aunt used to call it. How many times had she wished she could afford flashy apricot highlights, or maybe platinum. Maybe get a high-fashion cut and style to make her look chic. Only in her dreams. The last thing she'd ever be described as was chic, and hair coloring was completely out of the question these days.

She took another bite of her sandwich and noticed everyone zoning out again. The silence was too reminiscent of her childhood, being shipped from one aunt and uncle to another, and how they'd merely tolerated her presence out of duty. The sad memories drove her to start yet another conversation.

"Do you guys ever go out for drinks after work? I mean, I know I just said I'm counting my pennies, but seeing that it's my first day on the ward and all, well, I'd kind of like to get to know everyone a little better. You know, in a more casual setting?"

She saw the familiar gaze of people once again thinking she'd arrived from another universe. "How expensive could a drink or two at happy hour be?" she said. "And wouldn't we miss the rush hour on the subway that way, too?"

"You know, I don't even remember the last time we went out for drinks," the first nurse said, forking a bite of enchilada into her mouth.

"Have we ever gone out for drinks?" the second nurse asked, sipping on a straw in her soft drink can.

"I think once in a while we organize potlucks, but…" The respiratory therapist with a hard-to-pronounce surname on his badge said, scratching his head. "I wouldn't mind a beer after work. What about you guys?"

"That's a great idea," Polly said, making it seem like the R.T. had thought up the plan. "Count me in."

"Where're we going?" Another nurse wandered into the lounge.

"To O'Malley's Pub, a block down the street," the first nurse said. "I hear they've got great chicken hot wings on Monday nights, too. Spread the word."

Well, what do you know, she'd pulled it off. One moment the room had been dead, now somehow she'd managed to infuse some excitement into her co-workers as they made plans to do something different. They smiled and chatted about their favorite beer and mixed drinks, and laughed with each other.

It always felt good to please people. It had been how she'd survived, growing up. She had a long history of perfecting her talent, too. A set of narrowing brown eyes and a raspy voice came to mind. "So who's going to invite Dr. Griffin?"

All went silent again. Polly glanced from face to face to face as they stared at her with varying expressions, all of which implied she'd lost her mind.

"What? You don't invite your department head for drinks?"

The first nurse cleared her throat. "Maybe one of the residents but, uh, he doesn't socialize with us."

"Yeah. He merely tolerates us, and only because he knows he needs us to take care of his patients," the second nurse said.

"But isn't he the guy who approves your raises?"

Three sets of lips pressed into straight lines as they all nodded.

"I dare you to ask him to come along," the nurse who'd just joined them said, as she finished heating her soup in the microwave. She laughed with the others at the ridiculous dare.

"Double-dog dare?" Polly had never heard that expression before Dr. Griffin had said it that morning, but figured now was the right time to use it.

"Triple-dog dare," the last nurse said, taking her place at the table and leaning forward with a clear challenge in her eyes.

Polly knew a set-up when she saw one. Let the new girl hang herself with the boss. Well, she'd seen a different side of him that morning and couldn't believe they'd never seen it too. "How bad can a person be who makes balloon animals for his little patients?"

The four other people in the room looked at each other rather than answer the question. That meant one thing. Polly, the diehard, would have to find out on her own.

As the afternoon stretched on, Polly was surprised by how energized the staff seemed since they'd made plans for after-work drinks.

Even Brooke approved. "This is just the injection of fun we've needed around here. I may have to nickname you Pollyanna."

Polly made her goofy face and shook her head. "Please, don't." Even though that was better by far than being called Poor Polly.

At four o'clock, the first shift of the day had ended and had handed over to the next team. Word had spread about everyone going for drinks at O'Malley's for happy hour, and more than half of the staff had signed on. Some of the evening shift wished they could go, too. Not bad for her first day.

Polly tied her sweater around her waist and licked her lips. "I'll see you all down there in a few minutes."

She'd promised to invite Dr. John Griffin, and she always kept her promises. She walked to the far side of the sixth-floor hospital wing. Staring down the hall at his closed office door, she took a deep breath and strode onward.

Someone knocked at the door. John made a face because it interrupted his train of thought, thoughts he'd been avoiding all day. Just one day. That's all he asked. One day not to remember images from twelve years ago. One day without memories sweeping over him, wrenching his gut. Was it too much to ask for? There was a second knock. "Who is it?"

All he could hear was some whispery childlike sound, but he couldn't make out a single word. Irri-

tated, he raised his voice. "Come in. It's not locked."
He tossed his pen across the desk blotter and leaned
back in his chair.

Peering around the opening door were big blue eyes.
Those big blue eyes. Son of a gun, it was dumpling,
the young woman he'd mistaken for a teenage patient
that morning. Damned if he was going to be the first
to speak, he sat watching her enter his office. First her
head and shoulders came round the door. Next one foot.
Then the other foot cautiously followed suit. There she
was, as large than life, except in her case that equaled
a petite picture of youth and enthusiasm—the last thing
on earth, and especially today, that he needed. When
the hell had been the last time he'd actually felt enthusiastic about anything?

With one hand behind her back, she cleared her
throat. "Hi, Dr. Griffin."

He sat as still as a boulder. Sure, he'd heard the rumblings about everyone going out for drinks after work
that night, and little miss bright eyes being the instiga-
tor. Well, he wanted nothing to do with it. He didn't believe in fraternizing with his staff. It didn't set a good
example. And even if he changed his mind, today would
be the last day of any year he'd choose to break his hard
and fast rule.

"Um…" Polly edged closer one tiny step at a time
as he stared her down. "A bunch of us are going to
O'Malley's for some hot wings and beer, and…" She
scratched her nose, her eyes darting around the room
to avoid meeting his stare. "Well, I was, um, I mean,
we were hoping you'd join us."

"And why would I do that?" Even for him it came
out gruffer than he'd meant.

She studied her feet. "To help raise your staff's morale?"

"Morale? What's that?"

"When people enjoy coming to work, and work better because of it?" She looked all of fifteen standing there, thick wavy dark blonde hair gathering on her shoulders, saucer-sized eyes, chewing her lower lip, hands behind her back, yet somehow seeming courageous.

Normally, he wasn't into torture, but she'd been the one to come to him. It might be twisted, but making her squirm also distracted him from those morbid thoughts looping over and over in his mind.

"Are you their sacrifice?" he said. She glanced up, looking perplexed. "Did they put you up for the fall, being the new girl and all?"

"No, sir. I *wanted* to invite you. It was my idea."

Her near opaque aqua eyes finally found their mark, and the sight of this young woman staring at him made the hairs on his arms rise. His wife had had eyes exactly like hers. Earlier today, they had been the first feature he'd noticed about the new nurse. Everything else about her physically was completely different from his wife, except those eyes. God, he missed Lisa.

But all the wishing in the world couldn't bring her back.

"Do they need their morale raised?" he said, sounding dead flat even to himself. Who the hell was going to raise his morale? "Don't they have lives to go home to every day? Doesn't that raise their spirits enough without me having to babysit them in a bar, too?"

"They don't need a babysitter. We'd all like to share a drink together, that's all." He saw the pink blush begin on her cheeks and spread rapidly to her neck and ears.

He wasn't a monster. He felt bad that he'd made her feel so uncomfortable, but someone should have warned her about trying to involve him in anything social. Brooke had clearly fallen down on her supervisory duties.

All he wanted to do was go home, hide in a dark room, and bury his sorrow in a glass of perfectly aged Scotch. The world didn't need to know that today would have been Lisa's thirty-sixth birthday. How the hell would it look to be chatting in a bar on a day like this?

"I can't." He stood to signal their meeting was over.

"I double-dog dare you." She grimaced.

He folded his arms and one eyebrow quirked. Was she serious?

With a look of desperation she whipped her arm from behind her back, revealing the silly blue balloon sword he'd made for her earlier. "It's just that I was hoping to buy a drink for the man who saved my day, today. You and that jar of latex-free balloons on your desk."

By the earnest expression on her face he knew it hadn't been easy for her to come into his office and beg him to meet with his staff at a pub. A staff he kept socially at an arm's length yet depended on, no, demanded they give his patients the best medical care in New York. He'd always assumed their paychecks were thanks enough. Maybe dumpling had the right idea.

He didn't have a clue, neither did he care, what would make her need to include him. But the employees were all probably at the bar having a good laugh at the new nurse's expense about how they'd managed to set her up for failure. What a dirty trick. Some nurses really did like to eat their young and this Polly was definitely that. Young. Innocent looking. Fresh. Sweet. Ah, hell, be honest—attractive. He gave a tentative smile. She instantly responded with a bright grin and raised brows, and he was a goner. How could he let someone down with a reputation on the line?

Surely Lisa would understand.

"Okay," he said.

"Sweet!"

"One beer and you're buying."

She nodded, triumph sparkling in her bright blue eyes. "Gladly, sir." She pointed the way to the door with the balloon sword.

"That stays here," he said as he passed her on his way out.

She stifled her giggle when he impaled her with his dead serious stare.

One thing she'd already proved to him. This girl… er…*woman* named Polly was fearless. He liked that.

John had to admit the tall glass of house draft tasted great and felt smooth going down. His newest nurse, in keeping with her promise, had fronted the money to buy it for him, which made it taste all the better. She really wanted him there. When was the last time he'd been wanted anywhere other than in the orthopedic operating room?

The look of surprise on the faces of the group of nurses and techs when he'd walked into the bar had been worth the effort. Everyone had gone quiet for an instant before slowly winding back up to their usual pub noise. He could only imagine what they thought about him showing up, and wondered if anyone had taken bets. He and Polly had shared a quiet but victorious glance.

Chatty Polly had burned his ears on the stroll over, too. She'd practically burst with excitement explaining how much coming to New York and landing a job at such a famous hospital as Angel's had meant to her.

Good for her. The world could use more idealistic nurses. Yet he craved the silence of his apartment, where he could sit in the dark and stare out over the neighborhood—remembering the vacancy where the twin towers used to be, nursing his Scotch, which could never fill the bottomless hole in his heart. Shifting his thoughts to the here and now, he took another drink of his beer and gazed at fresh-faced Polly to help banish the image.

She sat beside him on a barstool, sipping pale ale that left a hint of orange on her breath as she continued to chew his ear. "I wasn't always interested in orthopedics. I saw myself as an emergency nurse." Her eyes went wide. Even in the darkened bar they sparkled. "That is, until I worked my first shift on a busy night with a full moon." She covered her face with long fingers and clear-varnished nails, and shook her head, then quickly peeked up at him. "I thought I was going to die!"

Was everyone this animated, or had he quit noticing? He'd be dead between the ears if he didn't admit she was cute, and likeable. She shrugged out of her sweater and he realized she'd changed her nursing scrubs, which had baby koalas patterned over them, for a clingy pink top that dipped just enough to reveal a full-grown woman's cleavage.

How had he not noticed that all day?

He took another drink and tried his damnedest not to stare. She removed her hairband and put it inside her combination backpack-purse, and those light waves curtained her face in an alluring way, coming to rest on her shoulders...which led his eyes back to her breasts.

He certainly wasn't dead. Just severely inactive.

But this wasn't right, staring down her shirt. He

needed to change his focus. "Bartender, the next round for this group is on me."

Everyone clapped and cheered, even a few people he'd never seen before in his life, and he took another drink of beer, feeling almost human again.

Polly wrapped her arm around his and squeezed. "Thank you!"

"You're welcome," he said, tensing, staring straight ahead, knowing his answer had come out clipped. He hadn't made contact with a woman like this in, well, longer than he cared to admit.

She must have sensed his tension and unwrapped her arm but moved closer on her stool. "So, Dr. Griffin, I've told you all about me, but I don't know where you come from."

The bartender delivered the drinks along the counter, and refilled the bowls with pretzels and mixed nuts.

"I'm a New York native."

"So your whole family is here, too?"

"My parents retired to Florida a few years back, and my sister lives in Rhode Island now."

"Are you married? Do you have any kids?"

If Lisa hadn't been killed he would have been a father of an eleven-year-old by now. But his world had officially ended the day he'd spent digging people out of debris as a first responder on 9/11. His always simmering emotions boiled and he snapped, "Look. I'm here for a drink, like you asked. My personal life is none of your business. You got that?"

A flash of hurt and humiliation accompanied her crumbling smile. One instant she'd been bubbling with life, the next he'd crushed it right out of her. Good going, Johnny. He had no business being around people.

She recovered just as quickly, though, straightening

her shoulders and sticking out her chest, eyes narrowing, as if this routine was nothing new to her. "Sorry for crossing the line, Doctor." She slipped off the bar stool and gathered her things and the glass. "Thanks for the beer." Then she wandered over to a group of nurses a few stools away and joined in with their chatter.

He chugged down the last of his beer, not touching the second glass. "How much do I owe you?" he asked the bartender.

He knew he had no business pretending to be like everyone else. He should never have let the pretty little nurse talk him into it. He was only good for one thing, and that was fixing kids with broken bones.

As for the rest of his life, well, that had officially ended the day his newly pregnant wife had gone to work and died on the twenty-second floor of the twin towers.

CHAPTER TWO

POLLY HAD SPENT the entire subway ride home seething over Dr. Griffin's sour attitude. What had she done to turn him against her? After a little cajoling he'd smiled and agreed to go to the bar with his staff. They'd had a brisk and energizing walk to the pub, enjoying the late afternoon sun and moderate June weather. He'd allowed her to buy him a drink, and he'd even made a grand gesture of buying the next round for everyone else.

All had seemed to go according to plan in the people-pleasing biz.

Then she'd asked about his family and the vault door had clanged shut. It hadn't been mere irritation she'd seen flash in his dark, brooding eyes, it had been fury. Plain and simple.

As she prepared for bed in her tiny rented room on the Lower East Side, where the shared bathroom and kitchen were considered privileges in the five-story walk-up, she couldn't stop thinking how she'd messed up that night. Clearly, she'd overstepped her bounds with Dr. Griffin. But how? Didn't everyone love to talk about themselves and their families? That was, everyone except people like her who had miserable memories of feeling unwanted and unloved, like she'd had since her mother had died when Polly had been only six.

She put her head on the thin pillow and adjusted to the lumpy mattress. Of course! How could she be so blind? The man was miserable with his staff. He didn't like to socialize. She'd dragged him out of his comfort zone and asked him about something very personal— his family—then everything had backfired. Something horrible had happened to that man to make him the way he was. Surely, no one wanted to be that miserable without a good reason.

She had to quit assuming that she was the only person in the world with family issues and that everyone else lived hunky-dory lives. Obviously, Dr. Griffin wasn't happy about his family situation and she'd hit a nerve with her line of questioning. Maybe he'd gone through a messy divorce. Maybe his wife had cheated on him. Who knew? But he'd attacked with vengeance when she'd dared to get too personal.

She'd let down her guard, let him skewer her with his angry retort, then, wounded and hurt, she'd brushed him off and moved on. In her world it was called survival, but he'd seen a flash of her true self the instant before she'd covered it up, just as she'd seen his. Well, touché, Dr. Griffin.

Polly folded her hands behind her head and in the dim light stared at the cracked ceiling and chipped paint—what could she expect from an apartment built before World War I?—and thought harder. Maybe she'd inadvertently hurt him as much as he'd hurt her, and, man, she'd felt his anger slice right through her. John Griffin wasn't a person to be on the bad side of. Somehow she'd have to make up for it.

Her eyes grew heavy from the two beers she'd enjoyed at the pub, but one last thought held out until she acknowledged it so she could drift off to sleep with a good conscience. She owed Dr. John Griffin an apology, and first thing tomorrow morning she'd give it to him.

The next morning at work, Dr. Griffin was nowhere to be found. Polly realized during report that Tuesdays and Thursdays were his scheduled surgery days, and felt a mixture of relief and impatience about getting her apology over and done with. She'd never make the mistake of including her boss in any social event again, even though the staff was already talking about another pub night in two weeks. Something else she noticed today was that everyone smiled at her, which made her feel good and far more a part of the team than she had yesterday. At least she'd succeeded in pleasing some people around here.

Her patient assignment was heavy, and although she only had two patients, each needed a great deal of care. Charley was sixteen and in a private room after he'd taken a header on his skateboard, breaking several bones and his pelvis. Her second patient was in surgery and would arrive later in the day after a short stint in the recovery room. Fifteen-year-old Annabelle would also have a private room, having undergone an above-the-knee transfemoral amputation for localized Ewing sarcoma of the lower part of the right femur.

Polly's heart ached for her patient. She'd already been briefed that a team of social workers, psychologists, occupational and physical therapists, as well as wound-care specialists, would be participating in her recovery. Polly would take care of the nursing portion, and for today it would mostly be post-operative care—basic and important for pain control and maintaining strong vital signs. She'd guard against any post-op complications, such as bleeding or infection, to the best of her ability. Tomorrow the reality of being a teenager with a leg amputation would require help from each and every member of that specially organized medical team.

"Here, Charley." Polly handed a washcloth lathered with soap to her shattered-pelvis patient. "You wash your face, neck and chest. I'll help with your back when you're ready."

She believed in letting patients do as much for themselves as possible. Fortunately, Charley had one good arm, and with the overhead frame with trapeze he could lift himself enough to allow her to change the sheets and replace the sheepskin beneath his hips.

She kept a doubled sheet over his waist to give him privacy as they progressed with his bed bath. "Do you miss school?"

He gave a wry laugh. "I miss my friends."

"How are you going to keep up with your studies while you recover?"

He scrubbed his smooth face and chest with the cloth. "They're going to send out a tutor or something. School's almost out for summer break anyway. What really sucks is I was supposed to start driver's training next month."

"Do people even drive cars in New York?"

"I live in Riverdale."

Polly didn't have a clue where Riverdale was but assumed it was a suburb of the city. She'd never, ever want to attempt driving in New York, where being a pedestrian was risky enough.

She washed his back and changed the linen, keeping casual and friendly banter going. "Have you got a girlfriend?"

"Nah. We broke up."

Uh-oh, here she went again, venturing into personal

information that might cause pain. Would she ever learn her lesson? At least he hadn't bitten her head off like Dr. Griffin had. "I'm sorry to hear that."

"It's okay. All she ever wanted was for me to buy her stuff, anyway."

Whew. "Sometimes teenage girls can be very superficial."

"Dude, tell me about it."

Polly gathered the soiled linen she'd heaped onto the floor and shoved it into the dirty-linen hamper just as the door swung open. "Well, look here, perfect timing. Lunch!"

The tall, bronze and buff dietary worker brought in Charley's lunch tray and placed it on the bedside table. Polly washed her hands and checked to make sure they'd delivered the right diet, with extra protein and calories for the growing and healing boy, then left him alone to eat with the TV on while she got his noontime medicine.

When she returned from her own lunch-break the ward clerk informed her that Annabelle was on her way up from Recovery. Polly rushed to the private room to make sure everything was in order then quickly checked up on Charley, who was fine and playing a video game. She explained she'd be busy for a while but made sure his call light and urinal were within reach in case he needed them.

Just as she exited the room she saw the orderly pull a gurney out of the elevator. At the other end was Dr. Griffin in OR scrubs. It was the first time she'd seen him that day and, taken by surprise, her stomach did a little clutch and jump. Would he still be furious with her?

Focused solely on the task, Dr. Griffin helped get

Annabelle into her room. Polly jumped in. "I'll get this, Dr. Griffin."

He let her take the end of the gurney but followed her into the room. She'd pulled down the covers on the hospital bed and had already padded the bed with a layer of thin bath blanket, an absorbent pad and had topped both with a draw sheet in preparation for her patient. She checked to make sure the IV was in place and had plenty of fluid left in the IV bag. Annabelle was in a deep dream state, most of her right leg was missing and the stump was bandaged thickly and thoroughly.

"Careful," Dr. Griffin warned the orderly as he lowered the side rail on the gurney and prepared to transfer the patient to the bed.

Polly rushed to the other side of the bed, got on her knees on the mattress and leaned over to grab the pull-sheet underneath Annabelle toward her. To her surprise, Dr. Griffin came around to her side of the bed and helped out.

"On the count of three," Polly said, as the orderly prepared to pass the patient over from the gurney while they all tugged her onto the mattress. After she counted, they made a quick and smooth transfer. The patient moaned briefly and her eyes fluttered open, but she quickly went back to sleep.

As the orderly left the room Dr. Griffin gave a rundown of Annabelle's vital signs, a job the recovery nurse usually did over the phone, giving Polly the impression of how important the operation and follow-up care were to this orthopedic surgeon.

He ran down the list of antibiotics and pain-medication orders as Polly listened and adjusted the pillow under Annabelle's head. Next she placed the amputated stump on a pillow, checked the dressing for signs of bleeding or drainage, circling a quarter-sized area with her marker and noting the time, then made sure the Jackson-Pratt drain was in place and with proper suction before pulling up the covers.

Dr. Griffin ran his hand lightly over his patient's forehead, gently removing her OR cap and releasing a blanket of thick and shining brown hair. Such a tender gesture for an angry man.

"I'll check back later," he said, giving Annabelle one last, earnest glance before leaving the room. Polly almost expected him to kiss the girl's forehead from that sincere, loving parent-type look in his eyes.

How could she stay mad at a man like that?

"I'll take good care of her, Doctor," she whispered.

He looked over his shoulder and gave an appreciative nod.

Seeing him in his scrubs, OR cap in place, untied mask hanging around his neck, she realized how fit he was, and that his shoulders and arms were thick with muscle. Where he might look stocky in his doctor's coat, he really wasn't. He was just big and solid. For a man she suspected to be pushing forty, he was in terrific shape, and she allowed herself a second glance as he walked away.

"Hey, Doc G., you haven't signed my cast yet!" Charley called out from the next room.

"I'll sign all three, Charley, my boy," Dr. Griffin replied in a cheerful manner, changing his direction and somber attitude on a dime.

How could a man who was so great with kids be so lacking in people skills? It just didn't make sense.

Soon lost in the care of her newly received patient, and also checking periodically on Charley, the afternoon flew by. Before Polly knew it she was giving report to the next shift and preparing to go home. But she couldn't leave yet. Not before she apologized to Dr. Griffin. She'd promised herself she'd make amends today, and she always kept her promises.

Now that he was back from the OR, she knew where to find him and marched far down the hall toward his office as a new batch of butterflies lined up for duty in her stomach. Refusing to be timid this time, she tapped with firm knuckles on the glass of his office door.

"Come in."

Mustering every last nerve she owned, she entered far more assuredly than she had the previous evening, noting the irony in seeing a huge jar of colorful balloons on the desk of a generally grumpy man.

"Is everything okay with Annabelle?"

"She's doing very well, considering." Polly scratched the nervous tickle above her lip. "I medicated her for pain just before I ended my shift." She glanced around the room, with requisite diplomas and awards lining the gray-painted walls yet not revealing anything personal about the man, and took a long slow breath. "What I came for. Well, what I mean is I came here to, you know, after last night and how I upset you, I, uh, I just wanted to stop in and…well…"

"Apologize?" He'd changed back into his street clothes and white doctor's coat. His eyes were tight and unforgiving as they stared at her impatiently. Had she expected anything less?

"Uh, yes." Why did he make her so annoyingly tongue-tied? "As a matter of fact, I did want to apologize for whatever I did to make you angry last night." Heat flared on her cheeks. Frustrated by how uncomfortable he made her feel and how he offered nothing to ease her distress by sitting there just staring, she bit back the rest of her thoughts—*but you were a jerk about it, and anyone with half a brain could tell I didn't mean any harm by asking about your family. It's normal to want to know such things. Sheesh!*

Adjusting the neck of her scrüb top, along with her attitude, and desperate for him to like her, she continued. "I overstepped the mark, practically forcing you to go out with the rest of us, then I thoughtlessly insisted you open up and tell me about your family." She held up her hand before he could growl or get angry with her all over again. "Which I understand, as the new girl on the ward, is none of my business. So, yes, I came to apologize. Profusely."

She sat on the edge of the chair across from his desk before her knees could give out. "And I hope you'll accept it, because I really want to be a part of this orthopedic team. I want to help you with special patients like Annabelle." She stopped short of wringing her hands, choosing to lace her fingers and hold tight instead. "I want to help make your job easier by you not having to worry about the level of care your patients receive. I want to be a top-notch nurse, Dr. Griffin. I want to be that for you, sir." Could she possibly grovel any more?

"Stop it already." He brushed off her apology with a wave of his hand. "I was needlessly sharp with you last night. I should be the one apologizing."

"But I started it, sir."

He gave an exasperated sigh. "Okay. I accept your apology. But knock off the 'sir' baloney and call me what my friends calls me. Johnny."

Stunned by his instruction, she could hardly get her lips to move. "Johnny?" For such a simple name it sounded breathy and foreign, the way she repeated it. How could she call the head of the orthopedic department Johnny? Wasn't that the shortened form for young boys named John? It seemed only families would continue to call a grown man Johnny, yet he said his friends called him that. Was he implying she was now a friend?

"Right. Johnny. Now get out of here. I've got work to do." The terse words fell far short of carrying a punch, in fact they rolled off her back. Maybe she'd really gotten through to him.

"Sweet." She didn't mean to say that out loud and couldn't stop the smile stretching across her lips. "Thank you, Doctor. Uh, I mean, *Johnny*." She emphasized his name. "Thanks so much." She stood to go, relieved beyond her wildest dreams. How had this mattered so much to her in such a short period of time? She shrugged. All she knew was that her apology and his acceptance of it did matter. "I'll see you tomorrow." *Johnny-boy.*

"Good, because I want you assigned to Annabelle for the rest of the week."

"You do?" He trusted her nursing skills enough to ask her to take care of an extra-special patient. This was definitely progress on their ultra-rocky-start.

"Yes. Now would you please leave, or I'll never get out of here tonight."

Still smiling, she looked him in the eyes. His had softened the tiniest bit, but she could also see a slight change in attitude. Yes, she could. "Yes, sir." When she reached the door, calm washed over her and she turned round. "See you tomorrow, Johnny."

Already back at work, he nodded while writing, rather than look up. "Let's keep that name between you and me."

She'd accept that, too. This desperate need for him to like her would have to stop, but for now she was pretty darned glad she'd fumbled her way through the apology, and wondered how many other employees got to call their boss by their first name, even if only in secret?

John had to admit the sputtering woman on the other side of his desk had been strangely captivating. Perhaps it had to do with the fact that she was easy on the eye, energetic, full of life, and had a nice ass, too. When was the last time he'd noticed something like that? Her earnest and unrehearsed apology had done strange things to a few nerve endings in forgotten parts of his body. Not that he was into dominance and submission, but he really liked her baring it all, as it were, by nearly begging him to forgive her.

Hell, he should be the one apologizing to her. He'd treated her badly and had seen a flash of anger in her eyes, which she'd quickly covered up, and instead of calling him an ass, which he deserved, she'd taken the high road. She'd brushed off his remark with a mere flutter of her eyelashes and moved on.

That showed grit, and he liked grit in a woman.

He reached into a desk drawer, withdrew a bottle of water and took a long draw. Her Pollyanna attitude of be-nice-to-everyone was far from his own style, and probably a cover-up for her insecurities. A wry laugh escaped his lips. Who the hell was he to analyze anyone? His style was more make-nice-to-no-one because he didn't give a damn. But he had to admit she had a special way with kids. And his staff.

Remembering how she'd given a horsey hip-ride to Karen in her clunky cast yesterday morning made John smile. She'd been in way over her head with that group of toddlers so how could he not have gone to save the day? He knew his kids. Knew pediatrics. That was his comfort zone.

Adults were the issue for him. He didn't particularly like most adults, merely tolerated them. He had to get along with them if he wanted to continue to run the orthopedic department, and for the past twelve years his motto had been, Do what you have to do to survive, the kids need you.

How had he survived all these years without his Lisa? He pressed his lips together, allowing one little thought about Polly to slip inside his head. She oozed life, something he'd given up on, yet her vibrant approach to things really appealed to him. Maybe he wasn't as far gone as he'd thought.

Looking around the ward that afternoon, when he'd returned from surgery, he'd seen a more cohesive staff. They had been talking to each other and helping each other, even joking. He'd never seen them so happy.

The question was, had his sour attitude spilled over to his staff, and had this Polly from Pennsylvania saved the day?

Her big blue eyes and trembling lips came to mind. Why had he had the urge to run his thumb over her lips to test how soft they were? More importantly, what was with the impulse he'd had to wrap his hand around the back of her neck and drag her to him to test those lips on his?

When was the last time he'd given a woman permission to call him Johnny? What was up with that? What else might he get her to beg for so he could grant her permission? Most importantly, what in hell were these crazy sexy thoughts she'd planted in his head?

Maybe Pollyanna wasn't nearly as innocent as she let on. *Well, guess what, dumpling, neither am I.*

He guzzled more water and scratched his chest, surprised by his thumping heart. Antsy to finish his work and get the hell out of there, he veered his surprisingly sexed-up thoughts away from Pretty Polly and back to dictating his surgery reports for the day. Before he left he'd check on his kids, each and every one—like he did every day before he went home.

Maybe that was the reason he had been out of sorts yesterday at the bar. Maybe it hadn't been because she'd gotten too nosey, or had threatened his resolve never to feel again, or because he'd wanted to go home and brood, which he had to admit was beginning to get boring, even for him. He'd blame it on not saying goodnight to his kids, because he hadn't been ready to admit he was a man clinging so tightly to his past he'd forgotten how to socialize with the living.

Polly had rushed him away from work and he hadn't had a chance to tell all of his patients goodnight, and things just didn't seem right when he missed saying goodnight to his kids.

Yeah, he'd use that as the excuse for his behavior last night, otherwise he'd seem far too pitiful the next time he looked in the mirror.

CHAPTER THREE

THE NEXT MORNING Polly rode the hospital elevator up to her floor. A vibration in her pocket alerted her that a text message had come through her cell phone: *B in NY in 2 wks. Have dinner with me? Greg*

Rankled, since *Greg* had dumped her for another girl over a year ago, and she'd been heartbroken as well as angry at the time, she wrinkled her nose and shut off her phone with a harrumph.

"Bad news?" A familiar voice came from over her shoulder.

"Oh." She turned round. "Dr. Griffin, I didn't see you there." There were several people she didn't know in the overcrowded elevator but she hadn't noticed him mostly because she had been lost in her thoughts and hadn't been looking at anyone. Aching from her lumpy bed, already dragging from the daily rush to the subway, getting pushed and bumped the entire commute, and now hearing from an unwelcome voice from her past, she couldn't begin to paste on a cheery face today.

John edged closer to her. "You don't look happy."

She lifted a corner of her mouth. "I'm not. Old boyfriend just texted me." What did she care if he discovered that little miss Pollyanna from Pennsylvania was a sham, that her carefree moods were manufactured from hard work and years of practice.

"Sorry to hear that," he said, sounding curiously sincere.

"About the boyfriend or not being happy?"

"Both."

"Really?"

"Don't act so shocked." He gave her a John Griffin style smile, which meant it was hard to differentiate the smile between a grimace and/or gas.

"Do you actually notice things like people's moods?"

"No. Not usually."

What the heck did that mean? Had her self-deprecating plea last night in his office put her on his pity list? Maybe she'd overdone it.

"Well, thanks anyway," she said, lifting her brows and glancing toward the neon numbers indicating the floors, having run out of superficial things to talk about. The elevator stopped and several people got off.

He moved closer and whispered near her ear. "You know, you don't have to put on your forever-cheerful act for me."

Had he seen through her already? "Gee, thanks." She didn't mean to sound disrespectful, but he'd just given her permission to show her true feelings, hadn't he? She glanced to where he stood. There was that gassy grimace-style smile again and a playful glint in his eyes. Why did she find it cute?

Cute? John Griffin?

Maybe it was his mouth, the way the marginally off-center bottom lip curled out ever so slightly, making her want to take it between her teeth and nibble… just a little.

Come on, Polly, the guy is way too old for you. Prob-

ably pushing forty. And gruff as a bulldog. Who needs the aggravation? Besides, there was no way he'd ever be interested in her. Yet…that goofy attempt at a smile could only be described as cute. Charming, even.

The elevator came to a stop on the fifth floor and everyone else exited. Once the doors closed, John leaned his shoulder on the elevator wall and looked directly at Polly.

"Let's make a deal," he continued to whisper. "I'll show you mine if you show me yours."

She lifted her head from staring at her scuffed white clogs with the image of nibbling his lower lip fresh in her mind. "What in the world are you talking about?"

"Our moods." So he had seen through her carefully crafted façade.

"Well, no offense, Dr. Griffin, but I think I've already memorized your moods. Moody. Grumpy." She used her fingers to tick off the list. "Gruff. Did I say moody?"

What do you know, she'd coaxed out a real smile. "Yes. Smartass." He squinted graciously under fire, his dark eyes showing signs of renewed life. "Don't forget Bashful and Sleepy, if you're thinking of naming all of the seven dwarfs."

"And Doc. You definitely qualify for that one." She sighed, realizing that whatever this silly game was she was playing with *Johnny,* many of her cares had already evaporated in the stuffy elevator. By giving her the okay to be who she really was, warts and all, he'd liberated her from being Pollyanna. It felt pretty darned good. Hmm, had he said bashful? Him?

"Bashful? Not you," she said.

"Oh, yes, I am."

"I don't believe it."

"You'd be surprised."

The elevator door opened and they got out and headed their separate ways, she giving a genuinely bright smile, thanks to his lightening her mood, and he, well, still looking gassy but with an added spring to his step. That on-the-verge-of-flirting look he'd just sent her way was bound to stay in her mind and keep her smiling the rest of the day. The little fizzy feeling that look had given her hadn't been half-bad either.

Dr. John Griffin. Bashful? As in let the woman make the advance? Just what else might she be surprised about with him?

As Polly walked to the nurses' locker room, one more thought popped into her head. Johnny smelled good, too, like expensive aftershave and clean hair. Combine that with his rugged, all-man features and her new interest in the shape and angle of his mouth, thinking it looked all too kissable for a guy with salt-and-pepper hair, for a head of Pediatric Orthopedics, and she lost her step and tripped on the doorframe.

All things considered, Johnny Griffin had done a great job of lifting Polly's spirits that morning.

"How's my girl doing?" John asked Polly, entering the hospital room shortly after she'd taken Annabelle's midday vital signs.

"Great! Thanks," Polly said. "Annabelle's doing really well, too." She caught and enjoyed the quick confusion in his eyes before he got her joke.

"You've got a real smart aleck for a nurse, Annabelle." He took his patient's thin hand, and the gesture squeezed Polly's heart.

Annabelle gave a wan smile, and John lingered over her bed like a fussing papa until she closed her eyes.

Polly had given her pain medication through a shot into the hip a few short moments ago.

"The nurses told me she'd had a rough night, complaining about phantom pains, and when she started mentioning them again just now, well, I wanted to make sure she was extra-comfortable today."

He folded his arms across his broad chest. "Good. We'll give her some rest now, but by later this afternoon I want her out of bed and in a chair for at least an hour."

"Got it."

"Physical therapy will start tomorrow, and the wound-care specialist should pay a visit this evening when her parents are here to discuss dressing changes when she goes home."

"Yes, sir."

"You can knock that stuff off, too."

"You don't want me to follow your orders, sir?" Why did teasing her superior feel so delicious?

He took a deep breath, as if trying to suck in patience from the room air. "Are you trying to bug me?"

"Am I doing a good job…sir?"

"Very."

"Good," she said, straightening out the bedspread and double-checking the IV rate. She didn't dare look over her shoulder, but she sensed he was enjoying her feisty mood. Would any of his staff ever dare to give him a hard time?

"There's no excess drainage from the surgical site, and I emptied thirty ccs from the drain at the beginning of my shift," she said, all business.

He checked under the recently smoothed covers and found the Jackson-Pratt bulb was nearly empty. The quarter-sized marking on the post-op dressing hadn't gotten much bigger either, as he soon noticed.

"Good." He lingered at the bedside.

She'd decided, after her pitiful, stumbling apology, and especially their ride in the elevator, that he was a good guy, even if he didn't know it. He'd had the patience of a saint while she'd fumbled her way through her monologue, and he'd rewarded her by telling her to call him *Johnny*. Who else on the staff got to call him Johnny? Not that she ever would, at least not in front of anyone else, especially as he'd asked her to keep it to herself.

"Hey, Johnny." Another doctor entered the room.

So much for the short-lived "special person privilege" fantasy.

"Dave. Come to admire your work?"

"Sure did."

Polly surreptitiously read the other doctor's badge. David Winters. Vascular Surgery. Of course, with the amputation they'd have to make sure the stump had proper circulation, and who better to assist the orthopedic surgeon than a vascular surgeon?

"I was going to wait until later to change the dressing, but there's no time like the present. Polly, can you bring some gauze, dressings, four by fours and paper tape?"

"Sure. Would you like me to bring the Doppler too?"

"Great idea," Dave said.

She knew it was never too early to make sure there was proper circulation to the wound, and the Doppler would let them hear the blood flowing through Annabelle's vessels. A lot rested on every step of the recovery. In order to have Annabelle fit for a prosthetic device she'd need to have a strong and healthy stump. The post op-team, including Polly, would do everything in their power to make sure of Annabelle's success.

After dropping off the supplies, Polly took a quick look at Annabelle's surgical wound as John had already removed the dressing, and was surprised how clean and healthy the skin flap already looked. Cancer of the bone was a curse, but at least Annabelle would be able to wear one of the state-of-the-art prostheses being created these days. One day, when she was back on her feet and used to everything, wearing slacks or jeans, secure in her gait, no one would ever know that part of her leg was missing.

Later that day Polly took Charley his pills. She noticed the three signatures John Griffin had left on the teenager's casts, which made her grin. They were big, just like him, and colorful, hmm, and he had much nicer handwriting than she'd ever imagined any doctor could.

"What's so funny?" Charley asked.

"Nothing. I was just admiring your autographs from Dr. Griffin."

"He's cool."

"Really? He seems so stern all the time."

"Nah, he's funny. And he's the only person who hasn't given me a lecture about my skateboarding."

"Well, I guess accidents do happen, but maybe you should be more careful so as not to tempt the fates."

"Yeah, I get it. And I've heard that before, but yolo, you know?"

"Yolo?"

"You only live once."

So said a sixteen-year-old. "True, but preferably longer than shorter. Right?"

Charley blew her off with a toss of his long-hair. She needed to change the subject back to something lighter, something more interesting for both of them.

"I never would have pegged Dr. Griffin as funny."

"No? You should see him do his Aquaman drowning imitation. And he can sing like that weird guy who got kicked off that TV *talent show* last season, too."

"Are we talking about the same doctor?"

"Definitely. He's a laugh all right."

"Never in a million years would I have thought Dr. Griffin was funny or talented. I mean, the man seems to take himself far too seriously, in my opinion." A second too late, she saw Charley's eyes go wide.

"Is that so?" Johnny Griffin's familiar voice flowed over her shoulder.

"Oh! Hey. We were just talking about you." Heat rushed to her cheeks.

"So I heard."

"I'm afraid you're going to have to do your Aquaman impersonation for me before I believe Charley here."

Charley smiled and, amazingly, so did Johnny-boy. A look passed between them like a secret handshake.

"Stop by my office after work and I'll be glad to give you the whole routine," he said, sounding as though he might be flirting. Really? In front of a patient?

She pointed at him. "I'm tempted to call your bluff on that, Doctor."

"I dare you," he said, a playful, sparkly glint in his otherwise dead-serious eyes. Eyes that were becoming more and more intriguing each time she dared to look into them.

The rock-steady gaze caused a response that zipped down her spine with a surprise destination. What was going on here?

She wasn't sure, but one thing she was positive about, she needed to leave the patient's room before Dr. Griffin got an inkling of how much he'd just excited her.

* * *

Polly's cell phone rang during lunch the next day and she was surprised to see who was calling. It was Greg. She hadn't responded to his text from yesterday. Why the persistence all of a sudden?

"What's up, Greg?" She tried to sound nonchalant.

"Did you get my text?"

"Oh, uh, I've been working a lot. I guess I missed it." She wasn't above lying to someone who'd lied to her. Repeatedly.

He went into his spiel about coming to New York in two weeks and how he hoped to take her out to dinner and maybe even to see a Broadway play. This couldn't be the Greg she'd once known. Would he actually want to take her to an expensive play on Broadway? Not likely. Unless he'd finally come to his senses about what a prize she was. Again, not likely. Maybe he thought he could come to New York on business and cheat on his girlfriend with *her* while he was here? As in letting history repeat itself.

She wouldn't put a sleazy plan like that past him.

One thing was sure—she wouldn't have to find out if she didn't accept his invitation.

"Can you give me a couple days to think this over, Greg?"

"Look, I understand I treated you pretty rotten last year, but I'd really like to see you again."

"Give me a couple days, okay?"

She hung up before he could say another word, desperate to talk over this invitation with someone else. Her best friend back home worked the evening shift and Polly didn't feel comfortable yet about opening up to anyone on staff about her personal issues.

She ate her lunch in silence, deep in thought, then

as she took a bite of her tuna fish sandwich she practically fell out of her chair when one person popped into her head. Johnny. He was the one person on staff she'd made a complete fool out of herself in front of. Now she'd advanced to being able to tell him exactly what she thought and how she felt, even in front of patients and other staff members, much to everyone's surprise. Hadn't he invited her to show him hers if he could show her his in the moody moods department?

She'd tested the waters and had had a great time being completely herself around him the last couple of days, and he had invited her to come to his office after work for the Aquaman imitation. She understood he had only put that invitation out there because of Charley listening in, but still.

Besides, the man had to be a good twelve or so years older than her twenty-seven, and there was no way on earth he'd ever be interested in her. So that wouldn't be an issue. Even if that look he'd given her yesterday had confused her and turned her on.

John seemed level-headed and world-weary. Why not run her dilemma by him? As a guy, he'd have good input for her. It might help her figure out Greg's true intentions, though she had her own strong suspicions. She'd bought herself two days before she had to get back to Greg.

Maybe Johnny could help her see things how they really were. Now, if she could only work up the nerve to approach him.

On Friday evening, for the third time in a week, a light tapping on John's office door interrupted his concentration on the computer. "Come in."

The best thing he'd seen all afternoon, well, since

the last time he'd seen her anyway, which had been two days ago, walked in.

Polly wore black, straight-leg jeans and high wedge heeled shoes with open toes. Red toenails seemed to smile up at him. Her bright blue top clung to her body in soft folds and outlined her breasts and curves in an inviting way. Since when had he noticed what a woman wore, or how much he liked it?

"Finally came to see my Aquaman imitation, did you?" He pretended not to be distracted by how fantastic she looked.

She smiled, a look that spread like warm butter across her face. "Not really."

"What are you still doing here?" he asked.

"I was going to see a movie tonight, and needed to hang around until eight."

She brushed her bangs across her forehead. The rest of her hair hung loose and free, something he hadn't gotten to see while she was on duty or since the bar on Monday night. The waves and curls accentuated her features, big eyes, straight nose, those well-shaped lips, forcing him to realize she was pretty. Damn, she was pretty. "I was just going to pick up some pizza, wondered if you'd like me to bring you a piece, as you're obviously still here at six-thirty."

The thought of pizza did sound good, but if she expected him to join her in the employee lounge, she had another thought coming. "You deliver, too?"

"Sure, if that's what you want."

What he wanted. Well, the picture of youth and suppleness in front of him gave a whole new meaning to what he wanted. Polly had started a domino effect of interest, attraction, challenge, and all-out lust since her arrival this week. He'd spent more time in the last five days missing and thinking about the wonders of sex than he had in all the years since Lisa's death. It wasn't right, but he couldn't stop himself.

For whatever reason, Polly had the right combination of charm and good looks to make his body involuntarily take notice. The thought was wrong on so many levels yet he couldn't give it up. She worked for him, for crying out loud, and what about Lisa? Well, that was a whole other matter.

Maybe having a piece of pizza with the new nurse and having his little fantasy of making love to her might add some long-overdue entertainment. That wouldn't be such a bad way to spend an evening, would it? Compared to his usual Friday nights, a tasty slice of pie and a few naughty daydreams about the new nurse would be a welcomed change.

"You'd actually bring me a couple of slices of pizza, no strings attached?" He could think of a couple of strings he'd like to attach to a place or two on Polly, but that would be wrong on so many levels.

"Sure."

"You're too nice for your own damn good, Polly-anna."

"What goes around comes around, right?"

"That's only when the world makes sense, and most of the time there's no rhyme or reason about what's going on in the world." Especially now with these crazy thoughts about Polly, which seemed to be growing stronger by the minute. Man, he needed to get a grip.

"Are we talking pizza or philosophy?"

He smiled, letting her youthful beauty warm up his innards and tease at that other kind of appetite he couldn't shake. "Maybe a little of both." He sat back in his chair and put his hands behind his head. Was right now one of those life moments a guy was supposed to grab with gusto, or was he going off the deep end? "Can I ask you a question?"

"Of course."

"Why don't I scare you off like I do everyone else on the staff?"

She smiled, took a few more steps toward his desk, and perched on the edge of the chair. He liked the way she kept her knees together when she sat, all prim and uptight. He liked the scent of whatever she'd splashed on her skin after work, too. "It takes a lot to scare me off." She went silent for a moment. "You want the truth?"

Did he really want to find out how a needy people-pleaser like Polly had become that way? It could ruin this perfect storm of a fantasy brewing in his mind. He glanced at Polly, so appealing and open. He needed to quit thinking only about himself. "Nothing but the truth. Lay it on me."

"My mom died when I was six and my dad couldn't handle it. He took off without me. Later we heard he'd been killed in a car crash. After that I got shipped from one aunt or uncle to another. None of them really wanted me, though they pretended they did. Even a kid can tell when someone isn't being sincere, you know?" She gave a wry, lopsided and totally appealing smile. "So it takes a lot more than what you dish out to scare me off."

Her story snuck around his chest like a vine and tangled up his already confused feelings. It messed with those more basic thoughts floating around in his head, too. She'd been kicked in the teeth, and she'd gotten used to jerks like him giving everyone a hard time. It didn't settle well on his conscience that, in her world, he was one of the bad guys. Why did one person get kicked in the gut and become unbearable, while another learned to be sweetness and light. Exactly what kind of a heel had he turned into since 9/11?

He had a sudden need to make up for all the times he'd been an ass to her. As hard as it would be, he'd banish those sexual thoughts she kept stoking in his head and show Polly some long-overdue respect. "I've got an idea. Why don't you let me buy you dinner? I know a great Italian joint round the corner."

"Oh, I couldn't let you do that."

"But you will." He stood, took off and hung up his doctor's coat on the rack behind his desk, and walked towards Polly. "Let's go eat. I promise to have you back in time for your movie."

She stood and looked at her backpack and lunch container, and the small plastic bag with her soiled scrubs.

"Leave that stuff here," he said. "You can pick it up later. I promise to get you back in time for your movie. Besides, I've got to come back to say goodnight to the kids."

Her widened eyes showcasing those baby blues looked as though they were calculating a gazillion reasons why she shouldn't let him take over her dinner plans, yet she stood mute. If she'd had any clue how she turned him on, looking at him like that, she would run for cover.

Wondering how long he could keep his poker face, he took her elbow and nudged her along. "Come on, come on, let's go, I'm hungry." He'd use being gruff as his cover, because right now the feel of her skin beneath his fingers set off a whole new list of thoughts he hadn't dared to think in ages.

She lifted her brows higher, which seemed impossible, as if she'd felt something in his touch, too. "Okay, Johnny."

The Italian restaurant named Giovanni's was less than two blocks away, and though Polly's wedge heels weren't exactly made for walking—she'd planned to change into flats before heading for the subway home—she enjoyed the exercise. Being in a big, noisy, polluted city, surrounded by skyscrapers and cement—albeit with many well-kept neighborhood parks, not to mention Central Park to soften the blow—made her miss home. John looked after her as they juggled their way through the passing crowds, ignored crossing lights, and jaywalked to their destination.

Giovanni's was everything she'd hoped for in a restaurant—quaint, quiet, romantic, with tall, thin breadsticks waiting at each table and a handsome young waiter ready and willing to serve the diners. For a Friday night, the place was half-empty, and Polly wondered if it had anything to do with the food. Or if the time being only six-thirty in the city that never slept might have something to do with the small turnout.

Johnny knew the waiter by name and ordered a bottle of Chianti and a medium cheese pizza plus two dinner salads, without giving Polly a chance to change her mind about pizza for dinner. The list of pastas and seafood was impressive, but she had said she was going out for pizza, so she didn't fault him for that. She even kind of liked John's take-charge approach to all things in life.

While in his office she could have sworn there had been a flash or two of something in his eyes, after he'd ordered he gazed at Polly as if noticing her for the first time that day. That interesting curl of his lip stretched into a regular smile, like he was surprised and happy at what he'd found sitting across from him.

"I'm going to be straight with you and say I like your hair down," he said, shaking out his napkin and putting it on his lap, sounding more like he was reading the first order of business at an admin meeting than paying her a compliment.

"Thank you." A warm flush moved in a wave up her neck to her cheeks. Polly couldn't exactly say the sensation was unpleasant, and by the appreciative glint in his eyes he must have found her turning red appealing, which made her face heat up even more.

She'd noticed a few things about him on their walk over, too. Like the fact that he filled out his slacks really well and his broad back made even a man of his size look like he had narrow hips. He walked like a guy on a mission, too, which made it extra-hard to keep up, especially dodging traffic and crossing streets in her wedge-heeled shoes.

The Chianti came quickly, and after downing half a glass of her ice water Polly looked forward to sharing a glass of wine with her boss.

"So," he said, crossing his hands on the table top. "How did your first week at Angel's go?"

"Really well, thank you."

He nodded then took a long draw on his wine, all the while staring into her eyes. He seemed to hold the wine in his mouth before swallowing, as if savoring the flavor and aroma. Oddly, his sensual care with the wine set off tingles across her shoulders. He soon diverted his stare over her shoulder and, she assumed, through the window to the busy street.

"I've got to say, I'm rusty with this sort of thing," he said.

"What sort of thing?"

"Taking a woman out to eat."

Dr. John Griffin didn't date? Even with his gruff shell, that surprised her. He was a good-looking man, a doctor with a gentle heart for his young patients, a… well, she wasn't sure what else he had to offer, but she'd figured he had a full life.

"Don't think twice about it. I practically forced you to do it, so…"

He hushed her by putting his hand on top of hers, and with a no-one-forces-me-to-do-anything look stared her down. "I wanted to."

His touch sent her reeling, and though she thought she might jump out of her seat, she settled and went all quiet, taking in the full significance of his message. Why would he want to spend time with her? She was a country bumpkin, a girl still searching for herself. Sometimes it was better to drop all the questions and just be polite. "Thank you, Doctor."

He shook his head. "Knock off the 'doctor' nonsense. We left that back at Angel's, okay?"

"Okay," she said, as she took her first sip of the strongly flavored wine. "Johnny."

That got an interesting look out of him, one that made her replay her earlier blush.

Midway into her second piece of pizza she'd finished her wine and let John pour her another glass. Another sip or two later, plus more pizza, and she remembered what had really been on her mind since earlier in the week, and why she'd gone to John Griffin's office in the first place.

"May I run something by you?" she said.

"Sure." His mouth was full of the best pizza Polly had tasted since she'd gotten to New York.

She took another drink of wine and placed the glass on the sparkling white tablecloth. "I'm in a dilemma about something and don't know what to do."

He, swallowed, looking very interested in her line of conversation. "Go on."

"I've had a bad history of men walking all over me and, well, last year I got dumped by a guy back home. I'd really had it with men after that, and part of the reason I moved to New York was to move on and start a whole new life."

She could read his body language. Shoulders hunched over the table, his chewing had slowed down. He squinted. This was not a topic of conversation he was interested in but she needed to discuss her options with someone, and tonight that someone was John Griffin.

"So, anyway, a couple of days ago I got a call from Greg, the guy who dumped me without warning last year. He's coming to town and wants to take me out to dinner. He doesn't mean anything to me any more, but I'm thinking he at least owes me a nice dinner, plus he mentioned something about taking me to a Broadway play, too. I know it may sound superficial of me, but I was thinking I deserved some kind of explanation and maybe he'd tell me what was up last year."

He sat perfectly still, hands fisted on the table for a few silent seconds, his expression impossible to read. "He wants to screw you," Johnny said curtly, before taking another drink of wine.

She winced from what felt like a slap in the face. "You don't think I should see him?"

"That depends if you want to get screwed or not." His irritated gaze delved into hers, sending a crazy mixed-up message right down her center. Had she just annoyed him? She sat straighter, using the table to help her balance. Did she want to have sex with her ex? Had she even thought about it in the last six months?

No.

Not until the last few days, that was…and Greg wasn't the face to come to mind when she did think about sex. Oh, cripes, could Dr. Griffin read her mind? Did he have any idea she had the hots for him?

"I'm sorry," she said, putting her napkin across her plate. "I should never have brought up the subject. It's just that I don't have anyone to talk things over with. The lady I rent a room from is probably eighty if she's a day, and my best friend works evenings in Pennsylvania, so it's not like I can pick up the phone after work and talk."

"You asked my opinion." He tugged on his earlobe. "I'm giving it to you straight," he said, his eyes darting around the room in an agitated way. "Unless you want to have sex with the jerk who dropped you last year, don't go near him." He looked at her as if she needed to have a psych referral.

"You're right. I was leaning in that direction, too," she said, mostly to her plate. "I won't even call him back or text him. Thanks for helping me see that more clearly."

Polly sensed a change in John's suddenly irritated mood when she spoke those last words. He inhaled subtly and took another drink from his wineglass, then glanced at his watch.

"We should probably get you back to the hospital to pick up your stuff so you'll have time to get to that movie," he said.

She lifted her chin and gave an exaggerated nod. "Right." She'd blown it. A perfectly lovely dinner with her boss. Until she'd opened her big mouth about some other guy. Could John be jealous? Of course not.

The walk back to the hospital was quiet between them, but the streets, which had come to life with people heading out for the Friday night, weren't. Across the way, Central Park looked hauntingly beautiful in the twilight. John strode on, not saying a word, hands in his pockets, a man on a mission. She did her best to keep up, but her feet were killing her.

"Thank you for buying dinner, Johnny," she said, the only words she could think of. Hoping to remind him he'd given her permission to call him that.

"Any time, dumpling."

That got a smile out of her. He was a paradox. She'd been around many gruff men in her life, but had never cared what they'd thought before. Staring at his profile in the dimming light, she saw a proud man, a talented surgeon, a man respected, if not liked by his peers, yet a man loved by his patients. A man she suspected hid something awful behind his gruff demeanor. Truth was, she found him more and more intriguing and attractive by the moment.

Beginning on Monday, she'd steer clear of him, especially after making a fool of herself by asking him for relationship advice. Whatever had made her think that was a good idea?

Since there was no way in hell she'd ever have a chance with a man like Johnny Griffin, what was the point of being around him? Because she liked him? Found him sexy? The thoughts caused her to pause on the pavement.

That's when he reached for her hand, wrapping his long, strong fingers around it, and pulled her brusquely along the crowded street toward Angel's.

CHAPTER FOUR

POLLY TAGGED ALONG behind John at a fast and challenging clip. They rushed through the hospital lobby towards the elevator, past the "welcome" clown pacing on stilts and the piano player, who was smack in the middle of "Old MacDonald". Diverse entertainment for visiting hours. He moved like a man with a single thought on his mind—how to dump his dinner date. Yet he never let go of her hand.

Still not saying a word on the crowded elevator trip to the sixth floor, he tugged her down the hall and, having left his office door unlocked, whisked it open, practically dragging her inside. Only then did he release his grip. She went directly for her bags and personal items, assuming he wanted her gone. Now.

Why had she thought that offering John Griffin pizza was a good ice-breaker in order to bring up her question about whether or not to go out with an old boyfriend? All she'd done had been to tick him off.

He stood off to the side, staring out the window, hands crammed into the pockets of his slacks, looking like he was doing battle with a slew of demons in his head. Had she done that to him?

"I feel like you're mad at me," she said, stating the unmistakable.

He turned abruptly. "I'm not mad at you, I'm angry about how you try to please everyone else and over-look yourself."

She bunched her hands into fists. "I've had a lifetime of practice. Old habits die hard, you know?"

He tugged his earlobe. "I know."

Relieved that he wasn't fuming at her but was more irritated at her situation, a wave of mismatched feelings swept deep, causing confusion in her mind and her eyes to water. She glanced away.

"If you don't mind—" her voice sounded congested "—I'll change out of these shoes for the subway first."

He turned and watched as she sat on the edge of a chair. "I thought you were going to the movies." The man had gone tighter than a stretched rubber band and the muscle at his jaw twitched as he blatantly ground his molars.

"It was a comedy, and I'm kind of not in the mood now."

He cleared his throat. "Sorry."

"It isn't because of you." She slipped off one shoe. "I guess I just realized how tired I am. It's been a long day." She stretched out her foot and toes. "A long week."

His gaze jumped all over her, from her face to her chest to her hips and legs and finally to her foot. His ex-pression changed from indecision and caution to longing and oh-what-the-hell. Something had snapped in him, some decision Polly wasn't privileged to know, yet his change was as plain as the sudden jangled nerves in her stomach. He made an abrupt move, came in front of her and dropped to his knees. Without a word he handed her his handkerchief for her teary eyes then removed her other shoe. His warm, strong hands caressed her foot, sending shockwaves through her.

Polly stiffened as the idea registered of John Griffin giving her a foot massage. She inhaled raggedly while he gently worked the ball of her foot and the arch with amazingly talented fingers. Soothing sensations tiptoed up her calf, causing tingles behind her knee.

Oh, my God, what do I do?

A crazy answer popped into her mind as she wiped away the tears from her eyes with his monogramed handkerchief. *Enjoy it.*

He splayed her toes and worked each joint right out to the tips of her nails. She tensed and sighed, and felt his touch all the way up the insides of her thighs, though his hands never left her foot.

"The problem with women these days," he said, increasing the pressure on her heel, "is they mess up their feet with these super-sexy shoes. All men want to do is get them off." She looked down at his short-cropped, silver-salted hair, discovering a small endearing cowlick in the middle. His voice sounded hoarse, strained, like maybe he really *was* mad at her. Yet his hands told a completely different story. Was he turned on? "I say that as an orthopedic surgeon."

That made her smile, his rubbing her feet in such a sexy way yet trying to pull off a professional manner. He was looking out for her well-being, though, wasn't he? His ministrations were so amazing she couldn't help but sigh again, so he reached for her other foot. Call her easy, but her shoulders slumped and her head dropped back, savoring the heat of his hands on her totally susceptible skin.

"You're too kind to me," she whispered, shifting her gaze from the ceiling to his serious face as he concentrated on the task at hand—her foot. Her incredibly lucky foot. Her mind wandered to what it would be like if his hands touched her everywhere like that.

"This isn't about being 'kind' and you know it." He stopped his massage and delved into her eyes as if measuring the level of her understanding. She concentrated on his mouth and the hair-thin scar above his upper lip on the right. The growing warmth between her thighs weakened when he stopped touching her, but she'd read his message loud and clear.

He wanted her.

Just as much as she wanted him.

At some point, as he'd stood by that window, he'd made a decision. She'd sensed it then and felt it with every fiber now. Saw it in the serious dark eyes staring at her. Whatever he'd needed to overcome, he had, and now…he wanted her.

A deep desire to break out of her usual by-the-rules role and not to let this magical moment pass made her lean towards him, take his life-weary face between her hands and press a kiss to his irresistible mouth.

Surprisingly soft, his lips were warm and responsive, and he soon took over the advance, proving her hunch had been right. He needed her as much as she wanted him. His hands clamped around her waist, squeezing with urgency as he deepened their kiss.

She ran her fingers across his short, springy hair then down his powerful neck as she kissed him back. Solid. The man was solid. She smelled his lingering forest-scented cologne and enjoyed the end-of-day stubble of his beard. His tongue found hers and she let him have his will, matching exploration for exploration and tasting a hint of Chianti. The warmth pooling between her thighs quickly renewed as her pulse thrummed throughout her body.

A sharp knocking on the office door shocked her out of her dream about kissing her boss. Oh, wait, it was really happening.

"Environmental Services," a loud voice called. "Dr. Griffin, are you still in there?"

"Just leaving, Constantine, give me a couple of minutes." His voice sounded heavy and forced. Heat radiated from John's darkened eyes as he stared at her. "I know a place we can go. Will you come with me?"

The question of the day—will you come with me?

Overcome with his no-nonsense sex appeal, his smoldering gaze, and their incredible kiss, there was only one answer she could think of.

"Yes, Johnny," she whispered, banishing from her mind their age difference and concentrating on their total attraction to each other.

He hastily gathered her things as she used the back of her hand to wipe her already kiss-swollen lips, trying her best to recover from the mind-bending introduction to making out with Dr. John Griffin. She could barely wait for more as he grabbed his jacket and her hand and led the way out.

"Goodnight," he said in a clipped voice to the janitor as they passed, as if he dragged a woman from his office every night of the week and Housekeeping should think nothing of it.

Was the fact that she was barefoot a dead giveaway to what they'd been doing?

The janitor had his back to them, concentrating on his cleaning cart, and she was grateful as John whisked her down the dark hall toward the stairs.

He led her through the back way and down a couple of flights to another deserted floor, then past half a dozen doors to an open on-call room. Rushing her inside, he hung up the "occupied" sign and closed the door behind them. Immediately, he dropped all of her bags and items into a chair and took her by the shoulders, walking her backwards against the wall.

"Where did we leave off?" he asked gruffly, digging his fingers into her hair before taking her mouth again.

His kisses were hot and wet and making her dizzy with desire. She bunched his shirt in tight fists, wanting him as much as he obviously wanted her. His hand wandered over her hip, skimming her waist and upwards until he found her breast. His other hand cupped her bottom and pulled her flush to his groin. She could already feel his arousal straining against her thigh. Knowing how she affected him excited her beyond any fantasy.

His kisses grew frantic and desperate, and his fingers found their way under her bra. Her breast was already tensed and peaked and he ran his thumb over the tip, which tightened her more. Tingles fanned across her chest, teasing her other breast. She angled the V of her thighs over his erection, and leaned hard into him, yearning for relief. He moaned and pulled her up, positioning her on top of his wedge. She slid over him, begging for more, hating the fact that they were still dressed.

Breaking apart only because she wanted to be without barriers, she raised her arms and he lifted her top over her head in record time. She reached behind and undid the catch on her bra as he unzipped his pants.

"Should we be doing this?" she asked, her eyes adjusting to the darkened room, seeing him stripping in front of her and realizing there was no turning back. Not for her, anyway.

"You started it." He kicked off his loafers and

dropped his pants. Thickly muscled legs, like those of a Grecian god, made her gasp inwardly.

"I didn't think it would get this far." Impatient to be skin to skin with him, she moved fast and jerkily while her clothes refused to co-operate.

"It has." He helped her break free of the bra then moved her into a beam of slanting streetlight that had snuck into the room, and took the time to look at her topless and vulnerable, conveying with his eyes how much he liked what he saw.

Her nerves were quickly overcome by her desire, and after an eager glance at him she definitely liked what she saw, too. A combination of jitters and excitement flitted along her skin. He clamped his mouth on a breast, kissing and sucking, while he pushed on the waist of her pants.

On board with the total program, Polly understood this would be no-frills sex but long-overdue passion that could only be released in a flash and never fast enough. Ready for anything, everything, she squirmed out of her tight jeans and underpants while trying not to lose contact with his body.

Soon back to having her pressed to the wall, he sealed his lips tightly to hers and his heavy erection pressed into her belly. The rush and aroma of hot skin and stimulation made her squirm with need. His hand slid between her legs, fingers quickly discovering how ready she was. He positioned himself and she lifted her thigh and wrapped her calf around his waist so he could find her entrance.

Angling his full erection, he hesitated. "I don't have a condom."

"I'm on the Pill."

Her answer seemed to satisfy him, and he launched

into her, releasing a sizzling sensation that spread across her hips. A few more thrusts and she'd molded to his length and thickness, her moisture slickening him more with each move. The internal burning turned to smoldering and soon fire as he pushed into her over and over, setting off bells, whistles and alarms on every surface he touched.

It had been over a year since she'd made love with anyone, and her tightness intensified the sensations rolling through her pelvis and soon connecting with the shivers in her breasts. She ached for more as he drove into her again and again, thrilling her, making her beg he'd never stop.

Under the hold of his strong arms, her body banged against the wall. He emitted deep, throaty sounds as he continued to bury himself inside her hard and fast, seeming desperate to have all of her. As if humanly possible, he grew harder with each thrust. Though wanting to ride with him all the way to his climax, she couldn't hold out. Her mounting thrill became too intense to control as crazy sensations spilled out and over her like demons storming through her body. She gasped and bit his shoulder as she came, helpless to stop the powerful release. His continued forceful rhythm extended her climax until she was as limp as a ragdoll against him.

With an "Ahh" he came and she felt his warmth spread inside. With spasm after spasm she adjusted her hips and drew him even deeper than he'd been as he crumpled against her. They stayed in that position, she limp, he holding her flush to the wall, locked tightly together until every last tingle and pulse from the top of her head to the tips of her breasts and all the way down to the soles of her feet completed their course.

Taking her chin in the V of his hand, he bussed her

lightly on the lips. Near feral eyes burned into hers when he drew back. "I'm not through with you yet," he whispered.

Too numb to speak, she stared at him mesmerized, completely willing to be with him again, however he wanted it.

Still bound together, he carried her just as they were against the wall towards the small bed, as if she were a feather. With her legs still wrapped securely around his hips, he slowly and gently placed her beneath him on the mattress, careful not to lose their point of contact. Amazingly, he was still firm.

With a serious-as-hell gaze he lifted her arms above her head and clamped one hand tightly around her wrists, binding her to the bed. He bent and took a breast into his mouth and cupped the other with his free hand. Minutes passed with his soft, sexy torture of kisses here and nips there, his intensifying touch drawing her nearer and nearer to frenzy. When she squirmed and tried to free her hands he held her firm, completely in charge. Already on overdrive, every touch, nibble and kiss sent her reeling. She wanted more and more.

After a few more minutes he grew harder inside her and slowly began to move in and out, each thrust building force. Still a prisoner to his hold, she moved the only part she could, her hips. She matched his pace, adjusting her position to bring him closer, being rewarded with amazing sensations gathering and tightening in her core. Within a few more minutes he was back to full strength, and as he drove faster and deeper, her thrills intensified, coiling so tight she neared another release.

As if he could feel her mounting climax around him, still clamping her hands over her head, he broke contact with her breast, accelerated his thrusts, and smiled devilishly at her. "There's definitely an advantage to having sex with a people-pleaser," he said, quickly finishing her off.

Embarrassed by how easy she'd been to conquer, again, she laughed while she came, a complete first for her. He let go of her wrists and rolled onto his back, bringing her along. She straddled his waist and held tight, soon taking him right where she wanted him, helpless to resist her and completely at her mercy, just as she'd been with him only moments before.

After he'd come, she smiled down at him, kissed and licked the crease of his curled lips. "I'm not through with you yet," she said.

It was his turn to laugh. "So I *have* died and gone to heaven, huh?"

She rubbed her breasts across his chest and nestled into the crook of his neck, taking his earlobe between her teeth. "I haven't even known you for a week, Johnny," she whispered into his ear.

His hands cupped her bottom and squeezed tight, sparking new desire. "Crazy, isn't it?"

"Crazy good?"

"Definitely."

Before dawn, Polly woke up tangled up in John's arms and legs. The word "crazy" occurred to her again as she disengaged, used the shower, dressed and snuck out before John woke up. As it was her weekend off, she couldn't be seen sneaking out of the on-call room by any of her co-workers arriving on Saturday morning for the day shift without stirring questions. Fully dressed, hair damp and on her shoulders, she tiptoed outside, but not before glancing over her shoulder at John, who slept peacefully, then she quietly latched the door.

Lying there, listening to Polly shower and dress, John played possum when she left. Truth was he didn't know what to say to her. They'd amazed each other with great sex half the night, finally collapsing from exhaustion in each other's arms only a few short hours ago. He'd never let go so soon or so easily with anyone in his life until Polly the people-pleaser had arrived on his doorstep.

He scrubbed his face to help him wake up. What the hell should he do now? It was so out of character for him to screw an employee. The thought of running into her on the ward would be awkward as hell after everything they'd done to each other. How could he keep professional with her now?

He wasn't looking for a relationship. She was too damn young for him. Too sweet for her own good. Too wild and crazy in bed for a man still pining for his wife. He would be just as bad for her as that jerk she'd come to talk to him about. Why did the thought of Polly being with another man make his blood boil again, especially now that he'd made love to her? What right did he have to feel possessive of her? Wasn't he as bad as that guy after the way he'd brought her here to the on-call room for the sole purpose of making love until the burning she caused inside him finally stopped?

Thinking about her this morning, he realized the desire for her hadn't come close to burning out. But it had to. John Griffin didn't have gratuitous sex, especially with someone vulnerable like Polly. Or someone he worked with. He sat at the side of the bed, ran his fingers through his hair as he stood and headed for the shower. What about Lisa?

There were too many questions, but only one answer seemed to solve them all. He'd avoid Polly as much as possible, and once he worked out in his head just what the hell had happened last night and why, he'd explain to her that it was unethical and could never happen again. She'd have to understand.

That was his plan, and he'd have to stick to it, because he wasn't about to change his just-getting-by personal life for a flighty young thing like Polly Seymour.

Polly got on the subway heading for the Lower East Side. Not knowing what to say to him, she hadn't been able to get away from John fast enough. What had gotten into her? Granted, he'd taken her to the on-call room after giving her the most incredible foot massage of her life and, well, they'd taken the natural course from there. And wow. She hadn't held back, and neither had he. Never in her life had she done such a thing, had sex with a man she hardly knew. A man she worked for!

Sitting on the hard seat of the subway train, she wondered if everyone in the car, which was thankfully only a handful, could see her flush until her ears burned. She rested her head against the cold window and stared out at the quickly passing darkness. She wasn't about to act needy around Johnny Griffin. No. That would turn him off quicker than her kisses had turned him on. She'd have to ride out this awkward situation, see where John took it. As far as she was concerned, it was up to him to approach her. After the way she'd made love with him, the man at least owed her a thank you.

Allowing her mind to drift back to the night before and some of the amazing things that had occurred, she remembered that "thank you" swung both ways. Holy cow, did it ever.

On Monday morning Polly arrived at work with trepidation. Her palms tingled and her stomach clenched at the thought of facing the head of Orthopedics. Doubt upon doubt had cropped up over the weekend. Was having sex in the on-call room how Dr. Griffin initiated all the new nurses?

In her heart she knew that wasn't true. He loathed interacting with his staff, and after a week on the job she hadn't heard any rumors about his personal life... just that he was a loner who preferred the kids on the ortho ward to adult company.

Surprised to see that Annabelle had already been discharged, she took report on all new patients. Today she'd be nurse to four pre-teens in various sizes and shaped casts in a group ward.

In the middle of taking vital signs she heard John's voice outside. Nerves unfurled through her center, making her hands shake. Still unprepared to face him, she prayed he'd stay out in the nurses' station area and not come into her room.

The deep, masculine tone carried over the usual noise of the ward as he spoke to Brooke. "Tell your nurses to get their kids ready by nine."

Polly was still getting used to the non-stop activities of Angel's Children's Hospital. They even had an on-site radio show in the lobby, and often the kids were the subjects of interviews. The play therapists didn't allow the patients to zone out on video games or too much TV. They kept them interacting with other patients with games and challenges where everyone could participate. If a child was too sick to leave their room, they'd come to them.

Volunteer grandmothers and grandfatherly types regularly came for one-to-one bedside reading, and the children ate it up. Especially with the man who looked like Santa on his day off in a Hawaiian shirt and golf cap reading *Harry Potter* cover to cover.

Polly snuck a look outside her room just in time to see John turn and walk back toward his office on the far side of the hospital wing. Though not a tall man, his broad shoulders reminded her how strong he was. A quick flash of him naked and carrying her to the bed in the on-call room had her cheeks burning.

"Why're you red?" the girl with waist-length black hair and a full leg cast asked. "Do you have a fever or something?"

"No. I'm fine. Don't you ever blush?"

"Not unless I'm embarrassed. Are you embarrassed?" Her insightful, inquisitive eyes made Polly's skin crawl.

"Maybe a little."

"Why?"

Polly glanced around the brightly decorated four-bed ward, where stenciled sports equipment and swaths of primary colors made the white walls pop, as she searched for either a dodge or a believable answer. One thing she'd quickly learned working with kids was they could tell when someone wasn't being straight with them.

"I just remembered something I did over the weekend."

"Did you get hammered?" The young one's bright black eyes suddenly seemed far too mature for twelve.

"No. And how do you even know what 'hammered' means?"

"My sister goes to college." She tossed half of her hair over her shoulder, in a gesture that advertised she knew everything about being a grown up and drinking too much in college.

As if that explained and closed the topic, Polly let the subject drop, but not before she noticed John Griffin's signature on the girl's cast and she felt her cheeks flush again. Did the man sign every single cast on the ward?

As promised, at nine o'clock sharp a raucous brass quartet blustered onto the ward playing circus music, as if a parade would follow. Polly had gotten each of her patients into wheelchairs and rolled them to the center of the ward just in time. One of her girls wasn't the least bit interested in the music, instead staring at her cell phone, until the trombone player swung by and hit a low note by extending the slide right under her chin. It shocked and delighted her and Polly laughed along with the patient, especially when the girl glanced up and saw a good-looking college guy, and her eyes brightened.

In mid-laugh, Polly glanced up and caught John's gaze from across the room. It seemed a trapdoor had opened in her chest, and her heart skidded to her ankles. Maybe it was the circus music.

She couldn't inhale.

Attempting and falling far short of the mark, she gave some semblance of a smile, and in return he gave that half grimace, half smile he was so adept at then quickly looked away.

Could things get any more awkward?

By Wednesday afternoon, having great sex with John Griffin had started to seem more like a figment of Polly's imagination than fact. He'd drifted in and out of the hospital ward like a ghost leaving hints of things out of place, or the tell-tale scent of his woodsy aftershave, or an icy chill spiraling down her spine. Not once did he try to confront her, and she'd vowed to steer clear of his office no matter how much she wanted to chew him out for being so cold and inconsiderate for leaving her dangling and insecure since Friday night.

On Thursday morning the pet therapy Dalmatian made rounds, stopping beside Polly's toddler patient, Eugenia. The child had fallen from a two-story window and broken both arms, and had been taken into protective services after being admitted to Angel's. She was withdrawn and moody, and Polly didn't know how to reach her or make her comfortable. But Dotty the Dalmatian brightened the child's gray eyes with interest, and soon a smile crossed her lips as Dotty licked her fingertips.

Warmth washed through Polly's down mood, and she grinned at her young charge, then was rewarded with Eugenia smiling back. Simple things. Small steps. This was the way to put a life back together, as Polly only knew too well from her own childhood.

"May I talk to you?" From behind, the familiar voice made her eyes go wide. It was John. Adrenaline sprayed like scattershot throughout her chest. She schooled her expression before she turned.

"Sure," she said, acting as if nothing, especially her ego, had been flipped sideways since they'd had mind-blowing sex.

Leaving her patient with Dotty and the pet therapy lady, she followed his long and purposeful strides toward the supply room.

When they arrived, he took a deep breath. "I don't want this to be offensive or anything," he said in a nearly inaudible voice, "but I think you should take some STD tests."

So this was all about medical business, about the messy little clean-up committee for being reckless with the new girl. He may not have wanted to offend her but pure insult made her send him a cutting glance. "Why, Doctor? Have you jeopardized me?"

"No!" he rasped. She could see the vein on the side of his neck pop out.

"But you worry I may have…"

"No," he said, in a strained whisper. "I'm just being practical."

She latched onto his eyes and stared him down. "For your information, I don't sleep around. I don't have any surprises to give you, so I'll skip. Thanks." She turned to walk away, trying her best to save what was left of her pride, but he caught her by the elbow and held her back.

"We were completely careless." He spoke quietly, directly into her ear. Even now, under the worst possible circumstances, the touch of his breath on her neck made her skin prickle. She looked up at him. His dark eyes peered into hers in warning. "As a doctor, I can't be negligent. I've ordered some tests for you."

"What about you?" she said, hackles fully raised and ready to fight.

He looked thoughtfully at his OR clogs. "I checked out okay."

"Then what's the point of me—?"

His flat expression warned she wasn't about to like his answer. "Because I'm not the one who can get pregnant, even if you're on birth control pills."

Stunned by reality, she swallowed around a dry knot. She'd already told him there wouldn't be a problem— didn't he believe her? Since he was being such a jerk about everything today, she wouldn't argue.

Desperate to save face, she shrugged free of his hold. "I'll handle the tests myself, thanks," she said as she walked away, trying her best to stand straight and look confident, while feeling anything but.

That night, still fuming, she stopped at the corner ma and pa grocery store and found a pregnancy test purporting to identify a pregnancy within seven to ten days after the missed period. But Polly hadn't missed her period, which wasn't due for another three days. Would she be able to hold tight and wait for three days then buy the test? The blood test John had ordered could tell much sooner than the urine test, but her pride had tripped her up and kept her from consenting. She was sure that just because John Griffin had ordered the test and the results would be sent to him, he wasn't going to be the first to know if, and that was a very big if, she was pregnant or not.

Of course she wasn't pregnant. She took her pills every night as directed.

For some illogical reason, that night when she prepared her dinner she made sure it was well balanced and nutritious as one short phrase whispered in her mind—*What if?*—which was quickly followed by a heavy brick of panic landing in her stomach and replacing her appetite.

Monday morning, officially late for her period, Polly showed up at work withdrawn and anxious. Dread trickled down her spine as she remembered the antibiotics she'd taken a few weeks back for a sinus infection. It was a known fact that antibiotics could interfere with the potency of birth control pills for up to two weeks. It had been more than two weeks since she'd taken them, though, and that kept her hopeful all would be fine.

"Hey, Polly, how's it shakin'?" the ward clerk Rafael asked as she passed the nurses' station.

"Meh," she said, and walked on.

"What? If you're not in a good mood, how the heck am I supposed to be?"

She stopped in her tracks and saw honest surprise in his dark chocolate-colored eyes. "I guess you'll just have to work extra hard at it today, Rafe ol' buddy."

"That's cold, forcing a man to be in a good mood for no good reason all on his own." He laughed. "See, even in a bad mood you make me smile."

"What's this I hear about little Miss Sunshine being in a foul mood?" Brooke said, approaching Polly and putting her hand on Polly's shoulder. She rubbed back and forth. "You okay?"

Did her face have to be an open book?

"I've been better." She should have gotten her period on Saturday, but so far there wasn't even a hint that it was on the way. She had a question she wanted to ask Brooke, but didn't want to be blatant about how a person went about getting a pregnancy test done at Angel's, so she decided to wait for a better time under less obvious circumstances.

On Wednesday morning, Brooke assigned her once again to Eugenia, who was constantly being assessed and visited by social services, play therapists, speech therapists, and just about every doctor on staff. Polly looked forward to spending the day with a little girl who needed love as much as she did.

During Eugenia's bed bath, Polly tickled and teased the child to get her to laugh, which she did more easily this week than last.

"Mornin', peanut," a woman with a heavy Texan drawl said. "How's my girl today?"

Polly looked up to see the beautiful blonde Dr. Layla Woods. "Can you say good morning for Dr. Woods, Eugenia?"

"Mun."

Dr. Woods smiled at Polly, then at Eugenia. "That's very good."

Polly loved her accent. As Dr. Woods warmed the child up with a game of peek-a-boo and then delicately did a quick physical assessment of Eugenia, Polly studied her flawless complexion and gorgeous Texas-bluebell-colored eyes. She'd seen her before on the orthopedic floor several times making general medicine rounds, always smiling and gracious. Always approachable.

Polly had heard rumblings about Dr. Woods and the head of Neurosurgery, Dr. Alejandro Rodriguez, the most gorgeous man on the planet. Bar none. But she didn't want to get caught up in hospital gossip and had paid little attention to the stories.

She looked back at the doctor, who'd finished up her examination of Eugenia with a tap on the tip of the toddler's nose. Dr. Woods could easily be a cover model or actress with her good looks, but there was an added ingredient, sort of like a secret sauce, that made the whole recipe of Layla Woods extra-special. Perhaps seasoned by her own life, the woman oozed compassion.

And that's when it hit her. No risk, no gain, right?

Polly cleared her throat and worked up the fortitude to ask the question of the day. "Dr. Woods, um, may I ask you a favor?"

"Sure, whatcha' need?"

"Could you order me a pregnancy test?" she mumbled, embarrassed.

"A pregnancy test?"

Polly wanted to shush her, but didn't have the nerve, instead lowering her lashes and staring at the floor. The perceptive doctor quickly caught on.

"Oh," she whispered, looking around. Thankfully no one else but the toddlers were in the two bed-ward. "Sorry. Certainly. I'll order that right now. You want a blood test, right?"

Polly nodded. "Thanks so much."

Dr. Woods winked, jotting down Polly's last name from her name badge, then Polly gave her medical record number.

"Your secret's safe with me. Good luck, whichever way you hope it turns out." She smiled and after pinching Eugenia's cheeks and kissing her forehead the lovely doctor left the room, heading for the nearby computer to input that order.

At the end of her shift Polly stopped at the lab to have her blood drawn. After a long day and a crowded subway ride home she was hot and exhausted and didn't look forward to taking those five flights of stairs up to her room. A room that didn't even have air-conditioning. If this was how it got in early July, how would she survive the rest of the summer?

While making a mental note to buy a big fan, she let herself into the apartment. Mrs. Goldman, her landlady, sat in the tiny, dim living room watching TV and didn't even look up, which Polly was glad about. The last thing she wanted to do was get sucked into one of her landlady's long and meandering stories tonight. After a snack she slipped into her room and took a nap.

A couple of hours later she decided to check her e-mails and saw the notice from Angel's hospital about her test results. Quickly accessing the hospital patient medical records program, she went into her account, eager to end this chapter in her book of life's mistakes. The sooner she knew all was clear, the faster she could close the door for good on John Griffin and move on.

She'd sweep her regretful actions into a corner and forget about them, like she had so many other things in her life. Though forgetting her incredible night with John would take a lot of effort.

Opening up her lab test page, her hopeful attitude got hitched to gravity and plummeted into an abyss. Positive. The blood test was positive.

Prickles of fear stormed like a battalion across her skin as her entire body went hot.

She. Was. Pregnant.

CHAPTER FIVE

FRIDAY MORNING, JOHN sat at his desk on the computer finishing up the last of his administrative work, the thing he liked least about being a department head. If he had his way he'd do surgery every day, but he needed to play fair and share the admin duties with his orthopedic surgical staff.

Out of habit, he glanced at the spot on his desk he'd always looked when in doubt, but it was empty. He'd already forgotten that he'd put the framed photograph of his wife in the desk drawer the previous week. He hadn't been able to look at her picture without feeling guilty since he'd slept with Polly...even though it had been twelve years since Lisa had died.

He wasn't a saint, he'd been with a woman here or there over the years, but never had he gotten involved, and he liked it that way. That was, until Polly and this alien desire to get involved. Very involved.

He thought about her every day, relived their love-making in his head at the craziest moments, and even though he'd handled everything monumentally badly, he still smiled when he thought about her lively blue eyes, sexy grin, and perky young body.

Polly the people-pleaser extraordinaire.

At thirty-nine he was too young for a midlife crisis,

wasn't he? With his elbow on the desk, he sank his chin into the palm of his hand and looked out the window. Damn, he'd become a moony teenager all over again.

Couldn't he just apologize to her for being so crass and start over?

Truth was he wanted to, and he'd never thought of himself as a coward…

The tap at the door yanked him from his thoughts. "Come in."

When Polly stepped into the room, looking tired and worried, something thick and cold dropped in his stomach and she got his full attention. Barely able to lift her eyes to his, she walked toward his desk.

He shot up from his chair. "Are you all right?"

She sighed and sat, finally lifting her gaze to meet his. "Yes, actually, I am."

He sat, not wanting to be a pushover. "Can you forgive me for being a jerk?" His mouth had gotten a jump on his cool-and-calm plan.

"That depends."

"On?"

"On how you react when I tell you something."

Another sinking feeling slithered down John's throat. What messy surprise was she going to spring on him? Would she tell him she never wanted to be with him again when he'd just realized how much he wanted to know her better? He sat perfectly still, keeping her in his line of vision, waiting for her big announcement. To cover his insecurity, he went the tough route.

"I'm a big boy. Don't worry about me." He thought about picking up his pen and pretending to continue to work on his papers, blowing her off, just to show her how absolutely fine he was with however she planned to dump him. Yes, he was a busy, busy man, who would hardly notice if she dropped out of his life.

Liar.

She put her fingertips over her mouth and watched him, as if gauging his true feelings. Shaking her head, she glanced at the floor then back up at him. "There's no easy way to put this."

He went still, sensing the heaviness in the room gather into a giant cloud directly over his head. This wasn't the Polly he knew. This Polly seemed like she'd been steamrollered by life, not the bright young woman she'd been when she'd first arrived at Angel's…before they'd made love.

Pretty lousy effect you have on women, Griffin.

Okay, he'd made a snap decision. He wouldn't mess up her life one more day, no matter how badly he wanted to get involved. She didn't deserve a moody old fart like him.

"I'm pregnant."

He'd let her go, break it off clean— What?

"You're pregnant?" He'd checked his lab reports every day and hadn't seen her results. "And you know this how?"

"I asked Dr. Woods to order a blood test for me." She raised her hand. "Before you say another word I want to tell you straight out that I will not end this pregnancy. And I don't intend to give up the baby for adoption." She looked into his eyes, hers shining from moisture. "I know how it feels not to be wanted…" her voice broke with emotion "…and I won't let my baby go through that." She swallowed and sat quietly, obviously trying to hold herself together.

He'd heard everything she'd said. He'd paid attention.

Yet he needed to repeat the words, to make them real, and help them sink in. "You're pregnant."

"Yes."

With his hands on his desk, perfectly still, he leaned forward, trying to get his mouth to move so he could ask the question *What do we do now?* but nothing came out.

"And no matter what you say..." she stared at him out of those determined, teary eyes, having the same effect as reaching into his chest and wrenching out his heart "...I'm keeping this baby."

His baby. She was keeping his baby. He'd never thought he'd have a chance at a family again. A nugget of hope planted itself in his heart, filling a long-forgotten hole. He almost smiled at the absurdity of how he'd become a father at thirty-nine—from one amazing night in on-call.

Not since his wife had told him she was pregnant had he felt such a flash of joy.

A baby. A family.

But that had been long ago, and six weeks before 9/11. When he'd loved and lost both his wife and unborn child. When he would have gladly given his own life in exchange for theirs.

A jet of fear shot through his chest and strangled the breath out of him. He couldn't speak as a flashback of the hopeless feeling that had nearly ended his life—and had surely ended his wife and future child's life—played out in his head. The horror of that day. The frantic need to find her in the rubble. The sinking feeling as reality had put one foot in front of the other and stepped ever closer to ripping his life apart, as it had for so many others. The desperation when hope against all the odds had lost out and he'd found out she'd been killed. That he'd never kiss Lisa again, never hold her, never welcome their baby into his arms.

Oh, God, he couldn't do this again. He couldn't bear the pain if anything happened to this baby…or Polly. He'd used up an entire life's worth of pain and sadness already. He couldn't spare one more…

"Are you all right?"

Polly's gentle voice broke through his thoughts. Even when confessing her predicament, she'd put him first. Was he all right? What about *her*? Was *she* all right with him getting her pregnant? Of course not! Yet, trouper that she was, she'd come to tell him she was keeping their baby, whether he liked it or not.

He tried to unclench his fists, to act as if he hadn't just relived the worst day of his life. Unfortunately, his expression must have been a snapshot of his true feelings, and Polly was a solid people-reader. Perspiration moistened his upper lip. He rubbed it away.

"Yes, I'm all right." He took a deep breath, knowing it would be impossible to invest emotionally in this pregnancy. At least he could be a civilized man and offer financial support. Surely she couldn't do this on her own without his monetary help. He ground his molars and lifted his eyes to meet her steady and earnest gaze. "How much do you think you'll need?"

His hands shook so badly he wasn't even sure he'd be able to hold a pen if she agreed to let him write her a check. He held onto the desk rim to hide his shaking.

He may as well have slapped her face by the way she flinched at his words. "Pardon?" Anger, like an off-shore squall, gathered in those luminescent blue eyes. Her face tensed, incensed. "You think I came here to ask for money?" Her voice quivered with barely controlled rage. "You want to pay me because you knocked me up?"

Of course she'd take it the wrong way. She didn't have a clue what he'd been through, and he sure as hell didn't have the strength to tell her now. He had to hold it together, to be the worst kind of bastard on earth in order to make it through this meeting. No matter what she thought of him, she at least deserved to be well taken care of.

He tugged his earlobe. "That's right." His jaw was so tightly locked the words had to squeeze themselves out.

Her obviously escalating fury forced her to stand. Her cheeks blushed red, her eyes looked wild. "You bastard!"

It was her turn to verbally slap *him*. "This pregnancy isn't some little problem you can clean up with cash. For me it's sacred!" She stormed out of the room and slammed the door, leaving the glass and walls shaking as much as his hands.

Ah, hell. He picked up his pen and tossed it across the desk. Could he have handled the situation any worse?

Almost a week later Polly helped her favorite LVN, Darren, start an IV he'd accidentally dislodged. She sat at the hospital bedside with her IV kit prepared and in reach. Children were always a challenge, and the little boy had started screaming the moment he'd realized what the "lady nurse" was going to do to him. Darren firmly held the six-year-old's arm to the bed, his other arm safely secured in a cast and sling. With Darren's free hand he pressed against the boy's knees to control the fidgeting legs.

Starting an IV on a child that was freaking out was

bad enough, but hitting a moving target was nearly impossible.

She wiped the skin with disinfectant and slipped on gloves. His wails escalated.

"Mikey, if you hold still for just a couple of seconds, this will go a lot quicker," Darren said. "Then I'll play *Battle Star* with you, I promise."

Fortunately, that morning the high school of performing arts had sent a troupe of street performers to their ward. A lanky kid in a fluorescent green shirt and a bright red beret appeared at the doorway, juggling neon yellow and blue bowling pins. He edged to the side of the bed, capturing the boy's attention.

The moment the child became distracted Polly slid the needle into the vein and anchored it with tape before Mikey's delayed protest made him squirm again. His mouth gaped as the juggler pretended, in an exaggerated way, to almost drop a pin.

"It's all over," Polly said. "Just need to tape it, Mikey." She wasn't even sure he was listening. "Then you can kick Darren's patootie in *Battle Star*, okay?"

The relieved child looked at his arm to make sure Polly hadn't lied, just as the juggler migrated to the next room.

Darren glanced at Polly, winked and smiled. She smiled back, then patted Mikey's shoulder. Teamwork. It was the only way to survive in a hospital.

Teamwork in a pregnancy was pretty darned important, too.

Leaving the room, she almost ran into John, who was holding a tiny patient and watching the juggler as he switched to multicolored balls. It had been a week since she'd told him she was pregnant and had stormed out of his office after he'd insulted her, and he hadn't lifted a finger to contact her since. She yanked herself back before they made physical contact, as her heart nearly hurtled out of her chest. "Oh, sorry," she said, by rote.

He handed the tiny patient to the nearby nurse then steadied Polly by holding her arms. "My fault. Wasn't watching where I was going."

She stared at his feet, rather than look at him, furious with him, the feel of his warm hands on her skin almost her undoing. What could she say that she hadn't already confessed in his office, and he'd frozen her out, tried to pay her off, leaving her hurt beyond comprehension? She'd calmed down since then for her baby's sake, and from now on her baby would be the only thing she cared about.

She stepped back, removing her arms from his grasp. The last thing she needed was for anyone on staff to become suspicious about them, or find out about their predicament. *Her* predicament, as he'd have nothing to do with it. The pregnancy would be apparent to everyone soon enough.

"How are you feeling?" he asked, under his breath.

"Fine. Thank you." She walked away, pretending her legs didn't feel like noodles, holding her head high. She felt his eyes on her, but refused to turn round.

"Dr. Griffin! Dr. Griffin!" a child's voice cried out. "Will you make me an elephant?"

"I'll make you two elephants, if you'll quit giving your physical therapist such a hard time, Nate."

Did he even give a damn about her?

The boy laughed, and Polly could practically see John messing his hair and pretending to punch him in the arm with the cast. The man was a natural with kids, yet he'd chosen to ignore his own child.

* * *

Later that day, when the opportunity came up to work a double shift, Polly jumped at the chance. She'd need to work lots of double shifts to earn as much money as possible while she could for her and the baby.

The evening staff had a whole different feel from the day crew. Gossip seemed to be their favorite pastime, and Polly got an earful from another RN named Janetta, a large woman with a loud voice. When Janetta spoke, everyone listened.

"You know that pretty new blonde doctor, Layla something or other?" Janetta said.

"Dr. Woods?" Polly asked.

"Mmm-hmm. That's the one. She talks weird."

"She's from Texas."

"That's right, honey. That's the one." Janetta leaned forward and looked around. "Guess who she's having an affair with."

Polly didn't have a clue, neither did she want to know, but something told her Janetta was about to tell her anyway.

"Dr. Dreamy himself. That hunk from Neuro, Dr. Rodriguez."

Come to think of it, Layla and Dr. Rodriguez would make a perfect couple, but Polly kept her thoughts to herself. "How do you know they're having an affair?"

"Everyone knows it. Where have you been? It's the talk of the hospital. Goes way back. I heard from a good source that it broke up Dr. Woods's marriage, too. It must be true, 'cos she's single."

The thought of her own and John's personal business getting spread all over the hospital like poor Dr. Woods and Dr. Rodriguez made her skin prickle.

From the corner of her eye she noticed John entering room number one. "Goodnight, Chloe and Sandra. Sleep tight. See you in the morning light."

She'd never been here before for John's nightly ritual.

He zipped into the next room. "Jason and Brandon, don't give your nurses a hard time or you'll have to answer to me. Have a good night's sleep and I'll be back to check on you tomorrow."

How would John hold his head up at work if their affair became fodder for the hospital gossip mill?

As for herself, she couldn't wait to be a mother, single or not. Finally she'd have a baby to love and cherish and they'd be a family, just the two of them. She thought about Dr. Woods and wondered if she had a clue what was being said about her, and decided not to participate in this grapevine.

She thought about telling Janetta that unless she knew for sure about something, she shouldn't pass it along, but didn't want to get on Janetta's bad side. Instead, she nodded her head and let Janetta give her the rundown on several other people having affairs in the hospital, while listening to John enter each patient room and wishing the children a good night.

Soon enough her name would be added to the jilted-lover list.

Polly kept her thoughts to herself and to avoid John went back to caring for her patients, thankful that visiting hours made the floor busier and noisier than usual. The chaos still wasn't enough to keep her from thinking about her own situation, though.

She'd have to get used to the evening staff as she planned to work at least two extra shifts a month from now until she went on maternity leave. She would have to in order to make ends meet, and there was no way she'd let John pay her for getting her pregnant. She'd never take his guilt money.

Thankfully, she'd get medical coverage through Angel's hospital after her probationary two months. She'd have to hold tight until then to have her first prenatal appointment. Since she didn't have a clue how to find a good obstetrician in town, she'd have to be discreet about getting a name without alerting the rest of the staff to her situation.

During her dinner break Janetta and someone Polly had never seen before joined her at the only table in the nurses' lounge.

"This here is Vickie. She's the receptionist up in hospital Administration offices."

Polly greeted her, but wondered what she was doing hanging around the hospital after hours. The look on Vickie's face made Polly think she was bursting with something to say.

"I thought we were going to be alone," Vickie said to Janetta.

"Oh, you can trust Polly. Now, spill. What's the big news you have for me?"

Vickie licked her lips as excitement widened her eyes. "You'll never believe what happened today."

"Go on, go on." Janetta practically rubbed her hands together with glee.

"Okay. Well, Dr. Woods got called up to the offices today. She showed up all solemn-faced and nervous. When they buzzed me and I told her to go inside, girl, she looked scared." Vickie took a big bite of bread and chewed quickly.

Janetta impatiently gobbled some of her dinner, as if not wanting to miss a single syllable. Polly wished she could disappear, but knew if she walked out Janetta would peg her as someone she couldn't trust with good old-fashioned gossip, which would make Polly an enemy, so she stayed in her chair, quietly nibbling at her meal.

Vickie's eyes brightened. "Okay, so a couple minutes after Dr. Woods is in the room, guess who comes barreling through the office doors?"

"Tell me, oh, tell me. Not…"

"Yes. Dr. R., and before the door can close I hear him say 'I insist Dr. Woods's name be cleared'."

"Cleared from what?" Janetta looked like she was sitting around a campfire hearing a famous urban legend being retold.

"I think this has to do with some surgery on a kid back in Los Angeles that they got sued for. But get this. I sort of got out of my chair and went over by the door so I could hear better. He says, 'She's a gifted doctor with much to offer our hospital, and she shouldn't have her name dragged through the media because of a surgery I agreed to perform'." Vickie put on a horrible accent, and Polly's stomach twisted with guilt, listening. "'I was the person who was charged in that malpractice suit, not Dr. Woods, and I was cleared.' He went on to say that he knew the surgery would be high risk, and if they wanted to lay the blame on anyone, it should be him."

"Oh, my God, this is something."

"Yeah, so next thing I know, Dr. Woods rushes out of the offices and out the door and Dr. Rodriguez keeps yelling at them. The last thing I heard was, '*No, you listen to me. The verdict was no malpractice. Make it public, then!*'"

Janetta was practically salivating over this news. Polly sat silent, watching the two women live vicariously through someone else's drama. It just didn't seem right.

Later, while exiting her patient's room, she noticed the nurses' station had gone quiet. She glanced up and spotted across the ward the very doctor Janetta and Vickie had been talking about at dinner. Polly waved and rushed to her side, not caring how it looked to her co-workers.

"Hi," Dr. Woods said with a genuine glad-to-see-you smile.

"Hi. I wanted to thank you for arranging my test, and ask another question if you don't mind?"

"Of course not. What's up?"

Polly guided Dr. Woods to a more private spot, noticing Janetta's eagle eyes watching. She lowered her voice. "I was wondering if you could recommend an obstetrician who is close by the hospital."

Layla raised a perfectly arched brow. "So the test was positive," she whispered.

Polly gave one solemn nod.

Layla patted her forearm. "Let me ask around, since I'm kind of new in town myself, and I'll get back to you, 'kay?"

"Thank you so much."

"Darlin', it's my pleasure. We girls gotta to stick together. You know?"

Overwhelmed by the doctor's care and genuine concern, once their hushed conversation had ended, Polly decided that regardless of the hospital gossip about Dr. Woods having had an affair with the head of Neurosurgery while she was still married, Polly would be Layla Woods's number one fan.

Polly could barely breathe when on the following Thursday the case involving Dr. Woods and Rodriguez went public at Angel's. She read the memo addressed to the hospital staff about a boy named Jamie Kilpatrick and a high-risk neurosurgery that Dr. Woods had recommended to Dr. Rodriguez. One thing stood out beyond everything else: Dr. Rodriguez had valiantly taken full responsibility for the boy's death.

One major question crossed Polly's mind. Why would Dr. Rodriguez put his career and reputation on the line to protect Dr. Woods? She didn't need to think for long. The man was obviously in love with her, just like Janetta had said. Wow, what must it feel like to have someone love you that much?

That night Polly combed the aisles of her local market, hunting for healthy food. Her routine in the mornings had always been to buy a couple of pieces of fresh fruit from one of the street carts near the hospital. She'd bring a yogurt from home for morning break, then a sandwich for lunch, usually tuna, and eat the second piece of fruit. Now she worried she wasn't getting enough vitamins. She grabbed a bag of baby spinach, deciding to sauté it with oil and garlic and serve it for dinner over the chicken breast she'd just picked up. Eating for two was a big responsibility, and she wanted her baby to have the best opportunity possible at a healthy start.

Eyeing a package of her favorite cookies, she steered away. This pregnancy business would be harder than anything she'd done in her life, but she was determined to have a successful pregnancy.

The thought of a healthy baby brought back the need to see an obstetrician in the next couple of weeks. With fingers crossed that Dr. Woods would come through for her, she paid for her groceries and headed home.

* * *

John stood over his six-burner state-of-the-art stove, grilling salmon. He'd gutted the old-fashioned kitchen when his parents had sold him their condo at a steal before moving to Florida. Now he had a kitchen that connected to the flow of the house, instead of hidden behind a wall. The 56th Street, near Sutton Place address was perfectly situated for work, plus he had the East River within walking distance whenever he felt like taking a jog. With two bedrooms and baths, a living room, which he'd expanded by breaking down a small third bedroom wall, and the new roomier kitchen, he lived comfortably for a New York City bachelor.

Tri-colored squash sautéed in a small pan and the brown rice steamed in another. He loved to cook and wasn't shy about letting people know. While cooking, he wondered if Polly was taking good care of herself, and how she might enjoy this meal. Flipping the fish, he realized he didn't have a clue what she liked to eat beyond cheese pizza. For all he knew, she hated fish.

She was carrying his baby. Every time he thought about it, the breath squeezed from his lungs.

With everything under control dinner-wise, and Polly solidly implanted in his mind, he dug out his cell phone and called a forgotten friend. "Geoff, it's John."

The old medical school colleagues went through a required, though brief catch-up time, then John broached the true reason for his call. "I was wondering if you'd do me a favor. One of my ortho nurses just found out she's pregnant, and she needs a good OB guy. I told her I knew the best. Any chance you could squeeze her in?"

Geoff asked John to hold while he flipped through his calendar and, taking this opportunity, John checked the salmon and veggies, then opened his kitchen catch-all drawer, hunting for a pad of paper and a pen. Soon Geoff was back on the line with an appointment date and time.

"Fantastic. Thanks so much." He tugged his earlobe. "Oh, by the way, send me the bill."

By the brief silence on the other end before Geoff agreed, John figured he hadn't pulled the wool over his old classmate's eyes. Yes. John Griffin had knocked up a nurse. His nurse. Polly.

On Friday afternoon Polly was in the middle of hanging intravenous antibiotics for her newest post-op patient when John appeared at her side. Her hand trembled as she placed the small bottle of potent medicine on the hook and opened the drip regulator. She got mad at herself for letting him have that much power over her and hoped he hadn't noticed. He was in his OR scrubs, having followed the surgical patient back to the ward.

Having already received report from the OR recovery nurse, she knew Emanuel had been in a car accident, had broken his left leg, and needed to have a metal plate and pins to secure his bones back in place.

"I wanted you to have this." John handed her a small piece of paper.

She stared at it instead of reaching for it, thankful that Emanuel was completely out of it and in a private room so no one else would hear them talk. "What's that?"

"It's an appointment with the best OB guy in the city."

Hesitant to take anything from John, she shook her head. "That's okay. I've got someone else in mind."

John tugged his ear. "You need to let me be involved in this, too."

"Why, John? The other day you wanted nothing to do with me or our baby," she whispered spiritedly over Emanuel. "You wanted to pay me off." She wanted to sound indignant, but it came out hurt.

"Look, there's a lot to get used to for both of us. I'm just asking you to give me time."

She snatched the paper from his fingers. "You think I don't understand how much we both have to get used to? And as for time, well, you've got approximately eight months to work it out." She glanced at the appointment, next Thursday at four p.m. with a Geoffrey Bernstein. It was perfect for her work schedule, she'd give him that. Then she noticed the address. Park Avenue? "Forget it. I can't afford this guy."

"It's all taken care of."

It stalled her for a second, but she quickly recovered. "I don't want your guilt charity." She handed back the paper but he refused to take it and left, grinding his jaws, without another word.

That afternoon Layla Woods crossed the ward, heading directly for Polly, looking far less confident than usual. Up close, Polly could see she had dark circles under her eyes, as if she'd been on call and hadn't slept. "I've got some information for you."

"Great. Thank you so much." Polly glanced around to make sure no one was within hearing distance.

"I've been told this guy is the best OB doc in town. The only problem is the wait list is long, and I think he's pretty pricey." She handed Polly the paper, and Polly opened it immediately. *Dr. Geoffrey Bernstein.*

Polly tried not to hide her disappointment because Dr. Woods had gone out of her way to help her out. "I can't thank you enough. I'll look into this right away."

They parted company and Polly watched the petite

doctor walk away as a hollow, aching path burrowed through her stomach.

Round one had gone to John. Not only had he found her the most expensive doctor in town, he'd made an appointment for her, too. And he was paying.

As her least favorite Uncle Randolph used to say whenever Polly had resisted her cousin's baggy hand-me-down clothes: *Don't look a gift horse in the mouth.*

So be it. For the good of her baby she'd take the appointment John had made for her, and because she'd been raised right afterwards she'd swallow her pride and thank him for it.

Three nights later Polly worked her second double shift. It probably wasn't a wise move as she still hadn't recovered from the first sixteen-hour shift, even though she'd had the whole weekend to do it. Now she dragged through another.

The pregnancy had zapped most of her energy. She'd also become aware that other early signs of pregnancy were cropping up. Her breasts were tender, and she wanted to sleep more. And she was hungry. All the time. Maybe she'd be one of those lucky ladies who didn't get morning sickness, but it was still very early along.

For her dinner break, to avoid another gossip-infused lecture from Janetta, she decided to go outside and eat on a bench in the hospital garden. She walked to the elevator feeling more than fatigued, eager to breathe in some fresh air. With all of the gossip at the hospital and speculation about her own situation, she felt as though she had a brick on each shoulder. While she waited for the elevator she rolled her neck around and lifted her shoulders, hoping to release some stress from the stiff muscles.

The elevator pinged and opened to reveal Dr. Alex Rodriguez inside. Alone.

Polly had never seen the man up close before. She entered and tried not to stare at his handsome profile or notice the waves in his thick black hair as it curled along the collar of his shirt.

He stood stoically silent, deep in thought, hardly noticing she was there.

The elevator stopped at the next floor and Dr. Woods got on. Polly's heart tripled in beats. Layla nodded at Polly, looking noticeably riled, then turned to Dr. Rodriguez. "Hi," she said, sounding breathy and unconfident as she pressed the button for the lobby, which had already been pushed.

"Layla." His all-business attitude threw Polly in light of what she already knew about the memo and their supposed past, through Janetta.

"Listen, I wanted to thank you for what you did the other day," Layla said. "Sticking up for me in the board room and all."

"It needed to be done." Curt. Businesslike.

Had *she* become invisible?

"Well, I want to thank you for that, Alex. It meant a lot to—"

With a quick gesture, he brushed her off. "It was nothing." He wouldn't look her in the eyes, and that must have bothered Dr. Woods. It sure would have if Polly had been in the doctor's shoes.

Layla punched the button for the second floor, obviously upset. "Both of us getting out of the elevator together in the lobby would only fuel the fire of the gossip around here." She tossed her hair over her shoulder and the moment the doors opened she started to get out, but Dr. Rodriguez stepped around her and exited first.

Holy cow. Polly hoped and prayed that Layla didn't think she had participated in the rampant gossip around the hospital. Especially after all she'd done for her.

Dr. Woods let him leave, watched him go, staring, even though the elevator doors had closed again. Polly didn't know what to do so she kept quiet, hoping maybe she really had become invisible. They continued downwards in silence, Dr. Woods deep in thought, until the doors opened to the lobby.

Straightening her shoulders, she glanced at Polly, the first sign that the doctor had remembered she was there. "He may think this is finished between us, but it isn't. Not by a long shot." With that, Dr. Layla Woods, looking determined and undeterred, exited the elevator.

Polly stood frozen to the spot, her mind swirling with what she'd just witnessed. It wasn't hatred or anger that fueled them, it was passion. Pure and simple. Those two were meant to be together, and somehow, some way, they'd both have to figure it out. Just before the doors closed Polly rushed out of the elevator and toward the garden exit.

As she ate her dinner, she made a vow. No way would anyone hear a hint of what had gone on in that elevator. Their secret was safe with her, and she hoped Layla was right, that whatever they had going wasn't over by a long shot.

At the end of her shift, completely exhausted, she went to the bathroom to splash some water on her face, hoping to pep herself up for the long subway ride home. Afterwards, she gathered up her belongings from the employee locker room and headed toward the elevator, the last person to leave from the late shift.

A lone silhouette stood at the other end of the hall.

White doctor's coat, broad shoulders, short-cropped hair, unmistakably John. Her heart fluttered at the thought of facing him after several days. He met her at the elevator door.

"What are you still doing here?" he asked.

"Did a double shift."

"Should you be doing that?"

She yawned, and covered her mouth. "No choice these days."

She noticed he festered over that response. He blinked and turned his head as if he had a thing or two to say to her, but had maybe thought better of it.

He looked at his watch. "I don't like the idea of you taking the subway home at this time of night."

"It really isn't about what you like or don't like, now, is it, *Johnny*." Yes, she could be a brat when she wanted to, make that *needed* to. Being pregnant had put her in a whole new frame of mind. Her baby came first, and John wasn't on board with her being pregnant. End of story.

"Let me give you a ride home."

"No way." But, man, oh, man, her feet were tired, and the thought of walking the required blocks just to get to the subway station did seem daunting at almost midnight.

"Look, I had early surgery today so I drove my car. I'm parked next door. Don't be stubborn *and* foolish."

Stubborn? Look who was calling whom stubborn. "Do you have any idea how big the gossip mill is at Angel's? People would have a field day if they saw us leave together." *And then found out soon enough I'm pregnant.*

"Look, dumpling, I don't give a rat's ass what other

people think. Right now, all I want to do is give you a ride home."

"Don't call me dumpling."

"Sorry."

If, and that was a big if, she decided to let John give her a ride home, it wouldn't be because she was giving in to him. No. It would be because she really didn't want to face that long subway ride to the Lower East Side. It had been almost two a.m. before she'd gotten in bed the last time she'd worked a double shift and, being honest, she worried she might fall asleep on the subway and miss her exit.

"Okay."

"Okay you accept my apology or okay you'll let me give you a ride home?"

"I'll take the ride."

He looked surprised, as if she hadn't put up nearly as big a fight as he'd expected.

Ten minutes later she slid onto the smoothest kid leather seat she'd ever seen in a fancy sedan like his. It was soft and cushy, too, and, oh, the headrest was adjusted perfectly to her neck. She touched the button to lower the head of the seat, making it like a lounge chair, and snuggled in after clicking her seat belt.

John didn't say a word, but she could see his cheek lift in that unbalanced smile of his. He'd won. He knew it.

But she was reaping the benefits.

Before he'd even exited the parking structure, she closed her eyes and drifted off to a sweet dream about being curled up on the softest sofa in the world, while the sexiest guy she'd ever met touched her knee and talked to her softly.

CHAPTER SIX

JOHN PARKED THE car, walked around to the other side, opened the passenger door and lifted Polly up and out. She slept sounder than his mother's cat, and only stirred when he pulled her to his chest.

"Shh, go back to sleep," he whispered in her ear, as he motioned with his head to the doorman of his building to let them in.

Marco the doorman gave a deeply inquisitive look but followed orders. John had been a resident in the building for three years now and had never brought a woman home in this condition.

"Drunk," John mouthed to Marco, who gave an affirmative *Aha* nod.

"Park the car in your usual spot?" Marco whispered.

John nodded, knowing his car keys would be left in the parking-garage office where he paid a hefty monthly fee for the privilege of driving and parking in New York City.

He punched the elevator button with his elbow and hoped Polly didn't wake up until he was ready. He'd driven the long way home around Central Park to make sure she'd fallen asleep deeply enough once he'd decided to bring her here.

As he rode the elevator to the ninth floor, he took

the liberty to study her close up—flawless skin, though maybe a little pale, ash-blonde hair with waves that made him want to dig his fingers in every time he saw her. Her thick brown lashes fluttered the tiniest bit under his scrutiny and her nostrils twitched as she breathed softly. She was sweet and tender, and he felt the urge to kiss her.

The elevator door opened, and though it was a bit tricky to unlock his door with one hand while holding Polly with the other, he balanced her on his thigh and succeeded, and had them inside in no time at all. Before anyone on his floor had a chance to wonder what in the world he was doing with a woman in his arms on a Monday night at this late hour. He chuckled inwardly, thinking how they'd never probably even seen him with a woman before, had probably assumed he was gay or celibate.

The condo was dark, but he knew his way around by heart and took her immediately to the guest bedroom, where he carefully laid her on the double bed. She stirred but only to reposition herself on her side. Not wanting to freak her out in case she woke up, which surprisingly she still hadn't, he laid a comforter over her, left the door ajar and went to the kitchen. There, he turned on the light and rummaged around the refrigerator for something to eat.

Three bites into a turkey and Cheddar sandwich he heard the gasp. "Where am I?"

He rushed down the hall to the bedroom. "Don't worry, you're at my place."

"Why am I here?" She came to the door looking groggy and very appealing with mussed-up hair and heavy-lidded eyes.

"You didn't tell me where you lived before you fell

asleep, and you looked so comfortable I didn't have the heart to wake you."

"So you thought you'd make me a prisoner at your house?"

"You're not a prisoner."

"Then you'll take me home?"

"If you insist."

She stood staring, obviously considering his offer. Maybe she needed some convincing.

"Look, I was thinking of your best interests. I've got the guest bedroom and you'll get a good night's sleep, then I'll take you home in the morning."

"I don't have to work tomorrow because I did the double shift."

"That's fine."

"Don't you have to be at work?"

"Not until nine. It's my clinic day."

"So you'll take me home before you go to work?"

He nodded.

She leaned against the doorframe looking drowsy and too tired to put up a fight. "Where's your bathroom, please?"

He gestured with his forehead towards the door down the hall, then took another bite of sandwich.

On her way back to the guest room she slowed down by the kitchen and gave him a suspicious glance. "Don't get any ideas about sneaking into that room tonight." She pointed to the guest room.

"I won't."

"Because what we did was a one-time deal."

He didn't bother to swallow his bite of sandwich. "By my count, that was a three-time deal."

Obviously too tired to put up a fight, she tossed him an aggravated look then went inside the guest room and closed the door. At least she didn't lock it. He took the last bite of sandwich and decided he'd got a kick out of riling her. Come to think of it, there was a lot about Polly he got a kick out of. Now, if there was only a way to get her back into his life on much better terms.

Early the next morning, John had a full breakfast prepared by the time he tapped on her door and woke her up. She rolled out of the room, stretching and yawning and looking even more inviting than she had the night before.

"What time is it?" she asked.

"Seven. Have some coffee. It's decaf," he said, before she could protest. Somehow he knew she'd take good care of the pregnancy. "I've scrambled some eggs and there's fresh OJ over there. Do you like wheat or sourdough toast?"

"Wheat," she said, before closing the bathroom door.

The fact that she didn't throw a hissy fit or make a major protest about getting home right this minute gave him hope, and that notion made him smile. Maybe she was back to being that people-pleaser he liked so much, though the feisty version of Polly definitely had its merits. He smiled and pushed some perfectly scrambled eggs onto a second plate then sprinkled some finely grated Cheddar cheese on top.

They sat on bar stools in companionable silence while they ate at his granite counter.

"Tastes good," she said, eating a second piece of toast slathered with blackberry jam.

"You're eating for two now, right?"

He'd named the elephant in the room, and she took her time to respond. "I don't need you to remind me." Her gaze was brief and filled with icy-blue warning.

"I want to be a part of this pregnancy, Polly."

"That's not the impression I got when I told you about it."

"I was in shock."

"You wanted nothing to do with me or this pregnancy. You tried to pay me off, as if I'd go away and never mention another word about it."

He reached for her hand and squeezed. "I didn't mean it to come off that way. I wanted you to know you weren't in it alone, and that you didn't have to worry about money. That's all."

She dropped her gaze toward her lap. "We're not for sale."

If that was the metaphor she wanted to run with, he'd play along. "Look at it from my perspective." He pointed to her stomach. "There's prime real estate inside there, and though you may be the landlord, I own half of it."

She made a face at him. "Have you always been this romantic?"

He shrugged. "It's a gift."

"You don't have the right to make it all neat and tidy like that. Like a business deal." Polly shoved another bite of egg into her mouth and stared straight ahead. Once she'd swallowed, she leveled a serious gaze at him. "I don't have a clue what your issues are, but since I believe you do need to be there for this baby I'll generously consider whatever part of 'being there for this pregnancy' you think you can handle."

He grinned. That was the people-pleasing Polly he knew. "Good. For starters, I intend to go to all obstetric appointments with you."

Her eyebrows dropped and furrowed. "That's a very private thing."

"And one doesn't wind up pregnant by not doing

a few *very private* things with the father of the baby, does one?"

She sighed. "Okay, you can come to the OB appointments."

"And you should let me cook for you at least twice a week."

"You cook?"

"What do you call these scrambled eggs?"

"A six-year-old can scramble eggs, Johnny."

She'd called him Johnny again, and he'd consider it progress. "I happen to be a good cook, and I want to make sure you get a balanced diet."

"Look, I may have gotten knocked up with little effort but I am not an idiot. I know how to eat healthily."

"There was a *lot* of effort involved in you getting pregnant, as I recall, and for the record you didn't get 'knocked up', as you so poetically put it, on your own."

Silence stretched on for a few seconds while he regrouped. How long would he have to keep pointing out to her that she didn't have to be in this alone? If he didn't handle things right this time, he could blow it all for good.

"I was on birth-control pills," she said. "I swear I was, but I'd taken antibiotics a few weeks back for a sinus infection."

"I see." He understood perfectly what she was getting at, she didn't want him to think she'd set him up. Antibiotics could interfere with birth control pills' potency and effect for a couple of weeks after use, enough to make a woman potentially vulnerable to pregnancy. Under the circumstances, and without added protection, which they'd completely blown off that night, pregnancy wasn't out of the question. Polly and her baby onboard were living proof.

John ate the remainder of his breakfast vigorously. The real question was, though, why hadn't she thought about that when they'd made love? Ah, hell, why hadn't *he* thought about anything but how much he'd wanted her that night? There was no point in making this a blame game. What was done was done. They'd had sex, hot sex, and made a baby.

Though there was no way on earth he could invest emotionally in the pregnancy, or be a proper father, he could at least be an ally for Polly during a time when she would definitely need a friend. As for after the pregnancy? He downed the last of his orange juice. Well, he was content to take it one step at a time for now, and she'd just have to understand.

"So I'll wait for you at the hospital parking lot on Thursday when you get off work, and take you to your appointment."

"Okay." She sounded like a teenager who'd given up on getting out of a major book report. "But can you take me home now? I'd really like to shower."

"Of course."

On Thursday, Polly ran a little late after change-of-shift report and had to run-walk to meet John at the car. He'd had the car brought up to the entrance and leaned against his silver sedan, checking his watch as she jogged his way.

"Sorry! We had some late admits and I couldn't just dump and run."

"I've already called the doctor's office and let them know we may be a little late. I'll drop you off in front then park."

"Great. Thanks." She fixed the flying strands of hair around her face, knowing her skin was probably shiny from working hard all day and that her colored lip gloss had long ago been chewed off. "I really appreciate it."

"It's the least I can do."

The least he could do, was that how he looked at it? Was he only trying to get away with doing the bare minimum so as not to come off as a deadbeat? Boy, had she been there and done that with her aunts and uncles after her mother had died. Every part of that equation made her skin crawl, yet here she was, riding in John Griffin's fancy car on her way to the doctor's appointment he'd arranged. She was sick of people going through the motions on her behalf, but that seemed to be the repetitious hand life had dealt her. Resigned, she'd just have to make the best of it this time, not for her but for her baby's sake.

Dr. Bernstein's nurse was ready for her the minute she walked in and whisked her into one of the examination rooms in the glamorous medical suite. She had no intention of letting John in on the actual examination.

The doctor looked to be around John's age and had gentle hands and an affable personality. He looked intently into her eyes as she explained her side of the pregnancy, and she believed him when he promised to keep her and the baby healthy and happy for the next eight and a half months.

"You can get dressed then meet me in my office," he said on his way out the door after the thorough examination.

Polly suffered a surprise when she entered Dr. Bernstein's office only to find John already sitting there, chatting amicably with "Geoff", as he called him. The moment Polly stepped inside the conversation stopped and John shot up. He reached over and pulled out the chair next to him so she could sit. She'd give him points for always being a gentleman.

"Polly," Dr. "Geoff" started right in, "you are a healthy young woman, and at this early stage in the process I'd say you're going to do well. Your uterus and cervix look good, the pregnancy is implanted securely in your uterus lining, and your pelvic cradle should handle the body changes just fine. I want to get some baseline lab work done for you and start you on prenatal vitamins. In a couple of weeks we'll do an ultrasound." He scribbled on a prescription pad, ripped it off and handed it to her, then sat back in his chair and steepled his fingers. "Do you have any questions?"

"My due date?"

"Right. My calculations show March twenty-eighth, give or take a day or two."

The skin on her shoulders and arms prickled. Somehow, this actual date of birth made everything come into focus. It was real. She'd have a baby and be a mom beginning March twenty-eighth. John must have noticed her emotional reaction when he put his arm around her shoulders and tugged her close. She couldn't help the brimming tears. She was going to be a mother in eight short months from now. Only because the long and stressful day had caught up with her, and she needed it right this moment, she accepted John's comfort as she buried her weeping eyes on his shoulder.

Back at the car, John grinned at her as he let her in the passenger side. "You agreed to let me fix you dinner twice a week, and I thought tonight would be a good time to get that routine rolling."

"You don't even know if I have food allergies or anything." She'd recovered from the emotional high in the doctor's office and had pulled up her guard again.

"Chicken tetrazzini with wholegrain noodles and a garden salad."

Her mouth watered at the description. "I hate onions. Does it have onions?"

"Not now. I hope you like garlic, though."

She bobbed her head as she slid inside the car. Hating having to hold back all her excitement about being pregnant, she tightened her jaw and ground her teeth for most of the ride back to John's condo.

Marco the doorman gave her and John a knowing nod when they walked inside, and it made her pause. Had she ever seen him before? The small but tasteful lobby gave her the impression that well-off, long-time New Yorkers lived in the building. What a difference from her turn-of-the-century walk-up.

Though John had overall masculine flair in his taste in interior design, a maroon leather couch and chair with glass and chrome tables got her attention, and across the room a surprising floral-upholstered overstuffed chair and ottoman looked beyond inviting.

"Have a seat," he said, gesturing to the living room that flowed naturally into his kitchen. "You need to rest as often as you can." He tossed her the newspaper he'd just sorted out of his pile of mail. "Read this while I get cooking."

"Don't be so bossy." At a little after five o'clock she was hungry and more than ready to eat, and decided not to give him a hard time, so she did what she was told and put her feet up, shaking out the newspaper and reading the headlines of the day, all of which were depressing.

She surreptitiously kept track of him while he cooked. He wore khaki slacks that fit in all the right places and a pale blue shirt. He'd removed the tie while he'd shuffled through his mail, and the open-collar look held her interest longer than she'd wanted. But most of all what kept her riveted to watching John was how he genuinely seemed to enjoy cooking. She liked discovering that about him.

He ran a tidy kitchen and was very comfortable in it, like cooking was a less sterile version of surgery. She thought of her living arrangement and the tiny out-dated appliances she shared. What she'd give to have such a gorgeous modern kitchen at her fingertips. The comfort of the chair and the simple dream of living in a place like John's soon had her closing her suddenly weary eyes…

"Dinner's ready!"

Polly sat bolt upright. What time was it? She glanced at her watch. Six o'clock. She'd taken a forty-minute nap. The hint of garlic, chicken and freshly drained pasta weaving their way from the kitchen and up her nostrils was heavenly. "Give me a sec to wash up, okay?"

"Of course." He whistled while he set plates and flatware on the bistro-sized table in the corner of the kitchen, and she stopped a couple of moments to enjoy the sight.

The food smelled fantastic and her taste buds went into overdrive, looking forward to the meal as she hurried down the hall to wash her hands.

He hadn't lied. John Griffin was a darned fine cook. Every mouthful sent jets of pleasure through her gastronomic senses. She could get used to these twice-a-week meals, maybe bargain for a third as time went on. Piecemeal, really, since that was all he was offering in the way of getting involved in the pregnancy. Far be it from her to want to ruin a delicious dinner, but really was that the best the man could offer? She continued to eat with a disappointed outlook.

After a few bites John put his fork down and cast a pressing gaze at her. She wasn't about to stop eating, but the daunting stare did slow her down a bit.

"I want you to know that I liked you right off. You know, that first week you came to Angel's. I, or we, did something crazy and out of character, and now we've been thrown together in some pretty astounding circumstances."

She wanted to ask him how long he'd practiced the speech, but decided, as he was finally opening up, not to be a smart-aleck.

He cleared his throat. "What I'm getting at is I know you're disappointed in me. I'm only skirting around the perimeter of our predicament."

She started to protest his calling her pregnancy a predicament, but when she opened her mouth he raised his voice a pre-emptive notch. "I don't think any guy would know how to handle it perfectly, but I'm not making excuses for myself. I'm just being honest with you, because I think you deserve it."

He got up, refilled his water glass, took a long draw and sat back down. "There's something you need to know about me. Maybe it will explain why I'm not all balloons and bubbles over your pregnancy."

Sensing his earnestness, she put her fork down and gave him her total attention. "Go ahead, John."

As if the words strangled and fought in his throat, John's pained expression made Polly brace for what he was about to say.

"I don't even know if I told you that I used to be married. Happily married for two years. My wife, Lisa, was a financial adviser." His voice clogged and he stopped every sentence or two to clear it. "Anyway, we were happy because she'd just found out she was pregnant."

The heavy foreshadowing made the gourmet meal in Polly's stomach suddenly feel like a large lump of paper maché. John talked to the table rather than engage her eyes.

"We'd stayed up late, planning, all excited about our baby, how our lives would change." He had to clear that stubborn lump in his throat again. His nose ran and he wiped it with his paper napkin. Instinctively, the hair on Polly's arms rose and John's profile grew blurry.

"We were going to tell my parents over dinner that night. I kissed her goodbye that morning and she went to work on the twenty-second floor of the World Trade Center on September eleventh."

Chills rolled over Polly's skin. Tears broke free from her eyes and she realized the implication of that fateful day. She'd been a high-school student at the time, eating breakfast and listening to the kitchen radio when she'd heard the news report. She grabbed John's knotted fist and squeezed tight. Oh, God, he didn't need to say one more word. She understood. He'd lost everything he loved and held dear on one historic day.

Polly got up from her seat and circled around John, banding her arms around his chest as she cuddled him from behind. He sat stoic, like the rock of Gibraltar he'd tricked himself into becoming—for survival's sake, she was sure, she understood that now. Bleeding emotionally for his loss, she stayed with him wrapped in her arms for several long moments as she mulled over their circumstances. She was willing to give him a pass for now, for not committing to their child beyond the neat and tidy logistics of appointments, well-prepared dinners, and finances.

Slowly, as she stood hunched over, holding him, a tiny thought wiggled and snaked its way clear of her emotional landslide on John's behalf. The thought gained power and implanted itself in the center of her head. *That was twelve years ago.* Was John determined to keep his life stagnant and take the loss to his grave? More importantly, would Lisa want that for him?

They may have made love under unusual circumstances, but something bigger than both of them had come out of it. They'd made a baby. He could never get his wife or child back, but she and John had made a little life that was growing inside her. A baby with a birth date. March twenty-eighth.

It was Polly's turn to clear her thickened throat. "John, please don't get me wrong, I realize how horrific your loss was. But twelve years have passed, and that's no excuse for abandoning your responsibility to *this* child." She stood straight and placed her hand on her currently flat abdomen, one hand anchored to his shoulder. "This baby needs you now. You're the father."

He sat staring at his plate rather than acknowledge her, and when she'd given up on him answering she dropped her hands from his shoulder and her stomach and cleared the dishes from the table.

"I'll take care of that," he said, belatedly.

"No, this is my way of thanking you for a great meal." As long as he held onto the past, she'd never have a chance to really get to know him.

John removed the remaining dishes and joined her at the sink. Together they worked in silence, cleaning the kitchen.

"Can you take me home now, please?" she asked, once everything was done.

"Sure."

Noncommittal seemed to be all the man could offer, and his history explained why, but that definitely wasn't something she'd settle for, and John really did need to let go of the past.

John watched Polly from across the kitchen. Her petite frame looked good in anything she wore, which happened to be hospital scrubs. She was right about so many years having gone by, he knew. He couldn't argue with the logic of being held captive by a time capsule, but the habit had become so deeply rooted into his being that he couldn't seem to break free. He'd been one of the first responders at the scene and to this day he had flashbacks of treating the injured and mangled, of staring into the faces of the dead, while desperate to find his wife. He'd taken risks amongst the falling debris and rubble searching for Lisa, but it had all been fruitless. She'd died and taken most of him with her. To this day he questioned why he'd lived and she hadn't.

When Polly had gathered her things, he got his keys and they headed for the elevator.

An hour later, due to heavy traffic conditions, when John dropped Polly off at her century-old building on the Lower East Side, a crazy idea popped into his head. She was the one accusing him of abandoning his responsibility to the child. She'd probably never agree to it but, what the hell, when the time was right, he'd make his pitch.

He'd double-parked and watched while she climbed the stoop stairs and buzzed herself into the building. The thought of her surviving during the long hot summer while being pregnant and living in the ancient brownstone walk-up didn't sit well. He couldn't offer his heart to a stranger, but he owed her the common decency of making sure she was comfortable and cared for.

Patience, John, give her some time to realize how hard things will get on her own, then you can make her the offer she can't refuse.

CHAPTER SEVEN

FRIDAY MORNING POLLY was measuring out liquid antibiotics at the medicine station for the three-year-old toddler in Room Twelve B when John appeared in her peripheral vision.

He pushed a small brown bag her way. "Here."

"What's this?"

"Your lunch," he said, already walking away.

"I made my own lunch."

"Save it for tomorrow. You'll like this better."

"How do you know that? Maybe I've been craving peanut butter and jelly all day. Maybe I've been dreaming about my home-made lunch since breakfast." When had she reverted to being a contrary teenager again? Could it be the hormones?

He stopped, turned and flashed that slanting smile, his dark eyes reminding her of milk-chocolate chips. Beneath his knee-length doctor's coat he wore a white shirt and blue silk tie, looking dressier than usual. She inhaled, the savory scent coming from the bag already making her mouth water. Something warm and spicy awaited her, thanks to Dr. Griffin, the father of her baby.

He'd gone out of his way to bring this to her so the least she could do was be grateful.

She mouthed, "Thank you". He dipped his head and

walked away. Truth was, she could easily get used to him catering for her, and wondered how abruptly it would end once she had the baby. She glanced around, noticing Brooke and Rafael giving her odd looks. Oh, man, what must they think? The last thing she needed was to get picked up for the gossip grapevine like that poor Dr. Woods and the neurosurgeon, Dr. Rodriguez. Thank goodness Janetta didn't work the day shift.

After finishing the obviously home-made minestrone soup with spinach and chicken meatballs, Polly found at the bottom of the lunch bag a large peanut-butter cookie with a note hidden behind it.

Meet me for an early dinner at Giovanni's tonight? See you there at five.

How could he be so confident she'd come running just because he'd told her to? She went back to work determined to blow him off. Let him sit there and wait for her to show up. She may be pregnant, but she was darned sure not to be taken for granted because of it.

As the afternoon wore on, she prepared a teenage soccer player for surgery on his left knee and right shoulder. She'd given him his pre-op medicine and shot and stayed close by until the transportation clerk could take him to the operating room. As his eyelids grew heavy and he dozed off, she thought about John and his sexy blue silk tie and that off-balance but charming smile. Did she really want to play games with him? He'd asked her to dinner, had seemed sincere enough, and she had no reason not to go, so why stand him up?

The man had been to hell and back over the past twelve years. Here he was getting a little sparkle in his eyes again, and the last thing she should do was give him a hard time. It wasn't in her nature to play games with men anyway. Besides, in her dating life the guys had always been much better at game-playing than she could ever compete with.

No, after work she'd take her time and freshen up then walk over to Giovanni's for another dinner with John. Memories of what had happened after the last time they'd eaten there made her lose her step but not stumble. She'd make sure it didn't happen again, and maybe she'd ask him to drive her home, just to make sure. Besides, lately the fumes in the subway made her feel nauseous.

To her surprise, John was already there, waiting, when she arrived. He'd ordered bottled water instead of Chianti, too, which was sitting on the table. He stood when he saw her, and the smile he gave was definitely genuine. So was the warm feeling inside when she smiled back at him. Without his doctor's jacket she could see his solid, football-player physique, and it spawned a quick flash of being naked in his arms and near bliss.

"If you like shrimp, I recommend the scampi," he said, sitting down after she'd shaken the sexy thought from her mind and taken her seat.

"So much for idle conversation. You say dinner. You mean dinner." She picked up the menu and scanned the specials.

"I'm sorry, is there something you'd like to talk about?"

She screwed up her face. "No. It's just, well, customary when meeting someone for dinner to start off with small talk like 'Hi, how was your day?' or something before getting right down to ordering."

"Sorry. I have an administrative meeting at seven."

"On a Friday night?" There went her chance for a ride home. "So why'd you invite me here, then?" If he wanted to get right down to business, so could she.

He poured both of them a glass of the sparkling bottled water then took a drink of his. "I want you to move in with me."

She almost spit her water right into his face, but instead she swallowed it wrong and coughed. He patted her back, looking concerned. She coughed and hacked for several more seconds, eyes bugging out, feeling embarrassed about how she must look. He looked on, earnestly trying to figure out how to help her. After she settled down she said, "You what?"

"You heard me right. I've been thinking about this and as we're having this baby together, it's the least I can do."

That warm something or other she'd felt momentarily when she'd first walked in and seen him smiling at her turned to ice. "The least you can do? Well, how kind of you, sir. Thank you for the magnanimous crumb." She stood, fully intending to leave. "As far as I'm concerned, you can take that crumb and shove it!" With the room melting down to nothing as her anger overtook every cell in her body, she stomped towards the exit. Before she made it to the street, a big, strong hand grabbed her arm.

"Hold on, hothead."

She yanked back her arm and kept moving, now outside the restaurant. He followed close behind. "Leave me alone. You're a jerk."

He managed to get in front of her, planted both hands on her arms and forced her to stop and look at him. "I know I'm a jerk. I can't figure out how not to be a jerk *or* how to handle this thing. Give me a break, will you? I'm trying. I want to do what's right, okay?"

The fury rumbling through her chest lost strength with each of his sentences. The man was being painfully honest, how refreshing, and she could see it in his tense yet imploring eyes. She blinked then glanced at the darkening sky. She'd made a point to never depend on anyone after the day she'd turned eighteen. Being a child at the mercy of uninterested aunts and uncles had been the most painful part of her life. She couldn't allow herself to depend on John, though she sure could use his help for a while.

Was it wise to get more deeply involved with someone she barely knew? No. Especially since she'd had a fierce crush on John until everything had gone to hell in a handbasket with this surprise pregnancy.

"Well?" John said, confusion with a touch of impatience in his stare.

"I'm thinking. Can't you give me a minute?" She glanced at him, reinforcing his jerk status, then went back to staring at the sky. She didn't know what the heck she wanted from John, yet he was offering to open his home to her. It wasn't all about herself any more. Nope. She had a baby to think about. Was there anything wrong with testing the waters where John was concerned? She wouldn't dare get her hopes up or anything, but maybe for a while staying with John in a strictly platonic way could be useful for both her and her baby.

"Okay."

He lightened his hold. "Okay what? You'll give me a break?"

"I'll move in." Why mess around with pretenses. She was knocked up. He was the father. She hated where

she lived, and he'd just offered her a room in his homey
condo—a beautiful apartment in a gorgeous part of the
city. Why be coy?

"Just like that, you change your mind. You're ready
to move in?"

"Yes. I'll try it out for a week, see how things go. It
will depend on whether or not we're compatible. In a
strictly platonic way. Got it?"

His shocked expression quickly turned to happy, then
ricocheted to suspicious. "Whatever you say, dumpling."

She slowly shook her head. Even if it was a crumb,
he'd offered to help, and though she'd been prepared to
make it through this pregnancy on her own, she appre-
ciated his gesture, knowing it was way out of his comfort zone. How often in her life had she been invited
into a home? Why not take advantage of a win-win
situation? A nice place to live. Good food prepared in
a kitchen without grease stains everywhere. A roomy
bathroom without leaky faucets, mildew, and cracked
tile. She could walk to work. Take walks by the East
River in the evenings. If she got sick there'd be a doctor in the house.

He tugged on his earlobe, a combination of relief and
shock registering on his face. "Okay, then. It's settled.
One week with the option to make it longer, okay?"

"Sweet."

"Now will you have the scampi?"

Against her will a laugh escaped her lips. "Sure, why
not?" He guided her back into the restaurant. "It isn't
every day a girl gets a proposition she can't refuse, *plus*
a shrimp dinner."

He ran his hand over his short hair. "Yeah, well, it
didn't come out the way I'd practiced."

She sputtered another laugh. "You practiced that?"

"Like I said…" He pulled out the chair so she could sit back down.

It did her heart good to see a grown man and skilled orthopedic surgeon, department head like John Griffin fumble and stumble over his words and actions because of her. Maybe she and the baby did mean something to him. *Don't let yourself go there. He's got a lot of proving to do first.*

She sat down and took another sip of water. There was only one way to find out if the man cared about her or not, and under these challenging and unusual circumstances she'd made a snap decision to find out.

By moving in for a week.

Saturday afternoon, John helped Polly move out of her tiny rented room and managed to fit everything in the trunk and back seat of his car. She'd decided to bring everything so she wouldn't have to keep running back to the old place for this or that as the need arose. Besides, there wasn't that much and why leave anything for Mrs. Goldman to snoop through while she was gone?

When she assessed all her worldly belongings, it made her heart feel a little heavier in her chest. The only precious item was a small cherry-wood jewelry box that had belonged to her mother. In it was a delicate gold locket with an enameled cover. It was heart shaped and opened to her mother's picture on one side and Polly's on the other. Thinking about her single cherished item from twenty-one years ago made her wonder what object John still treasured from Lisa.

Back at the apartment, she would set the boundaries right off—she intended to stay in his guest room rather than share his bed. Until he could move on from his past, there was no point in trying for a real relationship with John. It kind of hurt her feelings when he didn't put up a fight about their sleeping arrangements, but she let those thoughts pass.

For a reputed grumpy old department head, John had been polite and helpful the whole weekend, and she began to see the balloon-twisting, cast-signing side of him. The man all the kids on the orthopedic ward adored. He made coffee in the morning and breakfast after that. Before she could offer to make lunch, he beat her to it. Being in his home, he was more relaxed and extremely considerate about making her feel welcome. If only the rest of the staff could see through his shield, but children seemed to have that special gift of looking into the true heart of a person. As for her, she was happy for the new glimpse of him.

On Sunday afternoon John took her on a walking tour of his neighborhood, which was another way of making her feel welcome. Delighted to find a yarn shop, she talked him into letting her go inside. Not in the least bit interested, he waited outside, chatting with a neighbor he'd run into, and she made her purchase quickly, embarrassed to let him see what she'd bought. It was silly, she knew, but she hadn't knitted in a long time and, well, she was pregnant! She kept the items in a brown bag and his lack of interest made it easy to drop the subject so on they walked through the amazing and upscale neighbourhood of Sutton Place.

They ended the tour on a bench at a small park overlooking the East River. How different this part of town was from the Lower East Side. From a money standpoint, John lived a charmed life, but she knew the whole story—he was alone and hurting. Terribly alone. Even though it seemed he was the one with all the advantages, she knew she could bring something sorely missing into his life. Maybe, with this pregnancy, she could help him experience joy again.

As she stared at the Queensboro Bridge arching across the river, she hoped for any tiny miracle that could open John's heart again. If an unexpected pregnancy was what it would take to shake some life back into him, so be it.

Deep in thought, she jumped when he took her hand. "What do you say we head for home?"

Home? Did she really and finally have a home?

"I thought I'd make pasta for dinner tonight."

So far he'd cooked all the meals. "Why don't you let me cook tonight?"

"Let me take care of you."

Polly couldn't let herself dream too much. All the years she'd never let herself get too comfortable wherever she was staying had trained her to take nothing for granted. If she got swept up in this little fantasy of having a home, it would hurt that much more when reality kicked in, and in her life reality always stepped in.

"Besides, you're my guest. It's my job to make you feel at home."

So she was just a guest. She really needed to keep that in mind. She may as well let him wait on her, and while he made the spaghetti sauce she'd start her knitting project.

By Monday, Polly didn't know how the hospital radar had picked it up so fast but she'd noticed odd glances and hushed conversations that stopped abruptly whenever she got near. It wasn't in her nature to be paranoid, but she was beginning to wonder if someone had been spying on her and John over the weekend.

During lunch, while eating another carefully prepared meal by John, she cornered Darren and grilled him. "Is something going on I don't know about?"

"I think I should be asking you that," he said, taking a huge bite of an Italian lunchmeat sandwich.

"What's everyone whispering about?" She decided to continue to play dumb.

"We're all wondering exactly when you and Dr. Griffin found the time to become a couple. That's all."

"We're not a couple."

"You're not. A couple."

She thinned her lips and shook her head.

"Who made that lunch for you?" He used his sandwich to point at her wholewheat bread, sliced chicken with avocado and sprouts sandwich.

She thought about lying but that wasn't in her nature. "John—I mean Dr. Griffin did." She didn't want to come clean until she cleared it with John.

"And who'd you walk into work with this morning?

In a month or two it would be apparent enough that she was pregnant, but until then why rush to tell everyone? "I got kicked out of my apartment and Dr. Griffin said I could use his guest room until I found something else." Okay, it was a half-lie, but she didn't have to spill the beans about being pregnant just yet.

Darren leveled her with a you-can't-fool-me glare. "His guest room. Uh-huh."

She leaned forward and got in his face. "Yes, uh-huh, his guest room. And I'd appreciate it if you kept everything I've told you to yourself, Darren."

He stared into her eyes, as if assessing how serious she was, then seemed to make his decision. "My lips are sealed," he said, immediately taking another huge bite of sandwich.

Realizing her personal business would sooner or later

become a juicy story for workplace gossip made her feel queasy. She'd only managed to eat half of her own sandwich but had already lost her appetite.

The next morning Polly moaned over the bathroom toilet, experiencing her first full-fledged bout of morning sickness. Lord, how would she be able to go to work feeling as though she stood on the ledge of losing it all, just waiting for someone or something to nudge her over?

"Breakfast is ready!" John called from the kitchen.

Oh, God, that was all it took. She hurled.

"I'm not hungry." She'd come up for air and managed to call back between bouts.

A few seconds later determined footsteps down the hardwood hallway grew closer. He tapped on the bathroom door. "You okay?"

"If you call being sick to your stomach okay, then I'm peachy."

"Morning sickness?"

She moaned instead of replied.

He waited outside while she cleaned up, rinsed out her mouth and opened the bathroom door. "I think if you eat some dry cereal or saltine crackers before you get out of bed tomorrow, it might help."

The thought of eating anything made her stomach clench in preparation for losing more of its contents. She twitched her nose and put her hand over her mouth. "I'm sorry, but your cologne is making me more nauseous."

"I'll wash it off," he said, without giving it a second thought.

A few minutes later he was at her bedroom door with a plastic bag in his hand. "You might think this is crazy, but it used to help Lisa." He handed her the bag filled with lemon slices. "It helps to smell citrus or suck on peppermint if odors set off your nausea." He handed her a roll of peppermints. "You can squeeze the lemon into water, too. Oh, and I can get some bottled fruit juice and make popsicles for you to suck on so you won't get dehydrated."

She wanted more than anything to be grateful for the sweet gesture, but everything he said had to do with eating, and her nausea grew worse and worse. She walked backwards toward the bathroom, listening to him and bobbing her head, then quickly closed the door.

"I'll tell Brooke you're not coming in today. You can't go to work like this."

"I don't have sick leave yet. I won't get paid."

"That's the last thing you need to worry about. I'll handle it," he said, walking way.

And handle it he did. From the bathroom she could hear him all the way down the hall.

"Brooke? It's Dr. Griffin. Listen, Polly is having morning sickness and needs to miss work today. How do I know?"

Obviously, John hadn't thought through all the ramifications of him calling in sick on Polly's behalf. Now what would he do?

"Well, uh. Listen, this is strictly confidential. She's staying with me for now. Just keep that between you and me, okay?"

Polly moaned. Didn't he have a clue? The effect of his innocent honesty showed how out of touch he was with his own staff, and the phone call, coupled with what she'd already let slip with Darren, was nothing short of a department-wide gossip memo announcing they now lived together and she was pregnant with his baby.

So much for keeping the cat in the bag a bit longer.

As if feeling sick to her stomach wasn't enough, the realization that soon everyone at work would know her personal business sent her head right back into the bowl.

John wasn't sure he'd ever get used to the quick glances and whispers whenever he did rounds on the orthopedic ward, so he chose to ignore them. He did, however, have to admit that never in a million years would he expect his name to be linked to a sweet small-town girl like Polly Seymour.

Having her living with him hadn't taken nearly as much getting used to as he'd assumed he'd need. She was quiet and calm, and sometimes he barely knew she was there, especially when she went to her room and did whatever she did after dinner until she went to bed. He wished she'd come out of her room more often and spend time with him.

He sensed she didn't want to be any more of an imposition than she assumed she was. Truth was, she wasn't an imposition at all. He liked having her there, having someone to cook for and look after. Someone to talk things over with. He liked her gentle, sunny nature, too. He even got a kick out of the twangy country music she liked to listen to on the radio in her room.

His apartment had never seemed more like a home.

John walked toward a fourteen-year-old boy's room to talk with the mother about Thursday's scheduled knee and ankle repair. The young teen, named Eric Caldera, had injured it playing in the dark at summer camp in Maine. It would be a long procedure and involve pins and plates and possibly even a bone graft. He wouldn't know exactly how extensive the repair would be until he started surgery.

Eric's parents were estranged, making all consultations tricky. The father had visitation rights with Eric, but the mother preferred never to be in the same room with him. Cases like these at Angel's required social services to step in to work out the details so all involved, especially the patient, could have their wishes met. After seeing the mother, who wouldn't leave her son's bedside, he'd give a call to the father and repeat everything he'd said to the mother. It might be double work, but he believed both parents deserved to be informed.

On his way into the room his gaze met and held Polly's. Something odd fizzed through his chest, and he winked at her. Her sky-blue eyes got wide and she covered with her hand the smile threatening to burst free. He liked taking her by surprise…like that night they'd made love.

She looked cute in her brightly colored top covered in cartoon angels on clouds and those bright pink scrub pants. Pretty in pink. Yeah, his new roommate was pretty in pink.

Entering the patient room, his smile was wide. Well, wide by John Griffin's standards, anyway, because he had something special to look forward to. Later today he'd accompany Polly for her first ultrasound at Geoff's office.

Standing beside the procedure table in the darkened ultrasonographer's room, John was as interested as Polly in seeing the first view of their baby. An ultrasound this early in the game wasn't called for, but more than anything John wanted to make sure the pregnancy was well implanted.

Having followed the preparation orders to a T, Polly

had been dancing around the waiting room, swearing she'd wet herself if they didn't take her in soon. He'd laughed at her antics, wishing he could help her get comfortable some way, but knew this was totally out of his realm of expertise.

Polly lay on the table with a sheet over her abdomen, looking excited yet in pain from her extra-full bladder. When the tech pulled back the sheet and squirted the cold conducting gel on her belly, she glanced at him, raised her shoulders and grimaced, letting out a tiny squeal. How could that flat abdomen possibly house a baby? John wondered. He hadn't seen her smooth ivory skin since the night they'd been together, and his reaction of longing to touch her surprised him. But now was not the time or place to get hot for his live-in nurse.

He'd pulled strings to have the ultrasound this early along in the pregnancy. After all, it had been barely five weeks since she'd gotten pregnant, the baby's heart wouldn't even be completely formed or beating yet, but Geoff was more than happy to accommodate them.

"We'll only be able to see the gestational sac," the sonographer said as she moved the transducer back and forth over Polly's taut skin.

Polly reached out and on reflex John took her hand. She squeezed, and he mindlessly ran his thumb back and forth over her icy fingers. He wanted to kiss her, right there in front of the tech. He didn't give a damn. He wanted to kiss her.

But he didn't, choosing instead to squeeze back on her hand when the fan-shaped image of Polly's uterus first appeared on the monitor.

"There it is," the tech said. "That's the gestational sac. Oh, and see that tiny thing? About the size of an orange seed? That's the embryo."

John had to squint to see it, but it was there. Their baby. The hair on his arms rose as assorted feelings of awe and joy along with an ancient ache rolled through him. He was definitely going to be a father, and he remembered exactly how he'd felt when Lisa had told him the news all those years ago.

"Oh, my gosh, look at that, Johnny," Polly said on gust of breath.

Warmth enveloped him, reaching through layers of protection to the deepest part of his heart as he glanced first at the screen then into the face of an angel. His angel, who'd brought life back into his lonely existence.

"Looks like we're really having a baby, dumpling."

The look she returned, full of wonder, joy, and excitement, was worth every single one of those twelve barren years.

John took Polly to a restaurant in Central Park for dinner on the balmy August evening. Outside on the deck they watched swans and ducks, rowboats, and even a gondola drift by as she sipped lemonade. She ordered hazelnut-crusted East Coast halibut with asparagus, cherry tomatoes, mushrooms and some kind of divine vinaigrette, grateful her morning sickness always seemed to wane by early afternoons. He went for a curry with shrimp and scallops.

As they ate, things loosened up between them. Even more incredibly, John opened up to her about his family without Polly prodding him first.

"My sister Dana is going to be floored when she finds out I'm going to be a father."

"Is she close by?"

He shook his head. "She lives in Rhode Island. She's been on my butt to get married again for years." His eyes drifted away momentarily and Polly wondered what he was thinking. Certainly he wasn't thinking about marrying her.

"Uh, Johnny, we hardly know each other. Aren't we going to just wait and see how things work out?"

He pulled back from his brief mental absence. "Oh, of course. I was just thinking back to when I lost Lisa and how important Dana was in helping me get by. My mom and dad were as devastated as I was and, well Dana was this rock for all of us."

"She sounds like a great sister. I always wished I'd had a sister or brother."

"We hated each other growing up, but now we're like this." He crossed his fingers. "First thing every summer I give her and her husband, Jerome, a break by taking my nephews camping."

"That sounds fun. Where did you go this year?"

"Maine. Acadia National Park."

"I've never been."

"You've got to go. It's beautiful."

There were so many places she'd never seen. Dare she dream of having someone to travel with and share special moments? Her mind drifted far away to the land of dreams come true, and she hadn't a clue how long she stayed there but most of her dinner had been eaten and John was talking about his parents when she checked back in.

"My parents eat dinner at four-thirty every day in Florida. They drive around in these electric carts like everyone else in the retirement community, it's the funniest thing. I took my life in my hands when I visited last year and insisted on walking around the place. They need some kind of signage that says '*Pedestrians Be-*

ware'! I nearly got sideswiped twice." He gave that genuine cockeyed smile she'd come to adore.

Polly laughed, imagining John dodging electric carts in some distant retirement community.

When dessert came, she ventured into uncharted waters. "Do you think it's too early to think about names?"

"Mort," he said. "I like Mort." When John let down his guard he had natural deadpan humor. At least, she hoped he was being funny about this name business.

She threw a leftover piece of bread at him. "No way, dude." The impish expression on his face gave him away.

"Hey, my favorite uncle was named Mortimer." Such a tease John was.

"What do you think about Sterling?"

"It's okay, but only if I can call him Mort for short."

She rolled her eyes and glanced at the full moon hanging in the sky. Mr. Sterling had been her favorite teacher in high school, the one who had encouraged her to pursue the sciences. She'd always thought his last name would make a great first name.

"How about Caledonia for a girl? We could call her Callie."

Polly couldn't read John's face on this one. Was he kidding or...? Actually, Callie wasn't such a bad name. "Sweet. I like it."

"You do?" His brows tented together. "It was my grandmother's name." He tugged his earlobe then drank the last of his after-dinner coffee and leaned back in his chair. The night air and hint of jasmine helped engrave this more-than-fine moment in her mind. Because she didn't own a camera, she'd have to take a mental picture to remember for the rest of her life. Had she ever dreamed about casually tossing baby names around with a man before?

He'd also been by her side for the day's exciting test. Not because he'd made the appointment but because he'd wanted to be. They'd seen their baby together for the first time and celebrated with this romantic yet playful dinner by the Central Park Lake.

"I guess I'm a traditionalist at heart," he said, with that adorable half-lifted smile.

At that moment affection and something more flooded her heart for John, almost making it hard to breathe. She wanted this. So. Much.

"Why are you looking at me all funny like that?" he asked.

"I'm not looking at you funny."

"Yes you are. It's sort of like this." He imitated a goofy I'm-in-love-with-a-dove look and she burst out laughing.

"I've never made a look like that in my life!" She feigned offense.

He repeated the silly expression and they laughed together while he paid the bill and continued all the way out of the restaurant to the car.

Arriving back at his apartment, they strolled toward the doorman, holding hands. Marco greeted them with a broad and telling grin.

"Beautiful night," Marco said.

"It is," John said, lightly squeezing her hand.

All afternoon and into the evening Polly had thought she'd fallen through the looking glass into a parallel world filled with bright colors, good will, and dreams come true. John was by her side. He wouldn't desert her over the pregnancy, as she'd feared. He'd promised and she believed him.

Marco opened the door and Polly snuggled into John's shoulder as they got into the elevator, feeling like half of a real couple. The fact he'd called her dumpling earlier hadn't escaped her. He smiled down at her and brushed his fingertips across her cheek. She saw the look, the same one he'd let slip several times during dinner. He wanted her. Badly.

As he unlocked the apartment door, the only question left on Polly's mind was who would make the first move.

Before he switched on the lights he stopped her by the front door, brought his lips down to hers and kissed her tenderly. She'd missed kissing him and savored his smooth, soft lips surrounded by end-of-day stubble. He broke free from the kiss first and flipped the light switch. Under the entryway light, he cupped her face in his palms and looked deeply into her eyes with his hazel stare. She couldn't help but notice the tiny gold flecks around the pupils. They were kind eyes, and right now expressed desire. For her.

"Things will be different this time. I promise," he said.

She went up on tiptoe to reach his lips. "I liked it last time just fine." He enfolded her in his strong arms and kissed her thoroughly. She'd never felt sexier or safer in her life.

Once he'd kissed her into a mindless state where all senses vibrated on alert, he took her hand and led her down the hall, bypassing her room and heading straight for his bedroom.

She'd peeked into both his office and bedroom several times over the last week, but had never stepped inside either room. Never considered being in his bedroom again before now. It was a strongly masculine room, like him, with big, dark wood furniture and deep blue covers over the king-sized bed. The walls were pale gray and peaceful. Though peace was the last thought on her mind at the moment.

Her breathing quickened as he stepped toward her, removing her shoulder bag and unbuttoning her top. She'd brought a change of clothes to work, knowing they had a doctor's appointment and not wanting to wear work scrubs there. She started to help him with her blouse.

He stilled her hands. "Let me." Always in charge.

The thought of letting him have his way with her sent a second wave of heat across her skin and a subtle coiling in her core. She knew what letting go with John in control meant. As he unbuttoned more, the tiny raised bumps didn't go unnoticed by him, and one corner of his mouth lifted in appreciation as he delicately traced his fingertips across her clavicle. That set her nerve endings to humming all the way down to her waist.

With her top opened, he pushed it over her shoulders and kissed the side of her neck. The single kiss sprinkled more tingles across her chest, this time dipping down to her center. With nipples tight and tender, she couldn't wait for him to remove the bra she could barely squeeze into any more. He did.

One raised brow signaled he'd noticed the change in size, too. He took the weight of her breasts into his hands, gently lifting and massaging then kissing each one.

How much more could she take standing up?

He must have read her mind because he bent over and scooped her up behind the knees, carrying her to his huge bed. He pulled back the covers and lowered her then undid his buckle and removed his belt. She took the cue to take off her slacks.

"Uh-uh," he said, stopping her in mid-zip. "Let me do it."

He crawled over her on the bed, kissed her breasts again, taking longer this time, making her gasp with pleasure, then unzipped and peeled back her pants. He quickly unbuttoned his shirt and removed it then his undershirt, all the while looking at her with hungry eyes. Heat engulfed every surface of her skin in anticipation of what would follow.

She loved the sight of his body, thick muscles and broad shoulders, a wide patch of brown hair across his chest. Not the kind of man you'd see in a model's magazine but a man's man, solid, all testosterone and heat. Boy, could she feel the heat.

First taking a full and firm feel of one hip and cheek, he removed her French-cut underwear in record time. The man broke bones and realigned them for a living, his grip didn't go unnoticed. She glanced into his eyes and could tell that even now he was practicing restraint. In the next second his slacks were gone along with his briefs, and seeing him completely naked she remembered how he'd brought her to climax over and over their first night together.

She reached for his arousal but he intercepted her hand, giving her a firm look. He was taking control. Again. Fine by her. If he wanted to devour her, she'd let him.

As he dropped kisses across her chest and stomach, she arched and writhed in order to keep her hands to herself. When he reached the top of her thigh, gliding his tongue towards her center, she couldn't help herself and grasped his head, holding on for dear life as he kissed and licked her most sensitive parts. Unrelenting, he continued, and shivers rained across her flesh, exquisite sensations folding deep inside her, until she gasped and clenched her muscles uncontrollably, the release strong enough to make her buck against his mouth. He didn't let up, staying with her until she'd ridden the mind-blowing waves to the very end.

He came up smiling as she crossed her arms over her eyes and let out a long breath. "I won't survive if you keep that up."

"I'm a doctor, I know how to resuscitate." He scooped her up and began to roll onto his back, planting both hands firmly on her hips. She rolled with him, reaching for his face, kissing him, tasting herself on his lips. That deep hip and bottom massage continued seeding her desire as she lay on top of him, and she could feel his firm length beneath her belly. Before she knew it he'd hoisted her hip up and over his erection with one hand, guiding himself inside with the other. She straddled him as he slid along every sensitive spot she owned all the way inside.

"No need for a condom this time," he said, as he began to move inside her. Their gazes met and melded together in understanding.

She adjusted her hips so they fit closer together. As if it were possible, the early pregnancy made her even more sensitive to his touch, and she wondered if he felt the change, too. His powerful hips thrust upward, the strength of his thighs lifting her off the bed. She balanced herself by placing her hands on his chest, leaning into him for added pleasure. His hands cupped and squeezed her hips and soon the lazy lifts and rolls weren't enough and they turned to rocking. Faster. Firmer. Desperately penetrating.

He stopped abruptly, and in one quick move flipped her onto her back so he could drive deeper and faster yet. Jets of pleasure rocked through her with each surge. She was gone before he'd barely gotten started, the powerful grip of her muscles sending shockwaves to every part of her body. "Johnny!"

Dissolving into his determined rhythm, she wrapped her legs around his hips, urging him deeper, encouraging his release. Bucking together for several more minutes, he reawakened her need. His strength built fiercely inside as he slid in and out at a frantic pace, until he groaned and she gasped and he erupted with a growl, sharing the bliss with her one more time.

CHAPTER EIGHT

POLLY AND JOHN lay folded together in bed for several minutes. He kissed her forehead and lightly rubbed her back while he rested his eyes. She snuggled into his chest, cushioning her head on his well-padded, muscular shoulder, enjoying the thump-thump-thump of his heart.

"From now on you sleep here with me." He didn't ask, just stated how it would be.

He'd tugged his earlobe when he'd said it, the gesture she'd come to recognize whenever he spoke from his heart. Whenever he spoke the truth.

"I'd like that," she said, embracing the magnitude of his statement. Maybe it was the ultrasound, seeing their baby together, but Polly had felt the change in John tonight. He'd let down that wall between them and finally invited her inside.

He rolled her onto his chest and had a good look at her as if for the first time, playing with her chaotic hair, brushing it out of her face and hooking it behind her ears. "I can't get enough of you, Polly." His hands drifted downwards and he cupped her bottom. "It's like I've been dead and now that you woke me up, all I want is you."

With her heart swooning over this man who wanted

to be with her, wanted her to live with him, to sleep with him, to have their baby, she kissed him long and heartfelt. Afterwards their gazes met and held—his as dreamy as she knew hers must be. Was this love? Her legs came together over his, and she discovered he was a man of his word, he really couldn't get enough of her. She cuddled his building erection with the insides of her thighs, and soon he'd slipped into her again. They stared at each other as their easily coaxed passion mounted slowly but steadily.

"I've been waiting for you a long time," he said, his voice husky with desire.

"I never knew I could be so lucky," she said, wanting nothing more than to please him for the rest of her life.

After making love again, just before they finally settled down for the night John popped out of bed and padded down the hall to the kitchen. He came right back with half a dozen saltine crackers and a glass of lemon water, placing them on Polly's bedside table.

"How thoughtful," she said, tiny prickles of contentment breaking over her. "Thank you." The small gesture meant the world to her. No one since her mother had shown they cared by doing little things. He made her lunch each day, fixed dinner more often than she did, and always asked if she'd taken her prenatal vitamins and folic acid. It might not seem like a lot, but to her his thoughtfulness was everything.

"I've got to look out for you and our baby," he said, cuddling next to her, tucking the covers around them.

Polly drifted off to sleep that night grinning, happier than she could ever remember and thinking she knew for sure who the true people-pleaser was of the two of them.

* * *

The surgery on Eric Caldera had been long and difficult, but after four hours John was satisfied he'd repaired everything to the best of his ability. Twice the anesthesiologist warned that the vital signs, especially the heart rate, had increased and a small dose of beta blocker had fixed it. Eric had been watched closely after extubation to make sure all was well. Once it was established he was breathing on his own and his vitals were stable, they sent him to the recovery room.

John left the OR and yanked off his mask, leaving patient recovery to his nurses. His first order of business was to call the father in one waiting room and the mother in another. With everything having been carefully planned by social services prior to the operation, Eric's parents had agreed to wait in separate locations. That afternoon, he'd inform each of them that surgery had been a success. Their boy would be back playing whatever sport he wanted after several months of recovery and physical therapy. The mother would be first at Eric's bedside when he returned to his room and, though unhappy about playing second fiddle, the estranged father agreed to wait an extra hour before seeing his son.

Polly took report for Eric Caldera from the recovery-room nurse. "Vital signs are stable. No sign of bleeding. Unremarkable recovery."

Polly first jotted down her notes then awaited the arrival of her patient by tending to two little girls in a double room.

"I want Dr. Griffin to make me a monkey next time." The little one with red hair held her bright pink balloon princess crown from yesterday and smiled.

"I want a monkey," the second girl said. Both her

legs were in casts, one suspended above the bed in a sling. Polly noticed John had already signed both casts and added a goofy-looking happy face next to each signature.

"Dr. Griffin will be glad to make whatever kind of balloon figure you want, as long as you both take your medicine, okay?" She wasn't above making a good bargain, especially with some of the sour-tasting pills having been an issue for these two girls over the last couple of days.

"Okay," they replied in unison sing-song fashion. Sweet, it worked!

Darren stuck his head in the room. "Your post-op just arrived."

"Thanks, Dare. Could you ask Raphael to let his mother know?" With that Polly said goodbye to the girls and trotted over to Eric's room.

Still completely out of it, Eric merely moaned when Polly, Darren and the transportation clerk slid him from the gurney to the bed she'd prepared for him. In the middle of her initial assessment Eric's mother entered the room with a huge bouquet of flowers accentuated with half a dozen bright balloons.

"How's my baby doing?" Mrs. Caldera had either used extra body splash today or the star jasmine in the bouquet was emitting a particularly strong scent.

Mostly asleep, but responsive to touch, Eric crinkled up his nose as if he didn't care for the smell. His blood pressure and pulse were low, but that was to be expected with a sedated patient, and Polly remembered the recovery nurse mentioning something about beta blockers having been given to lower his heart rate during surgery. Placing the oxygen monitor on his finger, she waited for a reading.

"He seems to be doing fine." The news smoothed the deep crease between Mrs. Caldera's brows. The oxygen saturation was at the low end of normal but holding. Polly put a nasal cannula in his nostrils and turned on the wall oxygen at two liters.

After making sure Eric was comfortable, that the site of the surgery wasn't oozing blood, the IV was intact and flowing, and checking there was good circulation to his toes, she headed out to input his medication orders into the computer. On her way she spotted John heading her way, still in OR garb, looking downright sexy and authoritative. Working to control her reaction, she grinned at him then waved.

With the blue OR cap still on his head, he gave her the smile that crinkled the corners of his dark eyes, and never failed to send her heart beating double time. Also on a mission, he headed for Eric's room.

Polly set out for the medicine room to get afternoon meds for the two little girls in her other assigned room. Now that she'd bargained with them, she expected them to co-operate. In the middle of her getting the medicine, another nurse entered and she got into a conversation about a memo going around regarding blood-sugar testing and new finger-stick protocol. When the conversation ended and she'd finished pouring her meds, she heard a code blue over the loudspeaker.

"Code blue. Room 614. code blue. Room 614."

Eric's room! She rushed back to the ward only to find a crowd gathered around the door of her patient. What could have gone wrong in the few minutes she'd been away? Peering inside, she saw John was at the helm of the code in progress, calling out orders while working to re-intubate the teen. The ambu bag was in readiness in the nearby respiratory therapist's hands.

One of the medical aides assisted the mother out of the room. The woman was crying and visibly shaken. "One minute he was fine, the next he stopped breathing. What happened to my baby?"

Knowing the code team was there in full force, Polly rushed to Mrs. Caldera's side to offer support. "He's in good hands. If he's having trouble breathing, they'll fix him right up. Has your son ever been diagnosed with asthma?"

"No. When he was a baby one doctor said he had twitchy lungs, but he's never had a problem."

Could the boy have asthma and not know it? Could the sharp scent of those flowers have set him off? Or perhaps the latex in the balloons? She searched her memory for "latex allergy" on his chart, but was positive she hadn't seen any allergies noted. Latex was such a common allergy these days that John's balloons were all latex free, and the hospital had been a latex-free zone from the beginning, but who knew about florist displays? Polly was surprised Mrs. Caldera had gotten that bouquet past the hospital entrance.

Oh, God, Eric had been given a beta blocker in surgery for his elevated vital signs, if he was having an asthma attack that drug would make the effect much worse and would block the antidote. She knew John was well aware of all the medications given during the surgery, and the code team was top-notch, so she settled for worrying her lower lip with her teeth along with Mrs. Caldera.

Five minutes. She held the mother's hand and promised all would be well. Ten minutes. The rush and chaos inside the room continued in a tunnel of noise.

"We need more epi," a resident hollered from the doorway.

Leaving Mrs. Caldera with the medical aide, Polly shot across the ward to the med room to retrieve more medicine, wondering who'd been assigned to restock the crash cart that day. How could they run out of epi during a respiratory arrest? If they *had* gone through that much epi, it couldn't bode well for poor Eric.

With shaky hands Polly got the medicine and rushed to the entrance of Eric's room.

"All clear," John called out, holding the defibrillator paddles in place on the boy's chest and torso. He zapped Eric with enough joules to start a horse's heart. All eyes went to the heart monitor. No change. Flat line.

Polly delivered the epinephrine and went back to Mrs. Caldera, positioned close enough for Polly to peer through the door. They defibrillated Eric again with the same outcome.

The mood in the patient room had changed drastically. John stood sullenly at the head of the bed, head down, staring at his patient with deep remorse in his eyes. No matter that the respiratory therapist squeezed the ambu bag to force breathing, the flat-lined bedside monitor squawking its continual alarm told the full story. A young teenager had had a respiratory arrest, which had led to a full code, and he had died after surgery.

Never could anyone have foretold this outcome for a routine surgery on an otherwise healthy child, yet sometimes it happened. Truth was, surgeries were never routine.

With terror in her eyes Eric's mother sensed the change. "My baby. Is it all over? Is my baby all right?" She tore away from Polly and the medical aide and lurched for the hospital room.

Polly intercepted her but the mother's weight pushed

her off balance. Polly stood firm, held her in a hug. "Give us a second, Mrs. Caldera. Please."

In a desperate move the mother broke away. "I want to see my boy."

John stepped into the hallway just as she reached the threshold. He braced her by both shoulders, a grief-stricken look in his eyes. "I'm so sorry, Mrs. Caldera. He stopped breathing then his heart stopped. We did everything in our power to save him."

Her scream reverberated off the ward walls.

John held her tight and let her cry. He glanced over her shoulder at Polly with a grim expression. "Go and find the father in OR waiting room two and let him know what's happened. I'll explain everything to him when he gets here."

Dreading having to face a parent and tell them their child had just died, something she'd never had to do before and which wasn't normally an RN's job, she bit her lower lip and nodded solemnly, wanting some way, somehow to help John through this tragedy. Oh, God, what would she say to the father? How would she tell him the boy had been alive one minute and dead the next?

Rather than wait for the elevator, she hustled down the stairs, her legs shaky from the adrenaline pouring throughout her system. Arriving on the third floor, thinking her heart might just jump right out of her chest, she found waiting room number two. A tall, overweight, swarthy-looking man in a business suit paced the floor. The instant she arrived he looked up. "Are you Eric's nurse? Can I see him now?"

Her heart practically burst. How was she supposed to tell him? "There's been a problem, Mr. Caldera. Dr. Griffin will explain everything to you—"

He stopped in his tracks. "What do you mean there's been a problem?"

"Eric stopped breathing and—"

He grabbed her by both arms and squeezed to the point of pain. "You'd better not be telling me what I think…"

"I'm so sorry, Mr. Cal—"

He shoved her aside, exiting the room, and she bumped against the doorframe.

Rubbing her elbow, focused solely on her task, she followed him down the hall. "Mr. Caldera, it will be quicker if you take the stairs. Follow me."

With fury in his eyes, his jaw set, he came at her. She opened the door to the stairwell and he followed her inside. "It's three flights up," she said, stepping back for him to go first, "but much faster than the elevator."

"You killed him. You killed my son!" He glanced up the stairwell. "Are you trying to kill me, too?" Three steps above her, with a contorted, out-of-control, grief-stricken expression on his face, he kicked out at her, the leather sole of his shoe landing solidly on her solar plexus. It knocked the wind from her lungs and sent her hurtling down the lower flight of stairs.

Head over heels she tumbled, arms flailing, searching for purchase, enduring sharp pangs of pain as first her shoulder, then her head, then her back and bottom hit cement, all the way to the lower landing.

She couldn't breathe and clutched at the point of greatest pain, her stomach, as Eric's father raced out of the stairwell. If she could inhale she'd call for help, and warn John what was coming his way.

Trying her hardest to get to her feet, still unable to catch her breath, the dim stairway light faded to black.

* * *

Polly worked to open her eyes. Everything hurt. She wasn't at the bottom of the stairs. No, she was on a thin mattress. Cracking one eye open, the bright lights of the emergency department had her immediately snapping it shut. But not before she saw John, and felt the warmth of his hand over hers.

"How are you feeling, dumpling?" he asked, obvious concern in his voice.

"Like I got kicked down a flight of stairs."

"God, I'm so, so sorry." He leaned close, held her hand between both of his, lifting it to his mouth where he kissed her fingers. "Forgive me."

"I'll be okay." She tried an achy smile, which quickly turned into a grimace. She did a quick test—her arms moved, her ankles rotated, her knees bent, her neck twisted just fine. Of course it hurt like heck to do any of the movements, but she could move. That was a start. "I'll get over all these bangs and bruises in no time."

The rows of lines in his forehead and wary dark gaze told a different story. "I shouldn't have sent you to do my job," he said.

"John, you had your hands full with the mother. You'd just coded your patient. If the parents could get along they would have been there together. You can't do everything."

He shook his head, biting his lower lip. "I should have sent the resident to tell Mr. Caldera."

"You were in shock from the failed resuscitation. Your resident was busy with the clean-up." She reached up to hold him, and his desperate need to hold her tight warned something more was at stake. "I'm okay, I swear. I'm okay, John."

He pulled back, shaking his head. *She wasn't okay?*

The only thing she saw in his eyes was pain. "You're bleeding, sweetheart. The baby…" His voice cracked on the word. He shook his head again.

Her pregnancy was in jeopardy? Little Callie? "Did I miscarry?" Her eyes welled up as she said the word.

He shook his head—a world of weariness in his gaze. "No. They're keeping you for observation for now." One tear slid down the outer part of his left eye, soon followed by another on the right. "I'm so sorry."

She believed with all of her heart that he was sorry. But she was bleeding. Her hands covered her face as the deep emptiness of possibly losing her pregnancy took hold. Soon her hands were covered in tears as she rocked forward and back, unleashing the dammed-up tears of a lifetime filled with disappointment.

John held her and moaned. She used his shoulder to brace her forehead as she bawled until there was nothing left. The brightest spot in her life, her pregnancy, was in jeopardy.

CHAPTER NINE

IN THE CRAMPED and drab ER cubicle, John held Polly until she was ready to let go. Until she'd digested the awful news. She'd had the life nearly kicked out of her womb, and he'd been responsible for sending her to do his job. She could have been killed falling down those stairs.

The words "guilt" and "anger" didn't come close to how he judged himself.

"Can you help me to the bathroom?" she said.

"Of course." He hopped to her side and dragged the IV machine along with them. She felt so vulnerable under his care that it made his heart wrench. Against all odds he hoped this pregnancy would survive. They'd have a new start, get their chance to be parents. Hell, he'd even marry her before the baby was born. Yeah, that's what he'd do.

Would the Big Guy hear his prayer and promise?

If our baby survives, to make things up to Polly, I'll marry her and be the best damn father on the planet. If only you'll let our baby make it. Not for me, for her. No. That's a lie. For me, too. I want this. I really do.

Helping Polly into the bathroom, he closed the door and waited outside.

Soon her moan carried through the thin wall loud and clear.

"What's wrong, sweetheart?" He rushed inside to find her sitting on the toilet, dejected and bereft. "Are you okay?"

"I just miscarried." She whimpered the phrase so softly he didn't understand what she'd meant at first. As the words sank in, he dropped to his knees in front of her and put his forehead to hers. Was this some cruel joke? How many times was he supposed to lose everything dear to him? He ground his molars.

"Oh, baby, I'm so sorry. So, so sorry." Rather than call for the nurse, he helped clean her up and walked her back to the bed. He put on the call light for the nurse, then made Polly comfortable, but there was no way on earth anything he could do would take away her loss or her pain. She'd lost the baby. Their baby. Her tears ran without effort down her cheeks. So did his as sorrow wrapped around his chest and squeezed the last of his feelings from him.

When the nurse arrived he told her what had happened.

"We'll need to schedule a D&C," he said, knowing the routine protocol for such things.

"I'll get right on that, Doctor," the nurse said on the way out the door.

John held Polly's fragile body until she fell asleep. Pacing the tiny ER cubicle, thoughts stabbed at his conscience. He hadn't been able to protect his wife and future child before, and look at him now—he'd sent Polly into the eye of the storm. He hadn't been there for Lisa and now he hadn't been there when Polly had needed him most. Hell, it was his job to tell parents when their children died, yet distracted by the failed code, in partial denial, and concentrating on Mrs. Caldara he'd taken the easy way out and sent Polly to fetch the father.

She could have been killed! Now she'd lost her baby.

What kind of man was he?

A man who didn't deserve to be loved by Polly or anyone else on earth.

Her lids fluttered and cracked open. He sat straighter. "You need anything?"

She studied him for several seconds with reflective eyes, as if she could read his thoughts, then shook her head soberly and went back to napping. He reached for her hand out of obligation, his fingers nearly as numb as his heart had become over the last few hours, and he stayed by her side for the remainder of the afternoon. In limbo. Lost, without a tether. Prayers unanswered. His heart cracked apart. He had nothing left to offer.

"They're ready for her in the procedure room," the nurse said at the cubicle entrance.

John jumped to his feet, prepared to go along with Polly.

As if she'd sensed his rote response, she looked at him. "I'll be fine. You don't have to come along."

"Are you sure?" He didn't even put up a fight.

"Positive." She squeezed his dull grip and he kissed her forehead, though his lips were numb, too.

"See you later, then," he said, watching the gurney roll down the corridor, not sure he recognized his own flat and distant voice.

Polly put her stained work clothes in the plastic bag provided by the hospital. She'd changed into the clothes John had brought from home. "I'm ready," she said that evening.

"Okay." He stood, his eyes drifting everywhere but

to hers. "I'll bring the car round and meet you at the ER entrance."

The transportation clerk waited nearby with a wheelchair. Protocol was protocol, and Polly felt too weak and achy to fight it.

When she met him at the curbside of the hospital exit, John hopped out of the car ready to assist her from the wheelchair, seeming robotic and acting out of duty. Yet he was here, she reminded herself, attempting to hold onto the positive. At least he hadn't run away from their depressing mess.

His hand felt chilly to the touch when he helped her stand. Again, his eyes avoided hers and she curled her lower lip and chewed on it just to have something else to concentrate on.

Unable to think of a single thing to say, Polly remained quiet on the drive on Central Park South toward Sutton Place, choosing instead to watch the tree-lined streets they passed. Once they were back in the apartment, he helped her to the guest room, where he'd already pulled back the covers in readiness. He must have planned making the change from lover to guest when he'd come back earlier to get her change of clothes and the car.

"I thought you'd be more comfortable in here," he said when she'd sent him a questioning glance. The ball of emotion swelling in her chest sank to her stomach when she noticed how detached he seemed. Cold even.

Too weak and bumped up to protest, she got under the covers and let him tuck her in.

Every considerate thing he did felt distant and done out of obligation as the evening wore on. He brought her a tray with soup and crackers, helped her to the bathroom when she wanted to get ready to turn in for the night, and assisted her back to bed as if she were a fragile ninety-year-old woman. Making her feel nothing like the woman he'd made love to.

Polly had hoped to curl into his protective embrace tonight. To sleep next to him and feel his heat radiate over her, healing her. Together they could get through this by clinging close and comforting one another. She'd hoped to regain the strength that had hemorrhaged out during the course of this incredibly long day by being by his side. But John had sent her back to the guest room without even asking her, as if without the pregnancy he no longer had reason to make her a part of his life.

What they'd made together was no more.

She was plumb out of tears as she lay in the darkness, staring at the white ceiling.

Today she'd been kicked down the stairs, she'd lost her baby, and somehow during the horrific series of events she may as well have been kicked in the gut again, because now she'd lost John, too.

Three days later Polly insisted on going back to work. She couldn't bear the thought of being a prisoner in John's apartment another day, and longed for the distraction of a busy orthopedic ward. They'd hardly spoken since the miscarriage and she felt more like an obligation than a lover and a grieving partner.

At times he'd pulled so deeply inside himself that she'd felt like an invasive war lord, demanding attention whenever she'd tried to engage him in the simplest things.

"Want to help make a salad?" she'd said the previous night, insisting making her own dinner.

"You go ahead," he said. "I'm not hungry."

She ate alone while he sequestered himself in his

study. They hadn't taken one meal together since the miscarriage.

At work, word traveled fast. During the Monday morning report Polly accepted each and every hug from her friends and fellow staff. It felt good to be back. At least in Darren's and Brooke's eyes she saw genuine sadness, something missing from John's. When she looked into his eyes, the unfathomable detachment made it seem like he wasn't there. As if he'd checked out for good.

Piling the pain of losing John on top of the heartache of her miscarriage, she could barely stand up straight. The house had become heavy with silence, washed in colorless depression. At night she'd hole up in her room working on a bitter-sweet but necessary project.

Warm hands rested on her shoulders. For an instant Polly imagined John had walked up behind her. He'd barely touched her since she'd lost the baby. Maybe there was still hope? Maybe all could be well again? She turned to find Raphael, his kind eyes probing hers, and she tried not to look disappointed. "You've got a phone call," he said.

"Oh, thanks." Shaken out of her thoughts, she forced a shift in her attitude. She was at work and needed to give it her full concentration. She punched the blinking light and picked up the receiver. "This is Polly."

"Ms. Seymour, it's Mrs. Goldman." Her landlady. "I have someone interested in taking your room. I know you paid me for an extra month, but…"

"No. Please, Mrs. Goldman, I'd like to keep that room a little while longer. I'm paid up through August and September. If you'd like, I'll pay for October now, too."

Agreeing on a compromise, Polly hung up the phone

feeling less helpless in her current living situation by having another option.

"Who in the blazes messed with the bed traction in Room Twelve?" John sounded like an ornery bear as he headed toward Brooke at the nurses' station. His rugged, masculine appeal had vanished along with his civil mood.

"P.T. was in there earlier," Brooke said, straightening her shoulders and making her taller-than-average frame seem even taller.

"Get them up here, now!" he growled, and stormed off to the next room.

Brooke glanced at Polly, alarm in her eyes. How quickly they'd forgotten how difficult John could be. No longer an avowed people-pleaser, Polly shrugged, realizing she'd also lost her magic touch where John was concerned, and went seeking solace in her assigned patient room. A teeny-bopper with bright eyes and a lively attitude was just the distraction she needed. *Sweet.* And thank heavens for small favors.

"Who forgot to put Brandon Seamus in the CPM machine today?" John's baritone carried all the way across the ward.

Darren popped his head up as Brandon was his patient. "Last week we had an in-service from P.T. that said the continuous passive motion device didn't make a difference by six weeks post-surgery."

"Did I DC the order?"

"No, sir."

"Then get off your duff and put his knee in the machine. Now!"

Polly came out of her patient room, shaken and embarrassed for John. "There's no reason to speak to Dar-

ren like that. He was following the recommendation of
Physical Therapy."

"Did I ask your opinion?"

"I don't care if you asked it or not. You don't have
the right to talk to your staff like that."

He looked at her as if he hated her and everyone else
in the world, harrumphed and walked away. "I'll have
a little talk with P.T. about going over my head and dis-
regarding my orders," he said when he passed Brooke.

Knowing deep in her heart the pros and cons of using
a CPM machine after knee procedures wasn't the issue,
Polly felt queasy for John. She wished she could find a
way to reach him before he quarantined himself completely from the world of the living.

That evening John cooked again. Maybe it was his
way of apologizing? After having a well-prepared but
tasteless meal in silence, Polly finished putting the
dishes in the dishwasher. "I think I'll go for a walk to
the park." There were two parks nearby and the one she
had in mind overlooked the East River.

"I'll go with you."

She'd known he'd say that. Not because he wanted
to be with her but because he wanted to protect her.
From what? She'd walk to a beautiful park in a well-
to-do neighborhood. It was still only early August, and
it wasn't even dark out yet. But she'd depended on his
twisted sense of obligation to accompany her, to open
up the opportunity to talk. Maybe, while they walked
and enjoyed the evening, she could crack that ever-hard-
ening shell he was doing such a fine job of constructing.

The night air was still thick and humid. Polly chose
a brisk pace and John had no problem keeping up. If
anything, she had to widen her stride to match his.

"So, what's been going on?" she asked.

"What do you mean?" He gave her a look as if she'd just landed from planet crazy.

"You've been very bristly."

"I've bent over backwards to give you space, to help you heal."

Silence doesn't heal anything. She didn't want to go there right now. She wanted to intervene on her co-workers' behalf, before John drove them to resign one by one by one. The orthopedic kids didn't need to deal with constant staff turnover along with all their other ailments.

"I'm talking about work, about how you're chewing everyone's heads off, like before I came..." Her voice drifted off. She didn't want to suggest she'd had anything to do with his turnaround in attitude at work... before everything had gone to hell in a handbasket.

"Nurses are tough. They can take me. Always have." End of subject.

They entered the park lined with red bricks and bushes. She found an empty bench facing the river and sat. Inhaling, she realized the air was nothing like the sea. This humongous East River by the huge city smelled like life itself—of car exhausts, hot cement, hordes of people—yet the pewter-colored water overcame it all and offered a hint of refreshment. Polly needed to be refreshed. Living on this side of town with John, however briefly, this view had become one of her favorites in the city.

A jogger passed by. A hundred yards behind a woman with a stroller walked her baby. Polly had to look away, choosing to focus on the long steel sculpture of the Queensboro Bridge rather than lost possibilities.

"People can take all kinds of things, but they shouldn't have to. Your berating everyone wears skin thin." She reached for his hand, a gesture she'd given up on since he'd brought her home from the hospital. "You're hurting, John, and you're taking it out on the people around you."

It wasn't obvious, but she felt his hand recoil the tiniest bit. "Look, you handle things your way, and I'll handle them mine." She let go of his hand just as the woman with the stroller came by.

They sat for several more minutes staring at the river, thousands of necessary words going unspoken. How could she get through to John in his emotionally shutdown state, where the only feeling allowed to appear was anger?

"You ready to go back?" he said. "I've got an early surgery tomorrow."

With that, they walked back to his apartment in silence, Polly feeling as though she had cement bricks chained to her ankles.

By the end of the second day back at work and after several more outbursts from John towards the staff, Polly dreaded going home with him again. How much could she take of his foul mood while she grieved? And yet at home he'd become docile, so docile, in fact, she'd begun to suspect he was no longer alive.

"I think I'll walk home," she said, at his office door that Tuesday evening.

He stood and came around his desk. For the first time in days she saw an expression besides anger on his face, but she couldn't make out exactly what it meant. "But you're too weak to walk all the way home." With brows lowered, looking gruff, his words didn't match.

"I managed working all day yesterday and today without problems. I'll be fine."

"Only two days back at work, five since the miscarriage. All the more reason to let me drive you."

Obligation. Pure obligation. Though it was the first time he'd mentioned her miscarriage since the day it'd happened, and that struck Polly as progress. But not enough to want to spend another painful night in his presence, longing to crack his hardened shell, to get back to that wonderful man she'd known so briefly. John wouldn't allow it.

"So we'll have more time to sit in that dead apartment of yours and stare at each other?"

His brows shot up. Surprise tinted his brown stare. "I thought you'd appreciate some peace and quiet."

"More like rest in peace, you mean? Just bury me and get it over with, why don't you?"

He folded his arms. "I've done everything I possibly can to make you comfortable."

"Including shutting me out."

"I didn't think we needed to talk about our loss just yet."

"You banished me from your room, John."

With the topic becoming personal, he strode around her and closed his office door. "You can't stand the sight of me."

"What in heaven's name gave you that impression?"

"It's my fault you lost the baby. Why would you want to be anywhere near me, let alone sleep in the same bed?"

She shook her head. "You don't know me at all, do you?" With that, she swung open the door. Didn't the man know the meaning of comfort, both giving and getting, by sharing sadness? "I'll be home later, don't wait up," she said, and took off down the hall determined to find something to do to keep her busy until it was time to go to bed. Maybe she'd stop at the bookstore the next block over and read until she couldn't keep her eyes open. Oh, wait, there was that letter she needed to write, she shouldn't put it off another day. She could write the letter at the bookstore.

Anything not to have to face the man who'd checked out on her when she'd needed him most.

CHAPTER TEN

Two MORE DAYS of living with John had drained the flow of energy from Polly's core. She could barely lift her head off the pillow. Would this be the story of her life? Drifting from person to person, never really cared for, ever to be seen as an obligation and nothing more?

She sat bolt upright. No. She wouldn't settle for that. She deserved more. She was young, she could get pregnant again if she ever found the right man. Melancholy thoughts about what she'd almost had with John, how he could be "the right man", how her dreams of having her own family had been just within reach but had been snatched away at the last moment invaded her thinking. A cruel joke.

Getting out of bed, she grabbed her robe and headed for the shower. Passing the kitchen, she smelled fresh coffee brewing, piquing her senses. Now that she could drink coffee again, she'd pour herself a cup and enjoy it. She was damned if she intended to live the rest of her life like a ghost, the way John had chosen to do. In his case, an angry, bitter ghost.

She got into the shower and scrubbed herself to near shining, ready to take on the world again. But this time she wasn't going to fall back into her old ways. Nope. From now on the only person she intended to please was herself. This would be the summer and fall of Polly, and she wouldn't let an out-of-touch-with-his-own-feelings sad-sack like John drag her down one more inch.

As she toweled off and combed out her hair, she made plans. She'd ask Darren to help her move out over the weekend and she'd go back to Mrs. Goldman's and put this sad episode of her life behind her. Little Caledonia would forever have a special place in her heart, and she'd honor her miscarried baby by living each day, not merely existing as John had chosen to do. She couldn't be around negative people any more. She just couldn't.

The John she had glimpsed and fallen in love with was long gone. How could she possibly tie herself to a man who wasn't even able to tell her how sad he was after the miscarriage? He'd cried half a dozen tears at the ER, but since then an iron wall had been erected, and she could waste a lifetime trying to scale it but never succeeding.

No. There was nothing here for her at the 56th Street apartment. Striding down the hall, she came to an abrupt stop when she saw John in the kitchen, eating a bowl of cereal, and was perplexed by the pop of feelings in her chest. When he saw her there was a sheepish quality to his glance. Surely he knew—how could he not?—he'd become unbearable at work and to live with. Yet what was up with that tiny circle of softening in her chest? She had to ignore it, harden up like he had, or she'd never get away.

"Good morning, John," she said, as if she'd walked into a business meeting.

"Polly." He kept spooning the cereal to his mouth yet watched her move around the kitchen.

She poured herself a cup of coffee, spilled in some

creamer, took a sip and smiled. "Hmm, I've really missed this stuff."

His lips quirked but not enough to call it a smile.

"I've decided to walk to work today."

He'd finished his cereal and dropped the bowl into the sink. "It's supposed to get really hot, you may want a ride home."

"No, thanks." She rummaged through the cupboard to find a bowl and poured herself some cereal, too. They liked the same brand, just as they liked so many other similar things.

Didn't matter. That was the past. This was her future. The new Polly only lived for Polly now, regardless of a guy's taste in cereal.

"I've got surgery in an hour, so if you're sure you don't want a ride…"

"I'm sure."

He stopped before he left the kitchen, gray suit slacks fitting perfectly, white dress shirt tucked in over a flat stomach, his muscular arms apparent through the sleeves. She didn't want to notice any of it, but couldn't help herself. He turned round and studied her, as if seeing her for the first time. Maybe he was wondering what he was doing, letting a stranger share his home. Or maybe he sensed the new, determined Polly, the one eager to take life by the horns again. She honestly couldn't tell from the gaze he gave her. Neither did she care.

"I'll try not to make any scenes at work today."

Well, that was something anyway. She cocked her head and tossed him an it's-about-time look. "Good, because that stuff gets old, fast." Then took another drink of coffee, rather than let her heart soften one tiny bit more.

He twitched a sad smile with resigned eyes, and left.

She heard the front door click closed, and she ate the rest of her cereal feeling curiously alone. It didn't matter. She wouldn't be living here much longer.

Before she left for work, she ventured down the hall to John's study, deciding to check it out just this once. At first glance it was a typical office with dark wood desk, blotter, computer and printer. Piles of medical journals covered one section.

Something on the book case against the wall caught her eye. A small glass orb sitting on a solid gold holder with the inscription "Forever", and inside the orb two wedding rings lay overlapped. Not only did Lisa live on in his heart, she lived real as life itself in his office. Polly had wondered what precious object John had kept from Lisa. It turned out he'd kept the whole marriage. His vows had gone beyond "till death do us part." Evidently they extended for ever. She had never stood a chance.

"Darren," she said later that morning at work, "is there any way you can help me move this weekend?"

"That bad, huh?" The ex-navy man may have let his body go, but his posture was always erect. He turned to look into her eyes. "Are you sure it's the right thing to do? I mean, you just moved in."

"It's a long story, Dare. I just need to get away. I don't have much stuff. All I need is one car trip to the Lower East Side, otherwise I'll have to make a dozen trips on the subway."

He put his hand on top of hers. "I'll help you. Does he know?"

"Here's the deal. I want my moving out to have some impact. If I come out and tell him, he'll just say…whatever, and I need him to feel something. Other than anger, he's forgotten how to feel."

She folded her arms and chewed her lower lip. "I probably don't mean anything to him any more, but I want him to be hit by my not being there." She shook her head, giving a brief exhalation through her nose. "He probably won't even notice I'm gone."

Darren leveled a serious look at her. "You don't see it, but I do. That guy is crazy mad in love with you. Men don't process stuff the same way women do. Maybe you should be patient."

"I've been patient all my life, Dare. I'm done. All I've ever done was tag along, grateful to have a place to live, grateful for whatever crumbs I got. I need more than that now. I deserve it."

"We all deserve things. Life doesn't always co-operate, that's all. Take Dr. Rodriguez and Dr. Woods that everyone has been talking about these last several weeks. They were supposed to be in love and some lawsuit got in the way. Here's a little surprise for you—everyone has them broken up for good, but not me. Everyone say's they've got too much to overcome and they're both too stubborn, but not me. I see how he watches her whenever they're both on our ward. She acts all 'oh, he doesn't know I exist' but he's totally aware of her.

"That's how it is with Dr. Griffin and you. Polly, the man has lost everything in his life, now you're leaving him, too. I'm your friend and I'm asking you to think about not moving out. Maybe just give it some more time."

Surprised by how observant Darren had been, she stared at him and considered his caution.

"I don't have any more time. I'm a shadow in John's

house and I need to be so much more than that. Until he snaps out of it, I may as well be a ghost." She put her hand on Darren's arm. "I can't be a ghost any more. Thank you for being my friend and helping me move."

"Sure, kid. Someone's got to look out for a small-town girl like you in the Big Apple."

She hugged him and they spent the rest of their lunch hour working out the details. Polly knew John liked to go to his athletic club on Sunday afternoons for racketball, and she planned to be gone by the time he got home.

On Monday morning John waited for Polly to get up, but didn't hear a thing. He'd gotten home late last night as after racketball he'd gone out to dinner with Carl, his friend since childhood, had laid the whole sorry tale at the guy's feet and had gotten some insight on what a jackass he'd been. Most importantly, Carl had given him some solid advice. This morning John put his wedding rings inside a box and packed them away in the office closet. Lisa was gone. She was never coming back. Polly was here. Alive.

Her door had been closed when he'd come home last night, and he hadn't wanted to disturb her, even though he'd had some major apologies to make and had found it hard to wait to get them off his chest. Regardless, he'd gone directly to bed.

Why did the place feel so deadly quiet this morning? The hairs on his arms rose. He knocked and jiggled the doorhandle. "Polly?"

He opened the door to an empty room. Every breath of life she'd brought into his world had dissipated. The effect of negative air sucked the wind from his lungs.

She'd left him. After the total ass he'd been lately, why should he be surprised?

Entering her room, a pang of loneliness dug so deep it may as well have taken him by the lapels and thrown him against the wall. She was gone. Had left without saying goodbye.

He walked around the room, inhaling the tell-tale scent of Polly. Lemon water and flowery bath gel, and the bouquet of her gloriously wavy hair on the pillow. God, he missed her. He'd played his hand so incompetently he didn't deserve to have her back. But how could he go on without her?

He searched the room. Circling the bed, he found the table drawer ajar. Inside, something pink caught his eye. He pulled open the drawer and discovered a pair of tiny booties. One pink. One blue.

The air went out of his lungs again as he realized the significance, as his heart squeezed with anguish. With eyes stinging, the whisper of what John had lost became reality. Their baby was gone. He'd lost another part of himself to tragedy.

How much more could he bear?

Tears tracked down his cheeks as he sat on the bed and fingered the tiny slippers, perfectly knit by Polly. How long would he punish himself for his mistakes? Something crackled inside the pink slipper and he put his index finger inside, practically filling the entire bootie, and found a small folded piece of tissue-thin paper.

Opening it, he had to squint several times to clear the burning tears blurring his vision.

Dear Caledonia (Callie) or Sterling (Mort)

Oh, God, how was he supposed to be able to read the note? His heartache deflated and oozed out onto his skin, making him fragile and achy.

Polly had written a letter to their miscarried baby. He swallowed, unsuccessfully, the knot of anguish in his throat and continued to read.

I know it's foolish to write you this letter, but I needed to tell you how happy I was when I found out you were growing inside me. I've never been so lucky in my life. For once I would have somebody to love with all of my heart, someone who would look up to me and love me back.

I remember my mother, and I know how important a mother is. I miss her as much as I miss you. I'm so sorry I didn't get to know you, or to be your mommy. We would have been so happy...

Pain tore at John's throat and down his chest. He could hardly breathe it hurt so much. She'd taken the words he'd buried inside and put them on paper. He wanted to be a father more than anything, but had been afraid to admit it. He'd substituted his young patients for his lost child. How could such a young woman as Polly be so much wiser than him?

John clenched his jaws and cried silently over all he'd lost. Soon the intensity of his grief and loss overcame him. Foreign, keening sounds emitted from his throat over everything gone or dead in his life. Finally, he let it all out. He hadn't sobbed this much since 9/11.

Oh, God. But Polly was alive. He'd practically ignored her and now he'd let the best thing to happen to him in over a decade slip away. What a fool he was.

Polly was the most honest person he'd ever met. She'd been kicked in the gut by life yet had refused to lie down. She was optimism and energy and sweetness in the flesh. Instead of burying her feelings the way

he had, she'd put them on paper and written to her unborn child. She'd suffered terribly, losing the baby, and
when she'd needed him most, what had he done? He'd
pulled inward, sent her to the guest room, as if turning
his back on her.

How stupid could a guy get?

Maybe it was time for him to quit kicking himself.
Sure, he'd screwed up plenty, but Polly was living proof
that a life could change. He wanted to change for her.

He'd made so many mistakes—too many to count—
but he couldn't let Polly be one of them. He loved her.
Absolutely. He did. There was no doubt in his mind.
And he missed her, with all the enthusiasm and spirit
she'd brought to his dull life. He craved her, the desire
and lust she'd reawakened in him. She'd made his life
so much better on countless levels.

But more than anything, he needed her back.

She'd never felt wanted since her mother had died,
and he couldn't change that, but he sure as hell could
change her not feeling wanted by him! She deserved
to know without a doubt that she was loved, and cherished, and would be for the rest of her life if she'd just
give him a second chance.

There was only one way to get his point across. In
person. He picked up the phone, called work, spoke to
Brooke and made sure Polly was there.

He ran down the hall and splashed some water in his
face, then did everything in his power to make himself
look presentable. He wanted to look good the next time
he faced the love for the rest of his life.

Polly flushed the line in the IV piggyback after delivering the antibiotics to four-year-old Jeffrey Pomeroy
the third. The adorable little boy slept soundly even

though he was inside a body cast that defied the word "comfort".

When she'd disposed of the syringe she noticed Dr. Woods across the ward, looking at a computer. Not more than fifteen feet away stood Dr. Rodriguez, pretending to read a report, but he was watching her. How could the woman not feel that smoldering gaze? Before long, Dr. Woods's pretty blonde head lifted and her gaze drifted towards and locked with Dr. Rodriguez's dark and mesmerizing stare. Quicker than a hummingbird, her eyes flitted away, but it was undeniably there, that one intense second had said it all—they definitely weren't over by a long shot. Polly shook her head and smiled to herself. That Darren knew a lot more than he let on.

She went back into the patient room and prepared to give her second patient a bed bath. All the while she thought about Dr. Woods and Dr. Rodriguez, and the one person she couldn't get out of her head or heart, John.

"Polly Seymour?" She heard John's distinct voice echo off the walls. "Polly. Get out here!" He'd promised to behave after last Friday's outburst. Oh, God, had he lost it altogether? Would someone be calling Security and taking him away soon?

Sheepishly peeking around the threshold first, she ventured out of the patient room. Anything to quiet him down until Security could arrive. The poor patients and their families didn't need to be subjected to his unpredictable and escalating mood swings. The constant ache in her heart since she'd left him panged deeper.

Of course a crowd had assembled to watch the poor man's demise. Brooke and Rafael, Darren, not looking the least bit alarmed, and all the other nurses and technicians she'd grown to know and enjoy from working with them. Even Dr. Woods and Dr. Rodriguez were there, still exchanging quick passionate glances, while lingering on the fringes of the group, most likely wondering what was going on with their colleague. Everyone huddled around the nurses' station, watching John, who looked amazingly dashing for a man on the verge of professional suicide.

"Polly." He spoke the word now, softened the tone of his voice, as if her appearance had taken the edge off. He smiled an honest-to-God, no mistaking expression of his happiness at seeing her.

Though shaking inside, she hoped beyond hope that if she played it cool and calculated she could de-escalate his impending meltdown. Polly schooled her voice. "Yes, John?" She could humor him until the hospital security squad arrived.

"You forgot something."

She stood cemented to the spot, her heart rapping a wild rhythm all the way up to her ears, watching as he pulled out the booties from the pocket of his doctor's jacket. Heat started at her clavicles and traveled to her neck, soon invading her cheeks. He'd found them. He'd discovered she'd let herself get so carried away with loving and longing for her baby that she'd knitted booties. Booties for a baby who would never be born.

Did he think she was pitiful?

"I need you to finish these," he said. "No. That's not entirely true." His voice was now low enough for only those in the front row of the crowd to hear. Others got on tiptoe and leaned in towards the spectacle of their department chief confronting the newest staff nurse. "What I need…is you. You, Polly. The thing is, I finally realize I can't live without you."

He came toward her, took her hand, and that tender look he'd had after each time they'd made love was back in his eyes.

"I love you, Polly. You belong with me. You've got to finish these booties because we're going to need them. After you marry me and..."

Applause broke out. Time stopped. With her heart reeling, she quickly glanced around the room, catching Dr. Woods and Dr. Rodriguez smiling at each other. Beside them, Darren grinned first at the lovebird doctors then at her.

"I told you so," Darren mouthed.

Real time snapped back in, ungluing Polly from the spot, and she grabbed John by the elbow and whisked him away to the consultation room at the far end of the ward. She closed the door. What she had to say needed to be said in private.

"What makes you think I *want* to marry you?"

He wore a goofy grin and dreamy eyes, and she could tell there would be no reasoning with him. "Because you're a smart girl, and I love you, and I want you in my life." His fingertips traced the length of her jaw.

She dropped her head back and stared at the ceiling for guidance. No one had ever wanted her before, but that was no reason to let him seduce her with words.

He grasped her neck, brought her head up straight in line with his lips and delivered a tender, sincere kiss. Nothing fancy, just his warm lips to her startled ones, and she felt his touch all the way down to the tips of her toes.

"I was a total jerk after the miscarriage, but I've come to my senses." He dangled the booties before her eyes as if to hypnotize her. "You did this on purpose, didn't you? Left these behind."

She glanced at his delving, dark eyes and quickly studied a speck on his white doctor's coat. "Maybe."

He took both of her hands in his. "I know you've never really felt like you belonged anywhere, honey, but I'm the guy to end it. The buck stops with me. I'm your man. The one who loves you. I'm the man who wants to spend the rest of his life with you." He looked so deeply into her eyes she was positive he could read her brainwaves, which were dancing around erratically and happily over his proposal. "So I guess the question of the day is, do you love me?"

Tiny pins stabbed behind her eyes as tears that she'd sworn she'd never cry again for John Griffin materialized. "I couldn't bear it if you ever shut me out again, John. You have to promise me you'll always talk to me no matter how hard or how horrible your feelings are."

He held her arms and kept her steady. Steady as his warm brown gaze. "I promise to love and honor you, to share the good, the bad, and the ugly, whether you want to hear it or not." His lopsided smile appeared. "How's that for opening up?"

How could she not adore a face like that? A tiny laugh escaped her trembling lips.

"I do love you, Johnny."

His smile morphed into a huge grin and spread from jaw to jaw as he took her into his arms. "So it's settled, then." He grew serious and kissed her again, this time with much more gusto, enough to spread warmth across her chest and make her toes curl in her clogs. After several more seconds of deeply attentive kisses dazzling enough to make her head swim and her heart believe he truly wanted and loved her, he stopped.

"Then let's blow this joint and get married, dumpling. Do you like the sound of that? The married part, I mean?"

Staring into the eyes of the man she'd fallen head over heels in love with on short notice, the man she'd run the gamut of any other long-term relationship in her life, but this time on hyper-speed, she could only think of one succinct yet most appropriate answer.

"I do."

EPILOGUE

Eleven months later...

"BE CAREFUL!" JOHN SAID, jumping up to help Polly walk across the living room.

"I'm fine, Johnny, seriously." She held her swollen belly as if it might fall off her body if she didn't, and wobbled toward the kitchen.

John tagged along behind her. "How's the back?"

"Achy," she said, looking into the face of the man she loved and trusted more than anyone on earth, "but I'll survive."

"I've got your suitcase packed and ready to go, just like the midwife instructed," he said, hovering like a penguin on a newborn. "Say the word and we'll go to the hospital."

Polly put her hands on her back, the habit she'd developed during the last few months of her pregnancy, and smiled at John. "It's not quite time yet, honey-bunches, but thanks."

Once in the kitchen, she opened a cupboard and started to reach for a glass. John jumped between her and the glassware and got one down for her. "Water?"

"Yes, please."

"Sit. I'll bring it to you." He pointed toward the table and she obeyed.

Since she'd been on maternity leave for the last two weeks, with twenty-four hours a day of intense attention from John and a uterus that felt ready to explode, no one was more anxious to deliver the babies than she. Babies. Yes. Two. A boy and a girl. She pinched herself. It wasn't a dream. Polly liked to blame those pink and blue booties for the twins. Maybe if she'd stuck to one color she wouldn't feel as if she had a small crowd inside her. But with John's loving care, the four of them had been getting along beautifully over the past nine months.

If she didn't count the constant acid reflux and a diaphragm so under pressure that taking deep breaths was almost impossible, she'd say life was perfect.

Polly sat on the kitchen chair, and John was quick to pull out another so she could elevate her feet, then he handed her the water. Just as she swallowed her first sip, Callie and Sterling decided to take a run around the indoor gym and pool.

"Oh!" She quickly set the glass on the table and sat straighter.

"What is it?" John jumped to his feet again then dropped to one knee in front of her. The poor man hadn't had a moment's rest since she'd announced with pride he'd made her pregnant again. And Polly had never felt more wanted and cared for.

She couldn't talk as pain escalated like she'd never experienced before. Her eyes bugged out and she held her breath.

"Don't forget to breathe, dumpling, remember what

the birthing coach told you." John looked at his watch. These days she really did feel like a dumpling.

The labor pain began to let up and she relaxed into the chair. "How far apart are we now?"

"Four minutes. Are you ready to go to the hospital yet?"

She shook her head. "Let's walk a little bit first, okay?"

She loved her evening walks along the East River, even though it was hotter than usual this July. The last thing she wanted to do was show up at Labor and Delivery when she hadn't even begun to dilate, and a walk by the river might just be the ticket to moving her labor along. Dr. Bernstein was thrilled she'd carried the pregnancy the whole nine months, but with John's tender loving care she wasn't the least bit surprised.

John didn't look convinced that a walk during early labor was such a great idea but, as with almost everything else in their life together, he wanted to please her. "Okay, then, let's go." He helped her to her feet and they headed for the door.

By the time they'd reached the street, Polly was having another contraction. She stood perfectly still and tried to breathe. John rubbed her shoulders and lower back as she did.

"This time it was three minutes," he said. "Change your mind about going to the hospital yet?"

The contraction had lasted longer and felt more intense, and even though John was a doctor she wanted to be around the trained midwife and OB nurses when she delivered. She nodded. "Okay, call the hospital and let them know we're coming in."

John's eyes went wide as he dug out his cell phone

and pushed autodial. "It's really happening?" He squeezed her hand, excitement and fear registering in his gaze.

"Yes. Maybe you should get my suitcase."

"And leave you alone?"

"Marco can watch me until you get back."

John hesitated, but when Marco got a chair for Polly to sit on while she waited, he dashed back into the building, heading for the elevator.

Ten hours later...

John watched his wife snuggle with their newborns. Her hair had grown thicker and curlier with the pregnancy, and the sight of her holding the twins, well, she was never more beautiful. In awe, he looked on. The babies had tiny fingers and toes, and nostrils that couldn't possibly pass enough air to keep them alive. Amazing. Nothing short of a miracle.

His kids. His wife.

If he'd performed back-to-back hip replacements, he couldn't have been more exhausted, yet being with his new family energized him. Polly had worked like a trouper during labor, and he'd been by her side every step of the way. The sight of Caledonia entering the world had brought tears to his eyes and when he got to hold Sterling seconds after his birth, he'd thought he might pass out for fear of dropping or injuring his son.

What a team they'd been, Polly in mid-contraction breathing and pushing, John holding her hand, cheering her on. *You can do it. Don't give up.* Like a fearless warrior she'd gone through labor fighting her way to victory, eager to get to the prize. Now, watching his children with their mother, the abundance of love and blessings welling in his heart made his eyes go bleary. Nothing could ever match this most special moment in time.

"We did it," Polly said. "We made beautiful babies."

He cupped her face and saw his children squirm in Polly's arms. "With me as their father they only had a fifty-fifty chance of that beautiful part, you know."

She grinned and shook her head. "They'll be strong and smart because of you."

"And they'll always know they're loved."

"Yes. Just like I do."

After all the losses John had experienced in his forty years on the planet, through Polly he'd learned to trust that life could still bestow wonders and joy, too. She'd complained he was way too protective of her, but she'd slowly gotten used to it. She'd had no choice.

"Now I'll be on triple duty, watching over all of you," he said, pride ringing from each word.

"You poor man, you're bound to wear out!" She feigned worry, but he knew she was delighted he'd promised to always be there for his family.

"Never."

He snapped a picture with his phone and sent it to Brooke to share with the hospital staff.

"We're going to have to work as a team with these little dumplings," she said.

He'd been warned by younger colleagues that nothing was more difficult than being a parent.

"We'll be the perfect team," he said. "You. Me. Callie and Sterling."

John gazed at his family in the hospital bed while reeling with ever-expanding love in his heart. Since meeting and opening his life and love to Polly, becom-

ing a husband and now a father, he knew one thing
deeper and better than anything else in the world. No
matter how many curve balls life threw at him, as long
as Polly and the kids were by his side he would survive anything.

* * * * *

NYC ANGELS:
AN EXPLOSIVE
REUNION

ALISON ROBERTS

CHAPTER ONE

'*No.*'

The single word was as dramatic as the way the man had stormed into Layla Woods's office and slammed a piece of paper onto her desk.

As dramatic as the man himself.

Alex Rodriguez was clearly furious. The waves of his thick, jet-black hair looked rumpled—as if he'd pushed angry fingers through it. Eyes that were nearly as dark glared down at Layla.

A long way down. Layla had to fight the urge to leap to her feet so that she could feel taller. Braver. But that would be a dead giveaway that she was rattled, wouldn't it? And she couldn't afford to let Alex know the effect he was still capable of having on her.

With a satisfyingly steady hand, she reached for the piece of paper. The memo she had sent out that morning to all the senior staff members here at the Angel Mendez Children's Hospital.

'This is the agenda for the next monthly report meeting.'

'And you've put me down as being the first presenter.' Alex folded his arms. 'The answer's no. I decline the invitation.'

'It's not an "invitation",' Layla flashed back. 'It's the case I've chosen to open the meeting. I'm sorry if it's inconvenient but it's your patient, Alex, therefore you present the case. End of story.'

The head of paediatric neurosurgery made an exasperated sound, turning as if he intended to storm out of her office in the same way he'd entered. Instead, he stopped beside the large window, with the backdrop of a bright blue October morning. Was he taking in the fabulous view of New York's Central Park that this prestigious top-floor office had to offer?

An office befitting Layla's position as the new chief of paediatrics at this famous hospital. Her dream job. A position that had been in jeopardy a few short weeks ago until Alex had stepped in to protect her.

'What the hell are you playing at, Layla?'

The angry tone of Alex's voice must have carried because Layla's secretary appeared at the open door. Layla gave her a tight smile.

'Hold my calls, please, Monica.' The tilt of her head conveyed the message that she wanted more than her calls held to deal with this. The door was tactfully closed as her secretary retreated.

'Well?' Alex turned back to face her and this time Layla got to her feet.

Slowly.

She walked to the other side of her desk but couldn't go any closer to Alex. The huge can of worms that represented their shared history was blocking the way.

Or maybe it was the memory of what had happened the first time they'd confronted each other since they'd both been working here at Angel's. When they'd been close enough for the flames of a sexual chemistry that had clearly never died completely to flare into that scorching kiss.

It couldn't happen again.

Their past had been precisely what had put her new job in jeopardy. Had she really been naïve enough to think that it had been so long ago it couldn't affect her life any more? That she could take a high-profile position like this and it wouldn't matter that she hadn't disclosed her involvement in the malpractice suit that had nearly destroyed Alex's career five years ago?

Somehow they had to move past this. Learn to work together.

'I had intended discussing the agenda with you. You declined the appointment I tried to set up last week.'

'I was busy.' Alex held her gaze. 'As you would have noticed if you'd bothered checking my electronic calendar.'

Layla kept her expression carefully neutral. She *had* checked his calendar but he could have easily suggested another time. They both knew the real truth. He had been avoiding her.

Since that kiss.

He hadn't even let her voice her thanks for the way he'd stepped in and defended her at the board meeting when her integrity had been under examination and it had been highly likely that they would decide she was not the right person to oversee the talented staff that Angel's was so proud of.

Being thwarted in expressing her appreciation had been a putdown but Layla's aggravation went deeper than that.

Good manners had been drummed into Layla Woods since she'd been knee high to a grasshopper and saying thank you to someone who'd done her such a huge favour wasn't just about maintaining a good appearance.

It was the right thing to do.

The idea of using the monthly report meeting had been a brainwave. OK, choosing a time she'd known Alex was busy to offer a chance to discuss the agenda could be deemed unprofessional, but Layla had had enough. She was taking control.

She hadn't expected it to backfire quite so instantly. Why hadn't Alex simply continued to avoid her? He could have asked his deputy head of neurosurgery, Ryan O'Doherty, to present the case on his behalf.

'It's not a current case,' Alex added. 'And it was successful.'

Of course it was. Layla would hardly have picked a case that was presenting a current dilemma or, worse, one that had had a bad result.

The last thing either of them would want would be to go over *that* old ground. To the case of the toddler, Jamie Kirkpatrick, that had brought them together in the first place. To the cutting-edge surgery for a complicated brain tumour that had fallen disastrously short of being successful. Jamie had died. Alex had been sued by a distraught family looking for someone to blame. He'd been cleared but Layla hadn't been there to help him celebrate, had she? She'd ended their affair the night before Jamie's surgery.

She nodded at Alex's terse summary. 'That's precisely why I chose it. We don't just put up a current, complicated issue to get the benefit of input from different specialties. Or to dissect what went wrong in a case that wasn't successful. Sometimes it's a good thing to reflect on a triumph. And Matthew *was* a triumph.'

'There are plenty of other cases you could have chosen.'

'Not one that so many people are so interested in.'

The brain tumour in the nine-year-old boy had been so rare and complicated that surgeons all over the state had refused to touch it. Until the little boy's desperate parents had brought him to Angel's as a last resort and begged Dr Rodriguez to use his legendary skills to give their son a chance to survive. And that was why it wouldn't make any difference if Ryan presented the case. Everybody already knew who the real hero was.

'The criterion for picking a case to report is that it's out of the ordinary,' Layla continued. 'From what I've heard, this one was all that everybody talked about at the time and the staff involved in the recent follow-up appointment were thrilled by Matthew's progress. I also heard that you're writing the case up for a top journal. I thought it would be nice to share that.' The occasional triumph shared at the meeting was good for everybody. A counterbalance for the heart-breaking cases.

'Shine the spotlight on someone else, Layla,' Alex growled. 'Somebody's going to wonder why you picked on me and I've been talked about more than I'm comfortable with around here lately.' Alex turned to look out of the window again as he spoke but then his gaze swerved back to Layla. 'Gossip about the Kirkpatrick case was bad enough. What happens when people start talking about the fact that I was having an affair with a married woman at the time? How do you think that's going to help my reputation?'

The glare Layla received would have intimidated anyone.

Layla straightened her spine.

'I came to Angel's for a fresh start,' Alex ground out. 'I won't allow you to drag my name through the mud.'

Oh…Lord…

OK. The plan had been to make this a public gesture of thanks, whether Alex liked it or not. She knew that this case would earn him even more respect from those colleagues who didn't know all the details of the case, even though it had been breaking news on the grapevine in the months before she'd come to Angel's. She had also known that it would be a public statement of her own faith in his abilities.

But it was a huge leap to go from not wanting her gratitude or public support to accusing her of being prepared to damage his reputation. The attack was unjustified. Unfair.

'You're not the only one who's come here for a fresh start,' Layla snapped. 'And I'm sure you haven't forgotten but I *was* the married woman. I don't want that being common knowledge any more than you do.'

'So stay away from me, then.'

Layla let out an incredulous huff. 'You're the one who came storming into *my* office.'

'Because this needed to be dealt with.'

'What needs "to be dealt with",' Layla responded, 'is the fact that we find ourselves working in the same hospital. Again.' She took a deep breath. 'It's unfortunate, I agree, but you had your chance to get rid of me. You could have let me get fired.'

'I didn't do it to protect your job and keep you here, if that's what you're thinking.'

No. That idea had been farfetched enough for Layla to have dismissed it at the time.

Almost.

'So why *did* you do it?' she asked quietly.

'Because I'm not going to let my past dictate my future. The Kirkpatrick case did enough damage already. I stood up for you because...because it was the right thing to do.'

Thanking him had seemed like the right thing to do, too, but he wouldn't let her. Now Layla wasn't even sure she wanted to thank him. Had he just been facing his own demons? Making them a part of a past that didn't matter any more?

She had to look away. 'Well...we're going to have to work together. I'm not about to leave a job I've only just started.'

'Neither am I.'

He was still angry. Layla could feel the waves of it reaching her across the distance she'd been careful to maintain between them. She could also feel other currents mixed in with the anger. Like his determination to succeed and the fierce intelligence with which he was assessing his options. And beneath all of that she could feel his raw magnetism and power. The charisma that Alex Rodriguez wore like a second skin.

There seemed to be nothing left to say.

They were at an impasse. Both of them struggling to take control of their present by focussing on the future and dismissing the past.

Could it be that easy?

Layla had to make an effort to swallow. 'Fine. Then let's start as we mean to go on from now on. I've set the agenda for the meeting. I'll look forward to hearing your presentation, Dr Rodriguez.'

Alex said nothing. With no more than another searing glance, he turned and left her office.

* * *

Two days later and people were filing into the small lecture theatre tucked away on an upper floor, along with the operating theatres. Some were carrying Styrofoam cups of coffee and paper bags containing sandwiches and some were reading messages on their pagers. All of them would have a notebook and pen available.

Fellow Texan, neonatal doctor Tyler Donaldson came in, protectively ushering his now very pregnant fiancée, Eleanor, into a front-row seat where she would have plenty of room. Eleanor smiled at Layla.

'Don't mind me if I have to sneak out to the bathroom,' she said. 'My bladder capacity is shrinking by the day.'

'Yeah...' Tyler beamed proudly. 'And that little rodeo rider in there likes to work out and use it for a punching bag.'

Layla returned the smile but said nothing. She wasn't in the mood for baby talk and Tyler might be an old friend but it wasn't exactly professional to sit there holding hands with Eleanor, was it?

There was a quiet buzz of conversation going on and seats were being filled but there was still no sign of Alex. Layla gave Ryan a questioning look, her head tilted towards the door. As Alex's second-in-command, surely he would know where the senior neurosurgeon was? But Ryan merely shrugged and then turned to his companion, a smile on his face as he responded to some comment. The atmosphere in here was relaxed and why wouldn't it be?

There was no blame, no shame for unsuccessful cases but the discussion could get robust. What could have been done differently? What *would* be done differently next time? Hindsight was a wonderful thing when it could be used for a good purpose. You could never say they didn't learn from mistakes around these parts.

Could Layla say that about herself?

Professionally, of course she could.

Personally? Layla suddenly became aware that she was tapping her foot impatiently. How long had she been doing that? Had anyone noticed? Her foot stilled.

Of course she could say that she learned from personal mistakes.

She hadn't got married again, had she?

She had challenged Alex, though. She hadn't heard a peep out of him since that tense exchange in her office and she'd been left wondering if he would back down and appear to present his case. Surely he would guess that a non-appearance would start people talking even more than if he'd shown up as her star turn of the day?

There was an air of expectancy in the room now. These were busy people. They only had an hour to spare and they were all giving up their lunch-breaks to attend. There were a few empty seats but that was normal. Some people couldn't make it on the day, even if they were rostered to present a case, but that was OK, too, because they always had more cases lined up than they ended up having time to discuss.

She'd give Alex exactly one more minute to show up.

'Aren't you supposed to be at Monthly Report?'

'Yep.' Alex Rodriguez was facing his half-brother, Cade. Both men were semi-crouched and already sweating in the midday September sunshine that bathed the small area out the back of the ambulance bay where a basketball hoop was attached to the wall.

Alex had control of the ball right now, bouncing it in sharp movements as his body wove from side to side, looking for an opening to get closer to the hoop.

'So why aren't you?'

'Could ask you the same question.'

'Hey, I was only going to listen. Aren't you supposed to be presenting a case?'

Alex ignored the question. With a lunge, he dived sideways, scooping up the ball and firing it at the hoop. With a resounding thump it hit the backboard and went through the net.

'*Yes...*'

Both men went for the ball as it bounced on the tarmac. This time Cade made contact first and gleefully took control.

'You may as well give up, bro. Go and have a shower and make Layla happy.'

'What the hell is that supposed to mean?'

'*Whoa...*' Cade caught the ball instead of bouncing it and spun it on his hand. 'Who put the burr under your saddle?'

Using Layla's Texan drawl, along with a phrase they'd both heard her use, was like rubbing salt into the wound. With a move Cade didn't see coming Alex knocked the ball from his hand and took off across the court, scoring another goal.

Cade laughed. Game on. For several minutes they played hard, ignoring the heat and the sweat and how out of breath they were getting.

No way was Alex going to go to that meeting and *make Layla happy*. It wasn't so much that this was obviously a public pat on the back for a case that had gone so well, it was the string-pulling that he could sense going on behind it.

OK, he'd done Layla a favour but he'd done it in order to face his own demons, not to protect her. He didn't want her thanks.

Hell, no…

Because if she got close enough to thank him properly, he knew exactly what could happen. Had already happened. That chemistry between them would explode and they'd end up in a clinch, kissing like there was no tomorrow.

And, God help him, he was not going to let it happen again.

Who the hell did Layla think she was that she could pull a string or two and have people dancing to her tune?

He'd told her that he didn't want to present. She'd had plenty of time to back down and change the agenda and she hadn't done so despite knowing that it could kick off a fresh wave of gossip. Well…he wasn't even going to put in an apology for the meeting.

He just wasn't going to show up. They might have to work together again but was going to do it on his terms, thank you very much.

She could deal with that. By herself.

This was getting borderline embarrassing.

From her position on the podium Layla nodded at the group. It was time to begin. Her heels sounded loud on the podium, rapping smartly on the wood as she moved to the microphone attached to the lectern. She tapped it gently to check it was on.

'Howdy, folks. Glad y'all could make it.' Her smile was bright. Along with good manners, Layla Woods had grown up knowing exactly how to present the perfect public face, no matter what was going on inside her head.

Or her heart, for that matter.

'Looks like our first presenter is missing in action,' she continued, 'so let's get the ball rolling with our second case. Dr Donaldson is going to share one of our neonatal department's case histories.'

'Thanks, darlin'…' Tyler reluctantly let go of Eleanor's hand and strolled up to the podium. He winked at Layla as he inserted a memory stick into the data projector.

Layla kept her smile in place with difficulty. She knew what that wink was about just as clearly as she could sense the significant looks being passed between the people seated in the tiered rows in here. They all knew that Alex's name was on the top of the agenda. Now they were all wondering if he really had an emergency keeping him away or if there was something else going on. Were some of those rumours circulating about a romantic involvement between Alex and Layla true?

'Meet Madeline,' Tyler Donaldson announced, as a photograph of a tiny, premature baby almost hidden by wires and tubes came up on the screen. 'Born at a gestation of twenty-five weeks, this li'l gal weighed in at six hundred and eighty grams and measured thirty-two centimetres. She was intubated immediately after birth and given positive pressure ventilation due to her prematurity.'

To outward appearances, Layla was listening attentively to the presentation of all the complications this baby had had but in reality she was trying to unravel the knot of anger forming in her gut.

He could have put in an apology for the meeting. Or arranged for Ryan to present the case. They could have both kept their dignity intact and made a fresh start by putting their professional lives onto some kind of an even keel. The gossip would be fuelled by his non-appearance with no explanation. Layla didn't like being the subject of gossip. She didn't like the ashes of the past being raked over. Would she ever get away from the mistake she'd made in getting involved with Alex in the first place?

Don't you mean get over *him*?

That tiny voice in the back of her mind got ruthlessly silenced. Layla glared at Tyler.

This was all his fault, wasn't it? They'd known each other practically their whole lives. Ty knew how badly her marriage had ended and how strained her relationship with her family was. OK, maybe he hadn't known about the affair that had spelt the end of that marriage, or that Alex had been the man she'd had an affair with, but it had been Ty who'd persuaded her to apply for the job here at Angel's.

The job that meant she and Alex were working at the same hospital.

Again.

Layla took a deep breath and tried to tune in to what Tyler was saying about the complex surgery baby Madeline had had to go through. The fleeting thought that his specialty had to be harder now that his fiancée was pregnant with his own baby only led Layla straight back to her own personal issues.

Like how she was going to deal with the tension between Alex and herself. It wasn't just about avoiding damage to their reputations, was it? There was still something there. Something powerful. That kiss had been more than enough to make it obvious. And, despite what Alex had said, she didn't believe that doing the right thing had been the only motive for defending her against the management board.

Did he care about her on some level?

Did she care about him?

Not like that. Layla may have fallen in love with him the first time around but the disaster the affair had created in her life had been enough for those emotions to morph into simmering resentment at how thoroughly her life had been derailed. Whatever was still hanging around was about lust, not love. But, man, that sexual chemistry hadn't lost any of its power, had it?

She just needed to learn to control it.

Like she tried to control everything else in her life?

Good grief, that little voice was annoying. A control freak? Her? Well…Layla had to admit she'd engineered what had been supposed to have happened today but look how well that had worked.

She was already planning how to get around it, though, wasn't she? To take control some other way. Instead of thanking him now, part of her wanted to let Alex know just how aggravated she was with the way he had dropped her into covering for his absence and fielding the ensuing curiosity.

She wanted to demonstrate that she was able to stand up for herself.

Like she had when he'd put her aside just before little Jamie's operation?

When she hadn't been prepared to stand aside quietly and she'd taken control and told him it was all over?

Why had she chosen the night before the surgery to

take her stand? She could have contributed to why Jamie's case hadn't turned out to be the kind of miracle that the case she'd asked Alex to present today was.

The guilt was still there, wasn't it? Not just that she'd been cheating on her husband but that she might have made a difference to Alex's performance that day.

And maybe *that* was why it had seemed so important that she got the chance to thank Alex.

And why he didn't want to hear it.

Why did it matter so much, anyway? It had been years and years ago. They'd both moved on.

Or had they?

Impossible not to remember that kiss…

It had been the last thing she had expected.

No. Maybe the *last* thing she had expected had been the way she'd responded to it. To have stepped so far back in time to when her desire for this man had made her throw her caution to the winds, along with too many of the values she'd grown up believing she held. They'd been fried in the heat that one touch from Alex could generate. Even now, Layla could feel a flicker of that heat, deep in her belly.

Was she blushing? Was that why there was this sudden silence all around her and why everybody seemed to be looking at her?

No. On an inward groan Layla realised that Tyler had finished his presentation. They were waiting for her, as the meeting's chairperson, to move things along.

Her smile was bright. 'Sorry, folks… Such an interesting case, I got lost in my thoughts. Anyone want to ask a question or add something?'

Several hands were raised and heart surgeon Molly Shriver got the nod.

'Can you talk us through your choice of antibiotic to deal with the pneumonia? And did you consider a blood transfusion immediately after the first surgery?'

Layla couldn't help looking past Molly, up into the dimmer corners of the lecture theatre where someone could have arrived unnoticed during Tyler's presentation by using the back stairs.

Not that she really needed the visual confirmation that Alex wasn't present. She could feel it. Like a shadow blocking the sun.

Forced to stop the hard physical activity due to exhaustion, Alex bent over, palms on his thighs, fighting to catch his breath again. Cade mirrored his action.

'It's working,' Cade panted. 'Think I've pulled the burr out from *my* saddle, anyway. How 'bout you?'

Again, Alex ignored the query. 'So what was your beef?'

'I'm fed up,' Cade growled. 'I was in charge of my department back in L.A. I don't like being told what to do like I'm just an intern. Getting squeezed out of the best cases. Having my decisions second-guessed.'

'You knew you were going to be second-in-charge when you took this job.'

'Yeah…I just didn't know how much I wouldn't like it. I'm beginning to think I should have followed your example and tried the other side of the world to escape. Australia is looking pretty damned attractive right now.'

'You didn't have something big enough to get away from.'

'Wanna bet?' Cade had caught his breath. He was moving again. His expression suggested he needed to blow off a bit more steam. He certainly didn't want to expand on that cryptic comment.

Alex tucked it away. He'd find out. He knew better than to push his half-brother to reveal more than he was ready to. It was too fragile, this newly re-formed relationship they'd managed to forge in the wake of the recent trouble.

Cade scored another goal. He was well ahead of Alex now.

'Anyway...' he panted, letting Alex get the ball again. 'It's all sorted, isn't it? The whole deal with that malpractice suit. You know I'm sorry for letting the cat out of the bag but we're good now, aren't we?'

'Yeah...' Alex was standing still, taking aim at the basket. Better than he could have hoped they'd ever be, that was for sure, given their history.

'And it's all out in the open and they're not going to fire you. Any more than they're going to fire Layla after you stood up for her.'

Alex missed the hoop and swore softly. He grabbed the ball as it bounced and took aim again.

He just couldn't get away from it, could he?

Away from Layla.

Away from the memories.

The demons he'd tried to deal with by running away after the malpractice suit that had followed the Jamie Kirkpatrick case were only part of the story.

Cade was trying to distract him from shooting the goal. Standing in front of him and waving his arms. He was grinning. He didn't know that Layla was another demon.

He'd heard she was divorced now. Well...no surprises there. Alex could feel sorry for the mug she'd conned into marrying her in the first place. Had she just dumped him—the way she'd dumped *him* when she'd got bored with their affair?

Affair.

Nasty little word but there was no getting away from the facts. He'd had an affair with a married woman. He wasn't proud of it and he certainly didn't want people to start talking about it. Had Cade been getting away from something that bad?

Now wasn't the time to find out. It was too hot for this and they both needed to go and shower and cool off.

Alex took another shot at the basket and the ball went through without even touching the backboard.

'Nobody's getting fired,' he finally agreed. 'And the whole mess taught me something very valuable.'

'Oh?' By tacit agreement, both men were calling it a draw and finishing the match. They high-fived each other and started walking back into the hospital.

'You don't beat demons by running away from them,' Alex told his younger brother. 'You can only beat them by confronting them.'

The sound Cade made was dismissive and Alex couldn't blame him for his disbelief.

He wasn't exactly confronting the demons that Layla represented, was he? He'd been avoiding her like the plague ever since she'd tried to thank him for standing up for her and saving her job. And then he'd marched into her office and told her to stay away from him. How was that supposed to sort anything out? And had he been entirely truthful? He'd told her that he'd gone to that board meeting to defend her because the Kirkpatrick case had done enough damage and it should be left in the past, but weren't the feelings Layla stirred part and parcel of the whole Jamie Kirkpatrick business anyway?

It had been so hard to put her aside so he could focus on that little boy's surgery. And he still suspected, deep in his heart, that the body blow of getting dumped the night before that high-profile operation had been why he hadn't been completely on top of his game that day. Yes, the demons were so intertwined they were impossible to separate.

Which meant he hadn't really confronted anything, despite letting the whole thing get aired in public again. Maybe he'd made it worse by giving Layla a reason to be grateful to him. He certainly hadn't helped his cause by giving her something to be angry about today.

Deliberately avoiding her hadn't done the trick. Fronting up and warning her hadn't achieved much either. And Layla was right about one thing. If they both wanted to keep their jobs here, they had to find a way of being able to work in the same hospital.

A corner of Alex's mouth lifted in a wry smile. Maybe he'd subconsciously realised that what he needed was to have Layla avoid him. The way she had after Jamie's death when she wouldn't even acknowledge him. All that was needed was a good push to get her started and what better way than a public refusal to let her jerk his strings?

Alex stood under the cool shower, letting the sweat sluice away. Be nice if the demons could get washed away as easily but he'd soon find out if he'd made life any easier for himself by what he'd just done. Monthly Report would be well and truly over by the time he was dressed again.

* * *

The discussion about Tyler's case was taking off now.
They might finish a few minutes early but there certainly wouldn't be time for another case.

The gap left by the unpresented case would probably
be old news by the time everybody headed back to their
normal routines. They would all move on with ease.

The way Layla and Alex needed to if they were both
going to keep their jobs and work together.

Maybe what was stopping them was that it was unfinished business.

And if there was something that bothered Layla more
than being the subject of gossip it was having unfinished business hanging over her.

Mulling it over as she headed back to her office,
Layla realised that dealing with this particular business
would be dangerous. The tingle that kissed her skin as if
she could still feel Alex's presence in this private room
was enough of a warning. The way the memory of that
kiss was lingering rang an even louder alarm.

But facing something dangerous…and winning…
was kind of an attractive challenge.

And Dr Layla Woods had always found a challenge
irresistible.

Besides, it could be good for both of them. She had
a responsibility to try and ensure that the senior staff
members could work together on good terms, didn't
she?

Of course she did.

Layla took a moment to enjoy the view from her window. Plan B was beginning to shape up rather nicely.

CHAPTER TWO

EVERYBODY WAS WAITING.

Expecting Alex Rodriguez to be taken to task by the chief of paediatrics for failing to put in an appearance or even the courtesy of an apology for the monthly report meeting.

Alex had caught more than one oddly expectant glance from people over the course of the afternoon following that meeting. When his path crossed again with that of Layla for the first time he was in the cafeteria for lunch the next day, and the air of anticipation around him was palpable. A public arena and an attentive audience to witness a senior staff member being told off was gold for feeding a grapevine.

Alex gritted his teeth and waited for the kind of acerbic comment that would let him know by how far he'd missed the mark in his professional responsibilities.

Instead, he was treated, along with everybody else snatching a quick meal, to one of those thousand-watt smiles that Layla was so good at.

'Good to see you're finding time to eat,' she said, with that husky Southern edge to her voice that always made her sound vaguely amused about something. 'I hear you're busier than a one-armed paper-hanger over there in Neurology.'

He waited for the kicker. The jibe about being so busy that he couldn't have found the good manners to let her know he couldn't make the meeting. But that smile didn't dim. With a flick of those tousled, shoulder-length blonde waves, Layla continued moving towards the food counter, leaving nothing but a faint scent of something deliciously fresh in her wake. Apples?

Realising that he was sitting there with his mouth half-open, trying to identify what flavour shampoo Layla used, was enough to make Alex aware of the unpleasant burn of embarrassment, but he needn't have worried. Everyone around him was still watching Layla. Especially the men. And the collective gaze was laced with admiration.

Definitely apples, he decided the next day when Layla brushed past him in the recovery room to visit with a small patient of hers who'd just undergone open heart surgery.

He knew it was a coincidence that had placed her patient right next to the little girl he'd just operated on to correct a spinal abnormality but did she have to stand on his side of the bed? Did she really have to be here at all?

'I've been so worried about this wee man,' he heard her say to the nurse. 'I just had to come and have a peek.'

'He's doing just fine,' the nurse reassured her. 'We'll be transferring him to PICU any time now.'

Recovery was an extension of the operating theatre suite. Alex's turf. As Chief of Paediatrics, Layla often got involved with the more serious cases that came into

Angel's and he'd often seen her in places like the paediatric intensive care unit. Even when she was sticking to her own specialty of paediatric cardiology, she would often have small patients who spent time in there when their condition deteriorated or after they'd had surgery. But he'd never come across her in the actual recovery area and it felt like more than a professional coincidence.

Was he getting paranoid or was Layla trying to get in his face at every possible opportunity and…and *enjoying* it?

'Don't tell me…' Alex didn't try and erase the sardonic lilt to his words as the nurse sped off to attend to another patient arriving from Theatre. 'You're regretting your choice not to become a surgeon.'

'Not at all.' Layla's glance flicked the whole length of his body and Alex instantly felt at a disadvantage.

Underdressed, standing here in his loose-fitting scrubs. He still had a theatre cap on his head and he'd only broken the top strings on his mask so it was hanging around his neck like a bib. Layla was wearing a smart, close-fitting pencil skirt and a crisply ironed blouse under her spotless white coat. And she had her trademark high heels on. Alex was wearing white, plastic gumboots.

'I adore cardiology,' Layla continued. 'I get to make the diagnosis and I get to enjoy the follow-up and see the way lives improve after surgery. I don't have to do the messy, in-between bit of adjusting the internal plumbing.' Her gaze seemed to intensify. 'My surgical rotation back when I was an intern showed me that it wasn't where I wanted to be.'

That rotation had been when they'd met. When Layla

had become little Jamie's champion and she'd persuaded him to take on the toddler's complex surgery.

When they'd been together as far, far more than professional colleagues. Was that what Layla was really referring to here? Maybe he didn't want to find out. He backed down.

'I've just never seen you hanging around Recovery before,' he muttered. 'That's all.'

She knew, dammit. She knew exactly how uncomfortable he was with her presence in what had previously been a sacrosanct area for him.

We're colleagues. Her raised eyebrows managed to convey even more to the message. *We work in the same hospital. We are mature, professional people who are passionate about our careers. Deal with it*.

Fine. Alex *would* deal with it. He tilted his head towards the tiny patient in the bed.

'What was the procedure?'

'Just an ASD closure. But it was a big one and little Josh here is a real cutie. One of triplets.'

Triplets? Good grief… Why was nothing about Layla…*ordinary*?

Even this unusual visit was vaguely disturbing.

Any other doctor would be looking at the monitors or reading the recovery notes. Or at least quizzing the nurse. But not Layla. She was leaning over the tiny, unconscious boy. Finding a patch of skin that wasn't covered by an electrode for monitoring or tape that was holding an intravenous line in place. Stroking that skin with such a gentle touch that Alex couldn't look away.

'Hear what that nurse told me, honey?' he heard her murmur. 'You're doing just fine. You keep it up now.

Your momma and daddy aren't far away and they can't wait to see you.'

Alex forced his attention back to the monitors attached to his own patient but he couldn't ignore the knot in his gut. It tightened when he glanced back in time to see Layla on the point of leaving. She had two fingertips against her pursed lips and, having turned her head to check that the nurse wasn't watching, she took that tiny kiss and transferred it to the forehead of the unconscious toddler.

A tiny moment in time. A very personal moment. If Layla hadn't turned in his direction again as she'd straightened, she would never have known that she had been observed. Alex was busted. He wasn't going to pretend he hadn't been staring so he held her gaze steadily and it was gratifying to see the flush of colour that painted Layla's cheeks.

But she didn't look away. Her chin came up and the spark in her eyes was one of defiance.

So I get emotionally involved with my patients, the spark said. *Deal with that, too. I happen to think it makes me a better doctor.*

'See you later, Alex.'

'Yeah…I'm sure you will.'

The high heels of Layla's shoes beat a sharp tattoo as she exited the recovery room and, despite himself, Alex knew he was watching her leave with the same kind of expression that every male in the cafeteria had had the day before.

You had to hand it to her. Layla Woods had very decided opinions and more courage than you could shake a stick at to defend them. And that feistiness, wrapped up in such an attractive package, was the kind of challenge any red-blooded man would get drawn to.

Look at him. He knew the deadly consequences of rising to that challenge and he was still finding it difficult not to get sucked in all over again.

Alex looked down at his small patient. He had done the best he could for her with the surgery to correct the spinal malformation and he was confident that it had been a success. This little girl would soon be able to sit up and walk and catch up with the developmental milestones she had missed. Her parents were going to be thrilled and he would take a great deal of pleasure in following up on her progress.

He cared about her. A lot. But he wasn't going to start cuddling and kissing his patients. He'd learned long ago how dangerous emotional entanglements could be. Probably even before his mother had died.

Alex hadn't needed the gut-wrenching confirmation of that lesson represented by the disastrous notion that Layla might have been different enough to deserve his trust. And he wasn't going to lay himself open to the kind of heartache that came with losing a small patient that you'd got too attached to. He knew how to keep just the right amount of distance to make sure he stayed at the top of his game.

He just had to apply the same wisdom to his professional relationship with Layla, never mind how many times he found himself close to her. Or how many personal things he happened to notice.

Personal things like the kind of shoes she wore or shampoo she used were superficial and easily ignored. The personal detail he discovered about Layla a few days later nearly did his head in.

* * *

Plan B seemed to be going slightly astray.

The idea had been to show Alex that the past was well and truly behind them. That they could enjoy a professional relationship and put any lingering attraction behind them as well. Tuck it away, along with the malpractice suit and the way both their lives had been derailed.

But it seemed to be taking on a life of its own now.

Alex didn't like it that she was invading his space. Layla could feel the 'Oh, God, not *again*' vibe whenever she just happened to be in the same place at the same time. Like the cafeteria or Recovery or the intensive care unit or one of the wards. She was getting so good at this she didn't need to check his electronic calendar to guess where he might be next. Often her instinct put her in the right place. Or maybe fate was helping because her path seemed to be crossing with that of Alex far more often as she fulfilled her own professional duties.

Well, Alex had only himself to blame. The effect of her subtle campaign was magnified considerably by how successful Alex had been in trying to avoid her in the run-up to that meeting he'd stupidly decided to miss. This could have all blown over by now. She would have given Alex his moment in the limelight, taken the opportunity to say thank you in a heartfelt manner and they could have agreed that this was a fresh start for both of them.

Bygones could have been bygones.

But no... Alex had taken a stand and presented a challenge and she knew perfectly well that he would have been expecting her to front up and tear a strip or two off him because everybody knew that she didn't hang back from necessary confrontation. The perfect opportunity had presented itself the very next day, in fact, in the staff cafeteria, with the bonus of a built-in audience.

What a stroke of brilliance it had been, doing the complete opposite of what they had all been expecting. Her ultra-friendly smile and the way she had simply ignored the whole issue had thrown Alex off guard completely. He was still suspicious of her motives and she couldn't blame him for not liking what was happening. She was in control here.

The problem was that she was enjoying herself. A bit too much perhaps. She was quite confident of how aware of her Alex was. She could sense the way he watched her, like that time in Recovery. She could feel the intensity of that gaze like a touch on her skin.

No. The real problem was the flip side of that particular coin.

She was equally aware of him.

Just how unhelpful this awareness was became strikingly obvious a few days later after Layla had been called to the emergency department to consult on a 'blue baby' case that had been rushed in by ambulance. The mother had had almost no prenatal care so the baby's cardiac abnormalities had not been picked up prior to birth and, to complicate matters, the young mother had gone into labour and had given birth at home. With the baby safely intubated and stabilised and now under the care of the neonatal surgeons, Layla was free to leave the department to carry on with the rest of her duties when she spotted Alex.

He was standing just outside one of the resuscitation rooms where the more serious cases were assessed and

stabilised. Right next door to the one she had been in.
That small thrill of excitement and the way her heart
rate picked up was due purely to the stroke of luck crossing his path in such an unexpected place. Neither of
them had much to do with the emergency department
so what were the odds of them both being here at the
same time? That this would annoy Alex no end might
be a kind of a bonus.

Except that he didn't even seem to be aware of her
standing so close by. His attention was focussed on
the woman he was with. White-faced and sobbing, she
looked barely more than a teenager. She had long, dark,
wildly curly hair and she was talking fast and loudly.
In Spanish.

Alex was looking stunned. As though he had no idea
how to handle the situation.

Layla had never seen him look like this.

She'd seen him in charge of emergency situations
in Theatre. Running a resuscitation scenario in the intensive care unit. Dealing with distraught parents. But
never once had she seen him look as if he wasn't in
complete control.

Looking...vulnerable?

Well...she had once. When things had gone so disastrously wrong at the end of Jamie Kirkpatrick's surgery. She'd had to stand back and watch helplessly then.

She didn't have to now.

Layla moved swiftly towards them. 'Can I help
you?' she said to the young woman. *'Te puedo ayu-
dar? Digame lo que pasa...'*

Her Spanish was fluent. The woman grabbed her
arm in relief and sobbed out her story. Alex looked, if

anything, even more stunned when Layla turned back to him.

'Ramona says you're treating her baby. Felix?'

His nod was terse. 'He's got a skull fracture. I was hoping to get to the bottom of the story but the language barrier's suddenly got a lot worse.'

Layla asked Ramona a question and then translated the response. 'His brother hit him with a toy brick.'

She could see the total disbelief in Alex's face. 'I'm talking about a fracture here. A *broken* skull. An *unconscious* child.' His voice was so tense it cracked.

Layla's brain sent out the kind of alert signal that any Chief of Paediatrics would be wise to pay attention to. It had been known to happen, hadn't it? She'd read of more than one case where parents had had children taken away from them by social services and had been prosecuted for child abuse.

One sprang to mind immediately, of an eight-month-old boy whose sibling had hit him with a toy aeroplane and caused a fracture. And what about the Tommy Jenner case a few months ago when the child-abuse screen had been started and then they'd found that Tommy had actually been injuring himself because of the seizures caused by his brain lesion?

Alex needed to be careful of what he was saying here but Layla found that she was thinking of something else entirely as she stared at him. Had she really not noticed before how those glimmers of grey had crept into his jet-black hair? The way those lines at the corners of his eyes had deepened over the years they hadn't seen each other? Had she really forgotten the way those chocolate-brown eyes could darken when something emotionally intense was going on, like anger or…physical passion?

Heavens…they looked positively black at the moment.

Ramona had picked up the tone of Alex's voice. Looking terrified, she made a huge effort to pull herself together and change languages.

'No…don't say those words. No person hurt my baby. I…I *love* him.'

The anguish in her eyes and broken words was heart-breaking. Alex put his hand on the young woman's shoulder.

'Try and calm down, Ramona. I won't ask any more questions now. We've got Felix stabilised and we'll be taking him up to surgery in a few minutes.'

'*Què*? I…no understand…'

Layla translated but she couldn't look away from where Alex's hand was still resting on Ramona's shoulder. She could feel that hand herself.

'Ask her if her husband's on the way,' Alex ordered.

But Ramona understood that.

'Not husband. Boy…friend. I was…' With an impatient head shake and hand movements she reverted to rapid Spanish and Layla had to relay the information.

'She was already pregnant with Felix when she met him. He's bringing in her older son. She's scared that you're going to call the police and she doesn't want to get into trouble.' It was quite possible there was an issue concerning illegal immigration here. Layla bit her lip, wondering if this was another alert signal her new position meant she should be worrying about.

The hand had dropped now. Layla watched as Alex's fingers curled into a fist but that was the only sign that something was disturbing him very deeply. That and the sense of raw power he was exuding. Right now that power was all about anger on behalf of a defenceless small child. Did he know for sure that his little patient's head injury had not been accidental? Layla wouldn't want to be standing in his way if he was planning to do something about such a conviction.

When he looked at Layla, she knew he was barely aware of her.

'Tell her that my only concern is treating her son.'

Alex left the impression of power in his wake and it stayed with Layla long after leaving Ramona with one of the nurses. She was left with a whole kaleidoscope of impressions whirling around her head, in fact.

The tension in Alex's face. The image of his hand on Ramona's shoulder. The way those dark, dark eyes had seemed to look right through her.

Memories… That first time they'd made love in the wake of her being so wound up after a blazing row with Luke. The urgency and the mind-blowing *heat* of that encounter. The unbelievable bliss in which it had culminated…

The feel of his lips against hers, which she'd experienced again not very long ago. The sheer wanting that it could conjure up every single time…

Oh, yes. It was just as well Alex was nowhere near where he might be able to see what was whizzing through her head because any control Layla felt she'd had in following this fool plan of hers had just gone out the window.

Concentrating on what she had to do for the rest of her day was quite a tall order. Layla was still feeling out of kilter by the time she got to the end of her list, long after most staff members had finished their days and gone home for dinner. She always liked to pop into all the intensive care units before she went home, to make sure she was in touch with how all Angel's most seriously unwell children were doing.

Her little 'blue' baby was in the cardiac unit, having had surgery to correct the abnormality she had been born with. All was well in NICU, the neonatal intensive care unit. PICU was her last stop. Maybe because she was a little nervous at crossing paths again with Alex today?

A little nervous? Judging by the way she actually jumped when she heard the sound of his voice even before she saw him, she was as jumpy as spit on a hot skillet.

'For God's sake…a skull fracture with acute subdural and epidural bleeding. You can't tell me a two-year-old kid can throw a wooden brick hard enough to cause that kind of an injury.'

'Are there any other potential signs of abuse?'

Another male voice. And they were both talking quietly, probably confident that their intense conversation was private. Had they left the unit for precisely that reason?

Layla stopped in her tracks, unsure of whether to round the corner where she'd have to walk past them to get to the locked door of the intensive care unit. The indecisiveness was an alien sensation and she didn't like it at all. She shifted her weight from one foot to the other, fingering her security badge, which would allow her access through that locked door.

'I don't know.' Alex's voice was a growl. 'I haven't had a chance to check him over properly yet. I've been too busy trying to save the poor little tyke's life. My suspicions are more than enough to base a report on and it needs to be filed within thirty-six hours of admission.'

'You need to be careful. Do you remember the first time I went to the monthly report meeting? Who was that kid you presented the case on? The one who's been on chemo for months and you're going to think about operating on soon?'

'Tommy Jenner.' Alex sounded impatient now. He didn't want to change the subject.

'You presented that case as a warning, didn't you? Not to make assumptions that just might be wrong. The *last* thing you need is another malpractice suit on your hands.'

'Are you telling me to stand back and say nothing? You, of all people, should know better than that, Cade. We *both* know the kind of damage that can do, don't we?'

'Yeah, yeah…point taken. But that's exactly why you need to tread carefully, man. You're too wired to see the worst-case scenario. You know too much.'

Layla was standing very still now, her eyes wide. What on earth was all that supposed to mean?

'You're following protocol,' Cade continued. 'Treating the child is number one. You can order a child-abuse screen and do the other tests you need, like X-rays to look for old fractures. The kid's safe and you've got some time up your sleeve. You need to cool down.'

Having Layla appear around the corner probably wouldn't help Alex to cool down. She found herself backing away. Turning, ready to leave, only to find herself face to face with a man who had a small boy with him. The child was about two or three years old and he was a reluctant companion. The man had a grip above the boy's elbow and was half pulling, half shoving him along. With long, greasy-looking hair and the skin of his arms beneath his T-shirt barely visible between tattoos, the man looked distinctly menacing.

'Get a move on,' he snarled down at the child, ignoring Layla. 'We're going to find your mother and then I'm outta here. I'm done with babysitting someone else's snivelling brat.'

He swept past Layla and around the corner. He practically banged into Alex and Cade.

Layla was hot on the man's heels. She didn't need the strong whiff of alcohol that reached her nostrils to know that a very volatile situation was forming.

'Whoa...' It was Cade who held up a hand to ward off a collision. 'Take it easy.'

'I'm in a hurry,' the man responded. He ignored Alex and walked past Cade. 'What...is that door *locked*? What kind of a joint is this? I thought it was a hospital, not a bloody prison.'

Layla was watching Alex. She could see he had assessed what was going on with the speed and intelligence she had learned to expect from him long ago. He was also putting two and two together as fast as she had. A young man arriving at the intensive care unit with a small boy. His patient's mother was inside the unit with her son. The baby had an older brother who had, supposedly, caused his severe head injury.

Alex caught her gaze and she felt that tingle of connection. Of knowing they were on exactly the same wavelength.

But there was more to this than a surgeon worried about his patient or a doctor who found treating a case of child abuse appalling. The shadows she could see in

Alex's gaze created a flood of questions. She'd always been aware of that dark side to him, hadn't she? She'd never had the chance to find out how it had got there. She'd been happy to just let it add to the frisson of danger that had gone with getting close to this man. The excitement of the illicit affair.

And, right now, it was more than just wanting answers to those questions…she wanted to defuse this situation. Or was it more than that even? That squeezing sensation in her chest suggested that she wanted to… make it better somehow. For Alex.

As if he read something of that in her face, his gaze jerked away from her to the stranger.

'You're Ramona's boyfriend, aren't you?' Alex sounded calm. Dangerously so.

'Who wants to know?'

'I'm Alex Rodriguez. Felix's neurosurgeon. I'm the person who's been operating on Felix this afternoon. Getting some of the blood out of his skull before it did too much damage to his brain.'

'Good for you.' The man eyed Alex up and down. More up than down. Both Alex and his brother towered over this stranger by at least six or seven inches. Layla could see that he was practised in assessing another man's strength but if he was intimidated by his male company he didn't show it. He stepped closer to Alex. 'If you're a doctor, you can let me in through that door. I've got a right to see Ramona.'

Alex was taking a breath. Layla could see the way his eyes narrowed as he smelt the alcohol. 'I'd like a word with you first, if you don't mind.'

'I do mind.' Layla saw the way the man shoved the little boy to one side and then curled his fists.

The little boy staggered sideways and bumped into Cade, who caught him as he started sobbing. 'You're OK, buddy,' he said.

'Shut up, Cody, or you'll be sorry,' the man warned.

'Like Felix was?' Alex's query was almost conversational.

'Alex...' Cade's tone was a warning.

The men were squaring off at each other. Layla could feel the fury of Alex's stare even though it was fastened firmly on the man directly in front of him. The tension was indescribable. Any second now and all hell would break loose. Alex would flatten Ramona's low-life boyfriend and then what? She wouldn't be trying to thank him for saving *her* job. She'd be fighting a losing battle trying to save his.

Not going to happen.

Without pausing to think about what she was doing, Layla stepped in between the two men just as both men raised their fists.

The vicious shove she received from behind was meant to get her out of the way but, in fact, it slammed her against Alex's rigid body. He had no choice but to lower his fists to catch hold of her before she fell sideways. It still felt like she was falling but she was encased in an astonishingly powerful grip.

From the corner of her eye she saw the fist aimed at Alex, which would have connected with the side of her head if Alex hadn't hauled her out of harm's way.

He only held Layla long enough for her to feel that strength and all that leashed power. To feel the pounding of his heart against her own for no more than a second. And then he let go of her and moved so swiftly the attacker didn't have a chance.

'That's *enough*.' Alex grabbed the raised arm of the attacker and then twisted it behind the man's back.

'*Ow*…lemme go,' the man snarled. The words turned into a whimper of pain as Alex clearly tightened his grip.

Layla, Cade and little Cody were all staring, wide eyed.

'Call Security,' Alex told Cade. 'Layla, take Cody in to find his mother.'

Layla did as she was told. She held out her hand. 'Come on, honey. I'll just bet your momma is going to be so happy to see you.'

Behind her, she could hear Cade talking urgently to Alex. 'I'll sit on him till Security gets here. You need to go and cool down before you talk to them. I'll tell them you got paged.'

'No way…' The refusal was almost drowned by a stream of obscenities and threats from Ramona's boyfriend.

Layla used her swipe card to gain entry to the unit. As the doors closed behind Cody and herself she could only hope that Alex could control his fury. It didn't matter what the man was guilty of—a member of staff in an altercation with a parent figure would be a dismissible offence.

She found a staff member to take care of Cody and filled them in on what had happened. She even spoke briefly to Ramona and learned that Felix had come through his surgery with flying colours and everybody was very pleased with how he was doing. It was only a few minutes before she could head back to see what was happening on the other side of the door. With a curious mix of both relief and disappointment she found Alex was nowhere to be seen. Ramona's boyfriend was also gone from the scene and the security guard talking to Cade had finished whatever he needed to do.

'I'll go and have a word with the boy's mother,' he said. 'And I'll catch up with Dr Rodriguez when he's done with that emergency.'

Layla pinned Cade with a look that told him she wasn't leaving without some answers.

'Where's Alex?'

Cade shrugged. 'Gone. I thought he should cool off a bit before he started talking to the cops.'

There was a moment's silence as they stared at each other. Cade looked...defensive? As if he was challenging Layla to criticise Alex for coming on too strong. She weighed her words.

'I heard you guys talking,' she said carefully. 'What did you mean by Alex knowing too much?'

She could see the shutters come down. Cade shrugged again, a gesture that told her this was between brothers and none of her business. And then his eyebrow rose.

'Is it true what I've heard around here? That there's something going on between you and Alex?'

Was this a case of attack being the best form of defence? Or was it a brother looking after a brother? If Layla wanted an honest answer from Cade, maybe he deserved the truth first.

'Not now,' she told him. 'There's...history. We were together way back. At the time of the Kirkpatrick case. You'd know about that.'

A sharp nod from Cade. 'It's what made me get in touch with Alex after not seeing him for years. Not that

I got much of a chance to spend time with him before he took off to Brisbane.'

'It messed up a lot of things,' Layla agreed. 'But what's important right now is that I owe my job to Alex and I'm not going to let him get into trouble over what just happened here if I can help it.'

Cade's nod was relieved. 'Just as well. The creep's telling everybody that Alex started it. Just laid into him without any provocation.'

'I'll sort it,' Layla promised. But she wasn't letting Cade off the hook just yet. *'After* I've talked to Alex, that is. Now, are you going to tell me where he is so I can do that before the cops start looking for me?'

Cade sighed. 'He didn't say where he was going but I'd guess he's where he always is when he wants to burn off some steam. Where we both go.'

'Which is?'

'The hoop-shooting court out the back of the ambulance bay.'

CHAPTER THREE

THE SLAP OF the ball against the palm of his hand was hard enough to be causing pain.

Firing the ball towards the hoop with such aggression before he'd warmed up properly had ripped a bit of muscle, too, so that every subsequent attempt at a goal sent a stabbing sensation through his shoulder. On top of that, Alex had been going hard enough to be out of breath enough to make his lungs burn and create a satisfyingly deep ache in his chest every time he tried to suck in some more oxygen.

But he wasn't ready to stop yet. No way.

This felt like a fight to the death.

OK, he'd been wrong about Tommy but he'd known in his gut that Felix had been the victim of abuse from the moment he'd seen him. He should have had the cops there waiting for that creep of a father figure to turn up.

He'd wanted to kill the guy. Or at least hurt him enough to make him stop and think about what he'd done to an innocent child. Felix was a *baby*, for God's sake. He had no chance to defend himself in any way. He'd still feel the pain, though, wouldn't he? And the shock of such a betrayal from a person he had to trust because his survival depended on it.

His breath coming in ragged gasps, Alex did another circuit of the court at high speed, hammering the ball on the tarmac with every step, getting back to the point where he could make another leap and fire the ball at the hoop as fast as he could.

He'd been luckier than Felix. Ten years old and big for his age before the abuse from his stepfather had really started. Big enough to be fiercely determined to protect his little brother. Strong enough to stand up to a man who'd made it very clear he didn't give a damn about his dead wife's kid.

He hated this part of his job. Hated the memories that came with cases like this. Felt consumed with anger that his time and skills had to be used to fight something that should never, ever have happened in the first place. In a perfect world he could devote his life to being the absolute best in dealing with the kind of things that weren't preventable. The kind of complicated lesions that came out of nowhere and threatened to blow a loving, *real* family apart.

Everybody knew he was well on the way to being the best. What they didn't know was that he was driven to it by the mix of guilt and determination that he had to live with for ever. Guilt over what had happened in the little Jamie Kirkpatrick case. Determination that it would never, ever happen again. That nothing, and nobody, would ever put him off his game.

And that was under threat.

It wasn't just the anger about child abuse in general that Alex was trying to burn off here. Or the fury and disgust at coming face to face with the perpetrator in a single case. Part of what was pushing him on and on despite the pain right now was fear. This threat was huge.

Because of the guilt that had spurred his determination in the first place.

Because the reason he hadn't been on top of his game for little Jamie was back in his life again.

And because the pull of it was unbearable.

It had been bad enough earlier today when he'd heard her speaking *Spanish*, for God's sake...

He could probably have conversed with Ramona himself except that he'd shut the door so successfully on the language he'd heard so much of in his earliest years. The Rodriguez family had kept close ties with their culture but his mother had refused to speak Spanish after his father had died. Phrases had slipped out in emotional times, though, on the occasions she'd got cross. More often when she'd been happy, like when she'd been giving him a cuddle and kiss to say goodnight.

It was a language that touched something very deep inside Alex. It had roots in a happy time that was so long ago it was only a fairy-tale. Hearing Layla speaking it so fluently had given him a chill down his spine. Made him realise that there was more connecting him to this woman that he'd thought.

Pulling him back.

But he hadn't realised the terrifying power of that pull until a few minutes ago. When he'd been so consumed with that anger towards Ramona's boyfriend that he might have ignored Cade's warning about what the consequences might be until...until Layla had stepped between them and everything had changed in a heartbeat.

The need to protect her had come with the same kind of automatic speed that he'd practised as a kid, making sure that Cade wasn't going to get in the way of his father's fists. And *that* had become more important than anything else.

And then that low-life had pushed her and she'd slammed up against his body and, as inconceivable as it should have been given the circumstances, the awareness of her warmth and softness and...just that she was *Layla* had messed with his head completely.

The desire to hurt the creep had been diluted by the relief that Layla was safe. The memories were jangled and confused. Cade had been right. He'd needed to get away to cool off and clear his head.

Was he succeeding?

It didn't feel like it. Another circuit of the court and the muscles in his legs were burning now. Every pore was releasing sweat in a vain attempt to cool him down and he felt light-headed for a moment because he wasn't getting enough oxygen.

But he still kept going. The anger may have worn off but he still had too many other emotions curdling his blood.

He had to fight the threat. Find a way through it. He wasn't going to let his life get derailed again. He'd learned his lessons.

Not instantly, of course. He'd gone from his disastrous fling with a married woman to falling into bed with Callie Richards, one of his new colleagues in Brisbane. The lust had burned off fast enough, though, and he'd been left with a friendship he knew they'd have for ever. Callie was just like him. Burned by love to the same extent and determined that it would never interfere with her life again.

She'd tell him to do whatever it took to forget and then move on.

Like they had, after their fling had fizzled out. They'd been able to salvage a true friendship and work together without this gut-wrenching tension he was trying to get past now.

It was so hard fighting the past here. Especially now. The memories of Jamie. And Tommy. And now Felix.

And not just the *memories* of Layla. He had to deal with the *reality* of her. Every day. Every minute of the day it had started to feel like. That kiss. The feel of her body against his so recently upstairs. That disturbing, automatic need to protect her.

He had to deal with it. Or he'd have all his demons snapping at his heels for the rest of his life and he'd never find peace.

Alex was finally forced to stop moving and catch his breath.

Exhausted now, he could start to push everything out of his head. Except for the knowledge that he had to find a way through this and that he had no idea where to start.

Give him a case that was complicated enough to scare anyone else off and he was fine. He could make a plan. Step by step. A thorough investigation and then treatment with the goal of a cure lighting the path.

Work was great like that. But personal stuff?

Callie might know what he needed to do. She was a touchstone for advice.

Maybe Cade could help. He'd lived with the same background of violence and he'd only been protected until Alex had abandoned him and walked out when he'd been sixteen. Cade had been justifiably angry but they were sorting out that emotional minefield now. They were brothers again and that was thanks to Cade making the first move so maybe he would have a clue where you got started on a journey to make peace with the past and move on.

He certainly needed to talk to someone. If he didn't find an outlet for the emotions he couldn't suppress, he'd go crazy.

Things weren't hurting quite so much now. A few more minutes of this over-the-top physical activity and he could go and have a shower. With a bit of luck he'd be too tired to even think after that.

Layla had gone through the emergency department and out the automatic doors that led to the ambulance bay. There was a crew unloading a young patient who appeared to be having a severe asthma attack. He was sitting bolt upright on the stretcher, clutching a nebuliser mask to his face. His anxious parents gave Layla a hopeful look as if the stethoscope around her neck and perhaps the seniority her white coat advertised meant she would pause on her way and put things right, but all she could offer was a sympathetic smile.

She'd never been around the back of the ambulance bay before. As far as she knew, this was where all the rubbish skips were lined up ready for collection so there'd never been a reason to go there. Tucked into the corner, however, and brightly lit by the powerful security lights, was a good-sized patch of tarmac. The backboard and hoop were securely attached to one of Angel's walls.

Alex had clearly been working out without a pause since she'd last seen him. He was wearing nothing more than some shorts, a singlet and trainers, and his exposed skin gleamed with sweat.

And, oh, man…there was a lot of exposed skin.

Standing at the end of the line of rubbish skips and not directly under a light, Layla knew she was probably invisible. Alex was so focussed on his lonely game that he probably wouldn't have noticed her anyway, even if she was out in the open. She should call out or something because it felt suddenly as if she was seeing something private but when she opened her mouth Layla found it was inexplicably dry and no sound emerged.

Even if the overhead lights weren't picking Alex out from the surrounding darkness like spotlights, it would have been impossible to look away. This was the image of a very well-built, very fit man. There wasn't an ounce of fat on Alex Rodriguez. Muscles rippled and tendons appeared like ropes on his thighs and arms as he ran and twisted, changing direction and gathering speed before firing a shot at the goal. Layla found herself holding her breath every time, waiting for the crack of the ball against the backboard and the satisfying slide of it going through the net.

There wasn't a woman alive who wouldn't be impressed by Alex's body even when he was fully clothed and standing absolutely still. To watch him display this level of fitness and physical acuity was mesmerising. Erotic, in fact. She could hear the rasp of Alex's ragged breathing and the occasional grunt of effort. She could almost feel the body heat coming at her in waves and smell the salty tang of his sweat.

Her mouth might be dry but there was another part of Layla that most certainly wasn't. Her breathing rate had picked up as well and her knees were actually feeling weak, like those of some swooning heroine from a story like *Gone With The Wind* or something.

When Alex finally stopped to catch his breath, Layla ordered herself to get a grip and focus on what she'd come here for.

Which was what, exactly?

To talk about what had just happened outside the intensive care unit, of course. So that they could make sure they were singing from the same hymn book and that, if necessary, she could use her position to make sure Alex didn't get into any trouble over this.

And…if that went well enough, maybe she'd push him just a little bit and try and find out what Cade had meant about Alex knowing too much. What it was that had made him shut her out so convincingly.

Layla didn't like being shut out.

She pulled herself together enough to think she could manage to start this conversation but by then Alex had started running again. Not nearly as fast and furiously as he had been when she'd arrived. The anger he'd been burning off must be spent and that was a good thing. He probably wouldn't mind being interrupted now. Swallowing hard, Layla walked away from the rubbish skip and out into the open where he couldn't fail to see her when he started a new circuit after the next goal.

It wasn't so good that she'd have to talk to him while he was more than half-naked and dripping with sweat, given the ache of raw desire she could still feel pulsing in her belly, but Layla already had a plan in place. She'd tell him to have a quick shower and then they'd grab a coffee. She'd wait outside the door of wherever he was going to have a shower to make sure that she got to talk to him first.

The clock was ticking. The police were probably paging him already.

* * *

Alex became aware of Layla's presence the moment she stepped into the periphery of his visual field but he totally ignored her while he did another circuit of the court.

He could guess why she'd come looking for him. Well…she could stand there for another minute or two. The fact that the few items of clothing he was wearing were now dripping wet and clinging to his body didn't bother him at all. The physical activity and his success in burning off that anger made him feel powerful. In control. Layla, standing there with her pretty skirt and her hair getting ruffled by the warm evening breeze, looked feminine and fragile. Definitely on the back foot.

The final goal was accompanied by a snort of something close to laughter from Alex.

Layla *fragile*? Not in this lifetime.

With a final bounce Alex caught the ball. He turned and walked decisively to where Layla was standing. He couldn't miss the way her eyes widened as he got closer. Or the way her breath hitched, allowing just a tantalising glimpse of cleavage to peep over the scooped neckline of her blouse. She even averted her gaze when he got within touching distance.

Oh, yeah…Layla wasn't very comfortable right now.

'We need to talk,' she said.

Alex let one corner of his mouth curl upwards. 'Sure. Unless you'd prefer me to shower first?'

'That…would probably be a good idea. I…um… wouldn't want you to catch a chill or something.'

'I'll only be a minute.' Alex tilted his head towards the rarely used facility built into one corner of the ambulance bay. 'We often use the shower in the decontamination room over there.'

'Fine. I'll wait out here.'

The decontamination room was big enough to allow a stretcher to get wheeled in. It was designed to deal with a situation like people or equipment being in contact with a toxic chemical or potential infection. Completely tiled, there were overhead showers as well as hand-held sprays over a tilted floor with large drains. There were also big tubs and shelves that held stacks of clean towels and other items that might be needed, like gowns, gloves and masks.

Alex stripped off and got under the shower, pumping some soap from the container attached to the wall. He scrubbed some lather through his hair and then sluiced it off, letting the water rain on his face and onto his chest. He shook his head when he turned the water off but still had rivulets running over his skin as he stepped off the tilted floor to reach for a towel.

He felt the cool touch of the breeze on his back and knew the door had opened behind him. With a corner of the towel dangling from one hand, he turned to see Layla closing and locking the door behind her.

'What the *hell* do you think you're doing?'

She was leaning against the door now, facing him but with her eyes closed.

'There's a cop out there. The squad car's parked in the last ambulance slot. I didn't want them to see me yet. Or find you yet. I...couldn't think what else to do.' Layla opened her eyes. 'Sorry.'

Alex was trying to process this. She was hiding from the police? Because she had some misguided notion that she could protect *him*? Why did she want to do that?

In the time it took for the thoughts to take their turn Alex was also processing the way Layla's gaze dropped. Slowly. Travelling down his body and then up again. The way her pupils dilated. The way the very tip of her tongue appeared to moisten her lips.

Oh…God… What was it about the chemistry between them? This was way more intense than the atmosphere had been before that kiss. Alex could feel the oxygen being sucked out of the air around them. That final plunge before the electricity exploded. If he didn't do something…anything…right *now*, they would both be consumed by the flames and there would be no turning back.

But it was too hard to even think, let alone move.

He was as naked as a jaybird. With his hair all spiky and drops of water caught on the damp whorls of hair on his chest. Hair that arrowed down to where his fist was holding the edge of the towel.

She knew what was barely concealed by that drape of towelling. She knew what that hand was capable of doing when it wasn't busy holding something. Maybe if every cell in her body wasn't screaming for more than the memory of that touch she could have handled this. But then Layla's gaze dragged itself upwards until it snagged with Alex's mouth and she knew she was completely lost.

She couldn't look away. The only thing her brain was capable of was willing those lips to come closer. To touch her own.

A pager sounded. Hers? Maybe Alex's, coming from the pile of his clothing that was on the bench. They were both off duty so it was most likely to be something connected to the incident upstairs. Something that should have been enough to break the unbearable sexual tension in this small, clinical space.

It certainly broke the impasse but not in the way Layla had expected. With a muttered curse Alex moved.

Not to look for his pager.

Towards Layla.

His fingers caught in her hair as they curled around her neck. She closed her eyes, instinctively tipping her head back. Exposing her neck to him. Parting her lips. Waiting for *that* moment…The touch of his lips…his hands…his tongue. The moment when nothing else in the world mattered.

And when it came, it was better than she could have imagined. That unexpected kiss, weeks ago now, had erased the first shock of their bodies meeting again. This time it was all about what they knew they could give each other. What they craved like an addict denied his fix for too long.

How was it that the passion could be so white hot and desperately urgent and yet it could feel gentle at the same time? That buttons could come undone and not ping onto the tiles like bullets?

The sounds echoed around them. The fast breathing. The groans of pleasure so intense it was painful. Did the sound come from her own throat when Alex's hand cupped her breast, his thumb pulling the lace of her bra aside so that his lips could find her nipple?

Of course it did. But it was matched by the low growl that came from Alex. Her cry was much louder moments later when her skirt was hitched up and she was touched where she wanted it most.

It wasn't enough. Layla could feel the hard tiles

against her back. She had the hardness of Alex's body against her breasts and her belly. Her own hands sought the hardness she knew she would find. That she couldn't live without for another heartbeat.

This was wild. Irresponsible and totally, absolutely irresistible.

Layla felt her panties being dragged down.

Yes…

She felt herself being lifted. She wrapped her arms around Alex's neck and her legs around his hips. It would only be a matter of seconds before she got tipped off the world into paradise and maybe the bliss wouldn't last nearly long enough but…oh, *God*…nothing was this good and never could be.

For a long, long minute there was nothing but the sound of them both trying to catch their breath.

Not a word was spoken as they finally peeled apart. Layla fixed her clothing while Alex got dressed.

He checked his pager.

'Cade's looking for me.' Alex had to clear his throat. 'He's talking to the cops.'

'We still need to talk.' Heavens, her voice had come out all husky too, from the aftermath of passion.

'We'll do it on the way. Come with me?'

A bubble of wild laughter threatened to escape from Layla. *I just did*, she thought. And then the realisation hit her. Of what had just happened. How huge it was—to her, at any rate. Of how weird it was not to be saying anything about it. Of how enormous the new problem had just been created. What did it mean and, more importantly, what on earth were they going to do about this?

Maybe it was too big to know what to say yet. Layla stared at Alex and he held her gaze. She could see the kind of peace that only came from ultimate physical satisfaction. But she could also see confusion there. Regret, maybe? She didn't want to hear him say anything to confirm that.

'And, yeah…I reckon we do need to talk.' Alex still hadn't broken eye contact. 'We'll do that real soon.'

With a nod Layla followed him to where they needed to be now.

The promise was enough. Alex was a man of his word. They *would* talk soon and somehow, between them, they would be able to sort everything.

The tension between them had been resoundingly broken, that was for sure. Plan B had succeeded in a most unexpected way. Now all they needed was a new plan. One that would enable them to find a way forward.

A plan that Layla couldn't begin to formulate because it was going to be very different. And it required input from both of them.

CHAPTER FOUR

'YOU DIDN'T...' A gasp was followed by an echo of incredulous feminine laughter over the international
phone line. 'Oh, my God, Alex. You *idiot*.'

'Hey...I rang you for some advice, Callie Richards.
Not a character assassination.'

'OK. Sorry, mate. But...but *Layla*? Wasn't she the
final straw that drove you over to this side of the world?'

'Yeah...I *know*...' Alex scrubbed his fingers through
his hair as he stood, clad only in his boxer shorts, beside the open windows of his Manhattan apartment,
trying to catch a hint of breeze in the middle of this
sultry Indian-summer night. He sighed heavily. 'I *am*
an idiot. I thought I could handle it, you know? Stay
the hell away from her, even though we're working in
the same place. But there she was...'

'You were at *work*. Even *we* never did anything that
crazy.'

Being ashamed of himself was a very alien sensation for Alex. He tried to ignore the unpleasant squirm
in his gut.

'I hope some of your brain cells were still active and
that you used a...'

Alex had to cut her off. Callie may be an ex-lover

and his best friend but there were limits to how candid he wanted this conversation to be. 'No,' he snapped. 'They're not something I generally have on hand when I'm at work.'

There was a moment's shocked silence on the line. She didn't need to tell him how stupid he'd been. How irresponsible. That he was thirty-eight years old, not eighteen, and he should have known better.

'It just happened, Cal. I can't undo the past, no matter how recent. What I'm trying to figure out here is what the hell am I going to do about it *now*?'

Callie's voice had a sharper edge. 'What did Layla have to say about it?'

'That we need to talk.' Alex wasn't about to admit it, even to the woman he considered to be the closest friend he'd ever had in his life, but the prospect was terrifying. He didn't want to have that conversation with Layla. Didn't want to be that close to her again until he was absolutely confident he could handle it. And his level of confidence in that situation had been badly shaken. Destroyed?

'She's right,' Callie told him.

'I *am* talking,' Alex growled. 'To *you*.'

Callie's voice softened. 'And it's great to hear you, mate. I miss having you around.'

There was another short silence that seemed to contain a sigh of regret. Of them being a world away from each other? Sadness that their brief fling when Alex had first gone to Brisbane had burned itself out so convincingly that nothing more than the chance of friendship was left in its wake? Not that the friendship wasn't wonderful. They were so alike they could have easily come from the same genetic pool. Callie was a soul mate in the way a sister could have been.

'You've hardly called since you moved to the Big Apple,' Callie added. 'Not good enough.'

'I know. I'm sorry. It's been hectic.'

'Yeah, yeah…I know what you're like, Alex. But being a workaholic to escape personal stuff might not be the whole answer.'

It was Alex's turn to let a snort of laughter escape. 'That's the pot calling the kettle black.'

'So? I'm an expert.' Callie was unrepentant. 'I know what I'm talking about and I'm better at it than you.'

'OK. If you're such an expert, tell me what I'm supposed to do about this. I don't want to get tangled up with Layla Woods again. With anyone, for that matter.'

'That might have been your first mistake,' Callie said seriously. 'If you hadn't taken that vow of celibacy after our…after we…' She cleared her throat. 'Anyway…you're not cut out to be a monk, Alex Rodriguez. If you'd just had some fun now and then, it wouldn't have been all bottled up and ready to explode like that.'

'I didn't take a vow of celibacy. I just haven't met anybody else that…that spun my wheels enough.'

Because nobody had come close to being like Layla?

No. That was ridiculous. The world was full of gorgeous women. He just hadn't wanted the complications that came with even a brief entanglement. Work had been the answer. Satisfying enough, anyway.

Until now?

'Layla still spins them, then, I take it?' There was an odd note in Callie's voice. Wistful? No. More like resignation. This was more a sisterly thing. As though she was wanting to protect him from someone she knew had hurt him so much in the past.

'Obviously.' Alex's response was dry enough to evaporate instantly.

'Hmm. Well, at least it was just a quick shag in the shower. Nobody could say that was romantic.'

'No. I guess not.' Unbidden, images of Layla in a more romantic setting flashed into his head.

A big bed with rumpled sheets.

A soft rug in front of a crackling, open fire.

A candlelit dinner by a moon-touched sea.

Oh…God… It didn't matter that the images were so fleeting they almost hadn't touched his consciousness. They still left a drag of something way too close to longing in their wake.

He *didn't* want any of that. No way.

'And you didn't have a heart-to-heart and trot down memory lane?'

'We didn't get a chance to talk. The cops were waiting for us.'

'What? That was fast. How did they know what you'd been up to?'

Alex laughed and instantly felt better. Trust Callie to be able to break the tension like that. He filled her in on the incident with Ramona's boyfriend, which they'd managed to defuse completely with the solid wall of evidence from Cade, Layla and himself to refute the creep's claims that Alex had attacked him.

'And then I got caught up checking on Felix and by the time I'd finished, Layla had gone home so Cade and I went to O'Malley's for a drink.'

'Who's O'Malley?'

'It's an Irish pub. Close to Angel's so it gets used a

lot. You'd love it. Irish pubs are the same the world over. Could have been in O'Reilly's in Brisbane. Felt kind of like home, anyway.'

Except he didn't have a real home, did he? Never had. Maybe he never would. A shaft of a very melancholy shadow made him fall silent suddenly.

Callie didn't notice. 'And a good brotherly chat? You've really patched things up between you?'

'Yeah… Seems like it.' The shadow lifted. Maybe home was really about people, not places.

'So what did Cade have to say about you and Layla hooking up?'

'I…didn't get round to telling him about that.'

Callie made an impatient sound. '*Men*. What is with you and talking about personal stuff?'

'We talked about plenty of personal stuff.'

'Oh, yeah? Like what?'

'Cade's stuff.'

'Worse than yours?'

'Maybe.' Alex pressed his lips together. He wasn't about to break a confidence. And Cade's stuff had made him think his own worries were insignificant.

The worst that had happened to him had been that a girl he'd been crazy about had dumped him. She hadn't tried to trap him by getting pregnant and then punished him for not responding in the way she'd planned. Cade had had to deal with the guilt of this girl taking an overdose and then having a miscarriage.

'Anyway…' Callie had given up waiting for him to say anything more about the conversation. 'You working tomorrow?'

'It's Saturday and I'm not on call. I'll do a ward

round in the morning and was planning to catch up on paperwork after that.'

'Talk to Layla,' Callie ordered. 'If nothing else, you need to find out if she's on the Pill. Or whether you need to get screened for an STD or something.'

A curl of anger came from nowhere and was bright enough to make the night seem even hotter. 'Layla's not like that,' he snapped.

Why was the urge to protect her so automatic? What did he know about Layla these days? How on earth could he be so sure that he hadn't been put at risk despite doing something so irresponsible?

His rebuke had hit home. Callie sounded wary now. 'You still need to talk to her. Tomorrow. The longer you leave it, the harder it's going to be, and if you avoid her, you'll just be setting yourself up for another…um… shall we say, inappropriate means of dealing with the tension?'

A repeat of what had happened in the shower room? Oh…*yeah*…

Alex gave himself a firm mental shake. 'You're right. I'll catch her tomorrow and we'll talk about it. I'm sure she's as horrified as I am that it happened at all. Between us, we'll be able to figure out a way of making sure it doesn't happen again.'

'And…be careful, Alex.'

'How do you mean?'

'I'm not saying that Layla's not trustworthy or anything. Don't get me wrong, any woman that's managed to get under your skin the way she has must have a lot going for her. I'm just saying that maybe there's some merit in the whole "once bitten, twice shy" approach.'

Meaning he could get hurt. Again. As if he didn't know that.

'I get it,' he said softly. 'Thanks for caring, Cal.'

'No worries. Now, you need to get some sleep. What time is it over there?'

'Three a.m.' But Alex didn't want to end the call. Not while Callie was still sounding hurt by his defence of Layla's reputation. 'But I want to know how *you* are, Cal. How's it going at Gold Coast General?'

'Well...seeing as you've asked, I'm overworked and stressed out. If I don't get a new prenatal surgeon who's up to my impossibly high standards very soon, I will go stark raving mad.'

'Hmm.' Alex was only too happy to get completely distracted from his personal issues. He was also keen to do something to cheer Callie up. 'You know what? I might just be able to help you out there.'

'You're a neurosurgeon, Alex, not a prenatal surgeon.'

'True, but I might know one who could be interested.'

'Who? He'd have to be good.'

'He is. And I'm not just saying that because he's my brother.'

'You mean Cade? I thought he'd only just started at Angel's.'

'He has but he's finding it a bit frustrating. And I have to agree that he's too good to be second in charge. Funnily enough, he said something just the other day about thinking I had the right idea in going off to start a new life in Australia.'

With the benefit of hindsight, he could tell Cade that running away from some things didn't work. They could lie in wait for you and the ambush could be unexpected and very disturbing. He might be better to stay here and face his demons head on, if he had any. Except that maybe it *was* the answer for Cade.

Callie had picked up on his train of thought with her customary level of intuition.

'What's he running away from? If it's just his position on the ladder, there's nothing stopping him from finding a different hospital in the States.'

'Maybe he just needs to stretch his wings and see a bit of the world. He's young. Brilliant. Frustrated.'

'OK.' Callie was sounding much happier now. 'Tell me more, then. Just in case I need to talk to him.'

Finally, a puff of deliciously cool air came through the windows. Alex settled himself on the window sill. This was a conversation he was more than happy to have.

The one he would have to have tomorrow, with Layla?

Not so much. To put it mildly.

'Layla… Hey, wait up…'

'Chloe.'

The two women hugged each other in greeting. A paediatric nurse, Chloe Jenkins—no, Chloe Davis now that she'd married Brad—had been the first real friend Layla had made after arriving at Angel's.

'What's up?' Chloe pulled away to give Layla a questioning glance. 'You don't look like you're feeling great.'

'I'm just a bit tired.' Layla forced a smile. 'It was so hard to sleep last night with that heat. I need to ask my landlord to look at the air-conditioning unit.' She needed to change the subject quickly in case Chloe guessed she was trying to hide something. 'What are you doing in here on a Saturday morning when you're not on? I thought you and Brad were grabbing every chance you could get to go house hunting?'

'We are, but didn't you hear? Eleanor Aston had her baby last night.'

'Oh, wow…isn't that a bit early?'

'Yes, but they're both fine. Little girl. Tyler's over the moon.'

'I'll bet. What have they called her?'

Chloe laughed. 'I don't think they've decided. Right now, she's either "Peanut" or "Honey".'

'So Tyler's a daddy…' Layla shook her head. 'Astonishing.'

'Oh, that's right… You two go way back, don't you?'

'Since we were knee high to grasshoppers.' Layla was grinning now. 'I'll have to get him a cigar.'

'They might have chocolate ones in the gift shop. Come and have a look. That's why I'm here.' Chloe steered Layla across the lobby. 'I need to get a teddy bear or something before I go visiting and I've seen some really cute ones in our shop.'

'I've only got a minute. There's a queue of patients I need to catch up with this morning.'

'Must be a serious case amongst them.'

'Why do you say that?' Layla stopped beside a rack of cards. She could get one and send it to Eleanor and Tyler with Chloe.

'You look like you're on the way to give somebody some very bad news.'

'Oh…' Layla bit her lip. 'I guess I have got a conversation coming up that I'm not looking forward to.'

Chloe had reached out to pick up a teddy bear from

the shelf but her hand stopped in mid-air. 'I knew it. What's going on?'

Layla sighed. She picked up a card and pretended to read the message inside as she stepped closer to Chloe and lowered her voice enough to ensure she wasn't going to be overheard.

'You know how awkward it was seeing Brad at work after you two had slept together?'

'Do I ever. Oh, my God, Layla Woods.' Chloe's whisper became a gasp. 'Who *was* it?'

Layla was silent. Chloe's eyes widened.

'OK, you don't have to tell me because I can guess. It was Alex, wasn't it?'

It was Layla's turn to widen her eyes with shock.

'Don't worry.' Chloe touched her arm. 'It's not written all over your face or anything. I can guess because of the way I saw you two looking at each other when we had that girls' night out a while back.' She sucked in a deep breath. 'When did it happen?'

'Last night.' Layla felt the warmth of colour touching her cheeks. That was the only information she was about to share. Imagine if anybody heard about the actual circumstances? Oh...Lord...

'So what's the big deal?' Chloe picked up the bear and tested its cuddliness. 'You're single. So's he. He's *gorgeous*...and I'll bet the sex was...um...' she grinned mischievously '...memorable?'

'Oh, you have no idea,' Layla murmured. 'But it was a mistake. A big one.'

'Why?'

Why indeed?

Because they had to work together again now?

Because both of them were focussed so completely on their careers?

Because they had messed with each other's lives in the past so much they would never be able to trust each other?

That was more like it.

'Been there, done that,' Layla muttered. 'It wouldn't work.'

Chloe looked thoughtful. 'You can't know that for sure. If there's something there that's strong enough to pull you back together after…how many years?'

'Five.'

'Hmm. That's a pretty powerful something, if you ask me. Does Alex think it was a big mistake?'

'I don't know. We haven't talked about it.'

'Oh…' Chloe's grimace was sympathetic. 'No wonder it's awkward. Good luck with that.'

'Thanks. I think I'm going to need it.'

CHAPTER FIVE

It was later on that Saturday morning before Alex and Layla saw each other and when they did, it was so much like a stand-off in some old Western movie that Layla almost laughed aloud.

She'd stepped out of the elevator on the eighth floor with the intention of going into the neurology ward and finding Alex. She had expected to see him so she shouldn't have been so surprised. What she hadn't expected was to find him striding towards the elevators. That was why her breath caught in her throat and why her heart rate suddenly accelerated. Why her feet seemed to be glued to the floor.

Alex had stopped dead in his tracks with the double doors of the ward entrance still swinging gently behind him.

They were both frozen.

Who's going to reach for their gun first? Layla wondered. Her lips twitched at the ridiculousness of this and, with a determined inward shove she started moving. So did Alex.

Not exactly towards each other. By a kind of telepathic tacit consent they both moved in a V-shaped track that brought them together close to the big windows.

The view over Central Park from this height was spectacular. You could see from the park's southern border almost as far as the huge reservoir in the northern half of this massive area. Layla stared down at the park rather than directly at Alex.

'Gorgeous day, isn't it?'

'Mmm.' It felt like Alex was staring at her rather than the view. Layla's heart skipped a beat. She knew they needed to talk about what had happened last night but she wasn't ready. Nowhere near ready. She could feel her heart skip a beat and she had to dampen her suddenly dry lips.

'I love this end of the park,' she said brightly. 'It's got the best bits. I just love the bird sanctuary and the zoo and…and the sheep meadow.'

Oh, good grief…the sheep meadow? It was nothing more than a vast grassy space where people had picnics or threw Frisbees.

Alex cleared his throat. 'The lake would be a nice spot on a warm day like this.' His hesitation was almost imperceptible. 'Got time for a walk?'

'Um…yeah, I guess.' Layla risked a quick glance at Alex, wishing her heart rate would settle. It was crazy to be feeling this nervous. 'I've only got a bit of paperwork waiting for me and it'll still be waiting when I get back.'

'Same.' Alex met her glance briefly and Layla realised he was as nervous as she was about having this conversation. Was that why he was suggesting they have it well away from the place they both worked?

Oddly, the fact that Alex was nervous calmed Layla enough to make her smile. 'I could kill for a hot dog or something,' she said. 'I'm *starving*.'

A wash of surprise, or maybe relief, crossed Alex's features.

'Same.'

'Let's get out of here, then.' Layla led the way.

They had to share the elevator with a troupe of candy-stripers heading off to the cafeteria for lunch. If Alex was remotely aware of the increase in the amount of giggling and the eyelashes that got batted in his direction, he gave no indication of it.

The lobby was crowded with people. Weekends were a time when lots of visitors could get to Angel's and often there were special treats planned for the young patients. Today it looked as if a celebrity basketball player was making an appearance and he was being tailed by a television crew.

Alex and Layla still hadn't spoken another word to each other by the time they emerged from the front entrance of Angel's into the welcome fresh air and sunshine. Walking side by side, Layla turned her head as they passed the small statue.

Alex noticed the movement. 'You know who that is?' he asked.

'I got told by the taxi driver who dropped me here when I came for the job interview. It's Angel Mendez, a little boy who died of polio during the Great Depression. That's where the hospital got its name.'

'Did you know that his dad was a paediatrician?' Alex asked.

'No. I hadn't heard that bit. How tragic that he couldn't save his own son.'

'His name was Federico Mendez. He wanted to honour Angel's memory and try and make sure other parents didn't lose their kids. This was New York's first free children's hospital.'

'It's a great history.' Layla couldn't help reaching out to brush the statue with her fingers as she passed. She was by no means the only person who ever did that. The bronze of this much-loved statue had weathered to a greenish tinge but the hands of the small boy were shiny because they were on a level that could be touched. By adults like her, or by children being lifted up or climbing so that they could make contact with something they could identify with.

'Mmm.' Alex was a little ahead of her now. 'Kind of sums up what we're all about, doesn't it?'

The road in front of them was wide and busy. Ambulances were turning into the hospital grounds and yellow cabs were sprinkled thickly amongst the heavy traffic. A police car went by with its lights and siren blaring. Alex led the way as the lights changed. A horse-drawn carriage was turning into the park and open-topped, double-decker tourist buses were offloading passengers.

'Which way? Right to the bird sanctuary or left to the lake?'

'The lake,' Layla said. The draw of water in the middle of a late summer's day was irresistible.

So was the smell of hot food from the carts as they walked through the crowds in the shade of the big old trees. Layla shook her head at someone trying to sell her a balloon and at someone else who wanted her to buy a walking guide to the park but she couldn't go past a cart selling Mexican food.

'Nachos,' she breathed. 'My favourite. Even better

than a hot dog.' She smiled winningly up at Alex. 'Do you mind waiting?'

He didn't seem to mind. In fact, the corners of his eyes crinkled as he smiled back. 'Go right ahead. I'll go and grab a burger from that cart we just passed. Meet you back here in five minutes.'

They kept walking after buying their food and drink because it wasn't far to the lake now. And then they sat and ate under the shady trees, watching people in row-boats and elegant swans floating past. A group of hungry ducks emerged from the water to watch them eat.

'No way,' Layla told them. 'You wouldn't like corn chips, anyway.'

She scooped another mouthful of savoury beans and cheese into her mouth and closed her eyes from the sheer pleasure of it all. Then she opened them and blinked. She was enjoying this?

The cloud of the conversation she and Alex had to have was still there but, again by some unspoken agreement, they were putting it off until they'd eaten. For the moment this felt remarkably like…well…a *date*.

Here she was, in a gorgeous setting on a stunning day, having a meal in the company of the most attractive man she'd ever known.

What had Chloe said? He was single. So was she.

There was something between them that was clearly strong enough to pull them together again with the force of an overstretched rubber band being released.

Was it even remotely possible that they could make a fresh start?

Would she *want* to?

Layla found herself watching Alex as he broke a piece off his hamburger bun and held it out. A brave duck was edging closer, gathering the courage to snatch the morsel from those long, surgeon's fingers. But Layla's gaze travelled up his arm to where his shirtsleeve was rolled up far enough to show the bulge of muscle in his upper arm.

The skin was dry now, of course, but Layla could still see it glistening with the drops of water from his shower last night. And she knew exactly what that bunch of muscle would feel like if she gripped it really tightly.

Oh…yes…

She would want to.

The duck who was brave enough to take bread from his fingers probably wasn't expecting his friends to turn on him the instant he succeeded. The cacophony of quacking and the violent flapping of so many wings broke the peaceful, summer picnic vibe that Alex had been enjoying more than he was prepared to acknowledge.

Late summer suited Layla. The sunlight made her blonde hair glow golden and she still managed to look smart in her light clothing. The skirt that swirled around her bare legs. The soft-looking shirt that had rolled-up sleeves fastened with a little tab and button and was unbuttoned down the front so it was like a jacket over a camisole top that clung to her curves and had an eye-catching bit of beadwork around that hint of cleavage.

Those bare legs were stuck out in front of her as she sat on the grass, licking melted cheese and salsa off her fingers with a totally unselfconscious enjoyment of her food. The skin on her calves looked tanned and smooth but Alex had been successfully resisting the urge to touch them because he knew that, however smooth the bits on show were, they couldn't compete with the skin hidden beneath the folds of that pretty skirt.

Yeah. It was just as well the duck fight broke the spell and reminded him of the intended purpose of this outing. It wasn't a date. Somehow they had to clear the air and sort out a way of being able to work together.

Alex sat up from where he'd been lounging on the grass propped up on one elbow. He took a deep breath and turned to look directly at Layla, wondering just how to start this conversation.

She caught his glance and he could see the way she caught her breath. She knew what was coming and she was nervous about it.

Why? Why was *he* so nervous, for that matter? They had a common goal here. They both wanted the same thing, didn't they? Maybe Layla simply wasn't ready to talk yet. Not about the big stuff, anyway.

'I saw Mike Jenner this morning,' she told him. 'Tommy's dad. He and Gina had brought Tommy in to get the pre-admission tests done. I didn't realise that Monday's the big day.'

Alex made a noncommittal sound. Why would she? Tommy Jenner was his patient, not Layla's.

Except that the little boy's case had captured the imagination of the entire staff at Angel's once the story had got round of how close a call it had been for his father to be accused of abuse. And of how serious Tommy's condition was. Any kid with a brain tumour was enough to tug at the heart strings but this one was definitely special.

'Mike's really stressed,' Layla continued. 'Which was why he was so keen to talk, I think. There's so much riding on this.'

Alex could feel an unpleasant kind of pressure himself. Of course there was a lot riding on this. A little boy's life.

'He wants to ask Gina to marry him,' Layla said quietly into the silence. 'But it's not the right time. If things go well, then he can see it being part of the celebration later. A new future for Tommy. A new family. It's lovely, isn't it? That Mike and Gina found each other in the midst of all that worry and that they both love Tommy so much?'

Still Alex couldn't say anything. He didn't need to be hearing this. Didn't want the feeling of emotional blackmail that could colour the huge decision he had to make on Monday about whether or not to go ahead with the complicated surgery.

'It's just as well they have each other.' Layla sounded as if she was talking to herself as the soft words continued to spill out. 'How awful would it be when you have to pin the hopes for your future on a decision that would mean your baby had to undergo such a risky operation?'

And then, as though the implications of her words were only now sinking in, Layla ducked her head and bit her lip.

'Sorry...' she muttered. 'I...get a bit carried away, don't I?'

'No kidding.' Alex spoke more sharply than he'd intended. 'Surely you're experienced enough by now to know how unwise it is to get too emotionally involved in a case?'

'It's never unwise to *care*,' Layla retorted.

A bubble of something hot and nasty was expanding in his gut. Anger that was encased in a skin of confusion.

He didn't get it.

Layla had always become too emotionally involved. He'd seen that when they'd first met over Jamie Kirkpatrick's case—the little boy whose condition was eerily similar to Tommy's. She was so passionate about her job. Cared so intensely about her patients and their families.

And yet she could dump someone she was in a relationship with without so much as a second thought. Without even looking back to see what kind of damage she'd done.

Without *caring*.

'I'll make my decisions based on my professional expertise,' Alex said coldly. 'I'll look at the results of the MRI on Monday and judge whether the chemo has made enough of a difference to improve the odds of attempting a surgery that has the very real risk of ending Tommy's life immediately.'

The bubble was getting bigger. It wouldn't take much to burst it.

'I do not need anybody telling me just how much the future happiness of his father depends on the outcome,' he continued. 'I will make a rational, *professional* choice about the actions I take.'

'Oh…?' Layla's hands were curled into fists and her voice was laced with derision. 'Like you did last night, do you mean?'

OK, that did it. This might not be the way into that conversation that he'd anticipated but he wasn't about to hold back now. Except that Layla got in another barb first.

'Do you make a habit of having unprotected sex?'

'No.' Alex spoke through gritted teeth. 'Do *you*?'

Layla gave an incredulous huff. 'The last person I had sex with, other than my *husband*,' she hissed, 'was *you*.'

Alex had only just started to form a coherent train of thought through the mist of red-hot anger. Now he was stunned into silence again. How long had Layla been divorced? There hadn't been anyone since?

Why not?

'So you don't need to worry that you've caught any-thing unpleasant,' Layla went on scathingly. 'And I'm not pregnant. If I hadn't been right at the end of my cycle I would have taken a morning-after pill today.'

The clinical delivery of the information was chill-ingly impersonal. Alex couldn't meet the glare he knew was coming in his direction. He stared straight ahead. The ducks, realising that any prospect of food was gone, were filing back into the lake. In search of a more con-genial atmosphere?

'You don't need to worry either,' he told Layla stiffly. 'The only relationship I've had in the last five years was way back when I first arrived in Brisbane. I've been tested and cleared of any transmittable diseases since then, thanks to having to work as a surgeon.'

He could actually feel Layla digesting that startling piece of information.

There was a long, long silence. He could feel her cu-riosity building. He might be wondering himself why Layla was still single but he wouldn't ask her straight out. Layla wouldn't shy away from something like that, though. She just wouldn't be able to help herself.

Sure enough, she asked, albeit a tad hesitantly.

'Why not?'

Alex shrugged. 'Too busy,' he said, with an attempt at lightness. 'You know how it is.'

'Yeah...' The agreement encompassed something a lot bigger than a busy career. She knew.

Alex shot her a glance. 'And maybe I'm too well aware of the damage that emotional involvement causes. Professional *and* personal.'

Another silence. And then Layla sighed and the sound was like an admission of defeat.

'I'm sorry,' she said quietly.

'What for?'

'The...way things ended. That whole mess. I didn't think for a moment that anything would go wrong with Jamie's operation and that made it all so much worse.'

'Not for you.' Alex didn't care what the bitter words might reveal. 'You just walked away without a backward glance. *I* was the one who got slapped with a malpractice suit. *I* was the one left wondering if my unprofessional involvement with a colleague had somehow undermined my ability to do my job well enough.'

'You think I didn't feel guilty?' Layla whispered. Her voice rose. 'I was *married*, for God's sake, Alex. My life was falling apart.'

Alex had to get to his feet. How dared she suggest that that black time had been just as bad for her as it had been for him? He jammed his hands in his pockets and took a few jerky steps towards the lake. Then he whirled back to face Layla.

'So why the hell did you get tangled up with me in the first place, then?'

She looked...anguished. Her voice came out sounding as though she might start crying.

Layla Woods crying? Unthinkable.

'Probably for the same reason that last night happened,' she said, jerking her head sideways as she stopped speaking, as though it was taking an enormous physical effort to break the eye contact with him.

So she hadn't wanted it to happen? Simply hadn't been able to resist, despite knowing that it was, somehow, so wrong? There was a world of unspoken pain hidden beneath those quiet words.

Alex had to exert the same kind of physical effort he'd seen Layla display. To stop himself moving forward. Reaching for Layla's hands to pull her to her feet. So that he could wrap his arms around her.

And hold her.

The silence around them was broken by the far-away sound of children laughing and the much closer sound of a rowboat near the shore of the lake, the oars dipping and splashing. The sound make Alex think of more than water.

Of wet skin.

The slide of bodies that couldn't get close enough fast enough.

Layla was getting to her feet but she didn't come any closer. She just stared at Alex.

'It happened,' she said steadily. 'The point is, what are we going to do about it?'

He swore softly, under his breath. She was right. There was a physical attraction between them that was irresistible.

So powerful it had the potential to destroy them both.

'I don't know,' he said, his voice catching. 'I really don't know.'

Layla held his gaze. 'Neither do I.'

This was a standoff of a very different kind from the

one Layla had been aware of when she'd stepped out
of the elevator on the eighth floor of Angel's a couple
of hours ago.

This one wasn't funny at all.

'Do we just walk away?' Alex suggested. 'Pretend
it never happened?'

He still hadn't broken that intense gaze that was
locked with her own. No. They both knew that wasn't
going to happen.

'There's another way we could deal with it,' Layla
heard herself saying cautiously.

A tiny flash of interest—hope, maybe—brightened
the dark gaze in front of her. 'Which is?'

'Um... There's some kind of a spark between us,
isn't there?'

A huff of breath from Alex. Something halfway between a snort of laughter and a groan.

'And being around each other is kind of like having
a pile of fuel available.'

Alex was silent but he was listening. Carefully.

'Sometimes...' Layla swallowed hard '...if you throw
the fuel onto the spark and make a fire, the fuel runs
out and the fire just...goes out by itself.'

She could see Alex processing the idea. His face
went very still.

What was he thinking? Did he feel the *shower* of
sparks Layla could feel dancing in the air between
them? And the certain knowledge that the tiniest bit
of fuel, in the form of a kiss maybe, would ignite those
sparks into the hottest flames imaginable. And that
those flames could be healing. They could burn away
the resentment and mistrust that lay between them after
the way they'd parted five years ago.

'Is that what you want to do?' His voice was the rawest sound Layla had ever heard.

She couldn't say a word.

All she could do was hold his gaze, knowing that he would see her answer in her face.

She saw his chest expand as he sucked in a huge breath. Saw the way he dampened his bottom lip with his tongue and the sparks got so bright her vision blurred.

'It could work,' he added, as they both began moving, the spell that had held them so still now broken. 'But fire's a dangerous thing to play around with. There's a risk that someone could get badly burned.'

Layla nodded, far more slowly this time. It would probably be her, she thought.

Did she really want to put herself in such a vulnerable position?

Yes…

The tiny voice was remarkably decisive.

Because there was just a chance, wasn't there?

A chance that the fuel wouldn't run out completely. That the huge flames would burn with a blinding brightness but then settle and leave a glow that might…just *might*…be enough.

And if she didn't take that chance, she might regret it for the rest of her life.

CHAPTER SIX

LAYLA ARRIVED AT work on Monday morning as nervous as a long-tailed cat in a room full of rocking chairs.

Yesterday had to have been the longest day in her life.

The longest night, anyway.

What had she expected? That Alex would give it some thought, decide that it was a good idea to see if they could deal with their lingering attraction by indulging it and then be unable to wait another night until they could put the plan into action?

Yeah…maybe she had and that was why she'd been waiting for her phone to ring or, at least for a text message signal to sound.

Why her heart had leapt into her throat when her ringtone broke the increasingly tense silence of her Sunday evening.

Talking to her mother was the same as always. Gully-washing October rain had set in. Her father was planning to run for yet another term as mayor. Her ex-husband, Luke, was going to be a father again and there was even a whisper about town that it might be twins this time. Fortunately, the topic of conversation Celia Woods was most concerned about was how she was going to provide the best treats in town for the children who would come knocking on Halloween.

'I don't know, Momma.' If she was honest, Layla didn't actually care. Halloween traditions were the last thing on her mind right now but this was preferable to being reminded of the life she could have had if she'd stayed with Luke. 'Why don't you do some of those meringue ghosts or the cat-shaped cookies you did one year? They look pretty special when you wrap them up in Cellophane and ribbons. Can't you get food dye that makes things black now?'

'I do believe you can. That's a real good idea, honey. I'm gonna go and fix my shopping list right now.'

The silence seemed even heavier after that phone call.

Nothing changed in Swallow Creek and suddenly that was making Layla feel even more on edge about what was happening in her life. The new life she had come here to start. One that had been so full of promise.

One that she had just lobbed a grenade into and now she was waiting to see if Alex was going to pull the pin.

Maybe it would be better if he didn't.

And how long was she going to have to wait to find out? Mondays were always hectic. Surgery lists would be jam-packed and weekends had the habit of accumulating issues that could wait until somebody senior enough was available to make decisions.

Layla was caught up in meetings, one of which was with the committee dedicated to raising the funds for a new MRI machine. The meeting had barely started, however, before she received an urgent summons to the emergency department.

And that was when her day started to go downhill.

Not that she realised it at the time, but it took another dive when she sent someone to page Alex with an
even more urgent summons than the one she'd received.

It should have been Ryan O'Doherty that Layla had
summoned because the deputy head of the neurology
department was on call for emergency cases today. Alex
had arrived with the intention of telling Layla that but
one look at the determined set of her mouth and he knew
he wasn't going to be permitted to delegate.

'I need the very best surgeon we've got,' she said.

Was this some kind of play to weld something personal into the professional? Had Layla done her own
thinking and second-guessed the decision Alex had
come to last night? Was this was a clever counter-of-
fensive to make him change his mind? Now certainly
wasn't the time to set her straight but he couldn't leave
it much longer.

Taking a closer look, Alex could see that the fierce
passion making those blue eyes glow so brightly was
purely professional. Layla had no head room for any
kind of personal agenda right now. This was all about
a six-year-old boy called Matthew.

Alex had perched one hip on the edge of the desk
in the office Layla had commandeered in the ER. 'Fill
me in.'

'I met Matthew four months ago. It was my first out-
patient clinic day during my orientation week. He was
in the waiting room with his mother, Dayna. She's a
single mum. Matthew's father was killed in an indus-
trial accident before she even knew she was pregnant.'

Alex was tempted to tell Layla to cut to the chase.
The medical details. But the words were spilling out

with wobbly edges and she was using her hands a lot while she talked. This was pure Layla. The story of any patient had to include a picture of the whole person. He needed to be patient and simply listen for a minute because she was going to tell him the story whether he liked it or not.

'He'd found a toy aeroplane in the basket. One of those double-winged ones, you know? Like Snoopy uses when he's being the Red Baron?'

Alex felt one side of his mouth curl upwards and his impatience faded as he listened to the lilt in Layla's voice that always got stronger when she was passionate about something. He watched the emotions that flitted across her face and was reminded of what an extraordinary woman she was. Unique. If he could somehow distance himself enough to become merely a good friend, her company would be a joy.

'There was a battle going on. The Red Baron was gaining height, ready to dive-bomb something. Possibly his mother's foot because she was busy reading a magazine and wasn't paying enough attention to the battle. Anyway…I came round the corner and there was a…a mid-air incident and the Red Baron crashed into my leg.'

Alex's lips twitched. He could imagine the scene.

'Fortunately there were no major injuries but poor Dayna was mortified when she found me sitting in with the consultant when she came in with Matthew for his appointment. I told her it was a real joy to see one of our cardiology patients looking so healthy. Matthew was in for a five-year check because he'd been a patient at Angel's when he was a baby to have a major vascular anomaly corrected.'

Alex finally frowned. 'This is a cardiology case? Why the hell have you called me down here? I'm in the middle of—'

Layla held up her hand, cutting him off.

'Dayna asked for me when she brought Matthew into Emergency this morning, maybe because she remembered the way we'd met. She'd found Mattie banging his head on the floor of the bathroom 'because it hurt so much'. He vomited twice and was found to have neck stiffness and photophobia on arrival.'

Alex's frown deepened. 'Sounds like meningitis.'

'Spinal tap was negative. We wondered about a head trauma after that so we got a CT scan done.'

'And?' Alex had closed his eyes for a moment. He did not need another case like Tommy Jenner. A brain lesion in a small child that Layla cared about a little too much. Then his eyes snapped open. This was worse, wasn't it?

'A major cardiac vascular anomaly as a baby? He's got a cerebral aneurysm, hasn't he?'

Layla nodded, her face now a picture of misery. 'Dayna's beside herself. She thought they'd got through the worst that life had to throw at both her and Mattie. He's started school now and he's such a happy kid. He…he told me he's going to be a fighter pilot when he grows up.'

Oh…*hell*…

'You'd better show me the CT.' Alex knew he sounded cool and distant but he'd been sucked in, hadn't he? Lulled by watching and listening to Layla and now he had more involvement on an emotional level than he was comfortable with before he'd even met the patient.

And there would be no luxury of time to consider a decision here, like he'd had with Tommy. The CT results were crystal clear. The damaged vessel in Matthew's brain was at risk of bursting at any moment and the results would be catastrophic. Severe brain injury. Or death. The surgery could be equally catastrophic but it was his only chance.

Could Ryan perform this surgery? Yes. Did Alex want to pass it on? He *could* use his position as head of department and say that Ryan needed the experience of this case.

Layla had remained silent while Alex studied the CT scan images. She stood back when he went to meet Dayna and Matthew. Small for his age, Matthew had a very pale face, big brown eyes and spiky black hair. He was in pain and terrified.

'Hey, buddy...' Alex could feel something squeeze hard in his chest when he smiled gently at the little boy. 'I hear you're going to be a fighter pilot when you grow up?'

Huge brown eyes were locked on his face. He heard the suppressed sob that came from Matthew's mother, who was sitting beside the bed, holding her son's hand. And he could feel Layla's watchful gaze from somewhere behind him. Could feel the *hope*.

'I've heard that there's a special airplane bed somewhere around here,' he told Matthew. 'What say I arrange for you to fly upstairs to come and have the operation to fix that nasty headache you've got?'

He had to brush close to Layla as he went ahead to set things up. He hadn't expected her to follow him. He didn't want to see the gratitude in her eyes when she touched his arm and forced him to stop just as he got to the internal double doors of the emergency room.

'Thanks,' she whispered.

'Don't thank me.' Alex knew he sounded curt but he couldn't let this go on. 'This isn't anything personal, Layla.' He held her gaze and had the odd sensation that he was trying to use his own to push her as far away as possible. 'I've thought about it,' he added, 'and the answer's no. We're colleagues now. And that's all we can be. Anything else is a recipe for disaster.'

He saw the shock of his words but he had to hand it to Layla. If she was disappointed she hid it completely.

'You're probably right,' was all she said. 'I'd better get back to Matthew. Maybe I can catch you later to follow up.' She turned away. 'On the surgery, I mean.'

Alex pushed the doors open with a little more force than necessary. *Probably* right? What did that mean? And had she really needed to underline that talking to him later would be purely professional?

Hell…maybe she wasn't disappointed at all.

Scrubbing in for Matthew's surgery a commendably short time later should have been the end of any personal undercurrents in Alex's thoughts. This was always a private time when he could centre himself and focus completely on what was going to happen when he had finished this intensive preparation.

Except it was taking a lot longer than usual to get to that focussed space. The suds being formed by the small soap-impregnated scrubbing brush foamed all over his hands but he wasn't ready to rinse them off.

He kept scrubbing. Under each fingernail. In the webbing between each finger. In a world of his own during this automatic preparation for surgery.

When you looked back on your life, he found himself musing, sometimes it's easy to see a particular day that marked a turning point in your life.

He'd had quite a few of them.

Like that dreadful day when he'd been only ten years old, and his beloved mother had died of breast cancer.

The day he'd finally walked out on his abusive stepfather, when he'd been sixteen, having made the heartbreaking decision that it would be better for Cade if he removed himself from the picture.

The day he'd first set eyes on Layla Woods and had realised that, against all the odds, he *was* still capable of trusting someone else.

Of loving them.

The flow of warm water was like balm after all that scrubbing. Alex rinsed the foam off his hands and then changed the angle of his arms so that he could rinse from his wrists to his elbows without letting the foam touch the well-cleaned skin of his hands. He picked up the sterile towel to dry himself, still lost in his thoughts.

In a few seconds he knew he would be able to turn them off as decisively as the tap he'd just been using and focus with the same intensity on the job ahead of him, but he also knew that, to get to that point of focus, he needed to let this train of thought reach its conclusion.

None of those earlier, turning-point days had been clearly marked in advance so that you got the chance to think about it and weigh up the potential benefits and downsides. Like he had been able to do ever since he'd parted company from Layla after their time in Central Park. Ever since he'd seen that willingness in Layla's eyes to start something between them again.

The history he had with both Callie and Cade would colour whatever advice they might give him. The history he had with Layla made it impossible to think rationally when he was close to her, let alone talk to her and hear that sweet Texan drawl that had been one of the first things that had attracted him to her.

By late Sunday night Alex had decided that getting back into any kind of a relationship with Layla would be a bad idea. He'd been quite confident that, with the calming distraction of a heavy day at work, that decision would seat itself so firmly he would be more than ready to talk to Layla later and find another way to deal with having to work together.

He was still confident that the decision was right. He just hadn't bargained on this turning out to be such a stressful day.

OK, he'd known that making a decision about Tommy Jenner would be a tough call and his heart had sunk as he'd watched the MRI images coming up on screen this morning. The call was too close to make one way or the other right now. A professional and emotional tightrope. The hardest thing had been to face Mike and Gina in his office and tell them he needed more time. That, despite their desperate pleas, he couldn't tell them his decision until he'd given it a lot more thought.

And it had been at the end of that interview that he'd received the summons to join Layla in the emergency department.

Well...he'd told her his decision now. And she'd accepted it.

The worst was over.

Now he could focus properly and move on. Do what he did best and go into Theatre to try and save a young life.

* * *

Layla slipped into the observation area above the operating theatre.

She saw the busy team preparing the theatre around the tiny, still form that was Matthew lying there under the bright lights. The television screen up here showed a close-up of Matthew's head. A large patch of his adorable, spiky hair had been shaved off and a nurse was painting the skin with iodine.

She saw the moment the star of the show arrived, hands held carefully crossed in front of his body, using his shoulder blade to bump open the swing doors that separated the theatre from the scrubbing-in area.

Alex…

He could do this. He could save Mattie. Layla's teeth sank into her bottom lip so hard it hurt. It didn't matter about the decision Alex had come to regarding what they did about the attraction they had for each other. All that mattered in this moment was the life of the child on the table.

Please…

As if he felt the force of her plea, Alex looked up as he took his position at the head of the operating table. Layla was by no means alone in the observation area but his gaze went unswervingly to where she was sitting.

Could he actually see her face behind the wall of glass when the lights down there were so much brighter?

Possibly not. But he was aware of her, that was for sure.

Layla's heart gave a painful thump. Maybe she shouldn't be here. Could her presence, reminding him of the tension between them, distract him in any way?

The way she'd always believed it had in Jamie Kirk-patrick's case?

She'd put pressure on him back then, ending their affair.

She'd put pressure on him again now, suggesting that they revisit that affair as a way of dealing with their un-finished business.

If anything bad happened to Matthew today, that would be the end. Alex would never want anything to do with her again.

Had she realised how much she was putting on the line by insisting that Alex get involved with this case? Had she even thought that he might take the opportu-nity to get what he wanted to say over with?

Of course she hadn't. She had followed her heart.

The disappointment of hearing his decision had been a body blow that she was still reeling from but Layla was fighting back. She *shouldn't* be this disappointed. She'd never expected to have Alex Rodriguez back in her professional environment, let alone her personal life.

Why couldn't she learn not to be so impulsive? To take the time to really weigh up the repercussions of making emotionally based decisions? She'd done this too many times in her life already.

Like when she'd fallen into Alex's arms in the first place, all those years ago.

When she'd ended things between them because she hadn't been able to stand the guilt and the way he had been making her feel.

When she'd practically thrown herself at Alex and suggested they kept seeing each other. Intimately.

The emotional overload was unbearable but, thankfully, it coalesced into only an imperceptible moment in time.

The subtle nod that came from Alex was probably just as imperceptible to anyone other than Layla. He seemed to be acknowledging her presence.

And reassuring her that it wouldn't distract him.

The whole team was poised as Alex turned his attention to the exposed patch of Matthew's head. He held out his hand.

'Scalpel.'

The critical point of this surgery came when the blood supply to the brain had to be compromised to allow a permanent repair to the damaged vessel, which was a major artery. There was only a small window of time— four minutes—before the blood flow had to be fully restored to avoid the certainty of brain damage. If the repair hadn't been done well enough by then, there would be no second chances.

'Start the clock.'

The order was delivered with crisp precision.

Alex was ready.

A small boy's life depended on what he was about to do. The child's desperate mother was sitting in a waiting room not far away. Layla was sitting in the observation area of this operating theatre.

Part of Alex's brain was aware of all these things and their implications but none of them could even begin to intrude on his intense focus on the job in hand. The intricate and challenging clipping of this defective blood vessel without allowing it to burst or cause any collateral damage through the technique.

The clock kept ticking.

'Two minutes,' the anaesthetist warned.

Beads of perspiration formed on Alex's forehead. A nurse patted them dry with a gauze swab. He had to blink and refocus his vision through the magnifying lenses of his eyewear.

The clip was so tiny. Slippery. So hard to slip into exactly the right position and keep it there long enough to secure it.

'Fifty-eight seconds,' the anaesthetist said quietly. 'Forty-five…thirty…'

It was there. In place. Alex squeezed it shut.

'Stop the clock.'

Another minute of complete silence as Alex inspected his handiwork in minute detail and finally he could give the verdict that created a collective release of breaths being held.

'Looking good. We can close up now.'

It was done and he knew it had been done well.

Only now could Alex allow himself a split second of satisfaction before focussing on the automatic protocols of closing. A moment to take a deeper breath and know that he had made a difference. Saved a life?

Quite possibly, although there was still plenty to be anxious about until he could measure the steps to recovery that Matthew would need to take.

Still, he could look forward to telling Dayna that the surgery had gone as well as they could have hoped for.

He could imagine what he would see in Layla's eyes when they next came face to face.

Gratitude, for sure. Far more than he'd seen when he'd agreed to take on this surgery in the first place.

Admiration as well?

The bone flap was back in place in Matthew's skull

a short time later and the probe to measure intracranial pressure was secured and tested. The final stitches and bandaging were the only tasks to be completed. Alex could relax.

And it was then that the realisation hit him.

He had been aware of the undercurrent of emotional pressure of this surgery, not only for his patient and the family but from Layla's investment in this case. From having her right there, watching his every move.

And it hadn't made any difference. He had put it aside and done exactly what he'd needed to do, to the very best of his ability.

Maybe he could handle more than he'd thought he was capable of when it came to Layla.

If he was aware of the danger of real emotional involvement, he could overcome it. Just like he'd just demonstrated when he'd been concentrating on Matthew's operation.

If he heeded Callie's warning, he could make sure he didn't start trusting Layla too much. So that when the end came, as it would, he would be prepared for it and it wouldn't destroy him because he would have been in control all along.

Maybe Layla had been right all along.

If they threw fuel on the smouldering ashes of what had once burned so brightly between them, it could burn itself out for once and for all.

It had worked with Callie Richards, hadn't it?

And if it could burn itself out, he wouldn't be left for the rest of his life wondering what if...?

No wonder last night's decision had been so hard won.

It had been the wrong choice.

But he'd already told Layla so it was too late to change his mind.

Or was it?

As the final stitch was cut, Alex dropped the curved needle and its holder onto the instrument trolley and looked up to where Layla had been sitting at the end of the row of seats. As soon as he saw her again, he might know the answer to that burning little question.

The seat was empty now. Layla wasn't there.

Layla had slipped out of the observation area with much the same stealth as she'd entered it, only this time she was having to swallow past a painful constriction in her throat.

She was just so darned *proud* of Alex.

Not that she could tell him that. She needed to clear her head and get back into a space where she could tell him how well he'd done on a strictly professional level without revealing such a personal response. He wouldn't want to see that. It would spell the end of being able to work together without the kind of tension that would inevitably become too poisonous to be tolerable.

Keeping herself busy, Layla waited a couple of hours before going to the PICU herself, where she found Matthew resting comfortably, still well sedated, and Dayna exhausted but with her eyes still bright with tears of relief.

'Dr Rodriguez is brilliant, isn't he?'

'He sure is.'

'He said we won't know if there's been any lasting damage until Mattie's properly awake again. That he might have some hurdles with his speech for a while, or a weakness on one side. But that he's young enough to recover completely from anything like that and that it was so lucky we found the problem in time.'

'I'm so happy we did.' Layla shared a hug with Dayna. 'I'll come by and see how you're both doing again tomorrow morning.' She stood back to cast a practised eye over the monitors surrounding Matthew's bed and Dayna followed the direction of her searching gaze.

'Dr Rodriguez said it's all looking real good. You just missed him. He said he had to go and check on another patient on the ward. That it seemed to be his day for special little boys who needed big operations.'

Layla caught her breath.

Tommy.

Alex must have gone to give his decision to Mike and Gina about whether or not he would operate. She knew how big a decision that would have been to make because she'd seen those MRI results.

The tumour had shrunk thanks to the chemotherapy but it was still a nasty one and it was in a very difficult spot. Uncannily like the one Jamie Kirkpatrick had had.

She could understand if that was enough to make Alex shy away from the challenge but would it have made any difference, having had the success with Matthew today?

Layla had to find out. This wasn't personal so she had no trouble justifying the need to see him. She didn't even give herself the time to question the wisdom of doing so.

She went straight from the PICU to the neurology ward. To Alex's office.

The door was very slightly ajar and she could see the screen on the wall with an image from an MRI being displayed. Tommy's MRI.

Did he still have Mike and Gina in the office? She couldn't hear the sound of any voices but could they be sitting in stunned silence trying to absorb some very bad news?

No. Alex would have closed his door before having a conversation like that.

Indecisiveness was not an option here. Layla tapped lightly on the door and went in, pushing the door shut quietly behind her.

Alex was alone in his office. Standing by the window, clearly lost in thought, tapping the end of the ballpoint pen he was holding against his bottom lip. Papers were strewn across his desk and some of them had rough-looking sketches. The kind you might make if you were talking someone through what was going to happen in a complex operation.

Alex turned slowly to watch Layla as she looked up from noting the sketches.

'You're going to do it?' she asked softly. 'Tommy's operation?'

The response was a curt nod. 'Everybody understands the risks.'

'But it's worth a shot?'

Another nod. More considered this time. Alex was holding her gaze and Layla could see something that had nothing to do with any patient in his eyes. She had to take in a slow, steadying breath. What she was seeing now was very, very different from the way he'd looked at her when he'd told her his decision.

He looked as if…as if he'd changed his mind.

'What about us, Alex?' The words came out as a whisper. 'Do you really think we're not worth a shot too?'

For a long, long moment Alex didn't move a muscle. Didn't make a sound.

He took a step towards her. The ballpoint pen clattered onto the surface of his desk.

And then he took Layla in his arms and she closed her eyes as her head tilted back under the pressure of his lips on hers.

It seemed like she had her answer.

CHAPTER SEVEN

SOMETHING WAS VERY different this time.

Giving in to the overwhelming attraction between them had always been illicit. Tinged with the knowledge that it was dangerous. That somebody was going to get hurt.

That it was *wrong*.

Even the other night, when Alex had been blindsided by Layla appearing in the decontamination shower, the encounter had been just as illicit. It was dangerous to have unprotected sex. Wrong to be doing it in their place of employment.

Quite simply, any occasion that had involved physical contact between Alex and Layla had been…wild.

Snatched moments of time when nothing had mattered other than slaking a white-hot lust.

But this time it was different.

They had all the time in the world and that made them both oddly apprehensive about taking that next step. So, when Layla suggested they had dinner at the tapas bar where she'd gone with Chloe a while back, Alex agreed without hesitation. It was a reprieve from more than making a decision about where and when they would next be naked together. It was also a way of keeping this to themselves. If they went out together to O'Malley's, the grapevine at Angel's would have been buzzing with the news within hours.

Because this felt so different it seemed right to keep it private. This was their business. The unfinished kind, and whatever they were planning to do to see it through to its conclusion was not something anyone else needed to know about.

Except…wasn't this supposed to be about throwing fuel onto the smouldering physical attraction that had never died between them? All they needed for that was a room with a bed. A hotel or motel, preferably, so that things didn't intrude too far into their personal lives.

Why were they here, in a vibrant but softly lit bar, about to share food and drink and conversation instead of some nice, uncomplicated sex?

Alex sighed audibly. He really had no idea. It had seemed such a good idea at the time. A way to put a hard day's work behind him and catch his breath before facing this new turning point in his life.

'So…' He raised his glass of beer in a mock salute as Layla looked up from the menu she'd been studying. 'Here we are.'

'Mmm.' Layla's gaze slid away from his and she lifted her glass of wine to take a sip. 'We've come quite a long way to get here, haven't we?'

She wasn't talking about negotiating rush-hour New York traffic to get to the meatpacking district on the banks of the Hudson River. And it was an accurate statement. They had both taken very different routes through life to get to this point.

Funny that it felt like a huge circle all of a sudden.

'Head of Paediatrics in one of the country's most

prestigious children's hospitals.' Alex tilted his head to show his respect for Layla's achievements. 'Well done, you.'

'Head of Paediatric Neurosurgery in the same hospital,' Laya responded. 'I think being sought after as the person most likely to save a child's life tops my ability to boss people around and keep things running smoothly.'

The sound Alex made was dismissive. 'I'm just doing my job. The best way I know how.'

'Dayna wouldn't say that. Neither would I. I…um…didn't get the chance to congratulate you earlier. That surgery today was amazing to watch.'

'Thanks.'

'You didn't mind having an audience?' There was an unspoken question in Layla's eyes. She wasn't talking about an audience in general. She was asking him whether it had bothered him to have *her* in the gallery. Whether it had brought back memories of the last surgery of his that she'd witnessed. The disaster that had been Jamie Kirkpatrick's case.

The very idea of talking about that was enough to send a chill down his spine. He'd factored in the way his past with Layla was so inextricably linked to Jamie's case but he hadn't bargained on having to talk about it.

How stupid was that? Jamie had been part of their story right from the get-go. The reason they had met in the first place. And Layla pulling the plug on that relationship the night before Jamie's surgery might not have been the end of things if that surgery had gone well. Alex might well have tried to find out what had gone wrong. Tried to fix things between them. But it hadn't gone well. His world had shattered and the shards had driven him and Layla as far apart as it was possible to get.

But here they were again.

A huge mistake?

Quite possibly. Alex could almost hear Callie's voice in his ear.

I told you so, mate. You should've listened.

At least he could try and avoid the subject. It was easy to pretend he hadn't picked up on the subtext of Layla's casual query.

'I'm used to having an audience,' he said lightly. 'Might close the gallery for Tommy's surgery, though.'

Layla toyed with her glass. 'Have you set a date?'

'Not before next week at the earliest. There's a lot of preparation needed.' Like there had been before Jamie's complex surgery. Alex ruthlessly squashed the comparison.

'Let me know if there's anything I can do to help.'

His nod was offhand as he opened his menu. Alex didn't intend involving Layla. 'Food looks good,' he said a moment later. 'What are you going to have?'

'Maybe *costillas*.' Layla looked up with a smile. 'The barbecued mini-ribs. Messy but so tasty. And some *pimentos rellenos*.'

Alex raised an eyebrow. Her accent was perfect. Odd from someone with blonde hair and blue eyes and the face of a prom queen. She hadn't aged at all in the last five years. She could still be someone's high-school sweetheart. The girl next door, if next door happened to be some vast Texan ranch.

'They're peppers stuffed with rice,' Layla told him. 'Do you like shrimp? Try the *gambas a la plancha*.'

But Alex wasn't thinking about food any more.

'You never used to speak Spanish.' The statement came out almost as an accusation. 'I've been meaning to ask you about that ever since you stepped in to interpret for Ramona.'

The night that had shown him the depth of the connection he still felt with Layla. The connection that had blazed into that astonishing encounter in the decontamination shower. Hell…even the hint of a memory of that night made Alex wonder afresh why they'd come here at all instead of locating the nearest available bed. He had to suck in a slightly ragged breath and focus on what Layla was saying.

'I got a job in Miami.' She sounded offhand. 'There was a huge immigrant Spanish community and I got frustrated at not being able to communicate properly.'

'So you did something about it.' The lopsided smile Alex could feel tugging at his lips was tinged with a mix of admiration and…sadness? This was pure Layla, as much as the way she hurled herself into an emotional involvement with small patients. Show her a challenge and she grabbed it with both hands.

Like the way she'd approached him when she'd been merely a baby doctor, working different rotations to see what she might want to specialise in. He'd already made a name for himself so it must have taken guts for her to approach him. To tell him about Jamie Kirkpatrick and the radical new neurological procedure she'd read about that could possibly cure the toddler.

What had pulled him in so decisively back then?

This cute woman who'd had the courage not only to suggest the procedure but intelligent enough to have done her homework and to be able to discuss it at a level well above what he would have expected from her years and experience?

Or had it been something far less conscious? The appeal of someone who could care so much about a patient? A person who had a heart as big as her home state?

The echoes of that first meeting were disturbing. Alex needed to get his head back to the present. Back to at least a semi-professional space.

'Why Miami?'

He was expecting the conversation to move into the medical merits of a large city hospital and the work-load and experience gained. But Layla looked at him in silence for a long moment and then dropped her gaze.

'It was as far away as I could get.'

'From L.A.?'

A brief nod. '*And* Texas.'

Had she gone alone, then? She certainly would have had the courage to do that. Suddenly it was important to Alex to know *when* she'd done it. How soon after their affair her marriage had ended. Whether he needed to shoulder some of the blame.

'How long did you spend in Miami?'

'A bit over five years. Until I came to Angel's.'

The same time frame that Alex had spent in his own self-imposed exile.

And the last person she'd slept with, other than him, had been her *husband*?

Oh…*hell*…

A waiter arrived with fresh drinks and a notepad to take their orders. Alex told Layla to order for both of them and then listened to her rattle off the Span-ish names of dishes. She had a conversation with the waiter in Spanish that made them both laugh but Alex couldn't raise as much as a smile. He drank his beer and waited until the waiter had gone and the noise of the bar closed around them again to create an oddly private atmosphere.

'Was it our affair that ended your marriage?'

Layla's eyes widened. Then she shook her head. 'It was already dead in the water, Alex. The affair would never have happened if that hadn't been the case.'

He nodded slowly. She wasn't just saying that to absolve him of any guilt. He knew enough about Layla to know how focussed her passion for anything was. If she'd felt that passionate about a man, nobody would have been able to distract her.

How lucky would a man be, to have that kind of passionate commitment from Layla?

'I did think about trying again to make it work,' Layla continued quietly. 'When I talked to my mother about it, she told me to "stop being so ridiculous". That marriage is for life and if it wasn't working then that was only because I wasn't working hard enough at it.'

Alex snorted. 'So your parents had the perfect marriage, then?'

It was Layla's turn to snort. 'That's the thing. My parents' marriage was like my whole life growing up. It only had to *look* perfect. That was all that mattered. Daddy was the mayor of Swallow Creek. Everybody knew he cheated on Momma repeatedly but nothing was ever said. It's like the whole town was in some kind of movie and they all knew the part they had to play to get to the happy ending.'

Alex was appalled. 'And you? What was your part?'

'Oh, I just had to be the perfect daughter. The town's

"golden girl". To do well at school and be the captain of the cheerleading team and the high school prom queen.'

'So you *were* a prom queen?'

'Yeah… Why'd you ask?'

'Never mind. Go on.'

'Well, I married my high-school sweetheart, of course. No prizes for guessing that Luke happened to have been the prom king.'

'Sure sounds like a movie script.' Alex's comment was light but something like anger was building. How could anyone have tried to put Layla into a box and keep her contained?

She was far too unique for that. Too…*special*.

She laughed at his comment but there was no amusement in the sound.

'Yeah…but I lost my lines somewhere along the way. I got ambitions past being a stay-at-home mum and parading the mayor's cute grandbabies at every community event. I got a bee in my bonnet about being a paediatrician instead.'

Alex was watching her face. She'd had to fight for that ambition?

'Luke wasn't happy about it but I wasn't going to let anyone stop me. I even dragged poor Luke to L.A. with me and he was like a fish out of water. I couldn't blame him for being so angry. He was miserable. *He* knew his lines and what's more, he was happy to be a part of that damned movie.'

'Where is he now?'

Layla smiled. 'Back in Swallow Creek, of course. Married to another girl from our school. Sally. They've got two cute kids already. Another one on the way. Maybe even twins this time.'

The first dishes of their meal arrived. The sticky ribs came with bowls of water that had lemon slices floating in them because the ribs had to eaten with fingers and they lived up to their name in stickiness.

They were delicious and, for some time, they both ate with enormous enjoyment. For Alex, there was more than the taste to savour. Watching the enthusiastic way that Layla could eat. The expression of bliss on her face. The way she sucked the sauce off her fingers before she dipped them in the lemon-scented water.

Man…it was getting hot in here.

The heat wasn't just being generated from physical attraction. There was a warmth coming from something much deeper. Something else that was very different this time.

It was as if Alex was meeting Layla for the first time. This wasn't the doctor he'd worked with. Neither was she the lover whose touch had driven anything else from his consciousness.

This was the real Layla. The woman who'd been a little girl growing up in Swallow Creek. Who'd had parents and a boyfriend and a husband. Who'd had a script laid out for her life and who'd chosen to rebel.

Who'd become a woman he'd fallen head over heels in love with once upon a time.

Who'd crushed him unmercifully at the worst possible time.

Alex's appetite deserted him but Layla didn't seem to notice. He shook his head when she offered him the last rib and she was happy to pick it up herself.

He waited until she finished it.

'Can I ask you a question?'

'Shoot.' Layla rinsed her fingers and dried them on her napkin. She reached for her wineglass.

'What was it that made you so sure we were over?' Alex hadn't planned the question. The pressure had built so fast he couldn't seem to prevent the words escaping from his mouth. From his heart. 'And why did you have to pick the night before Jamie's surgery?'

Oh…God…

Layla's hand shook so much she had to put the wineglass back on the table. Just when she really, really needed a rather large swallow of that wine, too.

She hadn't seen this coming. Not this fast, anyway.

The arrival of more food gave her a brief reprieve but it was obvious by the way they picked at the dishes after the waiter had gone that neither of them were hungry any longer.

Layla's head was a mess but she only had herself to blame for being put on the spot like this after being so open about her childhood. Telling Alex stuff she'd never told anyone.

It was because this felt so different.

She and Alex knew each other physically as intimately as any two people could know each other but they'd never really got acquainted on any other level, had they?

Five years ago Alex had known that her marriage had been in trouble. How could he not when he'd overheard that horrible row with Luke that night when she'd abandoned her husband yet again to work late on the preparation for Jamie Kirkpatrick's surgery?

All she'd known about Alex had been that he was a sinfully handsome and incredibly talented young neurosurgeon who had been well on his way to becoming a leader in his field. Nothing had prepared her for the sizzling chemistry between them and, with her emotions at breaking point in the wake of that row, she had done the unthinkable and made the first move on Alex.

She had started that affair.

She had ended it.

It must have been a new and unpleasant experience for Alex Rodriguez on both counts but Layla had been confident that he would be able to dismiss the effects in no time given his established reputation that would have scared any sensible woman off.

She hadn't been surprised by the information that he'd gone straight into the arms of another woman when he'd stepped off the plane in Australia. Par for the course. That the fling had been over quickly was also no surprise. But there had been nobody since then?

That was…disturbing.

Even more disturbing given the intensity in that dark gaze when he'd voiced a question that had clearly been haunting him.

What was it that made you so sure we were over?

Layla had been open with Alex tonight because this situation felt so different. As though they were meeting each other on a new level. Not a professional one, as they had when they'd embarked on Jamie's case together.

Not a physical one either, as they'd had from the moment Layla had put her arms around Alex's neck, stood on tiptoe and touched her lips to his that very first time.

Could she stop now? Be less than honest with him?

No. Of course she couldn't. Not when the compulsion to stop being dishonest had been the real reason her life had fallen apart back then.

Layla pushed her food aside. It took courage to look up and meet Alex's brooding gaze.

'I was living a lie, Alex. I always had been so I should have been good at it but I'd added a new layer of deception into my life. I was a married woman and I was having an affair. I felt guilty and I also felt kind of sick about it because I was doing what my father had done so often and I knew how wrong it was. How hurtful.'

Alex said nothing but he was listening to every word. He didn't take his eyes off Layla, even when she had to drop her own gaze and focus on the table. Grains of rice had spilled from the spicy peppers and she moved each one back towards the platter with the tip of her finger, aware of the heaviness of being watched so intently. The expectation that she had more to say. And she did.

'The first time we…we were together,' Layla continued quietly, 'I knew there was no going back in my life. I thought I had something to go forward towards but then I wasn't so sure.'

'Why not?' The words had a bewildered edge.

'You shut yourself away, Alex. The closer we got to the date of Jamie's surgery, the more closed off you got. The case was the only thing that mattered. I was…just a distraction that you needed to avoid. It got to the point that I couldn't even see the man I had fallen for so hard.'

A swift upward glance in the wake of that revelation showed her that Alex had closed his eyes. Retreated inwards again?

'So I was stuck in the middle,' Layla said sadly. 'I couldn't go back to what I'd had because you'd shown

me what there could be and…and I didn't think there
was anything to go forward towards any more.' Her
voice wobbled just a tiny bit. 'It was a really lonely
place to be. A really scary place.'

Layla had to close her own eyes for a heartbeat. To
gather another dose of courage to answer that second
question.

'The night before Jamie's surgery? I was there, in
the same room as you, but it felt like we were on different planets. I couldn't believe how thoroughly I'd managed to mess up my life and…I got angry. With myself.
With you. With everything in my life that had led me
to that moment.'

Layla sighed. 'When I get angry, I have to do something about it. So I snapped and did what my heart told
me I needed to do. I'm hot-headed, I know that. Impulsive. I know that, too. I let my heart rule my head too
often and I know it's not professional. You don't have
to tell me that I get too emotionally involved with patients. I know that as well.

'But it's part of who I am and…even if I didn't know
it at the time, I made the decision to stop being part of
that movie the moment I met you. I want to live my own
life and I want things to be true on the inside, not just
look like they're true from the outside.'

Oh…God…if she said anything else, she was going
to start crying. She pushed back her chair.

'Excuse me,' she muttered. 'I need to…to powder
my nose.'

She pushed her way through the crowd of people in
the bar, making for the ladies room.

'What's the hurry, sweetheart?' A young man
laughed. 'Let me buy you a drink.'

Layla didn't even see his face. Barely registered the invitation. There were only two people in this scene right now and she'd just laid herself completely bare in front of the other one.

This kind of nakedness made her feel far more vulnerable than any physical exposure could have done. What would Alex be thinking at the moment? Would he realise that she'd offered her heart on a plate back there? That, if he felt in any way inclined to exact revenge on the way she'd treated him, he now had the opportunity to carve her heart up into tiny pieces?

Layla needed a few minutes here. She was quite capable of gathering every ounce of courage she possessed and wrapping it around herself like a force-field. She'd already proved she was a survivor so she could survive whatever Alex had to say when she returned to their table.

She just needed a minute or two, that was all.

Alex watched Layla threading her way through the crowd. He saw some young jerk try to catch her attention and he knew that Layla hadn't even seen him.

He couldn't move a muscle. Couldn't even blink for the longest time. Talk about being walloped with an emotional sledgehammer.

If only he'd *known*.

Oh, he knew he'd pulled away from Layla. It hadn't been an easy thing to do but he'd done it because Jamie's surgery was going to make or break his career. Success had represented the future and the way he'd felt about Layla had had the potential to undermine everything he'd thought was rock solid in his life up until then.

That his career was all that mattered.

That emotional entanglements had to be avoided at all costs.

And maybe part of him had been aware that success had a new connotation. That the future had to be good enough for Layla to want to be a part of it. But had he told her why he was pulling away and erecting barriers?

No.

Why not?

Because that would have meant admitting how important she had been to him. That she'd had the potential to change his entire life if he could bring himself to trust her completely.

And he hadn't been able to.

He'd proved himself correct in withholding that trust because Layla had proved herself untrustworthy. She'd hurt him.

But he'd brought it on himself, hadn't he?

If only he'd known about what made her tick. About the way she'd been raised.

About that lonely place between turning points that had scared the hell out of her.

And most of all about the way she'd felt about him. What had she said? *The man she'd fallen so hard for?*

Alex could see Layla coming back towards the table now. Her chin was held high but the vulnerability in her body language was heart-breaking.

You could never turn the clock back. But Layla had been so honest with him. If nothing else, she deserved as much in return.

She sat down, eyed the leftover food and grimaced and then, slowly, raised her gaze to meet his.

Alex swallowed carefully. 'There was a bright spot, you know.'

Those bright blue eyes clouded with confusion. 'Sorry?'

'In the whole disaster that was Jamie's case and what happened after it...there *was* a bright spot.'

'Oh?'

'That's how Cade and I reconnected. He saw my mug shot in the papers, read about the malpractice suit and it was enough to make him ready to talk to me again for the first time in nearly a decade.'

He could see the stream of questions that Layla was dying to ask. It must have taken a real effort for her to remain silent.

'Any dysfunction in your family was hidden under a pretty exterior,' Alex said quietly. 'The problems with mine were there for everybody to see. There's probably a fat file buried somewhere with photographs of all the injuries I turned up to the emergency department with.'

'Oh, my God...' Layla breathed. 'From your *parents*?'

'Not my mother,' Alex said swiftly. 'No way. The only thing she ever did wrong was to marry an alcoholic bastard after my dad died. Cade's father.' He paused for a moment. 'No, maybe the worst thing she did was to get breast cancer and die.'

Layla's eyes had already widened with shock. Now they took on a brightness that suggested tears. Alex had to look away. He wasn't doing this to try and garner sympathy. He just wanted things to be equally honest between them.

'How old were you?'

'Ten. Cade was seven. He was safe enough, being Tony's son. I was the unwanted burden. A stepkid he'd never wanted in the first place. Anyway...' Alex wasn't going to dwell on those dark years of abuse. 'I upped and left when I was sixteen because I couldn't take it any more. Cade thought I'd abandoned him and he got pretty angry. By the time I tried to talk to him on his eighteenth birthday he didn't want anything more to do with me. I thought I'd lost my only living relative for ever but, thanks to the case, he made the first move.

'I'll always be grateful that he stood up to be counted when I needed it so much. He was about the only person who did. We've cleared up a lot of stuff since then and…well, I feel like I've got my brother back. So, that was a bright spot.'

Alex's smile was tight. There was no flicker of a response from Layla's lips.

'I'm sorry.' Her voice was choked. 'I felt so guilty… about everything. Luke, you…Jamie… I had no idea what to do about any of it and so I took the coward's way out and did nothing.'

'You didn't have anything to feel guilty about as far as Jamie was concerned. If I hadn't always had the ability to separate my personal stuff from my professional duties I would never have become a surgeon in the first place. What happened was a complication that none of us could have foreseen and, even if we had, we wouldn't have been able to do anything about it.'

'But it was me who persuaded you to try that new procedure in the first place. Because I'd fallen in love with Jamie and had got too involved and I was so determined to grab at any straw.'

'He would have died within weeks without the surgery. Technology has got a whole heap better now and I've perfected that technique since then as well. I'll probably use it for Tommy's operation.' Alex wanted to erase the frown lines creasing Layla's forehead. 'So, that's another bright spot, isn't it?'

Layla stared at him.

'What?'

'I can't believe you're trying to put a positive spin on any of this. You have every reason to hate me. I thought—'

'I don't hate you, Layla,' Alex cut in as she struggled to find words.

It was true. He didn't.

He couldn't have said exactly how he felt about her now other than an overwhelming physical attraction because the trust he'd been prepared to give her had been shattered and Alex had no idea whether it was even possible to repair something like that.

Maybe it was just as well he didn't need to say anything else just then. The waiter came back and eyed the plates of food on their table.

'You guys all done?'

'Yeah…' When Layla nodded to back him up, Alex pulled out his wallet and produced a credit card. 'We're all done here.'

Outside the bar, it was immediately apparent that the only completed business between them was the meal.

'Time to head home?' Alex asked.

Layla nodded.

'I don't live too far from here,' Alex heard himself saying. 'Come home with me?'

Layla hadn't expected that invitation. He could see the surprise in her eyes followed by a glow of…what? Pleasure? *Hope?*

He didn't want to try and analyse whatever it was because if he did, he might be tempted to run for cover.

What had happened to the idea of a hotel or motel and some nice, uncomplicated sex?

Alex had no idea. And when Layla's hand connected with his as they started walking, he laced his fingers through hers. When he felt the warmth of her hand and the responding pressure he was aware of a wash of relief that told him he was heading down the right track even if he had no idea of the destination.

Whatever was happening here had become about a lot more than simply sex.

Yes…things were very different.

CHAPTER EIGHT

ALEX'S APARTMENT IN the midtown suburb was tiny. No more than a single, ground-level room in an old brownstone terraced complex but it was cleverly designed, with a kitchen tucked into a back corner and a comfortable living space featuring a huge couch and a widescreen television taking up two-thirds of the entire floor area. Bare wooden steps led up to a sleeping loft and beneath that was a closed-off bathroom and an open office that was clearly well used. The desk around the computer, like the coffee table in the living area, was strewn with papers and reference books festooned with sticky notes.

There was only one window but it was huge and above the heavy rectangle of the sash windows was a semicircle of coloured glass that gave the whole window the appearance of an archway. The original character of the historic building could also be seen in the richly polished floorboards and the rough whitewash covering the old brickwork of the interior walls.

Layla fell in love on the spot. When she came out of the compact bathroom a few minutes after her arrival she stood for a moment, soaking it all in. Alex hadn't turned on any lights but he hadn't drawn the curtains either and the streetlight gave everything a soft golden glow. Through the window she could see the wide steps that led into the building and the intricate wrought-iron fence that shut them off from the rest of the world.

Them?

Layla looked over her shoulder, expecting to see Alex in the kitchen.

He wasn't there and she caught her breath and held it, aware of spinning sensation that had nothing to do with how much wine she'd had to drink at the tapas bar.

'Up here.'

He'd only spoken softly but the small space seemed to catch Alex's voice and bounce it so it felt like his mouth was right against her ear.

'Waiting for you,' he added.

Oh…my… Layla kicked off her shoes and moved to the wooden stairs. *Stairway to heaven*, she thought, and almost snorted with laughter. Except that this didn't feel at all funny.

It didn't feel anything like it usually did when she knew she was on the verge of having sex with Alex either. Where was the heat that fried her brain and made her aware of nothing more than his scent? His taste? His *touch*…?

She climbed slowly and when she got to the top there was nowhere to go other than the bed.

And the bed was filled with Alex.

There was more than enough light to see the sheen of the olive-brown skin of his bare chest, the copper discs of his nipples amongst the scattering of dark hair that arrowed down to the crumpled duvet covering his legs. There was even enough light to see the question in his dark eyes. A sudden doubt. Was he suddenly as unsure about this as she was?

'Layla?'

She couldn't say anything. Couldn't even hold Alex's gaze because the heat wasn't there to fry her brain and it felt, ridiculously, like it was the first time they were making love and Layla was aware of an extraordinary sensation.

For maybe the first time in her life Layla was overcome by crippling shyness and she had no idea what to do about it. She felt completely lost for a moment. For as long as it took to raise her eyes and meet that dark gaze again.

For a long, long moment they held eye contact. And then Alex was moving. He knelt on the bed and held out his hands and Layla took them. He pulled her gently and her legs buckled and then she was kneeling on the bed too. Still holding her hands, Alex leaned in and kissed her lips. A soft touch. A wordless question.

Did she want this?

Oh…*yes*…

Layla's lips parted beneath Alex's and he took the invitation to deepen the kiss. With the first, exquisitely slow stroke of his tongue Layla knew that the heat was still there. It was all around them. Inside them. But, instead of an overwhelming conflagration, this time it was under control. They could play with it. Luxuriate in it. Take all the time they wanted and revel in every moment.

Still locked in that first kiss, Alex loosened Layla's top and they broke the kiss so that she could lift her arms while he pulled it off. And then his head dipped and she felt his lips on the side of her neck and she tipped her head back with a sigh as his kisses trailed down. He pushed the straps of her bra over her shoulders as his mouth reached the top of her breasts and then he kissed her lips again as he unfastened her bra. A one-handed movement that advertised a skill he might not have practised for a while but which he certainly hadn't lost.

Still kneeling on the bed together, Layla pressed her bare breasts against his chest and felt Alex's hand slip beneath her waistband to cup her buttocks and draw her even closer.

Oh, yeah…the heat was there all right. Layla could feel herself slipping, deliciously slowly, into the mindless pleasure that only Alex had ever been able to give her. Her fingers skimmed over the hard planes of muscle on his back, over the soft skin on the sides of his neck and then they buried themselves in the soft silk of his hair.

Alex's hands mirrored hers. She could feel a trail of fire from each of the fingers on his hands as they covered her back, his palms dipping into the curve above her hipbones. Touching her ribs and then that sensitive skin beneath her breasts on their way up. His hands became completely lost in the tumble of her hair and Layla could actually feel the ends of her pale hair tangling with the dark hair on Alex's arms.

She'd never known that touch could be like this. That every cell in her body could be *this* connected. *This* sensitive. She breathed in the air that Alex was breathing out and it seemed to have more oxygen in it. She could taste the spice of Spanish food in his mouth. Or was that just the taste of Alex himself?

The kiss went on. And on. Until Layla felt herself

being gently lowered onto the bed and Alex began peeling the rest of her clothing from her body. The process seemed unbearably slow and she tried to help but Alex caught her hands.

'I want to do this,' he murmured, and she could hear the smile in his voice. 'It's like Christmas.'

Unwrapping a gift?

He saw her body as a *gift*?

Oh… Layla couldn't have moved to help him now. Her head sank back into the pillow and she closed her eyes as a wave of an emotion she couldn't identify swept her away.

She had known how good it was to be touched by Alex. To touch him. Her body had never forgotten the ecstasy of ultimate closeness. But it had always had an edge of something frantic to it. An insane race to capture satisfaction before they could be discovered. Before something, or someone, in the outside world intervened and ripped them apart. It had never been like this.

Layla had never imagined someone honouring her body like this. Worshipping her with the touch of his hands. The tips of his fingers. The silky glide of his tongue. She wanted to do the same for him. To explore his whole body. Slowly. To touch and taste every inch of his skin. To elicit sounds from him like the tiny whimper of need she heard coming from her own throat.

But not yet. She couldn't wait that long. Alex might still have control over that burning desire but she was rapidly losing hers. She was on familiar ground now. Wanting Alex so much that she felt she might die if it didn't happen. Now.

'Alex…please…' She writhed under the unbearably

gentle onslaught of his lips and tongue as they touched the core of her being. 'I need you. Inside me. *Now...*'

He responded with the swiftness of a whip cracking. A few seconds' delay as he wrenched open the bedside cabinet and then ripped into a foil package and then he was there. Between her legs. Looking down at her and touching her face with his gaze as intensely as the hard heat she could feel touching the entrance to the place she desperately wanted him to fill.

Layla was drowning in his eyes. She reached up to pull him closer and couldn't recognise her own voice as she cried out his name.

Layla woke first, a little before dawn, knowing that she'd had nowhere near enough sleep to face a day at work, but she didn't care. The need to go downstairs to the bathroom had woken her but she let herself drift into consciousness without moving a muscle.

She let herself become aware of everything she could feel. The heavy weight of Alex's leg draped over one of hers. The ridge of his arm beneath her head. The rise and fall of his chest against her cheek. The heavy grunt of his breathing that was almost a snore because he was still so deeply asleep.

Layla hadn't intended staying here all night. She must have fallen asleep first, because if Alex had she would remember it. She would have agonised over whether to wake him up to tell her she was going or just slip away and leave him a note or something.

Shifting her head carefully so as not to wake him, Layla moved so that she could see his face. His lips were parted slightly. Long, dark lashes nestled on his cheeks.

She had never seen Alex asleep before. He looked so peaceful.

So young.

Something huge squeezed in her chest as she remembered their conversation of the night before and put the pieces of the puzzle together. She knew now what Cade had meant when he'd said that Alex knew too much. That he was too quick to jump to conclusions about a small patient who might have been abused. She could understand why Alex had been so angry. So ready to deliver a brutal blow to Ramona's boyfriend.

It broke her heart to think of any child being abused. But to know that *Alex* had been injured so badly, physically and emotionally, went beyond heart-breaking.

Tears stung Layla's eyes. She wanted to wrap her arms around him and hold him to her heart. She couldn't fix the past but she could protect him now.

She could let him know that he hadn't deserved a childhood like that. That he should have been treasured and loved. She had to move more now. So that she could lift her hand and touch his face. Just with a single fingertip. A butterfly's kiss on his temple. To let him know that he was loveable. That he *was* loved.

By her.

Oh…God…

Those tangled, dark lashes flickered and Alex's eyes opened at the same instant that the realisation hit Layla that this wasn't only about physical attraction. And it never had been. Not for her.

So much for throwing fuel onto the ashes of a smouldering lust to let it burn itself out. What Layla was feeling now was burning so brightly that she knew it would never go out. She never had, and never could, love anybody other than Alex like this.

Maybe it was just as well it took as long as it did for Alex to surface completely. That he reached for her while he was still more than half-asleep and that their slow kiss reignited their earlier passion. He would never know how tenderly Layla had touched him. Or see the tears that had filled her eyes.

Talk about mind-blowing.

Alex had often wondered what it would have been like to have the luxury of spending a whole night with Layla.

Now he knew.

Had he really thought that a sleazy motel room would have been a good idea?

Or that the sex would have been satisfying but uncomplicated?

Layla was in the shower now. Alex had pulled jeans on but nothing else and he was making a pot of coffee while he waited for his turn to freshen up. He'd been invited to share the shower. Nobody could have missed the flash of disappointment—confusion, even—at his swift turning down of the offer.

God knew, he'd *wanted* to share that shower.

So why wasn't he in there? Soaping Layla's gorgeous body. Wrapping her in a towel and pulling her into a kiss as steamy as the bathroom, while they were both wet and slippery and smelling like the soap?

Because it would have been a step too far, that's why.

And last night hadn't been? Alex shook his head, emitting an incredulous huff as he spooned ground coffee into the jug.

It wasn't supposed to have been like that.

So...*tender*.

It had never been like that before so he hadn't expected it. Hadn't expected to feel like that. As though he wanted to make it up to Layla for having had to live a lie for most of her life.

To show her that *he* was real. That *this* was real.

And it wasn't, was it?

What was eating at his gut right now was the knowledge that they hadn't been having sex for half the night. They'd been making love.

And that was a kind of lie all on its own because if you made love like that you were making some kind of promise about the future, weren't you?

And he couldn't make that kind of promise to anyone. Especially not Layla. She'd proved she could turn her back and walk off if it suited her.

The kettle boiled and he poured the water over the coffee grounds. The smell hit him and he breathed in deeply as he fitted the plunger. Time to wake up, Rodriguez, he almost snarled inwardly. Don't even think of going there.

Trust nobody. Except yourself.

It was the only way to stay safe.

The rap on his door was unexpected. Alex crossed the room and opened it to find Cade, who held up a large paper bag.

'Breakfast, man.' Cade was grinning. 'I've got news.' He entered the apartment with the ease of someone who knew they were welcome. 'Mmm. You've got coffee ready. Perfect timing.'

They both knew that the clunking sound advertised the shower being turned off. Cade was over by

the kitchen bench now, depositing the bag. His head
turned swiftly. He took in the fact that Alex was only
wearing jeans and that the button was still unfastened.
Then he turned to stare at the bathroom door.

'Oops. Sorry. Am I interrupting something?'

Alex shrugged, turning to push the door closed. He
didn't see the bathroom door opening.

'Nothing important,' he said lightly. 'I got lucky last
night, that's all.'

The shock of seeing Alex's half-brother standing directly in front of Layla as she came out of the bathroom
was nothing compared to hearing the dismissive words
that had just been spoken.

'Hey, Layla…' Cade looked embarrassed. On her behalf, perhaps, after hearing that she'd just been a play-
mate for the night? 'I should…um…head off and get to
work or something.'

'Nah…stay and have some breakfast, now you're
here.' Was that relief in Alex's tone? An escape route
from the intimacy of sharing a meal after the night
they'd had? 'Layla doesn't mind, do you, Layla?'

'Not at all. I'll just throw some clothes on.'

'And I'll jump into the shower. I'll only be two minutes.'

Layla dressed as quickly as she could. She was planning on skipping breakfast. Alex had company and, besides, she needed to get home and changed so she didn't
turn up at Angel's wearing the same clothes she'd left
in yesterday.

But Alex was coming out of the bathroom as she
went back down the stairs. He had a towel knotted

around his hips and an apology written across his features.

What was he sorry for? That they'd been busted or because he'd dismissed what had happened between them last night as 'nothing important'?

He watched her pick up her handbag and stepped closer.

'Don't go,' he said softly. 'Please? At least have a coffee?'

This was confusing. Maybe the intention of last night had simply been to indulge the physical attraction they shared in the hope that it would burn itself out, but they both knew that it had been bigger than simply sex. That something had changed.

That they hadn't picked up where they'd left off years ago.

They'd made a fresh start.

And this time it actually held the potential of going somewhere.

If they let it. If they wanted it to.

Layla felt a wash of that emotion she'd experienced watching Alex sleep. She knew how damaged this beautiful man had to be, whether he was aware of it or not. Did she really expect him to trust her straight off? To trust that what had happened last night was real?

Maybe she could take the first step. She could let him know that she wasn't about to run away if things got tough. That, this time, she was quite prepared to do whatever it might take to be with him.

She smiled at him. 'Coffee would be great. And some of whatever's in that bag, if there's enough, because it smells divine and I'm hungry enough to eat a horse.'

'Is that what they do in Texas?' Cade welcomed her into the kitchen with a grin. 'Eat horse for breakfast?'

'Only if there aren't any griddle cakes and black-eyed peas.' Layla eyed the bag he was ripping open. 'Bagels. Yum.'

'Help yourself.' Cade watched as Layla swiped a smear of cream cheese from the bag and licked it off her finger. 'You and Alex, huh? And there I was, tell-ing people that those rumours were rubbish.'

Alex had dressed himself with impressive speed. He was buttoning his shirt as he joined them but he paused to drape his arm over Layla's shoulder.

'Layla and I go way back,' he told Cade. 'Pre-Bris-bane days.'

'Ahh...' Cade looked as though he was retrieving some more of those rumours. The ones about Layla being married at the time, perhaps. Or maybe he was putting two and two together about the unpleasant legal repercussions of Jamie's disastrous surgery and com-ing up with a reason for them splitting up that nobody would want to talk about. He gave his head a tiny shake and cleared his throat.

'Speaking of Brisbane,' he said to Alex, 'I was busy myself last night. Having a long conversation with your friend Callie.'

Layla was trying not to watch as Alex tucked his shirt into his pants and did up his fly and belt buckle. There was something about the inflection on the word 'friend' that sent a shaft of something nasty through her belly. Was Callie the one that Alex had had the fling with when he'd arrived on that side of the world?

Jealousy. That's what that nasty sensation was. Layla

had no right to feel this possessive. Good grief...what was happening to her here?

'She's talked me into taking the job,' Cade continued. 'I'm heading off as soon as I can work out my notice. Couple of weeks, tops.'

'Wow...you don't muck around.' Leaving his top buttons undone and his tie hanging loose, Alex filled a mug with coffee and took a big swallow. 'You sure you want to do this?'

'I'm not a kid any more, Alex. I get to make my own choices and learn from them if they turn out to be mistakes.' His gaze flicked to Layla and then back to his brother.

Layla caught her breath. Was Cade actually saying that he thought Alex having anything to do with her was a big mistake?

No. The sudden tension between the brothers suggested that some button had been pushed that had nothing to do with her. There were probably all sorts of triggers buried in their shared, stormy backgrounds. A background that Layla needed to take into consideration for all sorts of things. Like being patient with Alex if it took him a long time to trust her. And understanding his passionate reaction to cases of child abuse. Accepting his need for his own space at times to focus completely on the career that had been his way forward from a horrible start to his adult life.

The comment led to an awkward silence that Layla felt compelled to break.

'I should get going,' she said. 'I've got a big meeting at nine a.m. We're trying to find sponsors to help with the fundraising to update our MRI machine and it's a biggie. We were supposed to do it yesterday but the meeting got derailed when I had to see someone in Emergency.'

'I thought that was already sorted,' Cade said.

'What?'

'The social committee put out a flyer last week. They're hoping everyone will attend the big Halloween party they've got planned. That's down as a fundraiser for the MRI.'

'Oh...I hadn't caught up with that.' Layla smiled at Cade. 'Thanks for the heads-up. It might help to encourage the sponsors. Any money from a hospital fundraiser will be great but we'll still need more. New technology doesn't come cheap.'

'It should raise heaps. Tickets are a hundred dollars and everyone's being asked to bring as many people as they can. It'll be Angel's staff and all the friends and relatives they can bring with them. The venue could hold a thousand people apparently.'

Layla blinked. That was some fundraiser. Why hadn't she heard about it already?

'You'll have to come,' Cade continued. He sent a crooked smile in Alex's direction and it looked like it was intended to be an olive branch. 'I'm heading out to a costume-hire place with a few others after work today. Want me to pick something out for you?'

'I don't do dress-ups.' The words were curt. And he was looking at Layla rather than Cade.

I'm not going to pretend to be someone I'm not, the silent message said.

Was he trying to tell her that he was real? That this—whatever was happening between them—was also real? On the inside as well as the outside?

'Neither do I,' Layla said, still holding Alex's gaze.

Then she looked at Cade and smiled. 'I'll be happy to buy a ticket, though.'

Cade shrugged. 'Well, if it turns out to be my farewell gig from Angel's, you'll have to come, costume or not.' His glance slid from Alex to Layla and back again and a corner of his mouth lifted. '*Both* of you.'

Was he giving his blessing to the idea of them as a couple now? Encouraging Alex?

This was doing her head in. It didn't matter where she stood with Cade but how Alex felt right now was very, very important. Did he still see this reunion as a means of putting out an old flame so that they could both move on and be able to work together without it creating any personal tension?

Had it really been her suggestion?

Yes. But she'd known, deep down, that there was more than just a flicker of hope that it could be more than that.

What had she done? She'd learned so much more about Alex, that's what. She'd stirred the ashes and discovered that she'd been in love with him right from the get-go and she'd only fallen deeper last night.

Had she set herself up for a devastating blow?

The thought was terrifying but there was nothing she could do about it. As far as she was concerned, the step they had taken now was irrevocable. It was Alex's call how it was going to play out because there was no way she could pull the plug on this.

Vulnerability was dangerous. It made you weak. Layla had learned very early in life that if you felt threatened you had to make yourself stronger. Take charge. Fake it till you made it and all that.

She lifted her chin. 'I really do have to go. Got a hospital to run. I'll see you boys later.'

At least with Cade there, the awkwardness of what to say or do in farewell was gone. There would be no lingering kiss. No promises of when they could be together again.

It was a good thing, Layla told herself firmly as she flagged down a taxi outside Alex's apartment.

A promise was only words and a promise could be broken.

Like hearts could?

CHAPTER NINE

IT WAS AMAZING how quickly you could get used to a new routine. How quickly you could become lulled into a false sense of security. Within days, almost, Alex and Layla both stopped worrying about the rumours that might be circulating through Angel's. Now they didn't even bother to try hiding the fact that they were arriving for work together.

Tyler Donaldson wasn't about to let a chance slide by when he saw them standing near the huge fish tank in Angel's lobby one morning.

'You guys look as happy as pigs in muck,' he announced. His grin widened. 'Life's good, huh?'

'Hey, Ty.' Layla seemed happy to greet her old friend but Alex had spotted another early arrival at the hospital.

'Jack! Hey...haven't seen you for ages.'

'Alex...'

The handshake between the two men instantly morphed into a typically male, one-armed hug that involved a bit of back thumping.

Jack Carter held his hand out to Tyler. 'I haven't had a chance to congratulate you on fatherhood. How's it going?'

'I'm lovin' every minute of it.' Tyler shook Jack's hand but raised an eyebrow at the same time. 'And didn't I hear a rumour that you're gonna join the sleepless nights and nappy brigade? How's Nina doing?'

'Glowing,' Jack said proudly. 'Nearly five months along now.'

'She certainly is glowing,' Layla put in. 'I only caught up on that news myself last week. You must be thrilled, Jack.'

'Oh…for sure.'

'She told me that you'd adopted Janey and Blake, too.'

Jack shook his head. 'I know. Single man one minute, father of three the next. Life's full of amazing surprises, isn't it?'

'Mmm…' Alex caught just the flicker of a glance in his direction. 'I wouldn't disagree with that.'

He made no attempt to join in the conversation, however, because he had the uncomfortable sensation that he had been left alone in a parallel universe here. He wasn't disinterested because Jack Carter was his oldest friend. They'd been through medical school together. It had been Jack who'd set up this job for him at Angel's. They hadn't seen so much of each other since Jack had left to take up a full-time position at the pro bono centre in Harlem. He'd been Jack's best man at the wedding, of course, but that had been a long time ago now. Jack still did the odd consult here at Angel's and Nina was still a social worker but their paths didn't cross often enough. Perhaps that was why he hadn't noticed Nina's shape changing. Not that he wasn't happy for Jack because Jack looked on top of the world.

He just couldn't imagine it for himself. In the wake

of his childhood—and Cade's—the responsibility of bringing a child into the world was not something he would touch with the proverbial bargepole.

Layla seemed to be more than happy to be discussing the expected arrival date and how Nina's younger siblings were feeling about the addition to the new family. There was something about the animation in her face that rang a warning bell for Alex.

Layla would want children.

The conviction came from nowhere and it felt curiously...disturbing. She may not have wanted to settle down and produce grandbabies for the mayor of Swallow Creek to show off but...hell...she *loved* kids. Given the way she got so involved with her small patients, Alex could imagine how fiercely she would love her own children. And she'd be an amazing mother.

Why was the thought so disturbing?

Because it would have to be another man who would be the father of those children?

He should be fine with that. This new...fling with Layla was not going to be permanent. They were just burning off a lingering physical attraction and he had absolutely no desire for it to become anything more than that.

It *couldn't* because that would mean trusting Layla to the same extent he had mistakenly trusted her the first time round. And she'd betrayed that trust and left him to fall into such a dark place that he was determined he would never go anywhere near there again.

What the hell had he been thinking, playing with fire like this again?

Totally unintended factors were sneaking into the

equation. Like the need to be with Layla as often as possible.

Like a flash of downright envy for the man who would be the father of her children.

Alex tuned back into the conversation between in time to hear Tyler excusing himself. Jack made an apologetic face as the big Texan doctor walked off with a wave.

'Sorry about that. Kids aren't really your thing, are they, Alex?'

Alex snorted, ignoring the odd glance that came his way from Layla. 'No. That's why I became a paediatric neurosurgeon. Speaking of which, I'm due at a ward round upstairs right about now. Maybe we can grab a beer at O'Malley's later?'

'Sounds good. But you don't get rid of me that easily. I'm heading upstairs myself.'

'Me too.' Layla stayed with them. 'How's it going at the centre, Jack?'

'It's great. I feel like I'm making a real difference.'

'I wouldn't mind getting involved myself. Would you have any use for a doctor who can speak Spanish?'

'Are you kidding? We'd snap up any free time you had.' Jack shot Alex a sideways glance. 'From what I hear, though, free time might be a bit thin on the ground.'

The reference to time prompted Layla to check her watch. 'Oh, help…I'm going to be late for that meeting.' She waved and someone moved to stop the elevator doors closing.

The elevator looked pretty full. 'I'm going to take the stairs,' Alex said. 'I'll catch you both later.'

'I'll join you.' Jack hung back as Layla raced off. 'I could do with the exercise.'

'You here on a consult?' Alex asked as they entered the stairwell.

'Not exactly. Nina's hoping to get a bit of free time so we can go visiting. She tells me that Tommy Jenner is on the ward.'

'Yep.' Alex didn't slow his stride as they climbed the first flights of stairs.

'And you're going ahead with the surgery?'

'Yep. Scheduled for Friday. We had to put it off because he picked up a bit of a bug last week.'

'I hope it goes well,' Jack said quietly. 'Nina's going to be holding her breath.'

'I might be, too.' Alex could feel his breathing now after three flights of stairs. He paused to take a quick glance through the window. You could see the end of the ambulance bay from here. And the line of rubbish skips. The basketball court was deserted. Maybe he could find Cade later and he could get a workout in. And maybe that would dispel this odd edginess that was building in the wake of those disturbing thoughts he'd just had about Layla's future family. No. Now that he thought about it, that edginess had had been building ever since that night with Layla.

That *first* night with Layla. They'd clocked up a few more since then.

And whatever it was between them didn't seem to be burning itself out. If anything, those flames were burning higher. Brighter. He'd issued the warning himself, hadn't he? If you played with fire, things could get out of hand. Somebody could get badly hurt.

Had he been so confident of his ability to stay detached that he'd assumed the person who got hurt wouldn't be him?

'It was your first day at Angel's, wasn't it?' Jack was looking out the window beside him. 'When you got caught up in Tommy's case?'

'Yeah… It was a memorable elevator ride with Nina in there, trying to calm Mike down when he was furious with people trying to take Tommy away for treatment.'

'Hardly surprising when you look back on it all. There he was, struggling to be a single dad to a kid who'd been so traumatised by being left in a house with his dead mother for days and everybody assumed he was abusing Tommy. It's no wonder he went off the edge but it did make it harder to see what was really going on.'

'Not for Nina.'

'No… But she's a woman in her own class of amazing.' Jack's smile held a tenderness that made Alex feel left out again. 'She loves Tommy to bits. She's taught me a thing or two about taking notice of more than the clinical picture we get from patients.'

'Hmm.' Alex watched an ambulance turning into the bay. Layla did that. Was it a female thing?

Or maybe Layla was in her own class of amazing, too.

'She's really excited about the prospect of him getting a new mother soon. Is it true that Mike got involved with one of the oncology nurses?'

'Yeah…Gina. She's lovely. He's planning to propose if the surgery goes well.'

Jack sucked in a breath. 'No pressure, then…?'

Alex grunted and turned away from the window.

He was more than ready to tackle a few more flights of stairs. Jack was half a step behind him.

'So…how's it working out?'

'With Tommy? We'll have to wait and see.'

'No…I meant at Angel's. That first day was a while back now and I haven't been around for months. You happy here?'

'Yep.' Until Layla had arrived anyway. And now that they'd found a way to deal with the tension, Alex had to admit he was feeling happier than he had in a long time.

Years. More than five years, to be exact.

They climbed the rest of the way in silence but paused again after Alex had pushed open the fire-stop doors on the eighth floor.

'I heard about the Kirkpatrick case hitting the grapevine,' Jack said. 'How on earth did that happen? I was quite confident that it was going to be buried.'

'Cade didn't realise it was being kept quiet.'

'Oh…' Jack's glance conveyed his understanding of the turbulent relationship the brothers had had. 'Problem?'

'Could have been,' Alex admitted. 'In the end it turned out to be a good thing. Gave us the chance to resolve a few issues that needed airing. Our relationship is better than it's ever been now.'

Jack's nod was pleased. 'That's great.'

'Yes and no.'

'Why no?'

'He's planning to take off. Follow my footsteps and go for a new job in Australia. In my old hospital, no less.' Alex rubbed his forehead. 'I've only got myself to blame. I told him that an old friend there was on the hunt for a prenatal surgeon.'

They could have left the conversation there and gone their separate ways. Jack was here to visit Tommy and Alex was going to be late to start his ward round but that edginess was suddenly boiling to the surface. Alex stayed where he was, with the safety of the wall right behind him.

'Do you ever get the feeling that life goes in circles, Jack?'

If Jack was disconcerted by the subtext, he didn't show it. Like the good friend he was, he simply moved a bit closer, giving the impression that he had all the time in the world to talk. Two men having a bit of a yarn. Or two doctors having a quiet word about a patient.

'Circles?' he prompted gently.

'Yeah. I had Cade in my life and then out of it for too many years. Back in it again when he saw the publicity about the Kirkpatrick case and then out of it when I took off to Australia. Now he's back but he's planning to take off himself.'

'You won't lose touch. Email's great. Phone calls by computer even better. There's nothing to stop you taking a holiday either. I'll bet you miss all the sun and those fabulous beaches.'

But Alex wasn't finished. 'It's the same with my job. Has it occurred to you that Tommy's case is horribly similar to Jamie Kirkpatrick's? That I'm back where I was all those years ago, about to tackle a surgery that could go belly up and wreck more than one life?'

'It's a tough call.' Jack's face was creased with sympathy. 'But you can't think about it like that. Be proud that you are one of the few people that can offer any hope at all in a case like this. Mike's not going to sue you if it doesn't go well. From what Nina's told me, he's well aware of the risks. He's incredibly grateful that you're even prepared to try.'

Alex shook his head. 'I'm not sure I should be. I'm not sure I could live with myself if it doesn't go well.'

'If you don't try, he'll die,' Jack said bluntly. 'Could you live with that?'

Alex sighed. He started to rub his forehead again but, instead, ran stiff fingers through his hair. 'It's not just those circles,' he admitted quietly. 'There's also…'

No. He couldn't say her name. Talking about it might mean he'd hear something he really didn't want to hear. He might have to admit what was really going on deep in his own heart.

He didn't have to say her name. Jack's gaze held a sympathetic understanding.

'Layla?'

That heat at the sound of her name was anger. Something very private was being exposed. Something Alex had been avoiding looking at too closely himself until this morning. 'How the hell did you find out about that?'

Jack's smile was conciliatory. 'You forget that I'm still involved with Angel's. That Nina still works here. We…ah…hear things.'

'Like what?' Oh, God…had the grapevine somehow got information about what had happened in the decontamination shower that night?

'Just that there's a certain vibe whenever you two are in the same room. A rumour that someone saw a stolen kiss somewhere. I wasn't sure I believed it until I saw you two together this morning. You may as well have a neon sign above your heads.'

'Oh…' Alex couldn't deny that vibe. It felt like the very air came alive with sparks whenever he was within sight of Layla. Hardly surprising that other people could feel the heat. Had he really been bothered a few weeks back that Layla was stalking him and that their paths seem to cross far too often? It couldn't be often enough now. He really was in trouble here, wasn't he?

'There you are…' The voice came from the nearby elevator as the doors slid open. 'I've been looking for you, Jack.' Nina came towards them, smiling.

Alex found himself staring at the elevator as the doors slid shut again. Stupid to be disappointed that Layla wasn't amongst the people left. Her elevator would have delivered her to the top floor long ago. About when he'd been staring out the window, thinking about shooting hoops.

'Hi, babe.' If Jack had looked happy discussing his impending fatherhood, it was nothing compared to the joy on his face now. 'How's it going?'

'Wonderful. I've got our tickets for the Halloween ball.' Nina laughed. 'The suggestion was made that I could go as a pumpkin and all I would need is an orange dress.' She patted her belly. 'What do you think, Alex?'

'I think you could go as something far more glamorous than a pumpkin.'

Nina was still grinning. 'A witch, maybe?' She pointed at Jack. 'Don't you dare say a word.'

Jack managed to look totally innocent and highly amused at the same time. He cleared his throat. 'You going to the ball, Alex?'

'Nah…though it looks like it's going to be Cade's farewell and he's got some idea of us going in matching costumes.'

'The Brothers Grimm?' Nina had clearly caught

the excitement that seemed to be taking over Angel's. 'Tweedledee and Tweedledum?'

Jack shook his head. 'Come on. Time to take you away. Let's go and see if Tommy's up for a visit.'

'I'll catch you later.' Alex could see Ryan O'Doherty coming through the ward doors. Looking for his senior colleague, no doubt, in order to get the ward round under way.

'We'll grab that beer.' Jack raised an eyebrow and his smile was encouraging. 'And you know what?'

'What?'

'Circles can be good. Sometimes they can take you back to a place you didn't know you wanted to be.'

Tommy Jenner was getting a lot of visitors today.

Mike was there, of course. He had taken time off work to be with his son for the duration of this hospital admission. Gina was rostered on as Tommy's nurse whenever she was on shift in the ward but she had other patients to attend to as well. Jack and Nina had been in this morning and Tommy's surgeons, Alex and Ryan, were checking up on their young patient at frequent intervals. As chief paediatrician, it was only to be expected that Layla was taking a special interest in this case as well.

The irony that the medical problem Tommy was facing was so similar to the one Jamie Kirkpatrick had faced and that this surgery was happening when she and Alex were in the fragile new stages of another relationship was lying more heavily in the back of Layla's mind every day, but it still seemed like a bonus to find Alex in Tommy's room when she made her own visit in the afternoon.

It was always a bonus when their paths crossed during working hours these days. Layla could see him in the room before she tapped lightly on the door and pushed it open so she hesitated for a heartbeat, just to enjoy the moment.

It was kind of like when you were a kid and you'd been given the most amazing Christmas or birthday gift, she decided. It wasn't that you necessarily wanted to play with it all the time but it was very important to keep it somewhere where you could see it as often as possible.

So you knew it was real.

The reality of this new connection with Alex could be found in the most fleeting glance or the hint of a smile. During a professional conversation that had a subtext only the two of them were aware of. It was delicious.

Addictive.

So much so that Layla knew the instant it changed and that happened the second she walked into Tommy's room. Alex raised his gaze from the notes he was reading to nod and smile an acknowledgment of her presence and the smile was the same as always, but Layla still knew.

It was the abrupt way the eye contact had ended. A split second in time, maybe, but it was enough to let Layla know it was happening again.

Alex was pulling away.

'Hey, Tommy.' Layla smiled at both Tommy and his dad. 'How're y'all doing?'

'Me an' Dad are having haircuts tomorrow. We're getting it *all* shaved off.'

'Wow.' Layla hitched a hip on the end of the bed.

Close to where Alex was standing, flipping pages on the chart, but he didn't look up. Was it her imagination or did he shift just a little further away? 'Both of you, huh?'

'Yeah...' Mike ran a hand through his own hair and then ruffled his son's. 'We're going to have a race to see who can grow hair the fastest after Tommy has his operation.'

Layla was quite confident she was the only person here who was aware of the tension emanating from Alex. Or that it had just increased a notch. Tommy would have to survive his surgery if his hair was going to grow back.

'I asked Gina if she wanted to shave her hair off too,' Tommy told her. 'But she said she didn't *really* want to.'

Layla laughed. 'I'm not surprised. It's a bit different for girls.'

'Why?'

'I guess we're not as brave as boys. And we like our hair too much.'

'Dad said he likes Gina's hair just the way it is. She's got pretty hair, so I guess it's OK if she doesn't do the race.'

Alex was scribbling something onto the chart and even his writing sounded tense. Layla could hear the scratching and tapping against the clipboard holding the papers. She wished she'd never told Alex about Mike's plan to ask Gina to marry him if the surgery went well.

Of course he was pulling away. The pressure was building and he needed to focus. It wouldn't be like the last time this had happened because this time she understood. She could give him space if that's what he needed. She was older and wiser now and she wasn't going to have a hissy fit because she felt she wasn't getting enough attention.

She was starting to feel a bit tense about it all herself, in fact. It was kind of unfair that life was throwing a testing time like this at them so fast. They needed more time to build trust. They were making a fresh start and it had a promise that was precious.

She had way too much to lose if things went wrong.

Could Alex feel the reassurance she was trying to project? If he did, he didn't acknowledge it. When he finally looked up from the chart, he looked straight at Tommy.

'There's another doctor who's going to come and visit you tomorrow, buddy. Dr Jill. She's an anaesthetist. Do you know what that is?'

'No. What?'

'She's the one who's in charge of helping you go to sleep so you can have your operation. It's called having an anaesthetic.'

Tommy's bottom lip wobbled. 'But I'll wake up again, won't I?'

'You won't even know you've been asleep,' Alex promised. 'You'll close your eyes and then it'll feel like you just open them again straight away but it'll all be over.'

'Will my head hurt?'

'We'll give you medicine to stop it hurting.'

'Will I have a big bandage?'

'You sure will. And you'll be in a special place called Intensive Care for a few days.'

Layla could see the way Mike's throat moved as he swallowed hard.

'I'll be there, too,' he told Tommy, leaning down

to give him a kiss. 'I'll be right beside you when you wake up.'

The tiny break in Mike's voice almost undid Layla and she could see a tiny muscle jumping in Alex's jaw. She forced herself to sound bright.

'You know what's going to happen next week?' she asked Tommy. 'What you've got to look forward to when you come back to the ward?'

'No.' Tommy was frowning deeply, as though trying to figure out how to respond to the charged atmosphere around him. 'What?'

'It's going to be Halloween. There'll be lots of decorations and some of the doctors and nurses put on silly costumes and have a parade. And there'll be all sorts of yummy treats for everybody to eat.'

'What sort of treats?'

'Candy,' Layla said confidently. 'And ice cream and…and…*spiders.*'

Tommy's jaw dropped. Then he giggled.

'I'll leave you to it,' Alex said, moving towards the door. 'I'll see you tomorrow, Tommy.'

Layla watched him leave.

And she had the horrible feeling that she was watching him walk away from *her*.

Which was ridiculous. Wasn't it?

They were in a better place than they'd ever been.

And she was going to do whatever it took to keep them there.

CHAPTER TEN

THERE WAS COMFORT to be found in a case that required going the extra mile.

It was a lesson Alex Rodriguez had learned long ago and he slipped into that totally focussed mode with practised ease.

By seven that night his office looked like a bomb-site. Open textbooks and journals lay scattered over his desk and parts of the floor with relevant passages marked by bright sticky notes. Illuminated wall screens had MRI scan images on display. A white board was covered with intricate diagrams and bulletpoint plans.

He was standing in front of the white board, tapping the end of the marker against his teeth, when Layla ventured into his office.

'Thought you might like a coffee,' she said. 'And some food.'

Alex turned slowly, wondering if her presence was about to pop this comforting bubble of concentration. To his relief, the skin of the bubble appeared to be thick enough to cope. Layla was on the outside. It was like seeing her from a different perspective. Through the eyes of a surgeon and not a lover?

Whatever. He could work with that.

'Great idea.' He nodded. 'I can only stop for a minute or two, though. I think I'm on a roll with planning this surgery.'

Layla was trying to find a space to put down the carry tray that held two Styrofoam cups. She gave up and offered the tray to Alex who took one. Then she handed him a bag. 'It's nothing flashy, I'm sorry. I got one of the chefs in the cafeteria to make some filled rolls with the roast beef they had on the menu.'

'Smells good to me.' Alex unwrapped the roll and took a huge bite, letting his gaze travel back to the white board as he chewed.

Layla followed his line of vision and then turned to take in the illuminated screens. 'This looks like absolutely meticulous planning. Want to talk me through it?'

Alex shook his head. 'Later, maybe. There's one bit I haven't quite worked through yet. A bit of distraction might be helpful. Unleash my subconscious or something.' He smiled at Layla. This was working. The bubble was being protected as a private space. 'Tell me what you've been up to since I saw you visiting Tommy.'

Layla swallowed the mouthful of her own roll. She was leaning her bottom, carefully, against the edge of his desk. Alex stayed standing, too wired to sit down.

'Long meeting,' Layla told him, 'with the dieticians and kitchen management. You wouldn't believe all the stuff they've got planned for Halloween. We had to make sure that nutritional guidelines were still being adhered to and that special diets could be catered for. It meant going through every item pretty much and deciding who could and couldn't get the treats.'

'Are there going to be spiders, like you promised Tommy?'

Layla nodded happily. 'Yep. Made out of chocolate-covered marshmallows with liquorice legs and eyes. There's gingerbread cookies, too, iced to have skeletons on them. And witch's hat cookies. Upside-down cupcakes with a pretzel handle that look like brooms. Ghosts made out of strawberries dipped in white icing. I got shown pictures of what they've done in past years. It's unbelievable what a big deal Halloween is around here.'

'It's a kids' hospital. It's a big thing if they're missing out on Halloween. Wait till you see what they do for Christmas.'

'It's certainly creating a lot of excitement. Good for some kids, I guess, but Matthew was crying because he's going to go home before it happens.'

Alex nodded. Matthew was due for discharge tomorrow if everybody was happy with his progress. His speech was still slightly slurred but it was improving every day.

'I saw Felix on the ward, too. Ramona was practically chasing him down the corridor. He can crawl amazingly fast.'

'He's overdue for discharge. Nina wanted him kept as long as possible to give Ramona time to sort out her domestic stuff.'

'She said that her boyfriend was in jail, waiting for the court appearance. She's planning to take the kids back to Mexico as soon as the case is over. Her mother's arriving tomorrow.'

Alex nodded but he'd finished eating the roll now and his thoughts were drifting back to Tommy's case. He looked up at the screens. The lesion was in such a tricky place. Was he really confident of the planned route to expose it without doing too much collateral damage?

Layla's voice was soft. 'He'll be the third.'

'What?'

'Good things come in threes. Special cases this time. Felix and Matthew and…Tommy will be the third.'

'Only if I get things absolutely right. And luck's on our side.'

'The luck came when you agreed to take on the case. Nobody else could do this.'

Alex shook off the reassurance. He didn't need it. Or, rather, he did but he didn't want it to come from Layla. What if it became something he relied on, like a touchstone?

'I'm going to head home,' Layla told him then. 'You'd be more than welcome to come over when you're finished here. I don't care how late it is.'

There was a note in her voice that threatened to burst the bubble. She was offering him more than the distraction of great sex here. She was offering solace. More reassurance. The comfort of being close to someone who understood the kind of pressure he was facing. Of being *cared* for.

'Not tonight.' Alex knew he sounded curt. Knew he was pushing Layla away.

Repeating history because this was exactly what he'd done in the run-up to Jamie's surgery.

And Layla hadn't liked it. She'd wanted more attention and there'd been a showdown. Would that happen again? Would this finish, once and for all, the night before Tommy's surgery, maybe?

Alex could feel an odd prickle on the back of his neck. He had to rub at it.

But Layla seemed completely calm. She came up to him. Stood on tiptoe and planted a gentle kiss on his lips.

'I understand,' she said. 'And don't worry, Alex. I'm not going to throw some kind of hissy fit because you don't have any time or energy for me right now. It's different this time.'

The skin of his bubble was being seriously dented now. Alex pushed back, trying to restore its shape. He turned physically so that he was facing the screens and the white board. Facing his work.

'I'm not caught between a life I don't want to go back to and a future that has been taken out of reach,' Layla continued quietly. 'I think the future I want exists and that's enough for me at the moment. I'm not in any rush to get there.'

Alex had to turn back. To try and decipher exactly what Layla was saying.

Did she see *him* as part of that future she wanted?

'I know it's too soon.' Layla started gathering up the rubbish from their impromptu meal. Her movements looked jerky. Nervous, even. 'There's no pressure here, Alex. Not from me, anyway.' She looked up and caught his gaze. 'Let's just get through this week. You do whatever you need to do. I'm here if you need me but I understand completely if you don't.'

Her smile was so sweet. So genuine.

'I believe in you, Alex.'

She believed in *them*. He could see it in her eyes. Could feel the pull of it between their bodies.

He wanted so badly to submit to that pull. To burst his protective bubble himself and get so close it would feel as if they were part of the same person. Like it did when they made love. A person with the strength to get through anything. Not just to get through but to succeed. Together, they had a power that was nothing like anything he'd ever been conscious of as an individual.

But what if that connection got broken? Again?

He'd lose a lot of what he had already. The strength and power that had been painfully accumulated again piece by piece since the last time his trust in someone had been shattered.

His trust in Layla, no less.

He couldn't risk it again.

Not now. Especially not now. Who was it who said history never repeated itself? Alex had no faith in that sentiment. It only didn't repeat itself if people could stop themselves being stupid enough to step back into the same set of circumstances.

He couldn't find the words to communicate any of his thoughts to Layla. Even if he could have found the words, he wouldn't have used them because that would mean they'd talk about it and Layla would have more of those sweet, seductive words of reassurance.

And he might not be able to keep up the fight. The urge to trust those words.

To trust Layla. To imagine a future like none he had ever envisaged for himself. One that involved so much trust. Loving someone with all his heart and soul.

A family, even.

The internal struggle was fierce. He wanted it but the forces automatically there to fight back were still winning. As they always had, with the one exception of letting Layla too close back then.

So Alex didn't say anything. He nodded to show that he'd heard what Layla had said but then he simply turned back to his work. He could hear Layla behind him, quietly collecting the rest of the rubbish and letting herself out of his office.

For a moment it felt heartbreakingly lonely being by himself.

But the bubble was still intact, thank goodness, and Alex drew it more closely around himself.

The gallery was closed for Tommy Jenner's surgery.

Layla hadn't expected anything else.

It was Cade who came to find her, late in the day, to tell her that it had gone well. Even better than Alex had hoped for.

'He thinks he got it all, with a safety margin. And that any damage from the surgery will be minimal. Another course of chemo should mop up any other cancer cells that might be floating around due to the surgery.'

'Oh….' Layla felt absurdly close to tears. 'I'm so happy to hear that.' The wave of relief made her feel almost euphoric. If history really had repeated herself and the operation had been a disaster, it would have been the end of the road for her and Alex. No question about that. But now? There was hope. More than hope. Confidence almost. 'Where's Alex now?'

'In ICU. I expect he'll be there for a while yet. He won't want to leave Tommy until he's confident he's completely stable.'

Layla nodded. She could visit, though, if things were going so well. It was too big an ask to stay away for much longer. She hadn't seen Alex since she'd taken him that food in his office the other night. When he'd pushed her away and she'd said she understood.

She did. But the surgery was over now. It had gone well.

That would have changed things, surely.

It certainly seemed to have, on first glance, when Layla made her way to the intensive care unit an hour or two later. There was a quiet satisfaction to Alex's body language as he stood there, scanning the information various monitors were producing. When he looked up to acknowledge Layla, she could see a gleam of relief in his eyes.

Mike was there. Looking absolutely shattered but peaceful, sitting very still beside his son. Tommy was in an induced coma and still on a ventilator. He would be kept like that for a day or two at least, to allow his doctors to control the potentially damaging pressure that any swelling of the brain tissues could produce. His head was heavily bandaged and he was surrounded by an impressive bank of high-tech monitors that could reveal what his blood pressure was beat by beat. And what the pressures were inside his small skull. Whether his kidneys were functioning normally and exactly what percentage of oxygen he was taking in.

Life support.

The bridge between winning and losing the kind of battle that Alex, and Layla, and all the other staff here at Angel's had dedicated their lives to fighting.

Layla didn't stay long. She didn't say anything directly to Alex either, but as she left, she touched his arm. And when he looked at her she hoped she was conveying that she was with him every step of the way. That there might still be a way to go but even getting this far was a triumph that Alex should be very proud of.

He had done it.

Against some very heavy odds, Tommy had made

it through the most complex surgery Alex had ever attempted.

Well…ever since Jamie's surgery, anyway.

And so far so good. By the time Alex finally left the ICU just before midnight, with strict instructions to the staff to call him if the slightest thing changed overnight, everything was looking as good as he could have possibly hoped for.

There was more than professional satisfaction to be found right now. Something almost like euphoria was trickling through Alex's veins as he strode through the lobby and out into the night. He had no intention of going home. He'd find something to eat and then use an on-call room to grab a few hours' sleep before he went back to check on Tommy again.

He needed to get out for a little while, though. To walk off this excess of energy. To come to terms with what had to have been the hardest day of his working life. Nobody could know just how hard it had been to pick up that scalpel and begin a surgery that had, at best, a fifty per cent chance of his patient being alive by the end of it.

Not that other surgeons didn't face that kind of difficult surgery but they hadn't been through what he'd been through in the wake of the Kirkpatrick case. The public disgrace of being accused of malpractice. Of being a failure. Of knowing that his career—the most important thing in his life—was hanging in the balance and could be totally destroyed.

Nobody could understand how big this was for him. Knowing that he'd done it. More than succeeded, because he'd exorcised a ghost that had threatened to haunt him for the rest of his life.

No. That wasn't quite true.

There was one person who could understand.

The person who knew him better than anyone else alive. The person who believed in him. Who was intimately acquainted with his demons and *still* believed in him.

Alex raised his hand and flagged down a cab, which wasn't hard at this time of night. He didn't give the driver his own address, however. He asked to be taken to Layla's apartment.

Would she be there? Would she understand that there was only one way that Alex could release the huge feelings that were choking him? That some of those feelings inextricably linked to the Kirkpatrick case were also about *her* and if he'd dealt with one of those ghosts today, he had to see what it meant in relation to the other one because…because it was so big. It felt like the picture of his future was changing. Getting brighter. But he couldn't separate those ghosts so it was also confusing.

And he felt wired. Would she understand that he felt proud and excited and incredibly nervous all at the same time?

He couldn't explain why, despite the huge success of today, he felt more vulnerable than he ever had, even as a child.

Would she understand that he just needed to be with her?

Layla hadn't expected to see Alex tonight, of all nights.

She had thought he wouldn't be able to tear himself away from the intensive care unit and the watch over Tommy. That if he needed a rest he would go no further than a nearby on-call room where he could put his head down for an hour or two.

But here he was. On her doorstep. Still wearing his scrubs, as though he hadn't had the head room to give what he was wearing a single thought. Looking...

Like she'd never seen him ever look.

As if every defence he'd ever perfected had been stripped away. He looked like...Alex. Pure Alex. As if his soul had seeped into his skin and filled his eyes.

Layla felt her heart split wide open.

And the crack was big enough to gather Alex in and wrap her heart around him.

So she didn't say anything at all in greeting. She merely opened her arms as well as her heart.

And Alex stepped right inside.

Layla's bed was rumpled because she'd got out of it to answer the tap on her door. She was wearing nothing more than silk boxer shorts and a camisole top and the scraps of clothing seemed to evaporate as easily as Alex's loose theatre gear.

The sex was as different as the way Alex had looked.

Fierce and urgent but so tender it broke her heart all over again.

There was no conversation between them at all but how many times had Alex said her name?

With the groan of desire as his lips covered hers. The almost reverent whisper as his hands stroked her clothing away. The cry of need as he entered her. The echo of something she couldn't define at the moment of ultimate satisfaction. And a whisper again, as they lay, still joined, waiting for their breathing to slow and their heart rates to get somewhere close to normal again.

A whisper that could have been the start of being

able to talk but the intimate sound was drowned by the strident notes of Alex's pager.

He ripped himself away from Layla and was out of the bed in the same fluid motion.

'Rodriguez.' The greeting was almost a bark. He listened for only a few seconds. 'I'm on my way.'

And then he was pulling the scrubs back on and it took only seconds.

'What is it?' Layla had to ask, because Alex wasn't telling her. She felt like she was suddenly on another planet and the contrast to where they'd been such a short time ago was brutal.

This felt…like she didn't exist for Alex right now. Like she was back in that scary place right before Jamie's surgery. When she couldn't go back to her past life but the future she'd been dreaming of seemed to have been suddenly taken away.

No. She could cope with this. She could see the bigger picture. She could make allowances for this intense focus that had nothing to do with her.

'It's Tommy, isn't it?'

A terse nod from Alex. 'He's had a seizure.' The words were heavy. 'Intracranial pressure has spiked.'

There was nothing more to say. A headline proclaiming potential disaster and they were both too far away to gather any more information.

Layla heard her front door closing. She even heard Alex's shout seconds later as he demanded an urgent response from a cab driver.

The shivering started then. Hunched on her bed, Layla pulled the covers up to her shoulders but the chill wouldn't go away. A short time later she pushed them aside and went to find her clothes. There was no point trying to sleep so she may as well go into Angel's and find out for herself what was happening.

And it was then that the curious way Alex had said her name in that most unguarded moment came back to haunt her.

Maybe the undertone hadn't been indefinable at all.

As it echoed in her mind now, she could hear the clear notes of something that sounded horribly like despair.

Alex fought harder than he'd ever fought before.

He juggled drugs and ventilator settings and didn't leave Tommy's side until the rise in pressure that had caused the seizure was under control. It took a long time and there were more seizures before he was happy that Tommy's condition was stable.

Happy wasn't the word, of course. This was a major setback and he could see the fear in Mike's face. In Gina's, too, because she was there by his side, clinging to his hand. Sharing this horrible vigil.

A vigil that stretched and stretched. When things had been stable for thirty-six hours, Alex decided it was time to lighten the sedation and get Tommy off the ventilator.

The drugs were tailed off and the breathing tube finally removed and everyone breathed a sigh of relief when the monitors showed that Tommy was managing to breathe on his own and his condition didn't deteriorate. Mike and Gina couldn't be prised away from his bedside now because he might wake up at any moment.

Except he didn't. Hour after hour went by and there was no flicker of returning consciousness. Tommy wasn't in an induced coma now. He was in a genuine coma and things were starting to look bleak. They looked even bleaker two days later when Tommy still lay still on his bed, totally unresponsive.

'Is he going to wake up?'

Why had Layla chosen the moment that Mike voiced his worst fear to visit the intensive care unit?

Alex shook his head slowly. 'We just don't know what's really going on. We know that the cerebral blood flow is fine now but we don't know what it was like when he was so unstable. The intracranial pressure is the same deal. His level of oxygenation is good. So are his electrolytes and fluid balance. The EEG to look for brain activity was inconclusive. There's some activity. We just don't know if it's enough. Or whether the readings were accurate. We'll run the tests again tomorrow.'

'But you must have an opinion,' Mike pressed. 'You've had so many cases like this. You're the best there is and you must have a gut feeling for how this is going to go.'

Alex had to shake his head again. 'I'm sorry, Mike, but all I can say is that I really don't know. I wish I could say something else, I really do.'

'But it's not looking good, is it?'

'No.' He had a responsibility to prepare parents for the worst possible scenario when it was looking more and more likely, didn't he? 'I'm so sorry, Mike. We have to wait and see but...' It was too hard to finish the sentence. Alex's throat felt like it was closing up.

'But don't get my hopes up?' There were tears in Mike's eyes but he was trying so hard to hold it together. He knew Alex had done and was doing the best he possibly could and there was no blame in his gaze. Just despair.

Alex could only give a terse nod. He gripped Mike's arm in a gesture of sympathy but then he had to look away.

And Layla was there, dammit. With those big, blue eyes swimming with tears.

Looking as scared and grief-stricken as Mike.

He couldn't help remembering what she'd looked like just before Tommy's surgery. When she'd told him that she believed in him.

Where was that belief now?

Gone.

She was scared. Under emotional pressure. What would happen if Tommy died? Would she snap? Had she lost her belief in a future with him along with her belief in his abilities? There was no getting away from how she'd tried to take control the last time she'd been scared like this.

Would she dump him? Again?

No. He wouldn't let that happen. Couldn't afford to, if he was going to survive.

Alex excused himself from the unit. He really, really needed some time to himself.

Why did Layla choose to follow him?

Was it fate? Giving him the chance to take at least some control of this horrible situation? A way to jump before he got pushed?

'Alex…'

'Not now, Layla.' Even now he was fighting it. Postponing the inevitable despite the fact that they were out of the unit now and there was no one else around. It might be the only opportunity to have a private conversation all day.

Layla ignored his warning. How typical was that?

'I just wanted to say I'm sorry. I…feel awful that you were with me when things started to go wrong. And…and I wanted to say…don't give up on Tommy yet. There's—'

'Don't say there's still *hope*.' Alex kept his voice low to control his sudden anger. 'You and I both know what the likely outcome is.'

Layla had tears in her eyes again. Her bottom lip trembled. That fear was back in her eyes again, too, and Alex couldn't cope with that.

'Will I see you later?' The words were a whisper.

'No.' Somehow Alex found the strength he needed. And the words. 'It's over, Layla.'

She went very, very still.

'You mean…*us*?'

A single nod but Alex couldn't meet her eyes. 'You were right.' How on earth did he manage to keep his tone so light? Conversational almost. 'All it needed was to use up the fuel.' He risked a lightning-fast touch of eye contact. 'It was a pretty good fire the other night. Unfortunate that I'd decided to take a break from my professional responsibilities but there you go. It happened. And that was when I threw the last bits of fuel on.'

He managed a longer glance this time. 'I'm sorry if it's not what you want but it's all gone as far as I'm concerned, Layla. It's *over*.'

CHAPTER ELEVEN

IT WASN'T OVER.

It *couldn't* be.

Alex might think it was but he was having a knee-jerk reaction to an emotional situation and he was taking it out on her.

Taking it out on himself, too, but he probably didn't realise that.

It was Halloween today and Angel's was buzzing with the kind of excitement that came with a special day. It was always a bonus when you could distract sick and hurting children from the frightening circumstances they found themselves in and occasions like Halloween or Christmas were gold.

There were decorations to distract a child with when something painful or scary was about to happen to them. Treats to promise for when it was over. The anticipation of the staff parade that would build all day and would not only break the normal routine for longer-term patients but make being in hospital a special place to be.

Normally, Layla would have become enthusiastically involved. She would have found herself a great costume to wear all day and had a bag of treats she could distribute to small, excited children. She'd thought about it. Tossed up between turning herself into a cowgirl to amuse the children or a witch to amuse the staff, but any incentive to play had been lost in the awful tension of Tommy's case.

And it had gone out the window completely in the wake of getting dumped by Alex four days ago.

Her secretary had been busy adding the spirit of Halloween to her office. Layla had to brush past a soft, fabric spider web hanging from her doorframe that had a very cheerful-looking plastic spider attached to its centre. A large, bright orange Jack-o'-lantern sticker on her window obscured a good percentage of the view. Not that Layla was going to be distracted by gazing at Central Park any more than by the invitations to share the fun of Halloween.

She had been so afraid that something like this might happen to destroy what she'd found with Alex. That Tommy's case was too like Jamie's not to bring the ghosts of the past out to haunt and sabotage the present. Somewhere in Alex's mind, maybe Tommy *was* Jamie. And he was bailing because he could see nothing but the rocks their relationship was doomed to flounder on.

A mirthless snort of laughter escaped Layla. It was Halloween. How appropriate that it was ghosts that were responsible for this new low point in her life.

But how *unfair*.

It shouldn't be happening because Tommy's case was *different*. Nothing had gone wrong in the surgery. There was no obvious explanation for why he wasn't waking up now. Nobody could say that Alex hadn't done everything possible. Much more than anyone else might have even attempted.

And what she and Alex had together was just as

different from what they'd had in the days of that illicit affair.

They hadn't thrown fuel onto the smouldering ashes of what they'd had together back then. They'd started a new fire the night they'd gone out together and talked. They'd revealed things to each other that made them *real* people. People with difficult, hurtful things in their histories. They'd found a connection that went far, far deeper than anything physical could have achieved.

She'd learned things about Alex that had shocked her but it had also shown her how good he was at hiding things like that. Yes, she'd been aware of the shadows but she could never have guessed how dark they really were. He'd had a lifetime of practice at hiding. At protecting himself from getting hurt again.

And that was what he was doing now.

Protecting himself by pushing her away, as hard and as far as he could.

Because he didn't trust her?

Did he really think she was going to end things between them? Ever?

She'd done it once, hadn't she?

Had it ever occurred to her to wonder how much that might have hurt him? What had happened so soon afterwards, with the horrible publicity and the shame of the malpractice suit had been enough of an explanation for everybody else for why Alex had been so miserable. Why he'd quit and gone to the other side of the world, but...but what if there'd been more to it than that? If the way she'd treated him had contributed to more than potentially affecting his concentration the day of Jamie's surgery?

Oh, *God*... Layla didn't think she could feel any

worse than she had been feeling for the last two days but she'd been wrong.

Sitting down at her desk, she ignored the pile of memos that would remind her of what she had to fit into today's routine. Instead, she rubbed her forehead with the base of the palms of her hands.

She'd had a premonition of precisely this, hadn't she? When Alex had walked out of Tommy's room that time and it had felt like he was walking away from *her*? That despairing note in his voice as he'd cried out her name at the climax of that extraordinary time together in the wake of the successful surgery?

She'd been so afraid of losing him.

Standing there beside Tommy's bed when Alex had been warning Mike not to hold out too much hope, Layla had seen more than the heartbreak of losing a small child. She'd seen what it would be like to lose Alex from her life and she'd been so afraid.

He'd seen that fear in her face, surely?

And yet he'd chosen that moment to run. To wall himself off emotionally so convincingly that Layla had done her best to stay out of his way. Knowing that another blow like that and what was left of her strength might desert her completely.

What would her colleagues think of their new chief of Paediatrics if they saw her sliding down the wall somewhere, to crouch in a sobbing heap, overcome by grief?

Layla raised her head. Her eyes were still closed but she took a deep, deep breath.

Not going to happen.

What was going to happen was that she would come up with a plan to take control of her own life again.

Somehow.

As soon as she could catch whatever it was that was swirling elusively around in the back of her mind.

Something that wasn't ringing true about any of this. That was adding a note of confusion.

Shining a tiny light that might feel like hope if she could just catch hold of the danged thing.

Alex was running on autopilot. There were surgeries to perform. Ward rounds to conduct. Patients to treat and parents to talk to. Any free moments he had between his duties were spent in the intensive care unit.

Checking Tommy. Going through every note that had been made. Analysing every reading any of the monitors produced. Calling experts from anywhere in the world that he could discuss the case with as he desperately tried to find an answer. A way out of this dreadful dead end.

Ryan had come into the ICU to check on one of his patients, a head trauma from a car accident earlier that day. Alex knew that underneath the theatre gown his second-in-command was wearing a pirate costume. He'd probably left his hat in his office and when he was finished here he would be heading off like everybody else to go to the ball. Halloween didn't make it into any of the intensive care units. Or into any of the operating theatres, and that suited Alex just fine.

He'd never felt less like being part of a party.

He didn't deserve to be having fun. Not when Mike and Gina were sitting here beside Tommy's bed, as pale and still as Tommy was himself. There was nothing to even talk about any more. They just had to wait. Tommy was breathing perfectly well. All his organs were functioning normally. The pressure inside his skull was back to what it should be.

He just wouldn't wake up.

And maybe he never would.

Like part of *him* never would again either. A big part.

He'd told Layla that the fire was out and there was no more fuel to put on it. What a lie. How could you put out a fire that was actually burning in every cell of your body? If you did put it out, something vital would die.

Right now that part of him was in a coma. Like Tommy. And what he didn't know was what would happen if it did die. Was it a part of himself he couldn't live without?

Would he be on autopilot for the rest of his life?

The thought was unbearably bleak. It was a relief to feel a tap on his shoulder and Alex turned, expecting to see Ryan.

But it wasn't. Cade had come into the ICU at some point as he'd sat here at the nurses' station, poring over Tommy's case notes.

'You need to get out of here for a while, man.'

Alex shrugged. There was nowhere to go. He wasn't on call and the day's duties were long finished with. He didn't want to go home because he'd be faced with an apartment that was filled with memories of Layla's company. A bed that tortured him with its emptiness.

'Come with me,' Cade suggested.

To shoot hoops? Alex shook his head. He wasn't angry or wired enough for that to be an attractive diversion. He'd never felt so tired in his life. So…sad.

'I've got your costume. Come and be someone else for an hour or two.'

Now that was an attractive option. But a costume

wasn't going to make it happen. Heading off to a new job or a new country, like Cade was about to, wasn't going to fix this either. Alex had already been there and done that. He had several T-shirts, come to think of it. And look at him now. Back to square one. Trying to figure out how he was going to get through the aftermath of a case going horribly wrong.

Of getting involved with Layla Woods.

'You have to come,' Cade said. 'It's my last night here. Might be the last time we get to have some time together for a while.' His hand gripped Alex's shoulder. 'There's nothing more you can do here for now and it'd mean a lot to me, bro.'

Alex closed the case notes. He looked over at Tommy's cubicle. A nurse was hovering, probably moistening the little boy's lips or adjusting his pillow or something. Gina had her head on Mike's shoulder and he had his arm wrapped tightly around her. His other arm was outstretched, his hand completely enclosing one of Tommy's. Cade was right. There *was* nothing more he could do here. Was he getting too emotionally involved with one of his patients? Like he'd accused Layla of being so often?

And then Alex looked up and caught the expression in his brother's face. Cade was leaving a lot behind him here as he gave up his position at Angel's to head for new horizons in Australia. Bad stuff, for sure, but he was also giving up the only family he had. For a moment he looked like the kid brother Alex had let down so badly in the past.

Stiffly, Alex pushed himself to his feet.

'OK. Just for an hour or two. And I'm not saying

yes to the costume if it turns out to be the back end of a cow.'

'No.' Cade's face lit up. 'Jack Carter helped me choose. You'll love it, man. Come on, we can get changed in your office.'

New York Children's Hospital was so quiet tonight.

Everybody who possibly could go had gone to the huge fundraising ball in the nearby venue.

Not Layla, however.

She'd come to the intensive care unit to share the vigil that Mike and Gina were keeping at Tommy's bedside. Just for a while. To let them know they weren't alone. That other people cared.

Their whispered conversation had died some time ago. Now they were all sitting in a silence that was broken only by the soft beeping of the machines watching over Tommy.

Layla's thoughts inevitably turned inwards again. She was still trying to catch that elusive thought glowing, tantalisingly, just out of reach. Her gaze was on Tommy's face but she wasn't really seeing him or thinking about him. There was just a background sadness that a such a young, much-loved child could be in such a situation. Children were so vulnerable. So *trusting*…

That was it.

Layla dipped her head, closed her eyes and held her breath as she finally caught the thought. It was the way Alex had looked when she'd opened her door the other night. When she'd been able to see everything that was Alex Rodriguez. Everything about the man that she'd wanted to wrap her heart around. To love.

Had she seen the brilliant surgeon? The breathtakingly gorgeous man that turned every female head? Yes, of course, she had.

But she could see past that as well. To a frightened, lonely child who was afraid to love because people that he should have been able to trust had hurt him.

He hadn't even been trying to hide anything at all.

And that had to mean that he *did* trust her. Or could. Maybe all he needed was reassurance but what had Layla done when he'd told her it was over? Stayed out of his way. Like she had after Jamie had died because she'd felt so guilty and hadn't known what to say.

Well…she knew what to say this time.

And she'd been right. That elusive thought offered hope.

Letting her breath out slowly, Layla opened her eyes to find herself looking at Mike. And, weirdly, the warmth of hope that was seeping through her veins like a potent drug to reach every cell in her body seemed to be contagious. Mike still looked completely exhausted but his chin wasn't on his chest any more. He was looking straight ahead and he looked completely stunned. Blinded almost.

Gina had caught it, too. Her mouth was open and she was also staring straight ahead.

At Tommy? What were they looking at?

Very slowly, Layla turned her own head. Her heart missed a beat and then thumped so loudly she could swear she heard it.

Tommy's eyes were *open*.

The little boy blinked. Once…twice. His mouth opened and then closed. And then it opened again.

'Dad?' The whisper was a hoarse croak. 'Is it over now?'

Mike's outward breath was a barely controlled sob. He had to fight for control as he leaned down to kiss Tommy.

'Yes, buddy. It's over now.'

Staff came running as the monitors tripped alarms due to the unexpected increase in activity. Layla helped with the initial assessment but just as his coma had been inexplicable so was this return to consciousness. He was still very drowsy but could be roused easily now. There was no sign that he might slip back into the coma.

'Somebody needs to find Rodriguez,' one of the ICU doctors said. 'He'll want to know about this.'

'I'll page him,' a nurse offered. But she came back a short time later and shook her head. 'He's not answering his pager or his mobile. Apparently he left word that he was going to the ball for a while but would still be able to be contacted. I guess he can't hear his phone.'

'I know where it is.' Layla was already heading for the door. 'I'll find him.'

The venue was within walking distance and Layla got there within minutes. She couldn't wait to find Alex. To tell him about Tommy, of course, but more than that. Much more than that, she had to find out if the hope she was feeling about her future had a real basis. If Alex could trust her.

Could love her as much as she knew she loved him.

She entered the huge space through a doorway draped with black curtains and guarded by ghosts that had been made by white sheets draped over helium balloons so that they floated convincingly overhead. It was only then that she realised that it wasn't going to be easy to locate Alex .

There were hundreds of people here and she couldn't even see anybody she recognised because they were all disguised in an astonishing array of costumes. Not only that, the only lighting was coming from Jack-o'-lanterns on the tables and the music was loud.

Layla stood still for a minute or two, getting accustomed to this very odd atmosphere. There were groups of people standing talking, lots of people dancing and some were grouped around tables that had black coverings cluttered with wineglasses and platters of snack food. She could see ghosts and devils, clowns and fairies, a Frankenstein and a skeleton. An extraordinary couple dressed as Adam and Eve walked past her, wearing pink skin-tight body suits with fig leaves attached in appropriate places.

'Wow,' Eve shouted with laughter. 'You've come as a doctor. Very cool.'

It took Layla a moment to click and then she groaned aloud. She'd rushed out of Angel's so fast on her quest to find Alex that she hadn't bothered to take off her white coat. In this dim lighting she probably stood out as much as that man in the flashy white suit who was coming towards her. He had cowboy boots on, too, and a white Stetson hat a mile wide.

'Hey, darlin'. You've come to join the party, then?'

'Ty…' It was a huge relief to recognise someone. 'Hey, you make a good Texan tycoon.'

'I'm just tryin' it on for size. Might use this for my weddin' outfit. You'll be coming, won't you?'

'Of course I will. Have you seen Alex tonight? I'm trying to find him.'

'Who's he come as?'

'He doesn't do dress-ups.' He'd said that, hadn't he?

She'd thought he was trying to tell her that what was happening between them was real.

It was. It still could be.

'I *have* to find him, Ty. It's really important.'

'I saw Ryan a while back. He might know. He's a pirate.'

'*Layla*, hi…'

Chloe looked adorable as Wilma Flintstone in her ragged-hem dress, a necklace that looked like it was made of out golf balls and a bright orange wig that matched Brad's 'Fred' costume.

'Have either of you seen Alex?'

'He's right behind you. See?'

Layla whirled round. There were three men right behind her. Dressed identically.

The three musketeers were all roughly the same height. They all had the same black trousers tucked into boots, white shirts with flowing sleeves and tabards with a Celtic cross on the front and a cape attached at the back. They all had shoulder-length, curly black wigs, huge hats with ostrich feathers in them, masks and pencil-thin moustaches.

Three peas in a pod but only one of them was looking back at Layla with an intensity she could feel right down to her bones.

'Alex…' Layla couldn't tell if he could even hear her with this background noise. 'I need to talk to you.'

'Hey, Layla.' She recognised Cade's voice. 'This is some farewell party, isn't it? Glad you could make it.'

Layla nodded. Smiled, even, but she couldn't look away from Alex.

'You don't look like you're here to party.' The third

musketeer turned out to be Jack Carter. 'Everything OK, Layla?'

'It will be.' Layla felt absurdly close to tears. 'Alex… Tommy's woken up.'

'What? *When?*' He didn't wait for a reply. Alex grabbed Layla's hand and pulled her after him, heading for the doors. Away from the crowds and crazy costumes and all the noise. Out into the night with the trees of Central Park casting huge shadows in the light from the streetlamps. They were heading back to Angel's, still hand in hand.

Suddenly Alex stopped. 'Tell me,' he commanded. 'Tell me everything.'

It took no time at all to bring Alex up to speed on Tommy. Layla expected him to take off again. To go and see for himself that what she was telling him was true.

But he didn't. He let out a long, slow breath, closed his eyes and pulled Layla into his arms to hold her very tightly.

'Thank God,' was all he said.

A car horn sounded loudly beside them and Layla could hear some ribald shouting. Even in New York it was probably an odd sight to see a musketeer embracing a doctor. Alex caught the gist of the comments and stepped back with a wry smile.

'You're lucky you're not in a stupid costume,' he said.

'I don't do dress-ups,' Layla reminded him quietly. 'I'm not into pretending to be someone that I'm not.'

She held his gaze. 'I'm not going to live a lie or follow a script. Things are different now, Alex.'

He was listening to her words but was he hearing what she was trying to tell him?

'It's not just that Tommy's woken up and he's going

to be OK that I had to come and find you tonight. I know you think you can't trust me because of what I did last time but things *are* different now.'

Alex was still holding her hands. Did that mean something good?

'I'm not trapped any more. I'm not in a marriage that was never right. I'm not feeling guilty or scared. I'm free and I get to choose what I want and…and I want *you*, Alex. I…I love you.'

He was staring down at her. Frowning. 'But you *were* scared. I could see it when Mike was asking about Tommy. You looked like…you'd stopped believing in me.'

Layla shook her head sharply. 'Yes, I was scared. Scared of losing *you*. I can't imagine my life without you in it now.'

She still believed in him.

She *loved* him?

The news about Tommy was a huge relief but this… this was way bigger. So big that words had deserted Alex. It was Layla who broke the new silence between them.

'I thought you didn't do dress-ups, either.'

'I don't.' Alex wanted to rip the hat and wig off his head but that would mean letting go of Layla's hands. 'I thought I wanted to be someone else for a while, that's all.'

'Oh…' She understood that he'd wanted to step out of his own skin to get away from everything that was happening in his life. He could see the fear in her eyes again. Fear that she really was going to lose him?

'But I was wrong.' The words came easily now. From

a place deep inside his heart. 'I don't want to be anyone else. Not even for a minute.'

'Because of Tommy?'

'No. Because of *you*.' Alex dipped his head so that he could kiss her and the soft, welcoming touch of her lips was all he needed to know that this was right. So right it felt like he'd been waiting his whole life for this moment. 'I love *you*, Layla. I always have. And if I was someone else I wouldn't have you in my life, and I'm not going to waste another single minute of that.'

'There's a lot of minutes in every day.' Layla was smiling. 'And in every night. Can we go and visit Tommy now and then maybe go home?'

'Oh, yeah…' But Alex didn't want to move quite yet. 'How many minutes in a week are there? In a month? In a *year*?'

'Not enough, I reckon.'

Alex had an odd lump in his throat. 'Would a lifetime of minutes be enough?'

Oh…he could drown in those eyes. In the love he could see. A love that he wanted to claim. To return. For ever.

'Marry me,' he whispered. 'Please?'

It seemed to be Layla's turn to be lost for words. But she was nodding. And crying?

Layla Woods didn't cry. Unless…

She was scrubbing her tears away. 'Don't mind me,' she told him. 'I'm just so happy…as happy as a clam at high tide. Yes, Alex. I would love to marry you. As long as you don't wear that outfit to our wedding.'

'I won't, I promise.'

'Or a white suit.'

'It's a deal.'

Laughing, and still hand in hand, Alex and Layla set off again. Walking towards Angel's.

Towards their future.

* * * * *

ST. PIRAN'S:
THE WEDDING
OF THE YEAR

CAROLINE ANDERSON

CHAPTER ONE

'OH, DR TREMAYNE, Kate left this for you.'

Nick stopped by the reception desk and took the sealed envelope from Sue, glancing at it in puzzlement. How odd...

'Is she still here?'

'Yes, I think so, but she's about to go. She has to pick Jem up from holiday club. Do you want me to find her?'

'No, it's OK.' He gave the envelope another glance, and with a curt nod to his patients as he passed them, he went into his room, closed the door and slit the flap open with his forefinger as he dropped into his chair behind the desk.

He drew out a single sheet, handwritten in her elegant, decisive script, and as he smoothed it out with the flat of his hand he stared at it in disbelief.

Monday 12 April

Dear Nick,

I've written to the PCT, and will tell Chloe and all my other colleagues and friends over the next few days, but I wanted you to know first that I've decided to leave Penhally and my post here as midwife. I'm putting my house on the market and Jem and I will move away from here over the summer, in time for him to start secondary school in September. It's the right time to go, as far as his education is concerned, and I thought we could move closer to my mother in Bristol.

I'll miss the practice and all the people in it, but it's time for us to move on. There's nothing here for me any more.

I would just like to thank you for all the support and kindness you've shown to me over the years.

Yours,

Kate

Stunned, Nick scanned the letter again. She couldn't leave. Where the hell did she think she was going? And taking Jem away…

He pushed back his chair and crossed to the window, pressing his hand against the cold glass and staring out numbly at the sudden squall that had sprung up. The rain was streaming down the pane in torrents, bouncing off the roofs of the cars outside, and people were running for cover.

Including Kate. She wrenched open her car door, and as she got in her head lifted and she met his eyes, holding them for a moment through the lashing rain, then with a tiny shake of her head she slammed the door, started the engine and drove away, leaving him staring after her.

He sucked in a harsh, juddering breath and turned on his heel, moving away from the window before he put his fist through it in frustration. The letter was lying there on the desk, taunting him, and he crumpled it up and hurled it at the bin. It missed, and he picked it up, crushing it tighter in his fist.

Why? Why now, of all times, when he'd begun to feel there might be a chance…?

There was a tap on the door and old Doris Trefussis popped her head round and came in with a smile.

'Cup of tea for you, Dr T., before you start,' she said brightly, 'and a couple of Hazel's fairings. I saved them for you.'

'Thank you, Doris,' he said tightly, and held his breath until she'd shut the door. The last thing he could do was eat, it would choke him, but there was no way he could tell Doris that. She'd kill him if he didn't eat Hazel's biscuits, he thought, dropping down into his chair and dragging his hands over his face before flattening out the crumpled page and reading the letter again.

It didn't make any more sense the second time. Or the third.

Maybe the tea would help.

He cradled the mug in his hand and stared blankly out of the window. It was slack water, the boats in the harbour swinging every which way in the squalling wind. He knew the feeling. He'd been swinging at anchor himself ever since Annabel had died five years ago, unsure of what the future held, of which way the tide would turn.

For a time he'd thought Kate was getting married, but then he'd heard on the grapevine that it was over now, and with Rob out of the way, he'd thought that maybe now, with both of them widowed—but then this, out of the blue. He'd never expected this. Never expected that she'd go…

She couldn't leave. She couldn't. She'd lived in Penhally for ever, her entire life. He'd known her since she was twelve, dated her when she was fifteen and he was seventeen, left her at eighteen to go to university, intending to come back for her—but then he'd met Annabel, and everything had changed.

Except Kate. She'd stayed the same—sweet, funny, kind—but those soft brown eyes had held reproach and disappointment ever since. Or maybe he'd imagined it, but all he knew was that every time she looked at him, he felt guilt.

He shut his eyes and sighed. God knows, there was enough to feel guilty about in the past thirty-odd years.

He folded the crumpled letter and put it in his pocket. He could go round there this evening, see if there wasn't a way he could convince her to stay—but there was no point, he thought grimly. She'd made up her mind, and maybe it really was for the best.

He'd miss them both, but especially Kate—Kate he'd depended on for her kindness and common sense when he'd been in turmoil, Kate who'd managed the practice for years before she'd returned to midwifery and become a firm favourite with the mums.

Kate he'd loved, all those years ago.

Had loved, and lost, because of his own stupid fault. His chest felt tight just thinking about it, and he stared out of the window again, trying to imagine the practice without her. His life, without her. She couldn't go. He couldn't let her.

There's nothing here for me any more.

Particularly not an emotionally bankrupt old fool like him. He had no choice but to let her go. No power to do anything else. The least he could do was do it with dignity.

He pushed the tea aside, strode to the door and yanked it open. 'Mr Pengelly, would you come in, please?'

He tried to concentrate, tried to give the man his attention while he described his symptoms, but the letter was burning a hole in his pocket and judging by the feel of it the acid was doing the same thing to his stomach.

'Sump'n's goin' on out there,' Mr Pengelly said, jerking his head at the window.

'Hmm?' Nick dragged his mind back into the room and listened, and then he heard it over the rain and his clamouring thoughts. The sirens wailing, the rapid footsteps as Oliver Fawkner ran to his car outside Nick's window and shot off up the road. He was on call today, acting as First Responder in the event of a serious accident as part of those duties, and he'd obviously been called out to the emergency.

'The sirens,' Mr Pengelly said unnecessarily.

'Yes,' Nick said, blanking it out of his mind as he examined him, weighed him, checked his blood pressure, listened to his chest. He was a heart attack waiting to happen, and if he had one, it wouldn't be Nick's fault. He'd given him sage advice for years, and it was time to lay it on the line.

More sirens. It was a big one, he thought, and eyed his patient firmly. 'Right, Mr Pengelly, I think we need to have another look at your lifestyle. You're overweight, you're unfit, you don't take your drugs regularly, and then you come in and tell me you have chest pain, but you don't seem to be prepared to do anything about it and if you go on like this you'll kill yourself. We need to check your cholesterol level again. It was high last time, and you're still smoking, aren't you?'

'Ah, but I've cut down, Doc.'

'To what?'

He hesitated, then under Nick's uncompromising stare he sighed and came clean. 'Only twenty a day now.'

Only? 'That's twenty too many. Make an appointment on your way out for a fasting cholesterol test first thing one morning, as soon as possible, and then we'll review it, but you need to start exercising and attend the stop smoking clinic—'

'Must be a big'un. There's the chopper coming now,' he said, gesturing at the window again, just as the phone rang, and Nick frowned and reached for it, irritated that the man didn't seem to be paying any attention.

'Excuse me a moment—Tremayne.'

'It's Sue. I'm sorry to disturb you, but Oliver rang. Kate's had an accident, and they're airlifting Jem to hospital. He said you'd better get over to St Piran's.'

He felt the blood drain from his head, and sucked in a breath. 'What's wrong—? How bad is he—is he—?'

'Head and pelvis, he said, but he was quite insistent that

you should go, Nick. Kate's going to need you. And he said to tell her not to worry about the dog, he'll sort it.'

The dog? He mumbled something and cradled the phone with a clatter. 'Um—Mr Pengelly, I have to go. I'm sorry. Make the appointment, if you wouldn't mind, and we'll talk again when we get the results.'

'So—do you want those biscuits?'

The man was a lost cause. 'Help yourself,' he growled, and got to his feet and went out to Reception, his legs moving automatically. 'Right, Mr Pengelly needs a fasting choles-terol ASAP with a follow-up appointment,' he told Sue. 'I'm going to St Piran's—can you get Sam to cover my surgery for me?'

And without waiting for her reply, without even pausing to pick up his coat, he strode briskly out of the doors into the lashing rain.

The drive to St Piran nearly killed him.

His stomach was in knots, adrenaline pouring through his veins, and with no one to distract him his thoughts were free to run over all the things that could be wrong, and all the things that could go wrong as a consequence.

The list was hideous, and just thinking it all through made him want to retch.

He called Ben's mobile from his hands-free. His son-in-law would be there today, in A and E, and he'd give him advance warning. He drummed his fingers on the steering-wheel, waiting impatiently for Ben to answer, and when he did, Ben got there before he did.

'It's OK, Nick, we're on it. I can hear the helicopter now, we're going out to meet it. Just drive carefully and meet us in Resus. I'll get someone to look out for you.'

'OK. Ben—check Kate over, could you? Or get someone to? She was in the car with Jem and I don't know if she's hurt. And tell her I'm coming.'

'Sure. Got to go. See you soon.'

The phone went dead, and he sliced through the traffic and in through the hospital gates, abandoned the car on the kerb and ran in. It would probably be clamped but he'd worry about that later.

He was met at the door and ushered straight through to Resus, and as the door swung open he froze for a second. He was assailed by memories, his emotions suddenly in turmoil. He couldn't do this. Not here, not this room, of all the places.

He had to. On autopilot, he looked around at a scene of organised chaos, Ben snapping out orders and the team anticipating him like a well-oiled machine. A machine that held the boy's life in its hands?

The same machine—and the same man—that had held Annabel's—and lost it?

Dear God.

They were cutting Jem's clothes off, slicing through the sodden fabric, peeling it away so they could get a proper look at him, talking reassuringly to him all the time, and it could have been any of his boys lying there, all skinny limbs and ribcage with only the pelvic binder left to hold his pelvis stable.

Don't let him die. Please, God, don't let him die...

'OK, let's cross-match for ten units and get five units of O-neg to start with, and some packed cells, and let's get some X-rays—a full trauma series, starting with head, spine and pelvis. What about pain relief?' Ben asked. 'What's he had already?'

'Three milligrams of morphine IV, but his blood pressure's dropping. Want to try—?'

The voices washed around Nick, only two things really registering. One was the bruised little face scarcely visible under the mask, most of Jem's head concealed by the padding of the neck brace; the other was Kate, sodden and bedraggled, standing a few feet away watching as they worked on her little son, her eyes wide with fear, her lips moving soundlessly.

Praying?

Probably. There was little else to do. He crossed over to her, and she gripped his hand and gave a tiny sob.

He squeezed back. He wanted to hug her, to say, 'It's OK, it's going to be all right,' but he wasn't sure it was, wasn't sure she'd want him to hold her, wasn't sure she'd believe him—and anyway his tongue was glued to the roof of his mouth.

He freed it with effort and concentrated on the facts. 'Have you done a FAST exam?' he asked, sticking to something safe, and Ben shook his head.

'No, we're just about to.'

'Fast?' Kate murmured.

'Ultrasound, basically,' Ben said. 'It might show what's going on.'

Such as free fluid in the abdomen. Blood, most particularly, from torn arteries, sheered bone ends...

Nick felt the bile welling again, and dragged his free hand over his face.

The radiographer was setting up the X-ray machine as Ben quickly ran the head of the ultrasound wand over Jeremiah's thin, slightly distended abdomen, and Nick watched the screen, wincing at the image. Free fluid. Lots of it. Damn.

They were handed lead aprons. Ben must have realised they wouldn't leave, and as the X-rays appeared on the computer screen a few moments later, Nick sucked in a breath.

Even across the room, he could see the fractures on the left side of Jeremiah's pelvis, the bony ends displaced, the damage they'd caused all too easily imaginable.

'OK, this needs fixation before he goes anywhere,' Ben was saying. 'Are the orthos free?'

'No. They're just finishing off so they're ready for him,' the charge nurse said. 'Want me to get Josh?'

'Please—and fast-bleep the anaesthetist, we need to get on with this.'

'Who's Josh?' Kate asked, her face white.

'New guy,' Ben said. 'He's good—don't worry, I've known him for years. He's done a lot of this—he's a bit of a trauma specialist. But we need to get this pelvis rigid before we move Jem and he needs to go straight up to Theatre if we can't stop the bleeding here. You need to sign a consent form for that. Why don't you do that and then get a cup of tea—?'

'His pressure's dropping.'

Ben frowned and bent over the boy. 'OK, Jem, stay with us, come on, you're doing really well. Let's give him a 250-mil bolus of O-neg and we'll see if he stabilises. Kate, I don't suppose you know his blood group, do you?'

She shook her head, her face terrified. 'No. No idea. I'm O-positive, if that helps.'

'Cross-match results are up,' someone said. 'He's B-negative.'

B-negative? Through the roaring in his head, Nick heard Ben sigh harshly. 'Damn. We used all our stock this morning. I don't know if it's been replaced yet.' Ben's eyes flicked questioningly to Nick's, and he swallowed.

'I'm B-negative,' he confirmed, the last traces of doubt obliterated from his mind with this one small fact. 'So's Jack. We're both regular donors.'

Ben didn't miss a beat. 'OK. Nick, contact Jack and ask him if he's able to donate today, then we'll get Haematology to sort it. That'll give us two units, and we'll salvage his own in Theatre and recycle it and give it back to him, and we can use O-neg if necessary until we get more, but if we get the ex-fix on, the bleeding may well stop anyway.'

Or it might not. 'You can take two units from me,' Nick said, and he saw Kate turn towards him, heard the hitch in her breath as she waited for what he was going to say. Not that. Not out loud, but he met his son-in-law's eyes squarely, and Ben gave a brief, imperceptible nod of understanding.

A door flapped shut behind him, and Nick turned and looked straight into Jack's eyes.

'Kate, Dad—hi. What's going on?' he asked. 'I was out in cubicles—they said Jem was in here.'

'He is,' Nick said, and Jack looked at the X-rays, winced and glanced down at the child on the trolley.

'Hell,' he said softly. 'Poor little chap. What's the damage?' he asked Ben.

'Pelvis, for sure, and maybe abdominal and head injuries. We were about to contact you,' Ben told him. 'We're short of B-negative. Have you given blood recently?'

'Um—about three months ago? No—just before Christmas, so nearly four.' Jack sighed harshly and glanced at the clock. 'I've got a meeting I should be at and I'm already late. Can you call me if you definitely need me?'

'We definitely need you,' Nick said, his voice deliberately low so that only Jack could hear. 'He's your brother, Jack,' he added, and watched the disbelief like a shockwave on his firstborn son's face.

'Jeremiah? Kate's son? He's—?'

'My son,' Nick said softly, voicing the words in public for the first time, and beside him he felt Kate squeeze his hand. His words hung in the air between them for a moment, and Jack's face was suddenly expressionless.

'Well, we'd better roll our sleeves up, then, hadn't we?' he said after a long pause, and Nick let out his breath on a shuddering little sigh.

'Thanks,' he said, but Jack turned to him, his blue eyes like chips of ice.

'Don't thank me,' he said, his voice deadly quiet. 'I'm not doing it for you.' He turned back to Ben. 'Give me five minutes. I just want to make a couple of calls.'

'That's fine, we're using O-neg for now. You've got a little while. We'll save cross-matched blood until he's stable.'

He nodded curtly and walked out, slapping the door out of the way with his hand, and Nick closed his eyes and swallowed. He'd known it would come out at some time, he'd known it would be hard, but like this, with Jeremiah's life hanging in the balance—

'OK, what have we got?' a new voice asked, and a man strode in, a man they'd never seen before, with a soft, lilting Irish brogue and that dangerous blend of rakish charm and lethal good looks that would leave trouble in his wake.

Nick knew all about that. He'd been like that in his youth; it had gone to his head, and look where it had got him. He almost felt sorry for Josh O'Hara, the new A and E consultant, but maybe this man wouldn't make the same mistakes he had. He'd have to try hard to do worse.

He was bending over Jeremiah now, smiling at him. 'Hello, Jem, I'm Josh. I'm just going to have a quick look at your X-rays, and then we're going to send you to sleep and fix you, OK? That'll take away a lot of the pain for when you wake up.'

Jem made a feeble sound of assent, and beside him Nick heard Kate give a little sob.

Nick tightened his grip on her fingers. 'It's all right,' he said, reassuring himself as much as her. 'He'll be all right,' he repeated, and hoped to God it wasn't a lie.

Josh looked up and met their eyes. 'Are you the parents?'

They nodded, the irony of it striking Nick like a hammer blow. Of all the ways—

'OK. You need to sign a consent form, and then I think someone needs to take you to the relatives' room and give you a cup of tea.'

'I don't want a cup of tea, I want to be here with my

son!' Kate said adamantly. 'I'm a midwife, you don't need to mollycoddle me.'

'We don't need to scrape you off the floor, either, and it's a sterile procedure. You can stay till he's out, then you go.'

Nick put an arm round her rigid shoulders, squeezing them gently. 'He's right,' he said, fighting his instinct to argue, to stay. 'You shouldn't be here. Not for that. And someone needs to take a look at you.'

'I'm fine.'

'We don't know that. Nick's right, you need your neck checked, Kate,' Ben said gently, lifting his head to meet her eyes. 'And your feet. I gather they were trapped. Let us sort Jem out, and then while he's in Theatre I'll come and have a look at you, hmm? And in the meantime, go and have something hot to drink, and some biscuits or something. You're in shock.'

She'd signed the form by the time the anaesthetist arrived a minute later, and Kate clung to her son's hand, pressing it to her heart and murmuring softly to him as he drifted off, then Nick ushered her away, leading her out of the room and down the corridor to the relatives' room, his reluctant feet tracing the familiar path.

'You can wait in here—I'll bring you both some tea,' a nurse said with a kind smile. 'How do you take it?'

'Hot and sweet, isn't it?' Kate said shakily, trying to smile back, but Nick couldn't say anything, because the last time he'd been in this room had been in the horrendous minutes after Annabel had died, almost exactly five years ago.

It came flooding back the shock, the horror, the guilt. He should have realised she was ill, should have done something, but he'd been so tied up in the practice he'd scarcely noticed she was alive. And then, suddenly, she wasn't. She'd had a ruptured appendix, and Ben hadn't been able to save her.

And yet again the guilt and the senseless futility of it threatened to swamp him.

CHAPTER TWO

KATE cradled the tea in her hands and tried to force herself to drink it.

'I hate sugar in tea,' she said, and looked up at Nick, trying to smile, trying to be brave, but his face was shut down, expressionless, devoid of colour and emotion, and she felt the fear escalate.

'Nick? He'll be OK.' He had to be, she thought desperately, his stark expression clawing at her control and threatening to destroy it, but Ben had seemed confident, Josh also, and there was no talk of ifs or buts or maybes, so he would be OK. Wouldn't he?

'Nick?'

He sucked in a breath, almost as if he'd forgotten to breathe for a while, and turned his head to meet her eyes. 'Sorry, I was miles away.'

Miles away? When his son was under anaesthetic, having his pelvis stabilised with an external frame so they could try and stop the bleeding that was draining the life out of him? Where on earth had he been, miles away? And with that look in his eyes...

He scanned the room, his face bleak. 'I haven't been in here for years. It hasn't changed. Still got the same awful curtains.'

And then she realised. Realised what he was seeing, what

this must cost him, to be here with her, and her heart went out to him.

'Oh, Nick, I'm sorry,' she murmured, and he tried to smile.

'Don't be, I'm all right. It was five years ago.' And then he frowned. 'More to the point, how are you? Were you hurt? What was Ben saying about your feet? I didn't realise you'd been trapped in the car.'

'It was nothing—just a pedal. I'm fine.' Her smile was no more successful than his, she supposed, because he came over and sat beside her, searching her eyes with his.

'So what happened?' he asked.

She shrugged. 'I was picking him up from outside the high school. It was my fault—I parked on the right, hitched up on the kerb and rang him, and he ran up and got in, and I pulled back out onto the road. I couldn't see a thing—the rain was sheeting down, but there were no lights coming, and I remember thinking only a fool would be out in this without lights, so it must be clear, and I pulled out, and there was an almighty thump and the car slammed sideways into the car I was pulling out around, and the airbags went off and—'

She broke off.

It had been over in an instant.

There had been nothing she could have done at that point, no way she could have changed it, but for the rest of her life, with the stunning clarity of slow motion, she knew she would hear the sliding, grinding crash, the scream of her child, and the thump as the airbag inflated in her face...

'Ah, Kate,' he murmured, and she looked up, into dark, fathomless brown eyes that normally hid his feelings all too well. But not now. Now, they were filled with sympathy and something else she couldn't quite read. 'I'm sorry. It must have been horrendous.'

She nodded, looking away because if she didn't she'd lose

her grip on her emotions, and she couldn't afford to do that, couldn't afford to succumb to the sympathy in his eyes.

'I can't believe I didn't see him coming.'

'You said there were no lights.'

'I didn't see any, and I was looking, but—'

'Then it's not your fault.'

She gave a soft snort. 'Tell it to the fairies, Nick. I pulled out in front of a big, heavy off-roader when I couldn't see, and Jem could have been killed. How is that not my fault?'

His mouth firmed into a grim line.

'He must have been speeding, Kate.'

'Very likely. It doesn't absolve me of blame.'

'Don't,' he warned, his voice strained. 'Believe me, don't take on the blame for this. It'll destroy you.'

As his guilt over Annabel's death had nearly destroyed him? She bit her lip, trapped the words, looked at the clock. It had hardly moved, and yet they seemed to have been in there for ever.

'He'll be all right, Kate. He's in good hands.'

'I know.'

She gave him another little smile, and reached up to touch his cheek fleetingly in comfort. The day's growth of stubble was rough against her fingers, ruggedly male and oddly reassuring, and somehow his strength centred her. She had to stop herself from stroking her thumb over his cheek, backwards and forwards in a tender caress, the way she would with Jem. With anyone she loved. She dropped her hand hastily back into her lap. 'Are you OK?'

His smile was crooked. 'I'm the last person you should be worried about,' he said gruffly, but it wasn't true. She always worried about him—always had, always would, and running away wouldn't change that, she realised. And even though it was tearing him apart, he was here for her now, when she needed him the most, just as he had been on the night her husband James had died. And he needed her now, too, every bit as much as he had then. So, yes, she was worried about him. She could never rely on him, not in the long term, but she worried about him.

'Don't be silly,' she said with a little catch in her voice. 'I'm really grateful to you for coming. I know it's really hard for you, being here. All those memories. It was such a dreadful time for you, and I'm sorry to have to put you through it again.'

'It just caught me by surprise, coming in here again, that's all. All a bit too familiar.' His smile was crooked and didn't quite reach his eyes, and he rested his hand over hers. 'He'll be all right, Kate,' he murmured, his eyes reassuring, his touch steadying her tumbling emotions.

The unexpected tenderness brought a lump to her throat, and gently she eased her hand away before she crumbled. 'I'm sorry about Jack.'

He shrugged slightly. 'I knew he'd hate me for it, but it's not a problem. He's hated me before, I can live with it.'

It was a lie, even if he was trying to make himself believe it, and she felt herself frown. 'He's a good man, Nick. He'll come round. And he'll be good to Jem. They all will.'

He nodded, sighed, and stood up, thrusting his hands into his pockets as he crossed to the window and stood staring out into the rain. 'Oh, they will. They'll close ranks round him and take him into their hearts, all three of them. They're like that. They take after Annabel.' He glanced down at the table, at the mugs sitting there, the tea growing cold.

'You haven't touched your tea,' he said, and she let him change the subject and picked up the mug, giving him room, not crowding him. He hated emotion, and he was awash with it today, trying hard to hang together through all the horror of it. It was all right for her, she thought, her eyes welling. She could cry her eyes out and everyone would sympathise, but Nick—Nick had to stay aloof and distant, hold himself back, because for him, today was judgement day.

And, boy, would they be judging, and talking, and there would be plenty to say. Nick had been well and truly married twelve years ago, at the time of Jem's conception, and the good people of Penhally held no truck with infidelity. When they found out…

Not that it mattered now. The only thing that mattered now was that her son—their son, she corrected herself—survived this, and lived long enough for Nick to build a relationship with him. She wondered what they were doing to him at this precise instant, and decided she'd rather not know. Midwife or not, there were things one didn't need to see.

She pressed her hand against her heart, and realised it hurt. It was tender where the seat belt had tugged tight in the accident, pulling on her lumpectomy scar and the still fragile skin where the radiotherapy had burned it, and she suddenly felt very uncertain. Dr Bower had given her the all-clear from her breast cancer in January, but it was very much an 'it's OK for now' result, and there were no guarantees for the future.

And if anything happened to her, Jem would need Nick. Assuming he survived—

'Nick, drink your tea,' she said, slamming the brakes on that thought, and he sat down beside her again and picked up the mug and took a mouthful, toying with the biscuits, crushing them to dust between his fingers, crumbling them all over the table.

'Josh O'Hara's a friend of Jack's from London,' he said out of the blue. 'I gather he's red hot. Ben used to work with him as well. That's why he sounded him out about the vacancy. And Ben won't let anything happen to Jeremiah—'

The door opened and Ben came in, and she dropped her mug onto the table with a clatter, fear suddenly closing her throat.

'How is he?' she asked, barely able to find the words. 'Is he—?'

'He's stable, his blood pressure's low but holding, so Josh and the anaesthetist have taken him to CT now to rule out any other injuries, then he'll be going straight up to Theatre. And we need to check you over. Come on.'

She tried to stand, and suddenly realised how weak she felt, how uncooperative her legs were, how very long she'd been holding her breath. She wasn't really listening any longer. All she'd heard was 'He's stable', and her mind had gone blank, unable to take in any more than this one, most important, fact.

Relief was crashing through her, scattering the last shreds of her control; she sucked in some air, but it wouldn't come, not smoothly, not sensibly, just in little jerky sobs, faster and faster, until at last the dam burst and she felt Nick's arms close around her, holding her firmly against a broad, solid chest that felt so good, so safe that she wanted to stay there for ever, because if she leant on him, if she stayed there, then surely it would be all right...

Nick stood there for a second—scarcely that, but it felt like an age before he came to life again and his hands gentled, cradling her head against his shoulder, holding her against his heart as he rocked and shushed her.

She must be going through hell, he thought, and then it hit him that this wasn't just her son, but his, too. Emotions slammed through him one after the other, but he crushed them down. There'd be time for them later. For now, he just had to be here for Kate, for as long as she needed him.

'Why don't you go and let them take the blood?' Ben suggested, once Kate had stopped crying and been mopped up and taken through to X-Ray. 'I'll keep an eye on her.'

'Isn't Lucy expecting you home?'

He smiled again. 'She was—two hours ago. Don't worry, I've told her what's going on.'

'All of it?' he asked, his heart jerking against his ribs, but Ben shook his head.

'No. I thought I'd let you or Jack do that.'

'She'll be disappointed in me.'

'I don't know,' Ben said thoughtfully. 'Maybe a little, at first, but she's said before how well you and Kate get on, and she knows you went out with her before you met Annabel, so I don't think she'll be exactly surprised to know you had an affair. In fact, she said only the other week that you ought to get together, now you were both free.'

His laugh sounded hollow to his ears. 'I hope she's not holding her breath for that. Kate's going. She's handed in her notice—she's leaving Penhally.'

'Wow.' Ben frowned. 'That's a big step.'

He shrugged. 'She told me today—well, she left a letter for me.'

She hadn't even told him to his face. That hurt, but he put it on one side, like all the other feelings that were swamping him.

'I'm sorry,' Ben said, and Nick blinked in surprise and met his eyes.

'Why should you be sorry?'

'You tell me,' Ben said softly, and Nick looked away from eyes that saw too much.

'She's blaming herself. She said she didn't see any lights, and she pulled out.'

Ben accepted the change of subject without a murmur. 'Visibility was awful, apparently, and I gather the other guy not only didn't have his lights on but he was speeding significantly, according to witnesses. He wasn't wearing a seat belt, either, and the car wasn't taxed. He's in overnight for observation, and the police have been in to talk to him already. It definitely wasn't Kate's fault. I need to check her out. You go down to Haematology and I'll see you when you come back.'

He nodded, and walked quickly down to Haematology to give the blood they would process and give to Jeremiah later, after his surgery, after he was stable. God willing. Jack was standing at the reception desk waiting, and turned to him, his eyes raking over Nick's face.

'Are you OK?' he asked, and Nick nodded.

'Yes. Ben's taking a look at Kate.'

'Have you eaten recently?'

Nick nearly laughed. For a moment there, he'd thought his son was enquiring after his emotional well-being, but, no, he was checking that he was OK to donate.

'Lunch,' he said, trying to remember and recalling a sandwich of some sort. He'd left half of it, and it seemed a long time ago. It had been a long time ago. He should have eaten Hazel's fairings instead of leaving them for Mr Pengelly. 'They gave us tea and biscuits in A and E, but I didn't have them.'

'Here.' Jack handed him a small packet of biscuits from his pocket. 'Eat those, and get a drink from that water cooler, otherwise you'll pass out when they take the blood from you.'

And without another word Jack turned back to the desk and spoke to the haematology technician who'd just come to find him. Nick followed them, grabbing a cup of water on the way, and then lay in the next cubicle to his son, the curtain between them firmly closed, while the technician set up the intravenous line and started collecting his blood.

'Can you be quick? I need to get back,' he said, and she smiled.

'It's a good job you're a regular donor, Dr Tremayne,' she said tolerantly. 'Saves all the screening. I take it nothing's changed since the last time?'

'No, nothing.' Nothing except his youngest son nearly

dying and Kate deciding to leave the county. 'Take two units,' he insisted.

She tried to argue, but Jack's voice cut across them both.

'Just do it. It might keep him quiet. You can take two from me as well.'

'Are you sure? I don't like to, but our B-neg donors in the hospital have all been called on recently and there isn't any available until tomorrow. Stocks are really low at the moment; we've got O-neg but obviously this is better. You're not still working this evening, Mr Tremayne?'

'No. I've finished for the day and I've got a light day tomorrow. My registrar can cover me if necessary,' Jack answered.

'And you, Dr Tremayne?'

'I'm not leaving the hospital until I know Jem's all right.' Nick replied.

If he was all right. Hell, he had to be all right. There was so much to say to him, so much lost time to make up for. It would be the bitterest irony if now, when he was finally beginning to accept that Jem really was his son and realise what he meant to him, he lost him before he could tell him.

Nick rested his head back, closed his eyes and prayed as he hadn't prayed since the night Annabel had died.

He couldn't lose another member of his family, and neither could Kate. It just wasn't an option. He pumped his hand to speed up the flow, so he could get back to her side as quickly as possible...

'She hasn't got any fractures, but she's sore,' Ben said softly, taking Nick to one side when he returned to A and E. 'Her right ankle's got a nasty bruise, and she's whiplashed her neck slightly, and her chest is a bit tender where the seat belt cut in. The skin's still a bit fragile anyway, after the surgery and radiotherapy last year.'

He realised he didn't even know if it had been the left

or right breast, and asked—not that it made any difference, or was anything to do with him, but he just wanted everything straight in his head, trying to make order of the chaos of the day, and this was another brick in the wall he could straighten.

'Left,' Ben said, not even questioning his need to know that stupidly irrelevant fact. 'I wanted to keep her here for a bit, let her rest, but she won't hear of it. She's very shocked, though. I've given her some pain relief, but she wouldn't let me give her a sedative.'

'No. She wouldn't. Stubborn woman.'

Ben smiled tolerantly, and Nick gave a short, ironic laugh.

'Pot and kettle?' he said, and Ben chuckled.

'Go in and see her, she's waiting for you. And give me your car keys, I'll get it moved. It's obstructing the entrance and the ambos are getting cross.'

He handed over the keys, thanked Ben and went to see Kate.

How long could he be?

Ben had insisted she should lie there for a while and wait for Nick, and frankly she didn't have the strength to argue. Anyway, there was nothing she could do for Jem now except will him to be alive, and she could do that lying down in A and E as well as she could hovering outside the scanner room in Radiology.

Once Nick was back, she'd get up and go and sit there, waiting for news, but for now, she was lying wide-eyed, alert, her adrenaline running flat out, her pulse rapid, her throat dry.

'You're a mess, Kate Althorp,' she told herself, and closed her eyes. She wouldn't sleep. No way. But she could shut out the light.

* * *

She'd dozed off.

Or so he thought, but as Nick stepped into the cubicle, her eyes flew open.

'Is there any news?' she asked, her face worried, and he shook his head.

'No. I've just spoken to Ben, but they haven't heard anything. Josh is with him in CT. Are you OK to go down there now?'

She gave a humourless little laugh that cut him to the bone, and tried to smile. 'Sure. My right ankle hurts, but I've got some arnica gel in my bag, I'll put it on later. Let's go.'

'Want me to do it now?' he asked, wondering how he'd cope with touching her, smoothing his hand over her skin, feeling her warmth beneath his fingers and knowing she wasn't his to touch, to hold—to love?

Would never be.

'Not now. Later, maybe. I need to be with Jem.'

'I'll get a wheelchair,' he told her. 'Stay there.'

'Don't be ridiculous, Nick,' she said, swinging her legs down and wriggling her feet into her damp shoes with a grimace. 'I'm perfectly capable of walking. I'm fine.'

She wasn't. She wasn't fine at all, but she had guts. He tried to smile, but his own guts were strung tight. He tucked her hand in his arm so she could lean on him, and walked with her to Radiology, glad they were moving fairly slowly. He was feeling a little light-headed and wondering if his stubborn insistence on giving two units had been such a good idea after all. It was a quarter of his circulating blood volume—enough to crash his blood pressure into his boots. He ought to get something to eat and drink, but now wasn't the time.

'He'll be out in a minute, he's nearly done,' the receptionist told them, and they sat and waited, Kate suddenly even more nervous because of what the CT might show up.

She thought her stomach was going to turn inside out it was churning so hard, and the painkillers Ben had given her didn't seem to be helping. Well, they were helping, but not enough. She rolled her neck slightly to ease it, but it didn't work. It was because she was tense, coiled like a spring, poised for bad news.

'I can't sit here, I'm going to have to walk around,' she told Nick, pushing herself to her feet just as the doors opened and Jem was wheeled out by Josh and the anaesthetist. The radiologist came over to them, nodded to Nick and then turned to her.

'Mrs Althorp?'

'Yes,' Kate said, trying not to fall down and feeling Nick's firm hand on her waist holding her in place. She dragged her eyes from Jem and the gap in the blankets showing the frame holding his pelvis rigid, and leaned against Nick, grateful for the support, both physical and emotional, wondering what was coming, hardly daring to ask. 'How is he?' she managed, her throat tight.

'Stable. No damage apart from the fracture—he's been lucky, and there's no sign of a bleed from the head injury, so they're taking him straight up to Theatre now. You'll need to go up with him and sign the consent forms, if you haven't already done it, and I imagine you'll want to wait up there for news?'

She nodded and looked at Jem. She wanted to talk to him—touch him, just touch him so she could reassure herself he was still alive, but he was unconscious, still under anaesthetic. She leant over the trolley anyway, and rested her hand on his cheek briefly, reassured by his warmth but frowning at the bruises as they walked towards the lift.

'Jem? It's Mum,' she said softly. 'You're all right, my darling. You're going to be OK, can you hear me? I'll be waiting for you, OK? I'll be here, all the time. I love you—'

She cracked, and Nick hugged her to his side as they followed the trolley to the lift and went up with him. They watched him go through into Theatre, and then Nick guided her to the chair-lined recess, and the long wait began...

'So that's your father-in-law?'

Ben grunted in confirmation, and Josh watched him. 'Interesting undercurrents between him and the woman. I thought he was the kid's father at first. It took me a minute to work it out. He seems OK—bit distant, but supportive. I take it they're friends?'

Ben sighed and put down his pen, and Josh propped his hips on the back of the other chair and raised an eyebrow.

'She's a colleague as well. He's known her for years.'

Josh nodded. 'I know you didn't always get on with him. Jack mentioned that he could be...'

'Difficult?' Ben supplied, his smile wry, and Josh grinned.

'He probably wasn't quite as polite as that.'

Ben gave a grunt of grudging laughter. 'Yeah. But that's all behind us now.'

'Is it? I passed Jack on the way into Resus, and he was steaming down the corridor with a face like the Grim Reaper. I take it they'd had words?' Josh waited, but Ben obviously wasn't being drawn. He capped his pen and pushed his chair back, changing the subject.

'Nice job, Josh,' he said. 'The ex-fix. Very neat. You're going to be an asset to the department.'

He took the hint. 'Thanks. Let's hope I can convince them all.'

'Giving you a hard time?'

He shrugged. 'Some of them. Not all. I'm the new boy. They're suspicious.'

'Well, they don't need to be. I'll have a word.'

'No, leave it. I'll win them round—I'll bring in doughnuts and smile a lot, work a bit late, you know the routine. A little of the blarney thrown in for good measure...'

'Well, don't expect it to impress me, I know you better than that, and they won't be fooled by it. Stick to what you're good at. Save a few lives—that'll win them round.'

'I'll do that for an encore,' Josh said with a lazy grin, happy that Ben, at least, seemed pleased to have him there. Shrugging away from the desk and putting the Tremayne family out of his mind, he went off to conquer some of the sceptics.

How could the time pass so slowly?

Kate watched the hands crawl round the clock face—a minute, two. She shifted yet again on one of the padded plastic armchairs, resting her head back against the wall with a fractured sigh.

'He'll be all right, Kate,' Nick said, for the hundredth time, and she just nodded slightly and flexed her ankle.

It was enough to make her wince, and she felt him shift beside her.

'Give me the arnica gel.'

She handed it to him and pulled up her trouser leg a little, kicking off her shoe, and he squeezed a blob onto his fingers and crouched in front of her, so she could rest her foot against his lean, hard-muscled thigh. That was all the running and walking he did, mile after mile over the moors, trying to outrun his demons. She could feel the muscles flex beneath her sole as he shifted his position slightly, and the open neck of his shirt gaped so she could see the pulse beating in the hollow of his throat, hard and fast, driven by the adrenaline that must be coursing through his body as it was through hers.

She lifted a hand and laid it against his shoulder, and he went still. 'Thank you, Nick,' she murmured. 'For everything.'

'Don't be ridiculous.'

'I'm not. Nick, we need to talk.'

He squeezed more arnica gel onto his fingers and smoothed it gently over the top of her other foot where a small bruise was starting to show.

'About?'

'Did you get my letter?'

He said nothing for a moment, just kept rubbing her foot, round and round until the skin was all but dry, then he stood up again and washed his hands in the sink in the corner.

She wriggled her feet back into her shoes, wondering how long the leather would take to dry, how she could have got so wet. Standing in the rain, of course, watching while they'd cut Jem out.

'Nick?'

He dried his hands, then like a caged lion he started pacing, from one side of the small waiting room to the other, then back again, ramming his hand through his hair and rumpling it further. It suited him, she thought randomly. The steel grey threading through it made him look distinguished, setting off his strong features—the features Jem had inherited from him. He was going to be a good-looking man, her son—their son.

Nick's son.

Finally he stopped pacing, sucked in a long, slow breath and turned back to her, scanning her face for clues, but there were none. Her warm, golden-brown eyes met his calmly, giving nothing away, as usual. She never gave anything away unless she meant to, and then it was usually disappointment in him. 'May I ask why you're going?' he asked, his voice carefully expressionless.

'Why? I would have thought it was obvious, Nick. I can't just be here for ever waiting for you to sort yourself out. Did you think I would? That I'd stay, to let you see your son a few times a year, in carefully arranged, apparently casual circumstances, so you can keep in touch without having to tell him you're his real father? Or, more to the point, so you didn't have to rock the boat and tell your other kids that we made love while their mother was still alive?'

'Once,' he said flatly. 'Just once. It's not as if we had an affair, Kate.'

'No, you're right. It was nothing so premeditated, was it?' she acknowledged gently, as if he needed reminding about anything that had happened that hellish night. 'We just reached out, to someone we could trust, someone who could trust us. But we were married—well, I suppose technically I was probably widowed at that point, but you weren't. And we did make love.'

And they'd made a child. Until Ben had told him about the blood group, there had still been an element of doubt in his mind, of disbelief. But not now. Not any more.

He looked away from the shrewd, understanding eyes that saw too much. 'Neither of us was thinking that night.'

'And you've done your level best to avoid thinking about it ever since,' she murmured. 'So I'm going to make it easier for you. Easier for all of us. I'm taking Jem away, and we're starting a new life.'

'With Rob?' he made himself ask, even though he'd heard it was off, but maybe it was back on, maybe that was why. 'Is he going, too?'

A flicker of distress crossed her face. 'No,' she said quietly. 'He deserves better than me. I'm like you, Nick. Scarred, broken, emotionally bankrupt. I'm no good to anyone. He's a good man. He was very kind to me, and to Jem.'

He said nothing. After all, she was right. Rob Werrick was a good man, a decent man, who'd stood by her last year during her treatment for breast cancer, who'd supported her through the most dreadful days of fear and uncertainty, a role Nick had sorely wanted to play, but all he had been able to do was sit, isolated from her, and pray for her. And Rob was the man who'd taken Nick's son to his heart and made room there for him, when the man who was his father had found he was unable to do so.

'So was it you or him who called it off?' he asked in spite of himself.

'Me. He asked me to marry him, and I said no. I don't love him—I can't love him, not in the way he deserves to be loved.' Her brown eyes were reproachful, her voice tinged with sadness. 'So I'm going, and we'll start again, and we'll be fine.'

His heart felt as if it was being crushed in a giant fist, but if this was what she wanted, to go, to leave, then maybe she was right. Maybe it was for the best. Easier all round. And away from the shadow of this guilt they both carried, perhaps she'd find happiness with another man.

He ignored the little twist in his chest and nodded. 'You're right. If that's what you want, then go, Kate. I won't stop you—'

'You can't stop me, Nick.'

'True. What about Jem? Will I ever see him?'

She gave a mocking little laugh that gave his heart another little wrench. 'What about him? He'll be fine. He doesn't know you're his father, it hasn't done him any harm not to know, so it won't in the future. I'll tell him when he's eighteen. I can't stay here so you can ignore him at close range. Anyway, you don't see him now—why would this make any difference?'

'Don't be ridiculous—of course I see him,' he denied. 'I see him a lot.'

'Only if you can't avoid it. Seeing him reminds you of your human frailty, and you don't like that.'

He didn't. He hated the constant reminder of what they'd done that night, of how he'd betrayed Annabel, tarnished the memory of James. But that didn't mean he didn't want to watch the child grow up, make sure he was all right—

'How the hell am I going to explain it to my children? They won't understand.'

'You could tell them you're human?' she suggested softly, her eyes so wise, so—so damn knowing.

He gave a quiet snort. 'Oh, they know that.'

'And this is about what they think of you?' she said, her voice heavy with reproach. 'What about what Jem will think of you when he finds out that he doesn't matter as much as your other children—your proper children, all respectably born in wedlock? They're no different, Nick' she reminded him, her words still soft and yet flaying his skin off with their accuracy. 'Conceived in haste, every single one of them. Story of your life. Well, I don't want to be a part of it any more, of the carefully constructed illusion of reality you fool yourself with every day,' she said wearily. 'I'll work my notice, once Jem's better, but then I'm off, Nick, and you won't hear from me again. It's better that way.'

Was it? He wasn't sure. He was suddenly filled with a cold, nameless fear for the future—a future without Kate, and without the boy, this last, unacknowledged and yet still infinitely precious child who, it seemed, he'd managed to love in spite of everything.

He sat beside her, the chairs so close he could feel the warmth radiating from her body, feel the air move with every shallow breath as her chest rose and fell.

'I thought you wanted me to be in his life?'

'I do—but not like this, giving him fragments of yourself from time to time. He deserves more from you.' Her eyes suddenly filled with tears. 'I can't do this any more, Nick. I'm leaving, and that's an end to it. Please. Just let me go.'

Let me go…

He held her eyes, watched the threatening tears well, watched in despair as one slipped down her cheek and fell to the floor. She never cried. Before today, the last time he'd seen her cry had been the night he'd taken her into his arms and held her. The night Jeremiah had been conceived.

Swallowing the bitter taste of regret, he stood up and turned away.

How could he let her go?

He couldn't—but how could he make her stay?

CHAPTER THREE

HE SAT down again a while later, but not for long, pacing restlessly, ramming his hand through his hair again and again until she thought he'd tear it out.

And then the doors swung open and Lucy and Jack came down the short corridor towards them.

'How is he?' Lucy asked, looking at Kate, avoiding Nick's eyes as if she wasn't sure how to do this.

None of them, in truth, knew how to do this. They'd just have to feel their way through.

'Still in there. They stopped the bleeding, they're just plating his pelvis. He's been lucky, apparently—'

She broke off, wondering how on earth what had happened to her son could in any way be considered lucky, but then she felt Nick move closer, his hand on her shoulder, warm and reassuring despite their earlier words. Unable to resist the pull of that warmth, she dropped her head against his side, listening to the steady thud of his heart, and above it, the tension coming off them in waves, she could hear their quiet, fraught conversation.

'I'm glad you came,' Nick said, and she saw Lucy tense.

'I had to, Ben asked me to give you back your car keys. It's in the staff car park.' She dropped them in his hand, then shook her head. 'I'm not here for you, anyway, I'm here for a little boy who's apparently my brother. I don't know what to say to you. All that fuss when Mum died, but all the time you'd been carrying on behind her back—'

'Lucy, it wasn't like that. It was just once, right after the storm. Kate was distraught, I was distraught. It just—'

'Happened?' she said, her voice a little hard, unlike her usual self, but then she would be, Kate thought. None of them were themselves.

Nick let Kate go and moved away a fraction, and she lifted her head and looked up at Jack and Lucy.

'It wasn't just his fault. It takes two, remember. I was as much to blame. And just as married, really. James had only just died. There was no decent interval, believe me. It was inexcusable, but it never happened again.'

'Not with you, maybe, but were there others?'

Jack's question made Nick suck in a sharp breath.

'No,' he said firmly. 'There were no others. Apart from that one occasion when we were both beside ourselves with grief and I didn't really know what I was doing, I was never unfaithful to your mother. I loved her.'

Jack snorted. 'Strange way of showing it.'

'Jack, leave it,' Lucy said. 'It's irrelevant to this. But what I can't understand,' she went on after a slight pause, 'is why you've never told us he's our brother—why you've kept it a secret for, what, eleven years or more?'

'Two. I didn't know about Jem until two years ago,' Nick said, and their eyes swivelled to Kate.

'So, did you know?' Lucy asked incredulously. 'Before then, did you know? I mean, you are sure about this? That James wasn't his father? Have you had a DNA test?'

'James isn't his father. You've only got to look at him, Lucy. Look at his eyes. Look at his mouth. He was just like Jack's little Freddie when he was three or four, just like Jack and Edward at his age now. And, anyway, James and I had been having fertility investigations. We were talking about adoption. Why would I need a DNA test? Besides,' she added, 'if I needed any other proof, I have it now. James was A-positive.'

Lucy sat down hard, her eyes accusing and filled with tears. 'So—for eleven and a half years you've been convinced he was Dad's child, and you didn't tell him until two years ago?'

Kate reached out a hand, but Lucy snatched hers away, and she gave a fractured sigh and dropped her hand back in her lap. 'How could I? He was happily married, he had three other children—who was I to throw all that into chaos?'

Jack gave a short, hard laugh. 'The mother of his child?'

She met his accusing eyes. 'Exactly. I wasn't Nick's lover, I wasn't his wife—I was the mother of a child. And I did what I could to protect my child, and you, his other children, and his marriage. There was no point in upsetting all of that. Two wrongs don't make a right. And we've been fine. Jem's had a good life, settled, and I've given him all the love he could ever need.' Her voice cracked. 'And now he could be dying…'

She felt Nick sit down beside her again and slide his arm around her, there for her, giving her his strength and support—at least for now. 'It's OK,' he said softly, turning her head into his shoulder and cradling it gently. 'Don't cry, Kate. He'll be all right. It's going to be OK.'

Was it? She hoped so, but she couldn't for the life of her think how she'd cope if it wasn't.

She felt Lucy sit beside her, felt the gentle touch of her hand. 'Kate, I'm so sorry, I didn't mean to upset you, I'm just— It's a bit of a shock, that's all. And I'm so worried about him.'

'I know,' she whispered, patting Lucy's hand reassuringly. She loved Nick's daughter, she'd delivered her babies—she hated it that Lucy thought less of her now because of this, but it was only what she deserved. She'd given Lucy's father the means to commit adultery, and it was every bit as much her fault as his.

But for now her guilt was directed towards her son, lying there on the operating table, his life hanging in the balance, hoping that when they opened him up they didn't find anything unexpected.

She concentrated her mind on him, focused all her thoughts, willing him to pull through, to make it, to be all right. And then the door opened, and her heart stopped in her chest, eyes locked on the surgeon as he approached.

Nick got slowly to his feet, and Kate held her breath, unable to move until she knew he was all right, but he was, she could see that from the surgeon's smile as he pulled off his mask, and with a leap her heart started to beat again, the slow, dull thud threatening to deafen her.

He acknowledged Jack with a nod, then crossed to her, his hand extended.

'Mrs Althorp—I'm Martin Bradley. I've just finished operating on your son.'

She shook his hand on autopilot. 'How is he?'

'He's OK.' He perched on the chair beside her, taking Nick's place. 'I'm sorry I didn't have time to talk to you before we started, but I was already scrubbing in and I'm sure Ben Carter will have explained what we were going to do. Under the circumstances I didn't want to make him wait. Anyway, he's fine, he's come through the operation well, we've managed to fix the fractures and I think he'll get a very good result. He's broken the two bones at the front of his pelvis on the left, hence all the bleeding, but the pubic symphysis, the cartilage joint between the two halves at the front, wasn't disrupted so he'll be back on his feet quite quickly. We've sorted out the vascular damage, plated the fractures, and in fact it's all come together very neatly. It shouldn't give him any problems once it's healed in a few weeks.'

'So—he'll be all right? He hasn't got any nerve damage?'

'Not that we know of. His left sacroiliac joint might be sore for a while, but it wasn't displaced and I'm confident he should make a complete recovery. We'll know more later, but it's looking good at the moment. We're running whole cross-matched blood into him now, and we salvaged the free blood in his abdomen—that's gone off to the lab to be cleaned up so it can be returned to him if necessary, and then we'll do some tests and balance the blood components over the next twenty-four hours, but that's all pretty routine stuff. Any questions?'

'No. I just want to see him.'

'That's fine. If you think of anything, don't be afraid to ask. I'll be around for the next couple of hours, just in case there are any problems. Jem's in Recovery now, so you can come and talk to him. He's very drowsy, but he's come round and he's fine. I'm sure he'll be pleased to see you.'

Kate nodded, her body suddenly turning to jelly, and she was glad she was sitting down. Nick helped her up, his arm around her as they went through into Recovery, and it tightened as she stood by Jem's side, sucking in her breath at her first sight of him.

He was linked up to a mass of tubes and wires and drips, a monitor blinking on the wall behind him, and his poor bruised little face was so chalk-white against the pillow he almost disappeared on it.

She took his hand in hers, wondering at how small and fragile he looked—somehow so much more vulnerable, with his eyes shut and all the tubes and wires. Where was her lively, vibrant boy, his gangly limbs and eager enthusiasm carrying him through life at a hundred miles an hour? Where had he gone? She stroked his hair back from his bruised forehead with a shaking hand and bent to kiss it.

'Jem? It's Mum. I'm here, my darling, right next to you. You're going to be all right. You sleep now, OK?'

There was a small sound that could have been acknowledgement, and his fingers flickered in her hand. She squeezed them back, and he seemed to sigh and go off to sleep again, and she felt her legs start to buckle with relief.

But Nick was there, holding her up, giving her moral and physical support. She didn't want to rely on him, but there was something about him, like a rock, an anchor in a world that had gone mad, and she leant against him and let him hold her. Just for now, just while she stared at her son and let herself believe he might live.

'You won't get much out of him,' Martin Bradley murmured. 'He's heavily sedated, and we've given him some pretty hefty pain relief, but he should be more comfortable now his pelvis is stable.'

'So what happens now?' Nick asked, staring down at the injured child who looked so fragile amidst the plethora of tubes and wires and technology, and he shrugged.

'He'll stay here for a while—an hour or two? Just until we're quite happy that he's stable and we don't have to take him back into Theatre. Then he'll be in PICU—Paediatric Intensive Care—for the night. He doesn't really need to be there, but they've got the bed available and they'll be able to monitor him more closely overnight while we balance his bloods, so we might as well take advantage of it. He'll probably move to the ward tomorrow, and then he'll be there for a couple of weeks, I expect, while we get him up on his feet again, and then it's just a case of getting slowly stronger. We'll have to see. The plates and screws will have to come out at some point, as he's still got a lot of growing to do, but we'll worry about that in a few weeks or months. Anyway, I'll be around, so we'll talk again tomorrow if I don't see you later. And try not to worry. He's going to be all right, you just have to give it time.'

Kate wanted to smile, but her muscles didn't seem to work. She realised she was still leaning on Nick, and she straightened up, moving away a fraction, distancing herself. 'Thank you,' she murmured, and held out her hand. 'You've been very kind.'

He shook it firmly. 'My pleasure. I'm glad to see you've got someone with you—the whole Tremayne clan, no less, including Lucy. I haven't seen you for a while. Are you well?'

'Yes, very,' she said with a smile, but Kate could see it didn't reach her eyes. 'Busy. I've got two children now.'

'Yes, so Ben tells me. Well, it's good to see you again, and it's nice that Kate's got so many friends around her supporting her.'

Nobody contradicted him, and he left them alone, nothing to break the silence but the soft beeps and hisses from the instruments, and the distant ringing of a telephone in another room.

Lucy broke the silence first.

'Um—I ought to go. I've left Ben with the children, and Annabel's had a cold, so she's a bit fractious, and Josh is teething, but keep in touch.'

'Yes, make sure you do that,' Jack agreed. 'I should go, too, I haven't seen the kids at all today, and I've only seen Alison under the edge of the duvet, so I'd better go home before they can't remember who I am. I'll come up tomorrow and see Jem, but if there's any change in the meantime, Kate, give us a ring, OK? Or if there's anything we can do?'

'Of course I will,' she promised, and they walked out, shoulder to shoulder, Jack putting his hand against Lucy's back to escort her through the door. And then it swung shut behind them and Nick let go of some of the tension that had held him for the last few hours and looked down at Kate with a fleeting smile.

'I told you he'd be OK.'

She dredged up a smile. 'Of course you did. I just didn't dare believe you.'

'Do you believe me now?'

'I might be starting to,' she admitted, and looked back down at Jem, her face drawn and fraught. 'You don't have to stay, Nick.'

Was she mad? 'Of course I'm staying. You can't believe I'd leave you alone now.'

'Why not? You heard the surgeon, he's out of danger. You don't need to be here, you've got to work tomorrow.'

'No. I'm not leaving you, Kate. I'm here for you, for both of you, for as long as you need me.'

She met his eyes, and they seemed sincere, but she'd thought that thirty-something years ago, and he'd left her. Left her and married Annabel when she'd become pregnant with the twins. 'I can't lean on you, Nick. I won't let myself. Every time I do, every time I think I dare, you let me down.'

'I won't let you down. I promise you, Kate, I won't walk away from this.'

She stared at him, at the serious expression on his face, the conviction in his eyes, in his voice. Dare she trust him? 'You always walk away,' she said at last.

'I didn't the night James died.'

She gave a soft huff of laughter and shook her head. 'No, you didn't, did you? Maybe it would have been better if you had.' But then she wouldn't have had Jem, and her life would have been empty and pointless. And she needed him now.

'I know I've let you down,' he said softly. 'I know I've let Jem down. But I'm here now, and I'll stay here for as long as you need me, and I'll do whatever I can to help you. Just give me a chance.'

She shrugged and looked away. 'I can't stop you. But I can't lean on you, either. I have to do this on my own.'

'No, you don't,' he said, trying to inject something into his

voice that she could believe in. 'And I'll prove that to you.'
Even if it took years. A lifetime.

Her shoulders were drooping, and his heart went out to
her. Poor Kate. She was exhausted, he thought, exhausted
and shocked and traumatised, and it was late. 'You ought to
eat,' he coaxed gently. 'Keep your strength up.'

She shook her head. 'I can't eat. Not when he's like this.
Maybe later. I could murder a drink, though. I wonder when
they'll move him to PICU?'

'An hour or so? Shall I go and get you something? Tea,
coffee?'

'Tea would be lovely. Do you mind? I really don't want to
leave him.'

'On one condition—you sit down beside him and rest, and
you eat something if I bring it back.'

'You're a bully, do you know that?' she said, but she was
smiling, an exhausted, rather watery smile that in a heartbeat
could have morphed into tears, and she sat obediently in the
chair he put there for her.

'I'm looking after you is what I am,' he said, and headed
for the door. 'Any special requests?'

'Tea. And a sandwich, if I must, but no cheese. I'm going
to have nightmares as it is.'

'OK. Back in five.'

He went through the door and down the stairs, pausing
halfway because he felt suddenly light-headed. Damn. That
was giving two units of blood, not drinking anything like
enough to replace the lost fluid or taking in any food—apart
from Jack's biscuits, he'd had half a cup of tea, a cup of water
and whatever he'd had in A and E in the relatives' room, and
that was all since his miserable half-sandwich and instant
coffee at lunchtime. And it was—good grief—a quarter past
midnight.

And the café, when he got there, was shut, with a sign
directing him to the main canteen some distance away.

There was a vending machine, and he pulled some coins out of his pocket with fingers that were starting to shake violently, and put them into the machine, pressed the button for a bottle of sports drink to boost his fluids and blood sugar, and twisted the cap to loosen it. And it sprayed him.

He swore, twisting it shut again, and suddenly it was all too much. He dropped his head forwards against the vending machine and resisted the urge to slam it into the gaudy metal case. Head-banging wouldn't cure anything.

'Is it broken again?'

The voice was soft and feminine, and he lifted his head and stared vaguely at the woman.

'Um—no. Sorry. Did you want the machine?'

'No, it's OK.' She tilted her head on one side, looking at him keenly. 'Are you all right?'

He opened his mouth to say yes, and then stopped. The woman was slender and delicate, but curvy in all the right places. She was probably younger than Lucy, her dark hair twisted up into a clip, and there was compassion and under-standing in her emerald-green eyes.

'A friend's little boy's just been admitted,' he said, gag-ging on the half-truth. 'They had a car accident. His pelvis is fractured. I was getting us something to eat, but...'

She frowned. 'I'm so sorry. Has he been to Theatre?'

'Yes—yes, he's had an op to plate it, and he's OK, he's in Recovery at the moment and then he's going to PICU, but he shares my blood group, and it's B-negative, and stocks were very low, so they took two units from me, and...'

'And you haven't eaten or drunk anything because you've been too stressed, and the café's shut, and now the bottle's got its own back on you.'

He smiled. 'Something like that.' He held out his hand, then looked at it ruefully and smiled again as he withdrew it. 'Sorry—it's a bit sticky. I'm Nick Tremayne.'

She flashed him an answering smile. 'Jack's father—of

course. You look just like him. I'm Megan Phillips. I'm a paediatrician, so I'll be looking after your friend's son. What's his name?'

'Jeremiah Althorp. Jem.'

'I'll keep an eye out for him.'

'Thanks.' He tried to unscrew the drink again, but his fingers were shaking so much now he fumbled the lid and it fell to the floor. She picked it up and handed it back to him.

'Come on, you need to sit down. Let me go and get you something to eat.'

'No, I couldn't.'

'Well, I'd rather you did, otherwise I'll have to pick you off the floor on the way to the canteen. I'm going to buy myself some sandwiches. Why don't I get you some? I can bring them up to you, I'm going that way.'

'I couldn't ask you to do that.'

'You didn't ask, I offered.' Her smile was gentle. 'Chicken salad? Ham and cheese? Tuna? There isn't a fabulous choice, I'm afraid.'

'Anything. One without cheese for Kate, and I don't care what I have, whatever's going. And two teas, if you've got enough hands. You're a star. Here, take some money.' He pulled a twenty-pound note out of his wallet and handed it to her.

She took the note out of his hands and smiled. 'I'll come up in a minute. Drink some of that before you go back up there, and I'll come and find you.'

He took her advice, downing half the cloyingly sweet drink, and after a moment he began to feel better. Less shaky and light-headed. He made his way slowly back upstairs, and when he pressed the buzzer a young woman let him back in, waving goodbye to Kate as she left the room.

'Oh—were they shut?' Kate asked, eyeing his all but empty hands in surprise.

'Yes. I was going to the main canteen, but I met someone. A paediatrician, of all things. She's gone to get something for us. She said she was heading that way anyway, so I gave her a twenty-pound note. At least I hope she was a paediatrician.'

Kate chuckled softly. 'Nick, you're so cynical.'

He gave a weary smile and offered her the bottle.

'Do you want some of this? I saved you some.'

Kate eyed him thoughtfully. 'No, I loathe it, thanks, you have it. What was her name?'

'Megan Phillips, Who was that, by the way, who let me in?'

'Jess Carmichael. She's a counsellor. She heard I was here and she's been working late so she popped in. I saw her for a while after my lumpectomy. She was lovely. Really kind to me. She gave me a lot of support when I needed it the most.'

He felt a little stab of pain to accompany the familiar guilt. 'I'm glad.'

Kate met his eyes, her own holding that particular brand of gentle reproach that she reserved for him. 'I could have done with your support then, too, Nick.'

He looked away, swamped with regret, but what could he have done? 'You had Rob,' he reminded her.

'That didn't exclude you.'

Oh, it did. 'I didn't want to get in the way,' he said. 'He seemed genuinely decent, very fond of you—I thought you might stand a chance of happiness, a future for you and Jeremiah with a man you loved. A man who could love you back. I didn't want to get in the way of that.'

'You wouldn't have done,' she reasoned, remembering how it had felt when he'd kept his distance—Nick, the only man she'd ever really loved, keeping her at arm's length when all she'd really wanted was for him to hold her and tell her it would be all right. Tell her that if it wouldn't, he'd be there for their son. 'You wouldn't have been in the way,' she told him, realising, even as she said it, that of course he would have been.

'You know that's not true,' he said gently, and she shook her head.

'Nick, I needed you—even if you weren't with me, I needed to know that you cared, but you never said a thing.' She laughed, but it came out slightly bitterly with the remembered hurt. 'I thought you'd brought me flowers, but they were from everyone at the practice, you were just the messenger.'

He gave her a wintry smile. 'Would you have accepted them if they'd been from me?'

And then she knew—realised, with sudden insight, that they had been from him—been his idea, his choice, probably even paid for himself. And him bringing them had been the nearest he could get to telling her that he was thinking of her, worrying about her.

That he cared.

He hadn't let her down, he'd just given her space, stepped back out of Rob's way. And she'd misunderstood.

Her eyes filled, and she nodded, just once. 'Yes,' she said. 'Yes, I would have accepted them. Thank you.'

'Don't thank me,' he said gruffly. 'I did nothing—just as I always do nothing. If I'd acknowledged Jeremiah sooner, if I'd done what I should have done, then I would have been supporting you financially, making sure you had a safer car, a car with side impact protection instead of a little tin box that crushed like an eggshell—'

'No!' she said, reaching for his hand, clutching hold of it so he couldn't avoid her, her voice no more than an urgent whisper in the quiet room. 'I won't let you do that! This is not your fault. This is my fault, my guilt, and I'm damned if I'll let you have it and add it to the endless layers that you hide behind! I had the crash, I bought the car—'

'Because of me,' he returned stubbornly. 'Because I didn't accept that he was my son. Because I was letting you down again, hiding from the truth, hoping it would go away, but it won't, will it? But you are, and you're taking my son with you.'

And he didn't want her to, he realised. He really, really didn't want her to.

He turned his back on her, and saw Megan Phillips at the door, beckoning to him. 'Looks like our food's here,' he said curtly, and went out.

Kate followed him, and the woman smiled at her.

'You must be Nick's friend. I'm Megan Phillips, one of the paediatric registrars,' she said. 'I'll be looking after Jem when he's in PICU and on the ward later. How's he doing?'

'He's all right. He's going to be all right. Mr Bradley said it's just routine now,' she said, trying to inject some conviction into her voice, and as she did so she realised that for the first time she believed that he might be all right, that he might turn the corner, might actually make it, and the relief nearly took her legs out from under her.

Megan handed over the food she'd brought up for them, gave Nick his change and then left them to it. Nick opened Kate's sandwich and handed it to her, pushing her into a chair.

'Eat that before you collapse,' he ordered gruffly, ripping open another packet and demolishing the contents, then he drained his tea and dropped his head back, rolling it towards her with a sigh. 'You're not eating, Kate. Come on. You need to keep your strength up.'

'I can't eat.'

'Come on, you promised.'

She nodded. She had, and he wouldn't give up until she'd eaten the darned sandwich, she knew that, so she took a bite, and he stopped watching her like a hawk and glanced at his watch.

'I need to make a call.'

'A call?' she asked, realising she hadn't told her mother yet. Or Chloe, or Rob. She ought to tell them Jem was all right—but not now. Not in the middle of the night. She'd call them tomorrow—except…

'Oh, Nick, the dog. I need to make arrangements. I hadn't even thought about it.'

'It's OK. Oliver said not to worry, they'll sort it.'

'Bless them. They're so kind.' She sighed with relief, then looked at her watch. 'Nick, it's awfully late. Who are you ringing?'

'Edward.'

His other son, currently in South America and still, presumably, unaware. 'Oh. Oh, Nick.' She reached for his hand and he squeezed hers reassuringly.

'Hey, I'm fine. I'll be back in a minute. Eat, and have some tea. It's just the right temperature.'

She nodded, and forced herself to finish the sandwich and drink some of the tea before going back into Recovery to sit by Jem's bedside.

They'd been monitoring him constantly, checking him every few minutes, and as she went back in, they told her he was ready to go through to PICU.

'We'll find you a bed if you like—are you staying?' the nurse who was moving him asked her, and she nodded.

'Yes—if I can. I'll sit in the chair beside him, though. I don't need a bed.'

'We'll see. Let's take him and get him settled, and you can decide then, but he's stable now and he'll sleep all night; if you take my advice, you'll get your head down, because he'll need you when he wakes up and being the parent of a sick child is very wearing. You'll need your rest if you're going to be any good to him.'

Sensible advice, but she wasn't happy to take it. She wanted to be beside Jem, couldn't bear to leave his side, and even if she did, she didn't think she'd sleep.

'Kate, you were in the accident, too, you need to rest,' Nick said firmly when she continued to protest to the PICU nurse after he was settled. 'I'll sit with him. Go and have an hour, at least.'

'Half an hour,' she conceded, giving in because she knew it made sense and she was at the end of her tether. And the nurse was right—if she was going to be any use to Jem, she needed some sleep. 'I could do with lying down. What about you? Are you feeling better? Less shaky since you ate?'

'I'm fine,' he said, telling her nothing, as usual.

'Did you get hold of Edward?'

He shook his head. 'Go on, go and lie down. I'll get you if there's the slightest change.'

'Promise.'

'I promise,' he said, and she didn't know why, but she believed him. Maybe because she had no choice. Or maybe because this time, at least, she knew she could trust him?

So she went, escorted to a tiny room nearby just big enough for a chair, a little bedside locker and a bed made up with crisp white hospital linen. She'd never been more pleased to see a bed in her life. Her neck was a little sore, she had a killer headache, probably from the stress, her ankle was aching where the pedal had been squashed into it and she was emotionally exhausted.

She took some of the painkillers Ben had given her, then crept under the covers with a shaky sigh. Oh, that was better. Half an hour of this and she'd be able to cope again. Rolling to her side, she closed her eyes and lay there in the quiet room, and as the tension drained out of her, the only thing that had held her together up to now, she gave a tiny sob and tears leaked silently out of the corners of her eyes and dribbled down onto the pillow as she lay there.

Jem was all right. He'd be all right. He would.

She told herself the same thing, over and over again like a mantra, and gradually she fell into a shallow, restless sleep.

CHAPTER FOUR

NICK closed the door softly and stood looking down at her.

He didn't want to wake her, but he'd promised her he would, and she'd had over three hours, not just the half hour she'd agreed to.

But she was sleeping so deeply, curled on her side with one hand tucked under her cheek, and she looked defenceless and vulnerable. He perched on the hard plastic chair by the bed and watched her sleep for a moment, then with a quiet sigh he leant forwards and stroked her hair. She didn't stir, and he let his hand fall to the pillow.

And frowned. It was wet, and in the soft glow from the bedside light he could see a damp stain under the edge of her cheek, below her eye. Salt trails had dried across her temple, and down over her nose from the other eye, and he realised she'd been crying in her sleep. He closed his eyes and took a slow, steadying breath, then touched her again.

'Kate?'

Her eyes flew open, and she started to sit up. 'What is it? What's wrong?'

'Nothing,' he said hastily, kicking himself for scaring her. 'It's all right, he's fine. He's asleep, but you asked me to wake you.'

She let her breath out on a shaky little sigh, and dropped

back against the pillows. 'Oh. Sorry. I must have dozed off—What time is it?'

'Twenty to five.'

'Five!'

She sat up again, pushed back the covers and slid to her feet, swaying slightly. 'Steady,' he murmured, standing up and putting his arms around her to support her, and she rested her head against his shoulder with a sigh.

'How's your neck?' he asked, and she gave a little shrug.

'OK.'

He was pretty sure it wasn't. A bang hard enough to do that to Jem must have shaken her up, and he slid his hand carefully around the back of her neck and massaged the taut, tired muscles under the soft waterfall of dark hair. She shifted so her forehead was propped against his chest, just above his heart, and if he'd bent his head a fraction he could have dropped a kiss on her hair.

But he wouldn't. Of course he wouldn't. She wouldn't want it, and he wouldn't embarrass her by doing anything so stupid, but he held her head, his hand curved protectively round it, steadying her as his fingers worked slowly, gently on the muscles.

'Better?' he asked, and she nodded slightly, so he eased back and let her straighten before he moved away. 'Go and sit with him and I'll get us a coffee. Do you want anything else?'

'Tea. Tea would be lovely, and maybe a pastry or something. Thanks, Nick.'

'Any time,' he said, and backed away, leaving her to straighten her clothes and freshen up while he made the round trip to the canteen. He could do with stretching his legs, and a change of scene wouldn't hurt after hours of staring at his son's bruised and swollen face and wondering how the hell to tell him he was his father.

More to the point, wondering what Jeremiah would make of the news. He suspected not a lot. All in all, it was probably shaping up to be another thoroughly bloody day…

She sent Nick to lie down when he got back with the hot drinks and pastries, and he nodded and went without a word. He looked exhausted, she thought. Drained and stressed and emotionally threadbare.

She'd never seen him like this, even when he'd lost Annabel. He desperately needed a shave, and for a man who usually dressed so fastidiously, he was falling apart. His shirt was creased and open at the neck, the tie long gone, and his usually immaculate suit was crumpled and weary.

And despite it all, he was still the best-looking man she'd ever seen, the only man she'd ever really wanted. Apart from necessity he hadn't left her side since he'd arrived in Resus, and she didn't know how she would have got through it without him.

Although, of course, even though the biggest hurdle had been overcome in that Jeremiah was still alive, there was still the next obstacle to deal with, the one they'd been avoiding now for years, and she had no idea how Nick would be when the time came. One thing she knew for sure, he couldn't bottle out now, and maybe it wasn't the right time to go away. Her letter to the PCT was still in her bag, waiting for her to post it after she'd picked Jem up, only of course that had never happened, and now…

Oh, what on earth should she do? It had been complicated enough before this, but now…

She sipped her tea, hands cradling the paper cup, fingers tracing the ribbed cardboard holder round it, chafing it rhythmically as she sat with glazed eyes fixed on her sleeping son, watching the slow rise and fall of his chest, the occasional flutter of his eyelids, the trace of his heartbeat on the monitor, and prayed that when the time came, he could forgive them both for what they'd done to him.

They woke Jem at six, when they came to check his obs, and he smiled at her a little wanly. She'd never been so pleased to see his smile in her life.

'Mum,' he croaked, and she felt her eyes well with tears.

'Hello, darling. Good morning.' She leant forwards and took his free hand, the one that wasn't wired up to the drip, and kissed his bruised cheek gently. She'd studied his notes, and he'd had several units of blood overnight. She wondered if any of them had been Nick's, if his father's blood was now circulating in his veins. Or Jack's.

Like blood brothers cutting themselves and swapping blood, but on a grander scale and one-way. Would it bring them all closer? She hoped so. Apart from her mother in Bristol, and James's brother, the man Jem called Uncle John, there was no other family. It would be nice for him to have the family he should have had all along, but she wasn't going to make assumptions. Maybe they wouldn't want that level of involvement. She couldn't blame them. And there was still that hurdle to overcome, of course.

She stroked her thumb lightly over the back of his hand, and his fingers tightened a little. 'What time is it?'

'Six in the morning.'

'Oh.' He thought about that for a moment, then gave a tiny sigh. 'Can I have a drink? My throat's sore and my mouth's really dry.'

She glanced up. He was still nil by mouth, but she could give him a mouthwash. She spoke to the nurse, and a minute later she was swabbing his lips with the cool liquid, wiping away the dried secretions so he'd be more comfortable. 'Better?' she asked, and he smiled and nodded.

'Mmm. I'm sore all over, Mum.'

Her heart contracted. 'I bet you are, my love. You've

been through the wringer. Do you remember what happened yesterday?' she asked him softly.

He shook his head. 'No. The last thing I remember was making you a pot.' He frowned. 'Did I tell you I'd made you a pot?'

She nodded, thinking it might have been the last thing he'd done, the last thing he'd said to her, and she struggled not to cry. 'Yes, you did. A yellow one. I'm looking forward to seeing it. Do you remember me picking you up? Or the helicopter?'

He shook his head. 'Helicopter? No. I don't remember anything after making the pot. Did I go in a helicopter?'

'Yes. The air ambulance brought you here.'

'And I don't remember,' he mumbled, looking disgusted. 'I've always wanted to go in a helicopter. So what happened to me? Why am I so sore? Did we have a car accident?'

'Yes. I pulled out, and—'

She broke off, just as Nick appeared on the other side of the bed. 'Someone was going too fast,' he said firmly, 'and ran into the side of the car. It was his fault.'

'Oh,' he said, but she could see he was flagging. 'I can't believe I don't remember the helicopter,' he mumbled drowsily, and then looked at Nick and his brows clumped together in a little frown. 'Uncle Nick, why haven't you shaved today?'

She heard the quiet rasp as he scrubbed his hand over his jaw. Emotions chased across his face, and he pressed his lips together briefly. 'I haven't had a chance, I've been here all night,' he said. 'We both have.'

'Really? Why?'

Because you were sick. Because we thought you were going to die—

Kate met his eyes, and Nick reached out and brushed his knuckles over his son's thin, pale cheek and tried to smile. 'We were worried about you. You've been pretty sick. You had to have an operation.'

'Why did I need an operation? I don't really understand. I'm just really sore all over and I can't move, it hurts too much.'

Her fingers tightened involuntarily. 'I know. The surgeon will come and see you later—he'll explain. You had some broken bones, and they had to fix the ends together, to keep them still so they can heal and stop them hurting.'

He frowned. 'I can remember it hurting,' he said slowly. 'Much worse than this. And Ben—was Ben there?'

'Ben was there,' Nick confirmed. 'Don't worry about it, it's all over now and you're on the mend. You just need to rest and get well again, and then you'll be able to go home.'

'When?'

Kate swallowed. 'Not for a little while.'

His face fell. 'I'm going to miss the rest of holiday club, aren't I?' he said, looking worried, and she nodded.

'I'm afraid so. You could be in here for a few weeks.'

'Oh. Can Matt get my pot for you? Will you ask him?'

'You can ask him yourself. I'm sure he'll come and visit you soon.'

She saw Nick stiffen, but she couldn't pander to his feelings. Rob and his son Matt were an important part of Jem's life, and although she wasn't going to marry Rob, she wasn't going to avoid him, either, or his son. For Jem's sake, he needed to keep some continuity in his life.

Nick would just have to get over it.

Martin Bradley came to see Jem just before eight, and decided he could be moved into a side room on the paediatric ward just down the corridor as soon as it was cleared.

'You're doing really well, we're very pleased, so you can have a nice room to yourself for a few days so you can rest quietly until you're feeling a bit brighter, then we'll move you down into the other ward with kids of your own age, to give you some company. I'm going to increase your pain relief, because you're obviously quite sore, and once you're a bit more comfortable you'll feel a lot better.'

'Thanks,' Jem murmured, and his eyes flicked past Kate to the door, and he grinned weakly. 'Hey, Ben,' he said, and Ben came into the room and perched on the end of the bed.

'Hi, tiger. So, how is he, Martin? Will he live?'

'Oh, I reckon. Nice work, that pelvic fixator, made my job a lot easier. Did you do it?'

'No, that was Josh O'Hara. He's going to be a real asset. I had a look at the X-rays—it's looking good.'

'Mmm. It went back nicely. I'm pleased. Well, I'll leave you all to it. I'll catch up with you later, Jem.'

'So, how's it feeling, young'un?' Ben asked, and the boy shrugged.

'Sore.'

'Yeah, I'll bet. Still, you'll soon be up and about. Look on the bright side, you won't have to go to school for a few weeks.'

Kate frowned. Of course he wouldn't. And that meant she wouldn't be able to go to work, because there was no way she was leaving him with anyone else until he was better.

'Kate, don't worry, they'll get cover,' Nick said softly, reading her mind. 'I'm going to have to go in and sort it all out shortly, but you're not to worry, it'll be fine.'

She nodded. Of course it would be, but there were so many patients she wanted to be there for—Gemma was a few days overdue now and she didn't want to hand her over at this stage; she was one of their own, a practice nurse who was married to one of their GPs, Sam Cavendish, and Kate hated the fact that she'd have to bail on them at this stage. And there was a woman she'd seen—heavens, only yesterday—who she'd been a bit worried about. She couldn't even remember her name, but Chloe would sort it for her. As the only other midwife based in the practice, she'd have to.

'Nick, I need to speak to Chloe. There's a patient—'

'I'll get her to come and see you. She'll want to, anyway. They all will.'

Of course they would. They were a fabulous bunch of people, and she didn't know how she would have got through the last year without their support. She nodded, and turned back to Ben, who was making Jem laugh weakly with a dreadful joke. She smiled at him, and he winked and stood up.

'I need to get back to work, but I just thought I'd come and touch base. And Lucy'll be in later. She's going to leave the kids with me at lunchtime and slip up for a minute. You might want to shave by then.'

His teasing eyes met Nick's, and Kate thought she could read reassurance and support in them. Had Lucy come round? Maybe Ben had been able to listen to her and let her talk it all through last night, and maybe she'd softened her stance a little. Goodness, she hoped so. She didn't care if Lucy never forgave her for her part in it, but that she shouldn't forgive Nick—that was unthinkable.

She was his little girl, the apple of his eye, and he adored her. He'd be gutted if there was a permanent rift between them.

And then, when Ben had hardly left the room, Jack came in and grinned at Jem and perched on the end of the bed where Ben had sat.

'Hi there, kiddo. How're you doing?'

'OK. Bit sore.'

'I'll bet.' Jack glanced up at his father, and winced at the state of him. 'Dad, you look like a tramp. I think you need a shower and a shave. I've got a clean shirt here—do you want it?'

'No, it's OK, I'm going to go shortly and sort some stuff out at the surgery, so I'll have a shower then. Thanks, anyway.'

'Don't thank me, I just didn't want you scaring the children,' he said, but this time his voice was kinder, less condemnatory than the last time he'd told his father not to thank him, over the blood donating issue, and Nick gave a wry smile.

After a few moments of banter, Jack, too, left them alone, and it wasn't long before the nurses came to move Jem through to the paediatric ward.

'All ready to go?' the staff nurse asked cheerfully, and he nodded as they kicked the brakes off the bed and wheeled it through the door, down a corridor and then into a bright, sunny room off the children's ward that looked out over the gardens below.

'There are ducks down there,' Kate told him, peering out of the window and trying to find something normal to talk about as they sorted out his oxygen and monitoring equipment and pushed his locker back into place. 'A mother duck and some ducklings. You'll be able to see them when you can move around a bit more.'

'How many ducklings?' he asked, but she couldn't really tell.

'At least five. Not sure. We'll count them together later. They can't go anywhere, they're in a courtyard.'

'What, trapped?'

'Until they can fly. I expect someone's looking after them, but they'll be safe from any cats and foxes, at least.'

'Mmm.'

His eyelids were wilting, and it was obvious he was still very far from well. The move from PICU to the little side room had been more than enough for him, and Nick glanced at his watch. Ten-fifteen, give or take.

'I need to go to the surgery, sort a few things out, and if you're staying, you could do with some clothes and wash things, and some stuff for Jeremiah. Give me your keys, I'll sort it.'

She stared at him blankly. 'I haven't got my keys,' she said slowly. 'They must be in the car still.'

'Has anyone else got a key?'

She nodded. 'Yes. Chloe. Take her with you, she'll know what to get. And tell her I'm sorry about Bruno. If she can't manage, then I'll have to—'

'I'm sure they can manage the dog between them,' he said reassuringly. 'They said you weren't to worry. I'll be as quick as possible, ring me if you need to or if you think of anything specific you need.'

'Thanks.'

He found his car in the staff car park, and drove straight to the surgery, even though he was desperate for a shower and a change of clothes. There was a tie in his jacket pocket, and for a moment he contemplated it, but he was in a hurry now. He probably should have gone home, but for some reason he just needed to be here, amongst his friends, and it was nearly eleven, so with any luck the patients would have gone by now so they didn't have to see him looking like this. He walked in, straight up the stairs past a couple of waiting patients and the startled receptionist, ignoring their concerned questions, and into the staffroom.

It was crowded, and they all turned and stared at him, Sam Cavendish getting to his feet and breaking the silence first.

'Nick! How is he?'

'He's…' He couldn't finish, couldn't find the words, and Chloe gasped and covered her mouth with her hand. 'No! He can't be—'

He shook his head. 'No. He's all right,' he said hastily, and there was a collective sigh of relief. 'He's stable now and out of Intensive Care. It's been…um…'

He didn't know what to say, but they were clustered around him, gathered there as if they'd been waiting, and he lifted his head and met their eyes, seeing the love and concern and support there for him, for Kate, and for Jeremiah. And there was only one thing that mattered, one thing he needed to tell them, these people who were his friends, first and foremost, although they might well not be when they knew.

'It's been a bit of a worry, but it looks like he's going to be all right,' he said, and then he added, 'Actually, we're both going to need some help in the next few weeks with cover. There's something you should know, something I'd rather didn't leave this room. Jeremiah's my son.'

If he'd expected a shocked reaction, he didn't get one.

There was no condemnation, no gasps of horror, just acceptance and support.

It turned out that most of them had worked it out—some, like old Doris Trefussis, cleaner, tea-lady and general all-round good egg, years ago. Sam Cavendish knew, certainly, and when everyone had dispersed and left them alone, Sam put a mug of coffee in his hand and sat down at right angles to him, his bad leg stretched out and propped on the other ankle, a mug cradled in his hands and his eyes thoughtful.

'You can do it, you know,' he said, surprising Nick.

He frowned. 'Do what?'

'Be a good father to him. You were more of a father to me in my teens than my own father had ever been, and I know you've been good to my brother in the ten years I was away. And you love the boy. That means more than anything else.'

Nick gave a soft huff of laughter, and smiled tiredly at Sam. He'd been fond of him since he'd been a boy, and he'd been more than happy to take him on at the surgery when he'd come home wounded after a run-in with insurgents in Africa. And he was glad he had, because Sam had ended up back with Gemma, one of their nurses and his childhood sweetheart, and their baby was due any day. 'When did you get to be so wise, Sam?' he asked softly, but Sam just smiled back and ignored his remark.

'We need to sort the rota out, because Gemma can't go on

much longer. She's been having contractions off and on for days and every morning I wake up and think, How can she still be pregnant? So it won't be long, and we'll need another locum if you aren't going to be here.'

'Why not? I can still work most of the time.'

'No—because you'll be at your son's bedside,' he offered gently. 'Does he even know yet?'

Nick felt emotion well in his chest and cleared his throat. 'No. We're going to tell him when he's a bit stronger. To be honest, I'm dreading it and I'm happy to put it off as long as possible.'

'Don't leave it too long,' Sam advised, as if he hadn't already done that very thing, then he tilted his head on one side and raised a brow. 'You look like hell, by the way,' he said conversationally, and Nick growled softly under his breath.

'If one more person tells me that today I'm going to—'

'What? Go home and shower? Good idea, Nick. You could do with a seriously close shave, a shirt that's seen an iron in living memory and trousers that haven't got more wrinkles than an elephant's hide.'

He looked down at himself and remembered what he'd looked like less than twenty-four hours ago. How could that be? It seemed a lifetime ago. Nearly had been...

'We'll sort out the rota,' Sam was saying. 'I'm booking myself off now for a fortnight, because Gemma was looking iffy this morning, and I'll make sure they book you off, too, and we'd better have open-ended cover for Kate. I think Chloe might already have organised that, but I'll check. Kate's dog is being looked after, so all you need to worry about is your family. Go on, go and sort yourself out and get back to them. Have you had any sleep at all?'

'I had an hour this morning.'

'You might want to get your head down as well, then.'

He shook his head. 'No time. I can't leave Kate without back-up. Oh, and I'll need Chloe to find some stuff for them both. She's got a key to Kate's place. Kate's house keys were on her car keys, and they got left in it. I expect the police have taken them. I need to follow that up.'

He got to his feet with a sigh, put his mug on the draining board and paused at the door. 'Sam—thanks.'

'What for? I owe you more than I can ever repay, Nick. You go and look after your son, and leave the practice to us. We can manage.'

He laughed. 'Easy for you to say, you're booking yourself out on paternity leave as of now!'

'The others can cope. They love a challenge. Go on, shove off.'

He shoved. Half an hour later, after a rapid shower and a desperately-needed shave, dressed in clean trousers and an open-necked casual shirt and feeling a little more human, he headed back to the hospital, armed with Chloe's love for Kate and Jeremiah, the spare key to her cottage and a bag of toiletries and clothes for each of them, which Chloe had kindly picked up while he had been sorting himself out.

He got back at a little after one-thirty, and found Kate sitting by Jem's bed, her face exhausted.

'How is he?' he asked, putting the bags down by the chair, and she shrugged.

'The same, really. He's in a lot of pain—they've just given him more painkillers, and he's gone to sleep at last. Jess came and sat with me for a while, she's very kind. Oh, and Lucy popped in a little while ago—she's going to come back later when you're here. She sends her love. And Jack's been up again.'

He nodded, his eyes welling up. Lucy had sent her love. And Jack had been back, too, giving up his time to a brother he hadn't known he had. It didn't surprise him. His twins were both kind and generous to a fault, and he was immensely proud of them.

'Have you had lunch?'

She shook her head. 'I didn't like to leave him. Have you?'

'No—but he's asleep now, so why don't we pop down to the café and grab something while the going's good?'

She nodded, and got stiffly to her feet, easing out the kinks and giving him a wry smile. They told the nurses where they were going, then she fell into step beside him as they headed for the café.

'Oh, it's nice to move. I've been so afraid to make a noise in case I disturbed him.'

He smiled ruefully. 'I'm sorry I was so long, but I had to sort out the fallout at the surgery, and I got sick of everyone telling me I needed a shower. So, do I look better?'

She smiled up at him. 'Just a bit.' Actually, she'd quite liked him with the roguish stubbled look, but it was better to have him back with her—much better. She'd missed him. He'd been gone what felt like ages, and it had been a bit of an emotional roller coaster watching Jem in pain. It was good to step off the ride for a moment now he was comfortably asleep.

Nick looked up at the menu, then glanced at her. 'What are you having?'

'Oh, I don't know. Vegetables! All I've had in the last twenty-four hours is sandwiches. I'm sick of bread.'

'They've got salads.'

'Perfect.'

'I'll get you one. Go and sit down over there by the window and relax,' he ordered, so she went, and a few moments later he set a laden tray down in front of her.

She tried to summon up some enthusiasm. 'That looks nice,' she lied. 'What do I owe you?'

'Owe me?'

'For my lunch.'

He scowled at her. 'Don't be ridiculous. I got you a fruit

smoothie as well as the salad because I know you like them and I thought you were probably sick of tea and coffee, too.'

'I am.' She gave him a tired little smile, all she could manage. 'Thank you, Nick.'

He scowled again. 'Don't keep thanking me. I've made a complete fist of everything I've ever done for you. It's high time I started balancing the books.'

If only. She gave a quiet sigh and picked up her knife and fork, wondering how long she was going to be based at the hospital and when she'd be able to go home and lie down in her own bed, just for an hour or two. She was so tired, so very, very tired...

'Kate?'

She pushed her plate away. 'I'm sorry. I'm not really hungry.'

'You're exhausted. You should be in bed.'

'I can't, Nick. I have to be here for him. Tomorrow. I'll go home tomorrow—maybe in the morning, once we've seen Martin Bradley and we know if he's happy with him. I could go home then and have a rest.'

'OK. But if you're doing that, you're eating your salad now. Come on, you can do it.'

And so, with him coaxing and cajoling her, she finished most of it, drank the smoothie and then realised she was feeling more human. 'You're so sickeningly right always, aren't you?' she said with a smile, and a fleeting frown crossed his face.

'Now I know you need sleep,' he said gruffly, and stabbed his fork into the last slice of tomato on his plate and put it in his mouth.

She laughed at him. 'That's better,' she said softly. 'You sound more like the old Nick.'

He pushed his plate away and thought about it, realising

she was right. 'I feel better. It's amazing what a shower and a square meal can do. I've brought you some things, by the way. Chloe sorted them out—she sends her love. Well, everyone at the practice sends their love,' he amended with a smile that felt distinctly crooked. 'I told them he's my son,' he added, his voice low. 'I hope you don't mind. I asked them to keep it quiet.'

'How did they take it?'

He shrugged. 'It was odd. They didn't seem at all surprised. In fact, they were incredibly supportive. Chloe had arranged cover for you for the rest of this week already, but I've told her I'm writing you off sick for four weeks—'

'Four? Why?'

He smiled again, this time a little wryly. 'Because you've got whiplash,' he reminded her.

'No, I haven't.'

'I'm sure you have. You're having four weeks to get over it, whatever,' he told her, and, actually, she found she didn't mind his high-handed approach this time, because she needed the time to devote to Jem, and it wasn't entirely false. Her neck was a little sore.

She rolled it, wincing slightly, and he found himself aching to ease it for her, to massage it gently until it relaxed so she could get some relief. 'Sam's signing off on paternity leave—and, no, Gemma's not in labour, as far as I know, but he wasn't quite sure if she was on the verge this morning so he's booked a locum anyway.'

'She's a week overdue,' Kate said, biting her lip. 'I should be there for her.'

'Don't worry. Chloe's there, she'll look after her. And Sam is a doctor. They should be able to cope without you. And Sam's getting a locum to cover me for the next week at least, unless they really can't manage without me. I want to be here for you both,' he added, when she started to protest.

She said nothing for a moment, then sighed softly. 'Thank

you. I don't know how I would have coped without you yesterday and last night.'

'I would have been here anyway, Kate,' he told her quietly. 'Even if he wasn't my son, I would have been here for you.'

She nodded. 'Yes, I know you would. That's the funny thing about you, you're so generous, so kind, so helpful, but if anybody dares to realise it, you get so uncomfortable—look, you're doing it now.'

She shook her head slowly, carefully folding her paper napkin for something to do with her hands, because it would have been so easy to reach out to him, to take the hand lying on the table, fiddling with the little sugar packets.

'We ought to tell Jem, I suppose,' he murmured. 'Nobody in the hospital apart from Jack and Ben knows, so it shouldn't leak out, which means we can tell him when the time's right.'

He carried on fiddling, piling up the sugar packets and pushing them into straight lines with his fingertip. 'I'd just like to do it when I've had a chance to build a relationship with him—made friends with him, got to know him a bit better. You're right, I haven't ever really talked to him, or spent meaningful time with him, and it's time I did. Time I gave him a chance to get to know me, too. And it'll give you a bit of a break as well, if we're sharing the visiting. It's going to be a long haul.'

She nodded. 'Yes. Yes, I know. It should be better once he's on the mend, though. They have lessons and activities and he'll be doing physio, and there will be other kids for him to talk to. And his friends'll be able to visit in a few days' time, so that'll take the heat off us, too.'

And who knew? They might even find some time to be together themselves. That was a novel thought, but probably not one that would lead to anything. She'd do well to keep reminding herself of that fact, because it would be all too easy to fall into the habit of relying on him only to find he wasn't there when it came to the crunch.

She was sure he meant well, and maybe this time he really thought he could do it, but she wasn't holding her breath.

CHAPTER FIVE

MEGAN PHILLIPS, the pretty young paediatric registrar who'd been on call overnight, was waiting for them at the nursing station.

'We've got his blood results,' she began, and Nick felt his heart stall.

Don't let him have a problem. Not thrombocytopenia, he thought. Please don't let it be that, don't let him have DIC.

'He's OK now, but the biochemistry was a bit skewed. We needed to tweak some of the components, but it probably explains why he was feeling a bit rough. We've started an infusion and he should be fine now. We'll check it again in a while, OK?'

Relief hit him like a wall, and he smiled and thanked her, wishing, as a doctor, he didn't know so much. Ignorance would be bliss, he thought as he ushered Kate back into the side room where Jem was still sleeping. She stopped in the doorway and put her hand over her mouth for a second, sucking in air, and he squeezed her shoulder.

'He's all right,' he murmured.

'I know, but he looks so vulnerable, so fragile lying there like that,' she murmured.

'He'll be fine. You heard Megan,' he said firmly, and watched as she perched on the edge of the armchair by the bed.

It was upholstered in a hideous pink—wipe-clean vinyl, of course—and he found himself wondering how many parents had sat on it and watched their children.

He sat on the arm, laid his hand on Kate's shoulder and watched his son sleeping...

Megan reached out her hand to pick up the phone, and it fell back to her lap, nerveless with shock.

No!

It couldn't be him! She'd heard there was an O'Hara starting in A and E, but it had never occurred to her it was him, that he'd be here in Cornwall, of all places! She'd thought she'd be safe here, never have to see him again, never have to be reminded...

Her heart raced, and she shrank back into the chair, trying to get away, retreating from the sight of him. She must be mistaken, she told herself. It wasn't Josh. It couldn't be.

But it was him—tall, lean, more attractive even than he'd been eight years ago. He was the most good-looking man she'd ever seen, so sure of himself, so at home in his own skin that he exuded an almost tangible aura of confident masculinity. Alpha man. A man that women couldn't resist. A man who only had to crook his little finger and stupid, senseless little girls would abandon all their brains and follow him to the end of the earth.

He glanced over and caught sight of her, his body arresting momentarily, then excusing himself he walked towards her, resting a hand on the top of the counter and looking down at her with those extraordinary indigo-blue eyes, and she couldn't look away, for all she wanted to.

'Megan?'

His voice was shocked, his eyes dark with a host of emotions she couldn't even guess at, but it wasn't his emotions she was worried about, it was her own, tumbling in free-fall as she stared back at him, mesmerised, horrified, memory after memory crashing through her and robbing her of speech.

She unglued her tongue from the roof of her mouth and tried to remain professional.

'Hello, Josh.'

Just the two words. It was all she could manage, all she could force out through lips that were stiff with shock.

His hair fell over his forehead, and he threaded his fingers through the glossy black strands and raked it out of the way, making her suck in her breath. She could still remember the soft, silky feel of it between her fingers. 'I didn't know you worked here,' he said, that soft Irish brogue rippling over her nerve-endings like little tongues of flame. 'How are you?'

He looked vaguely stunned, his eyes wary now, concerned. As well they might be after what he'd done...

'I'm—I'm fine. Busy. Excuse me, I need to make a call.'

'That's OK, you can do it in a moment. I'm looking for a patient who's had surgery for a fractured pelvis—Jem Althorp? I put on the ex-fix in A and E.'

'He's fine. There's a minor problem with his bloods, that's all. He's in that room there. Now, I need to deal with this, Josh, and I don't need to deal with you. Excuse me.'

And picking the phone up again with shaking hands, she rang the haematology department, conscious all the while of Josh standing there, until with a quiet sigh he turned on his heel and walked away.

She nearly wept with relief.

The rest of the day dragged for Kate and Nick.

Josh O'Hara had popped in briefly, but he'd seemed distracted and hadn't stayed long. Just long enough for them to thank him for the procedure that might well have saved their son's life.

Jem's blood was quickly sorted, as Megan had promised, and he was feeling better, but by the evening Kate was at the end of her tether, and Nick sent her off to bed at nine, when Jem had drifted off to sleep again.

'I'll sit up with him.'

'But you haven't had any sleep either,' she protested. 'I've had more than you.'

'I haven't been in a car accident,' he said firmly. 'Go on. I'll get you if there's the slightest thing to worry about, but there won't be.'

'But how will you know?' she asked, fretting. 'You don't know him—you don't know how he sleeps, and what's normal—'

'Kate, he's just a child, like any other,' he said gently. 'If he's sick, I'll know. He'll be fine. Go to bed before you drop to pieces.'

So she went, reluctantly, and he settled down in the hateful pink chair and watched the monitor blinking steadily, watched the nice, even trace of Jem's heartbeat through the night, while the staff came in and did hourly obs and brought him endless cups of tea.

And then at three Kate came and took over, sending Nick off to grab some sleep, and he went into the little room where she'd been sleeping and lay down on the still-warm bed, her scent all around him and the residual heat of her body seeping into him like a soothing balm, sending him into a deep, restful sleep.

Jem woke shortly before six, and Kate could see at once that he was stronger.

'Morning, soldier,' she murmured, and, leaning forwards, she stroked his hair back off his forehead and smiled at him. 'How are you?'

'I feel better,' he said. 'I don't hurt so much, and I don't feel so sick. I'm hungry, though.'

He'd graduated from nil by mouth to sips of water, and so Kate poured a little into the beaker and held it to his lips.

'Maybe they'll let you eat something light later on. I've got some wash things for you. You'll feel better after we clean your teeth and wash your face with nice hot water,' she said soothingly. 'Grandma sends her love, and so does Chloe and everyone at the practice.'

'Where's Uncle Nick?' he asked.

She stroked his hair. 'He's here. He spent the night next to you in this chair, and then I got up and swapped over. I expect he's still sleeping. Why?'

He shrugged his skinny shoulders. 'Just wondered. I thought he might have gone home.'

She shook her head. 'No. He wouldn't leave you,' she told him, and she watched something terrifyingly like hero-worship dawn in his eyes.

But all he said was, 'Oh,' and then his eyes drifted shut again and he lay quietly for a while.

Behind her the door opened and closed, and she knew it was Nick without turning round.

'How is he?'

'Awake. Better. He was asking where you were.'

'I'm right here, son,' he said softly, the irony of it catching her in mid-chest as he perched on the foot of the bed and laid his hand lightly on Jem's ankle 'How are you?'

Jem opened his eyes. 'OK.'

'Good.'

Kate saw Nick's shoulders drop a fraction, and knew he'd been worried. 'He's hungry.'

'That's a good sign,' he said, and his shoulders dropped a little further.

'My bruises hurt,' Jem mumbled from the bed. 'My leg's really sore, and my side hurts, and my elbow's sore, but it's not like it was yesterday.'

'It'll feel better soon.'

There was a tap on the door, and a nurse popped her head round. 'We were going to give Jem a bit of a wash, if you two want to get some breakfast,' she said, and so they went down to the café that was fast becoming their second home, and had bacon rolls and pastries and lashings of coffee.

'One day I'll get home and start eating proper food,' she said, pushing the last crumbs around the plate. 'I never have anything like this for breakfast. I have yogurt and fruit.'

'You could have had yogurt and fruit,' Nick said with a frown, but she just smiled.

'I know, but I wanted a bacon roll, and I couldn't resist the pastries.'

He laughed, and, reaching out his hand, he covered hers and enfolded it in his warm, gentle grasp. 'Crazy woman,' he said, his thumb stroking slow circles over the back of her hand, and she felt the ice inside her starting to thaw, replaced by a strange heat that warmed her from deep inside, somewhere in the region of her heart.

'You need to go home this morning,' he went on gently. 'You're exhausted, and you need a shower and just to get out of here. Once the doctors have been round and they're happy, I'm going to take you home—and don't argue.'

She smiled a little unsteadily. 'I won't. It sounds wonderful. I could really do with a change of scenery, just for a little while. I ought to sort my car out, too, really. I need the keys.'

'We can phone the police, get that organised,' he said. 'I'll contact them. And you'll need another car.'

She rolled her eyes. 'I have no idea how long that'll take.'

'We'll get you one today,' he said. 'What do you want?'

She frowned at him. 'Why should you do that?'

'Because he's my son? Because you need it to transport him? I'll get you a bigger one, a stronger one.'

'No! I'll get it, and, besides, it can't be big, I have to be able to park in tight spaces.'

'So I'll get you a small stronger one.'

She sighed. 'Nick, that other driver must have been going at well over forty. Nothing's that strong. And I need it to do my job as well. Maybe I'll have to get a contract one through the PCT after all.'

'They can't do it that quickly. I can get you a car today—or at least organise it.'

She sighed again. 'Nick, it's very kind of you, but I don't really need it in a tearing hurry if I'm going to be stuck here for days.'

He shrugged. 'So you can have one in days. Just tell me what you want.'

She gave up. Sort of. 'I'll think about it,' she told him, and changed the subject.

The doctors were pleased with him. The blood setback seemed to have been resolved—routine, as Martin Bradley had said—his wound was healing well, and he was happy for them to leave the hospital—for a short while.

'Don't be too long,' Jem said, having a little wobble just as they left, and she hesitated, but Nick's hand on her arm was firm, and she promised they wouldn't be long and let him lead her out.

They went via the police station to pick up her keys and the items that had been in her car, and Nick put the bag in his boot and drove her home. It was the first time she'd been back since the accident, and it felt like for ever. She walked inside, picking up the post as she went, and then looked around.

The place was littered with Jem's things. A book on the stairs, his sports bag in the hall, a jumper dropped on the floor in the sitting room.

It caught her totally unawares, and she stared at the things numbly. What on earth would it have been like to come back to this if he'd died?

'I need a shower—put the kettle on and make yourself a drink,' she said, and hurried upstairs, needing to get away from Nick, to hide herself away in the shower where the sound of water might drown the threatening sobs that were rising in her throat.

She stripped her clothes off, the sobs starting to break free, and stepped into the shower, turning her face to the wall and slumping on it, her hands pressed over her mouth to hold in the pain that had been bottled up for days, the pain she couldn't hold inside any longer.

She could so easily have lost him. Just another couple of miles an hour...

A wrenching sob ripped through her, and she folded over, propping herself up under the pounding spray.

She was crying.

He'd heard the sound before. She'd done the same thing when James had died, and he'd brought her home from the headland and sent her to shower and warm up.

He couldn't go there again—not in the shower with her, holding her—but how could he leave her? How could he have left her then, torn apart by grief?

He went up.

She hadn't locked the bathroom door, and he opened the shower cubicle and turned off the water. She was huddled in the corner, and he reached for a towel and crouched down, draping it round her as he lifted her out, sitting down on the floor with her curled into his lap, her tears giving way slowly to fractured sobs that tore at his heart.

'He could have died,' she said at last, her voice fragmented by emotion. 'I came in and saw all his things, and I thought, What if I'd come back here, like I did when James died, and his things were everywhere—and...'

She broke off, fisting her hands in his shirt, and he held her closer, rocking her gently, hot tears scalding his eyes again as she clung to him, sobbing. 'Shh. He's all right, Kate, he's getting better now. He's going to be all right, sweetheart, he really is. You have to believe that.'

She nodded and sniffed, the sobs dying away to random hiccups. Every now and then there was another little bout, but he just held her close and let her cry, let her get it out of her system until at last she lifted her head and let go of his shirt, then swiped the tears from her face with shaking fingers.

'I'm sorry.'

'Don't be.'

'I always do this, don't I? Hide in the shower to cry.'

He shushed her again, smoothing the damp strands of hair back from her face and pressing his lips softly to her tear-stained cheek.

'All right now?'

She nodded slowly, and he eased her out of her arms, rescuing the towel as it slid down and tucking it back round her.

'I'll leave you to wash. I'll be downstairs,' he told her, and, standing up, he pulled her to her feet and kissed her cheek again. 'I'll make you a cup of tea.'

'Thanks.'

She came down a few minutes later just as the kettle boiled, dressed in clean clothes, her hair still damp and combed out over her shoulders and her smile wry.

'Sorry about that,' she said, looking a little sheepish. 'I just lost it.'

'Don't apologise, you've had a hell of a couple of days. You needed to get it off your chest. And talking of which, I'm a little underdressed. There's a bag of clean clothes in my car that I keep there for emergencies—could you do the honours while I shower? Since I'm already drenched?'

He'd taken off his sodden, crumpled shirt, but the trousers clung to his legs and her eyes scanned his body. Comparing him to Rob? He wouldn't come off well. He took care of himself, but Rob was a fitness fanatic and a PE teacher. And an ex, he reminded himself, and took small comfort from that.

'Sure,' she said, and took the keys, and he went upstairs to the bathroom. When he emerged from the shower a few moments later, the bag was there, just inside the door, with a clean, dry towel. She'd come in, and he hadn't noticed. Just as well, he decided, because when that towel had slipped he'd had a whole plethora of inappropriate thoughts and frankly he wouldn't trust himself with her at the moment.

He went back downstairs and found her sitting at the kitchen table with a cup of tea, and she ran her eyes over him again and smiled.

'It's a good job you keep spare clothes in your car,' she said, pushing a mug of tea towards him, and he gave a rueful laugh and sat down.

'Well, more or less. Trousers and shirt, at least, for predictable accidents. I don't tend to carry underwear.'

She chuckled, then sat back and eyed him thoughtfully. 'Are you telling me you're going commando, Dr T.?' she asked softly, raising an eyebrow and trying to stop her mouth from twitching, and the inappropriate thoughts leapt into his head again.

'That depends who wants to know,' he murmured, feeling the smile tug his own mouth, and the twitch got worse.

'Are you flirting with me?'

He felt his smile fade and searched her beautiful, teasing brown eyes. 'Would that be such a bad thing?' he asked softly.

The teasing look vanished, and there was a moment of breathless silence. 'I don't know—would it?'

'I'm not sure. It might be fun. It would make a change—we haven't had fun like that since our teens.' He glanced down at the mug, lined the handle up carefully exactly at right angles and then met her eyes. 'How about _it_?'

'How about what?' she asked carefully, and he thought she was holding her breath.

'Us.'

'I'm not sure that would be a good idea,' she said, after a seemingly endless pause. 'Maybe we'd just better concentrate on Jem for now.'

She'd hesitated, and in that time he'd held his own breath. He let it out now and gave a little shrug. 'If you want.'

'I want. Things are complicated enough.'

He nodded, and she gave a quiet sigh of relief. She didn't want to rush into anything. There was, however, another worry that was playing on her mind, a more immediate problem, and she raised it now.

'Nick, how am I going to manage when he comes out of hospital? I don't have a downstairs bathroom, or even a cloakroom, and stairs could be really difficult at first.'

'You could come to mine.'

She shook her head instantly. 'No. Not to Annabel's house,' she said softly, and watched the guilt flash across his eyes before he looked away.

'No. You're right, it wouldn't feel appropriate and, anyway, it's not exactly off the beaten track. So—perhaps we could rent somewhere? A bungalow or something, neutral ground. Just for a while, until he can manage the stairs again. I'm sure there are things out there. It's only April. It might be harder in August with the tourists, but I'm sure we could find something now and it needn't be for long. A few weeks, maybe.'

A rental property? 'It's worth a try,' she said, feeling the weight of that worry lifting from her shoulders with relief. 'I would never have thought of that.'

His smile was a little crooked. 'You see? I can have my uses, slight though they might be. I'll call the agents now.'

He made a couple of calls while she dried her hair,

and when she came down he was fizzing with suppressed excitement.

'There's a single-storey barn conversion. They've been trying to sell it, but it hasn't gone because it's quite pricy and the owners have been unrealistic, but they've now decided to let it, but only to people who don't want a long lease, which we don't.'

She nodded slowly. 'OK. Where is it?'

'On the way to Ben and Lucy's, so only about three miles out of the village. It's got a distant sea view, apparently—it's U-shaped, two-storey in the central section, with a courtyard garden and surrounded by farmland. Worth a look?'

'Definitely,' she said, then hesitated, not sure how to ask but just knowing that she had to, that this needed to be set out in black and white. 'Nick—is this just for me to stay in, or were you thinking of being there, too?'

He gave an enigmatic shrug, his eyes veiled. 'That depends.'

'On?'

'You, Jem? I don't know. If you want me there, I'd like to be there, but I don't want to confuse him or pre-empt any decision you might make in the future. I know Rob lived with you, but—'

'No,' she corrected hastily. 'Rob didn't live with us. He and Matt came to stay after I came out of hospital, but the boys shared Jem's room and Rob was on the sofa bed downstairs. We didn't share a room. It didn't feel right, when it came to it.'

He wasn't sure why, but that made him feel better. Not much. He knew they'd had an intimate relationship, because he'd gone to talk to her one night about a year ago and seen them through the window. He could still picture Rob bending his head to kiss her in the kitchen, and then the lights going off and coming on upstairs. Not that there was any reason why they shouldn't, but that had been before her surgery. Maybe that had changed things. Was that what she had meant about it not feeling right?

'I don't have any ulterior motive, Kate,' he told her. 'There are four bedrooms there. Two upstairs, each with en suite, and an en suite guest room, another bedroom or snug and a study downstairs in one of the sides. It's got a big open living space with a sitting room one end, a kitchen at the other and an open vaulted dining hall in the middle, with the stairs off it, and the third side is utility, workshop and garaging, apparently. We'd have plenty of space.'

She blinked. 'It sounds amazing.'

'That's what I thought. I've asked the agent to meet us there in twenty minutes.'

Her eyes widened. 'Wow. OK. You don't hang around, do you?'

'Is that a problem?'

'No. No, no problem, it's been worrying me to bits. It would be great if it was any good. The only thing is, how much is the rent, because I can't afford a fortune.'

'You let me worry about that.'

'Nick, I can't—'

'You can. It's not for you, it's for our son, and God knows I've done precious little for him in the last eleven years. Just let it go, Kate. Please. Don't argue.'

She opened her mouth, thought for a moment and then gave in. 'OK. But don't get in the habit of doing this.'

'What? Caring for my son? Why the hell not?'

There was a look in his eyes she hadn't seen for years, a purpose, a passion, and it was as if this whole course of events had brought him back to life.

She smiled. 'Shall we go and look?' she said, and he grinned and tossed his car keys in the air.

'After we've been via mine and I've got some underwear

on,' he said with a mischievous twinkle that gave her heart an unexpected lurch, and he ushered her out, closing the door firmly behind them.

It was fantastic. Perfect.

Built of granite, it was solid, tucked down in a fold of the land to shelter it from the prevailing south-westerly wind, and he couldn't find a single thing wrong with it.

It was to let fully furnished with every necessity and equipped to a very high standard, with king-size beds in the main bedrooms, lovely battered leather sofas in the sitting room and invitingly luxurious bathrooms with showerheads like dustbin lids.

He hadn't felt so excited about anything for years. He'd made his mind up after the most cursory walk-through and an exchanged glance with Kate, who was looking slightly stunned. It was wonderful, and he couldn't imagine why it hadn't sold instantly.

He said as much to the agent, who just shrugged. 'I don't know, either. It's been a second home and their circumstances have changed and they want to sell it, but they want a lot for it. The only thing I can assume is that it's too expensive for a holiday cottage and there aren't enough people living around here who can afford to buy it. As far as I can see, there isn't a single catch apart from the price, but the market's been a little odd recently. Maybe that's it.'

Maybe. And it was expensive, but Nick was doing some quick calculations. He wasn't a big spender. He'd been careful over the years, he was sitting on the cash he'd got for his parents' house when Ben had bought it at auction for Lucy, and if he sold his own house, he'd have enough to buy it.

Not that he was going to do anything rash just yet, but it might be worth having a word with the agent to see if he could have the option on it as they were renting. And maybe, if things went well...

'What do you think, Kate?'

Her smile was enigmatic. 'I think we need to talk.'

He frowned, as if he couldn't see what on earth they might need to talk about, and then with a slight shrug he turned to the agent.

'Can we have another wander around for a few minutes, talk this through?' he asked, and the agent nodded.

'Sure. Take your time. I've got a few calls to make, I'll be in the car.'

He left them, and Nick turned to Kate.

'Well? Come on, let's hear it, you've obviously got something you want to say.'

She smiled at his impatience, but she wasn't going to be railroaded, no matter what she thought of the house. 'I think it's wonderful,' she told him honestly. 'Absolutely gorgeous. I also think it'd be impossible going from this back to my house when he's better.'

He gave her a level look. 'Maybe you won't have to.'

'Because I'll sell up and move away?'

'I wasn't thinking of that. I was thinking you might stay on, live here.'

'Nick...' She gave a little, despairing laugh and shook her head. 'We can't just live here for ever.'

'Why not?'

She felt her eyes widen. 'Why not? Because it's outrageously expensive! I can't even afford to rent it, let alone buy it—'

'But I can. I could buy it, and you could stay here.'

'No.' She backed away from him a step, shaking her head again but in denial this time. 'Nick, no. Don't try and buy me, please. Or Jem. Especially not him. I'd rather carry him up and downstairs or put his bed in the sitting room with a commode beside it than let you do that. Please. I mean it.'

He sighed and rammed his hand through his hair. 'Kate,

I'm not trying to buy you, don't be silly. I'm just talking through the possibilities.'

'Well, how about possibly finding a simple, small bungalow somewhere with three bedrooms while he recovers?' she suggested bluntly, not sure she could picture him in that setting but pushing him just to see if he'd go for it, for his son's sake. For hers.

He stabbed his hand through his hair again and gave an exasperated sigh. 'Look, forget the money, forget the value, because it's not about that, it's not about impressing you, or Jem. It's about giving us somewhere to get to know each other, all of us, somewhere calm and safe, tranquil, somewhere we can all heal, because I'm under no illusions about it. When we tell him I'm his father there will be some wounds that need healing, Kate, and we'll need somewhere to do that in peace.'

He was so right—of course. He took her hands, meeting her searching gaze with troubled eyes, eyes that were filled with sincerity and pain. 'That's why I've held back, Kate, why I haven't involved myself with Jem, not because I didn't want to rock the boat with my other kids, but because of what it would do to him. I thought, when there was a possibility that you'd marry Rob, that he might not ever need to know, that he could have a stepfather who'd love him and keep him safe, and the knowledge that his father had died a hero. But now you aren't going to marry Rob, and it was only with the blood group thing that I realised there was no question that he was mine, and that he had to know.'

He dropped her hands and turned to the window, gesturing at the courtyard garden. 'Look at it, Kate. It's warm, sheltered, with flat paths where he can walk safely while he heals. Your garden's terraced at the back, your drive slopes up to the house and there are steps to the front door. My garden's the same, and it's so public there—so many people who'd make it their business to have an opinion and to express it.

If I'm ten minutes late taking the milk in, there's someone there with it in their hand, ringing the bell and checking up on me.'

'And you don't want people to see us together? Is that it?' she asked, a hideous sinking feeling in her chest. 'Are you ashamed of him, Nick? Because if you are, this stops now. I'm not having my son thinking you're ashamed of him—'

'Kate, no!' he exclaimed, his face horrified, and she knew instantly that he wasn't lying. 'Of course I'm not ashamed of him! I think he's a great kid—and I'm really proud to be his father. I just dread the impact it'll have on him when it gets out, and if there was anything I could do to protect him from that, to prevent it happening, I would do it, believe me, but I can't. I can just be there for him, to fend off the gossips, and the easiest way to do that is to avoid them. At least here we'd be free to explore our relationship in peace, and can you think of a better place to do it?'

He was right, of course, but even though she was reassured about his motives, she still had doubts.

'I don't want him to know you're thinking of buying it, Nick,' she said slowly. 'Not at first.'

He lifted his hands in a shrug. 'Why not? I'm still his father, I still intend to be part of his life, and maybe it's time to move on from the home I shared with Annabel. He can come and stay here with me. And if you move away, he'll be staying for longer—weekends, weeks...' He broke off and rammed his hands in his pockets.

'I don't know if I am,' she said slowly. 'Moving away.'

His eyes narrowed. 'I thought you'd handed in your notice to the PCT?'

'Not yet. I didn't get round to posting it. And now—well, now, maybe I should stay. That depends on you, on your relationship with Jem, on how you get on once he knows you're his father. We'll have to see.'

'But—'

'Nick, don't push it,' she warned, too emotionally fraught to make sensible decisions about their future right then. 'I need time to think this through, and I don't want to feel under pressure.'

'I know. And I want to give you that time. Please don't feel pressured, Kate. I don't want to do that. I'm just trying to give you all the options, and this might be one of them, if you think you'd like it to be.'

'You obviously would,' she murmured, watching his face, and he turned and gave her a crooked little smile.

'I would. I love it here. The moment I stepped inside, I felt it wrap itself around me. I know it sounds crazy, Kate, but I felt as if I'd come home, for the first time in my adult life. And I want it—the whole package. All of it.'

The whole package? Did he mean them, too? Or was she reading things into his words that didn't exist? Whatever he meant, when she searched his eyes she found nothing but a burning sincerity. For all his flaws, Nick Tremayne was nothing if not honest and honourable, and she knew he was only telling her the truth. If he said he'd give her time and not pressure her, he meant it. Whatever his ulterior motives.

And so she nodded. 'OK. We'll try. We'll tell Jem it's just rented, that it's only till he's better, so there are no carrots dangling in front of him, nothing to influence him in any way, and we'll see how it goes. All right?'

His mouth quirked into a wry smile, and he nodded.

'Sure. Sounds good. Let's go and tell the agent he's got a deal,' he said, and she followed him, wondering if it would work, hoping that it would and that it wouldn't all turn out to be the most hideous mistake...

CHAPTER SIX

THEY shook hands on the deal, agreed they could take possession of it as early as the next day and went back to the hospital, Nick still with that air of suppressed excitement about him, Kate assailed by doubts.

Their track record wasn't great. What if this was just another disaster in the making?

Think positive! she told herself, and walked with him up to the ward.

They found Lucy at her new-found brother's bedside, Jem propped up a little, a games console in his hand and an intent expression on his face. Lucy looked up at them with a smile. 'Hi.'

'Hi. Everything all right?'

'Fine.'

'OK, I'll see you in a few minutes, I've got some calls to make,' Nick said, and headed for the door. 'I won't be long.'

Kate perched on the chair by the bed and leant over towards Jem. 'So what's this?'

He grinned at her. 'Lucy's lent it to me—it's Ben's, and it's really cool. And I made her cry.'

Lucy looked a little sheepish. 'He was so sweet—he said he'd wanted one for ages, and it just got to me.'

'Oh, Lucy.'

She shrugged, smiled and carried on watching him as he got to grips with it, and moments later Nick came back in and sat on the chair beside her, perching on the arm with his hip against her side and the subtle scent of his cologne drifting over her, carried on the warmth of his body.

She thought of sharing the barn with him, and a little shiver of anticipation swept over her skin.

'So what's that?' he asked, and she looked up at him and smiled.

'Lucy brought him in a games console,' she said softly. 'He was so thrilled, he made her cry. He's wanted one for ages and we just haven't been able to afford it.'

Jem caught sight of Nick then and grinned excitedly. 'Hey, look what Lucy's lent me, Uncle Nick,' he said.

'I'm looking,' he said, deeply touched that his son wanted to share his excitement, but—Uncle Nick? 'That looks cool.'

'It's not just cool—it's awesome,' he said, stretching the word and making Nick's lips twitch. 'Absolutely epic! Lucy's lent it to me. You can do all sorts of things with it.'

'That's kind of you, Lucy,' Nick said, feeling a little choked and also inadequate because he'd been in such a hurry to get back yesterday he hadn't brought him in anything, and today he'd been so preoccupied with the barn that a simple thing like a present for his child hadn't even entered his head.

Lucy tutted. 'Don't be silly, Dad—it was lying around at home and we hardly ever use it, but don't imagine you're keeping it, half-pint, because it won't happen.'

She ruffled his hair gently, and he grinned and ducked slightly out of her way as she bent to kiss him, but she followed him and blew a raspberry on his forehead and made him laugh and grimace.

'You be good, and no giving the nurses trouble, or I'll set Ben on you, OK?'

'OK,' he agreed, and smiled at her a little shyly. 'Thank you for bringing it in. It's really nice of you.'

'My pleasure. You take care. I'll see you soon.' She hesitated by Nick, and then, going up on tiptoe, she kissed his cheek. 'Bye, Dad. I'll see you later. We need to talk,' she added, and he gave a brief nod.

'Yes, we do. Soon. Bye, Lucy. And thank you.'

'I want to try the face thing later,' Jem said as she went out. 'It's got a really cool thing where you can take pictures of people and it shows how they're the same, like eyes and stuff. And Lucy says you look like Jack, so we're going to try it when he comes to see me again.'

Nick swallowed. It wasn't only he and Jack that looked alike, he realised now that he was able to admit it, and Lucy had obviously thought of that, too. 'That sounds really interesting, I'll have to have a look at it some time. You seem much better,' he added, quickly changing the subject and relieved that he was sounding so much perkier, even though he could see he was beginning to flag now Lucy had gone.

'It doesn't hurt so much any more. They gave me some stronger painkillers just before Lucy came. My leg still aches a lot, though.'

'I'm not surprised. It got thumped pretty hard.'

'Is the car completely trashed?' he asked Nick.

'I don't know. I haven't seen it.'

Kate thought of the state it had been in by the time they'd cut the roof and the doors and the front wing off.

'Completely,' she said, shuddering inwardly. 'The boot was full of stuff, and it all got wet when they cut the roof off.' She laughed and felt herself colour. 'The boot's always full of stuff, but I'd sorted out all kinds of things for the charity shop, and I hadn't got round to dropping them off. And it'll be getting mouldy, it's still in the back of your car in a bag, Nick. I ought to deal with it.'

'Don't worry,' he told her, wondering how she could get

worked up about something so incredibly trivial in the face of her son's injuries. Or maybe it was because it was trivial that it was safe to worry about it. Safer than thinking about Jem? 'We can sort it out tomorrow.'

She smiled at him and agreed, and then looked at her watch.

'Have you had lunch, Jem?'

'Yes, there was shepherd's pie and peas and jelly and ice cream, but I could only have toast and jelly and ice cream, but I'm having pasta bake tomorrow 'cos I can eat properly then, they said. The jelly and ice cream was nice, though.'

'Good, I'm glad. And it's good news you can eat properly tomorrow, but you should be resting now. Why don't we leave you to sleep, and Uncle Nick and I—'

She broke off, hesitating over the Uncle Nick thing, and looked at him in mute distress, but he just smiled and said, 'We'll go and grab some food while you have a bit of a zizz, and we'll be back. OK, Jem?'

'OK,' he said, and he held the game out to Kate, his eyelids drooping. 'Can you stick that in my locker so it's safe? I don't want it to fall on the floor. I promised Lucy I'd look after it.'

'Sure. Sleep well,' she murmured, and bent over and brushed her lips over his forehead, her stumble over Nick's name reminding her all too forcibly of the conversation that was to come.

'I don't care if you both still call me Uncle Nick,' he said quietly as they walked down to the cafe. 'I don't care what he calls me. It's not what matters.'

Kate felt a little stab of pain for him. 'I know. I'm sorry, it's just—you've been Uncle Nick for years, and—'

'Kate, it's all right,' he said, squeezing her fingers with his free hand. 'I don't need to be anything else. I was happy being a surrogate uncle, and if that's what he wants when we've told him, I'll carry on. All I ask is the chance to be part of his life.'

'You are part of his life, Nick. You always have been, I've made sure of it. And you always will be.'

She heard him sigh softly, and paused on the stairs, her hand on his arm. 'Nick, it'll be all right. We'll get there.'

'Will we?' he asked doubtfully. 'I hope you're right, Kate, because I've suddenly realised how much I want it, and the thought of losing it all now is untenable.'

The day dragged slowly by.

Jem slept for most of it, still not allowed any visitors apart from family, and Jack and Ben came in turn during the afternoon, when they had a moment.

He was sleeping when Jack arrived, and Kate excused herself for a moment and left the men to talk. God knows, they had enough to say to each other, she thought.

'I'll be back in a few minutes, I just want to make a few phone calls,' she said, and slipped out of the door, pulling it ßbehind her.

Jack met his father's eyes, his own guarded, and Nick sighed quietly. It had taken him a while to rebuild his relationship with Jack once he'd returned to Cornwall, and he was desperately sad that it now seemed in peril again.

'Jack, I—'

'I'm not stopping. I've just come to tell you we want to see you. Tonight, Lucy's house, eight o'clock. Be there—and no excuses.'

And without giving him a chance to argue, he walked out, and Nick sat down heavily on the awful pink vinyl armchair beside the bed and stared unseeingly at his son's face until Kate came back.

'He didn't stay long.'

'Long enough to say what he came for. I've been summoned,' he told Kate softly, standing up again and giving her the chair. 'Eight o'clock tonight, Lucy's. Will you be all right if I leave you to go there?'

She smiled sadly. 'Of course I'll be all right. I've just heard Gemma's been admitted. I might take a walk up there and see how she's doing. You go and see them, Nick, and try and build some bridges.'

He nodded, wondering how he could be in two places at once and only really wanting to be here, by this injured child he was beginning to realise he loved more than life itself...

Ben came by on his way home after his shift finished, by which time Jem had woken up in pain again.

'I've got the most amazing bruises,' he told Ben, but although he was trying to sound as if he was showing off, Kate could tell he was frightened by them, and she wasn't surprised. When he turned back the blankets and showed his side to Ben, she winced yet again, the sight making her curl up inside.

'That's impressive. I'm not surprised you're hurting. I'll go and find someone.'

He went out, coming back a few moments later with Megan Phillips. They consulted the chart together, and she chatted to Jem about his pain, and then she turned to Kate.

'We want to get the pain under control because we don't like him hurting, but also because we'd like to get him up soon. We might start sitting him up on the side of the bed tomorrow and see how it goes, and if he tolerates that we'll move to the chair, and so on. It'll be slow, but you'll be in control of what you can manage, Jem. We'll let you guide us. And Mr Bradley wants your physio to start properly from tomorrow, so all your muscles don't forget how to work, but very gently at first, so nothing to worry about. Anyway, I'll talk to you in the morning, and I'm on all night if you're worried about anything, Mrs Althorp. Just get them to call me.'

'Thank you,' she said, smiling at the lovely young woman,

her dark hair held back in a clip out of the way, the thick curls trying hard to escape. She was kindness itself, but there was something lurking in the back of her eyes today, Kate thought, that hadn't been there yesterday. Something sad and desperate and a little lost. Her heart went out to her.

'I'll go and update your notes right now, Jem, and get someone to come and give you the extra pain relief shortly, OK? And if you're still really uncomfortable, press the bell and they'll get me and we'll have another look at things.'

'Thanks,' he said, looking relieved, and after she'd gone out he looked up at Ben again. 'Thanks for asking her, Ben.'

'Any time. Right, I'd better go home. Apparently I'm cooking tonight. I'll see you later, Nick?'

'Yes. I'll be there.'

Ben gave him a fleeting smile, murmured, 'Don't worry,' and left them alone with their son.

'Here you go, my gorgeous—jelly and ice cream,' a nurse said, putting it down on his bed table with a smile and helping him sit up a little.

Nick glanced at his watch, and realised it was suppertime. He looked at Kate. 'Why don't you go and have a rest for an hour or so while I sit here with Jem?' he suggested gently. 'Or you could go and get something to eat, as I'm eating at Lucy's.'

For a moment he thought she was going to argue, but then she smiled slightly and went out, and he settled himself on the edge of the pink chair and looked at the instructions for the games console while Jem ate the jelly and ice cream and told him how to work it.

'I don't know how you guys work these things out,' Nick said, frowning at it, and Jem laughed and took it from him.

'It's easy, Uncle Nick, but don't worry, Rob couldn't work out how to use Matt's, either. It's because you're too old for this kind of thing,' he explained innocently.

'Is that right?' he asked, taking the machine back and

having another go. So Rob couldn't work it? He ignored the voice that mocked him for his childish urge to be better than the other man, and got Jem to show him once again. And finally, finally, he cracked it.

After that, dealing with Lucy and Jack didn't seem nearly so daunting...

He left Jem's bedside at seven-thirty, just after Kate came back to sit with him. She'd had a rest, and something to eat, and she looked more like herself.

'I'll come back later and update you,' he promised. 'And I could stay, if you like—take turns, like we did last night.'

'We'll see. Have a lovely time,' she said, but her eyes were saying, Good luck, and he gave her a fleeting smile and left.

It took fifteen minutes to get there, and he parked the car outside and went in through the kitchen door, the way he'd always gone into his family home. He braced himself for the reception committee, but it was only Ben in the kitchen and he greeted him with a smile and a glass of wine. 'Here—I thought you might need this.'

'I'm driving.'

'Not for a while, and it's only a small glass. They're in the sitting room, go on through. And, Nick? Don't worry. They aren't going to skin you, they just want to understand.'

He nodded, and, taking the wine with him, he walked through the familiar house, feeling like a condemned man going to the gallows. Crazy, because in many ways this was none of their business, it was between him and Kate and Jem, and the only other person he owed an explanation to was Annabel, and she was dead.

But he supposed they felt they were acting as her representatives, and of course there were financial implications. Jeremiah, as his son, was entitled to an equal share of his estate, so each of them would lose a percentage of their stake.

Maybe that was what they wanted to discuss. Although he doubted it. His children weren't like that.

Shaking his head slowly, he straightened his shoulders and went through into the sitting room, and the conversation stopped dead.

'Well, don't mind me,' he murmured, and Lucy coloured.

Not Jack. He stood up, looked his father in the eye and said, 'You'd better sit down. We've got Ed on the webcam.'

He nodded, glad that he'd be able to talk to his other son at last, and sat down opposite the laptop on the coffee table, with Jack and Lucy across from him, visible over the top. So he could see them all, and they could all see him. It was like an interview panel, he thought. Or a jury.

I swear by Almighty God...

'Dad.'

He glanced down at Edward, his face moving a little jerkily but still very recognisable.

'I've been trying to ring you,' Nick told him.

'I know. I didn't answer because I don't know what to say to you,' Ed told him, his voice puzzled and hurt. 'I can't believe it—what the hell were you thinking of?'

Nick sighed and ran a hand through his hair. 'There's nothing I can say or do to change what happened, and I'm not going to make excuses,' he told them all, 'but I meant my vows to your mother, Edward, and I swear it was the only time.'

I swear by Almighty God...

'It's not that. That's between the two of you. I just hope she never knew. It's him I'm thinking about, a boy who thought for years that his father was dead when you could have been taking an active role in his life. Sure, it would have hurt Mum, but we were grown up, it was none of our business, and we could have spent time with him and made him feel wanted.

That's what's so gutting, that he didn't have any brothers or sisters there for him when we could have been, so easily.'

Nick shook his head. 'I didn't know. It was Kate's decision not to tell me, and she made it for good reasons. Wrong ones, maybe, but still out of consideration for everyone involved, and there weren't any right ones—'

'Don't palm it off on Kate. You've known for two years,' Jack retorted, cutting in. 'That's two lost years he could have had a father. You should have said something sooner, Dad.'

'How?' he asked. 'And when? She was with someone all last year, and she's been ill. You know that. She's had breast cancer. We could hardly tell him then, could we, with his life in turmoil and another man there ready and willing to act as his father? And before then, well, I guess I was still coming to terms with it—still in denial. I'm sorry you're so angry with us, but the only person I can worry about at the moment is your little brother, and I'm afraid he's taking all my time and thoughts right now.'

Edward frowned. 'How did he take it?'

'He doesn't know yet. He's still in a lot of pain. We're going to tell him later, when he's stronger, and when we've had some time to get to know each other. I'm hoping that with time we'll be able to get to know each other better and he'll learn to forgive us both, but I'm going to be part of his life now, come hell or high water, so I'm glad you've all accepted that, at least.'

'Don't worry about us. We're big enough and ugly enough to take care of ourselves. It's Jem we're all worried about.'

He pinched the bridge of his nose, pressing his thumb and forefinger against his eyes before dragging his hand down his face. 'Who the hell do you think I'm worried about?' he asked hoarsely, scanning all their faces. 'At the end of the day, I've done my bit for you lot. I haven't even started with him. I owe him so much I don't know where to begin—'

'That's what we want to talk to you about. You need to

change your will, to make provision for him,' Lucy said, and he glanced across at her and wondered if this had been her idea, his little girl, his peacemaker.

'I already have,' he said quietly. 'I did it yesterday, as soon as I found out—as soon as I was sure. The amendment to the will is with my solicitors in St Piran waiting for my signature.'

'And what about his schooling? We all went to private school. Where will he go?'

'Wherever he wants, Jack. I would think the high school in Penhally, with his friends. I don't want to change his life, I don't have the right to interfere.'

Jack snorted, and he met the condemnation in his eyes with new understanding.

'Is that how you saw my involvement in your lives? As interference?'

'Somewhat,' Edward said bluntly. 'It was "My way or the highway". No middle line, no grey areas, just black or white.'

Nick frowned. 'That's not how I see it at all. I did my best to be a good husband and father. I gave you guidelines. I thought that was what being a father was, but this—I don't know how to deal with this, how to be a father to him now.'

'Is that why you haven't?'

He looked at her and let his breath out on a long, ragged sigh. 'Yes. Yes, that's exactly why. I want to be a good father to him, to all of you, but I just—I can't seem to do it right, apparently. And with Jem—I didn't even get the chance until recently, and it was so nearly too late...'

He broke off, squeezing his eyes shut, pinching the bridge of his nose again, determined to hold it all together in front of them, but it was all still so raw, the image of Jem lying there in Resus while they cut his clothes away and poured fluids into him etched on his memory in acid.

'I still don't understand how you ended up sleeping with Kate when you were married,' Jack said, sounding so like him that at any other time it might have been funny. 'All the morals you rammed down our throats as kids, and yet you could do that—and you ended up with a child you won't even acknowledge! It's just so damned unfair. At least we knew you loved us—and we thought you loved our mother.'

'I did—and I love Jeremiah,' he told them earnestly. 'Don't imagine for a moment that I don't, and I fully intend to show him that, given a chance.'

'You're changing the subject,' Jack said. 'I want to know how the hell you came to have a random one-night stand with another woman totally out of the blue!'

'I don't think that's any of your business,' he began, but then he sighed and sat back, giving up the unequal struggle. If he ever hoped to make them understand, he had to explain at least some of it. He looked up and scanned their faces in turn.

'You want to know? All right, I'll tell you.'

'Dad, you don't have to,' Lucy protested, but he shook his head.

'I think I do—because it wasn't totally out of the blue at all. Kate and I go back thirty-five years.'

'We know you dated her.'

He smiled gently at Lucy. 'It was rather more than that. I'd know her since I was fourteen, but I was seventeen when I first really became aware of her; she was only fifteen, though, so we took things slowly—walks up on the moors, swimming, surfing, going for picnics. We went to the cinema, I took her to a rock concert—all pretty innocent stuff. And we fell in love.'

He hesitated, remembering those halcyon days, and then he sucked in a breath and carried on. 'I was in my last year at school, and I'd got into med school in London. We talked about me going away, and I promised I'd come back for her.

She was sixteen by then, I was eighteen, and although we still weren't sleeping together, that was pretty much a technicality. By the end of that last summer, I knew Kate's body as well as I knew my own, and I cherished it. But I was going away, and people change, and I didn't want to do anything that might hurt her later, so we held back from that last step. And then I met a girl during Freshers' Week, a beautiful girl with stunning blonde hair and the most incredible blue eyes, while we were being dragged round on some crazy pub crawl in fancy dress, and somehow we ended up in her room. I woke up in the morning feeling sick and ashamed and appalled at what I'd done, but it was too late. She came to me a few weeks later in floods of tears and told me she was pregnant, and I didn't know what to do. I just knew I had no choice but to ask her to marry me, and to make it work.'

'And Kate?' Lucy asked softly. 'What happened about Kate?'

'I came down and saw her, and for the first time ever I lied to her. I told her I'd met someone else and fallen in love, and I was going to marry her. I told her she was pregnant—and Kate was devastated. So was I, because I loved her so much—I never had to explain anything to her, I still don't. She still understands me as no one else ever has, anticipates me, and somehow forgives me. She actually sent us a card, saying she hoped we'd be very happy together. And I did everything I could to be fair to Annabel, to be good to her, because it wasn't her fault I'd got her in that mess, and she was lovely. It was no hardship being married to her, and if I didn't think about Kate, it was OK. But even though I did everything I could to make it feel right, I couldn't, not entirely, because my heart was with Kate and always has been. And even though I was with your mother, I always knew what was going on in Kate's life—we went to her wedding to James, we saw them socially from time to time, and I managed to convince myself that we'd both moved on. Only I never really did, of course, and I don't think she did.'

He tried to smile at them, but his mouth felt frozen. 'I don't know that I can explain what happened that night—the night of the storm. It was a few hours after my father and your Uncle Phil had died, and Kate's husband had been washed out to sea.'

He filled in the details of the day, the rescue that had gone wrong and led to the death of three men, the horror of it. 'Later that night your mother told me to find Kate, to see if he'd been found, and he hadn't. She was still on the clifftop, so I took her home and tried to look after her, but she was falling apart, devastated, and so was I, and we just reached out to each other. We've never needed words, and we didn't need them that night. We just hung on while the storm raged all around us, and afterwards I put her to bed and left her, and went back to your mother and tried to carry on.

'And that's what I've done for the past twelve years,' he said, 'tried to carry on, to keep going, keep putting one foot in front of the other and not hurt too many people along the way. And then I find I have another child, a son, and we're going to have to tell him, and yet again I'm going to hurt someone I love.'

He stopped, unsure what else, if anything, he could tell them, but there was nothing more of any relevance, so with a long, deep breath, he sat back and waited.

He'd told them things he'd never told anyone, not even Kate, and there was a long silence until Lucy knelt up beside him, put her arms round him and rested her head on his shoulder. 'Dad, I'm so sorry,' she whispered, and he could feel a wet patch forming on his shirt from her soundless tears.

He hugged her back, and she dragged in a shuddering breath and sat up. 'Ed, are you OK?' she asked.

Nick looked at Edward, clearly moved even on the jerky picture.

'I'm sorry,' he said. 'We had no right to make you go through that. You were right, it was none of our damn business. Look, I'm going to go. Just—look after him, could you, and send him my love? I'll write to him. You can give him the letter when you think he's ready.'

'Thanks.'

The screen went blank, and Lucy shut the laptop and leant back with a sigh, and he glanced across and saw Jack, stony-faced and silent, but he was far from unmoved, however tight his control.

'Well—I suppose we ought to eat,' Lucy said at last, and, unfolding her legs, she got off the sofa and went out. Seconds later, they heard her crying, and Ben's voice murmuring quietly as he soothed her.

'I'm sorry, I probably shouldn't have told you all of that,' Nick said softly, but Jack made a dismissive noise and shook his head.

'No, I'm sorry. I owe you an apology. I thought—'

'That it was some dirty little affair? That we'd gone out and got drunk? Believe me, that would have been easier to deal with.'

'I'm sure. How's Jem doing?'

'Oh, he's all right, I suppose. Still sore, still got the drain and the catheter, and I don't think that pleases him, but maybe he'll have them out tomorrow.'

'Probably,' Jack agreed. 'Are they going to get him up?'

How odd, Nick thought, that Lucy could hug him and then go and cry, but Jack was here talking about his treatment, hanging onto normality. So like him, so ready to push his emotions aside if they became inconvenient or embarrassing.

But this business with Jem was teaching him a lot about

his emotions, most of it uncomfortable, and he was learning to deal with them.

Ben appeared in the doorway. 'Supper's ready when you are. There's no rush.'

'It's OK, we're ready,' Nick lied, because his guts were so knotted with tension he didn't think he could possibly eat again.

'So—what happens now?' Lucy asked, and he shrugged.

'I don't know. We're taking it a day at a time. I've found a converted barn to rent—it's near here, you probably know it. St Adwen's. It's been for sale, but they haven't managed to shift it, so they're letting it, and it's mostly single storey, with two bedrooms upstairs and two down, so when he comes out of hospital we're going to stay there for a while until he recovers. It'll give us a bit of privacy and time to be together as a family, without the pressure of having to buy anywhere.'

'What about your house?' Jack suggested. 'That's got a room downstairs he could use as a bedroom, and a shower room next to it.'

'Neither of us would feel comfortable there, under the circumstances. It's very much your mother's house, but maybe it's time I moved on.'

'Meaning?' Lucy asked, looking at him keenly.

He set his fork down, very precisely, and met her eyes.

'I'm thinking of asking Kate to give me another chance. We're going to see how it goes with Jem, but if I think we could make a go of it, I might ask her to marry me.'

Her eyes flooded again, and she got up and came and hugged him. 'Oh, Dad. I'm so pleased. I've been so worried about you on your own, and Kate's so lovely, and now we know how much you love her—'

'Hey, hey, don't jump the gun, I haven't asked her yet and she certainly hasn't said yes. It could all fall apart if Jem throws a hissy fit at the idea of us living together.'

She sat down again and propped her chin on her hand. 'Do you think he will?'

He shrugged. 'I really have no idea. He doesn't know I'm his father yet, we still have to cross that hurdle, and I have no idea how he'll react.' He sighed. 'Although with my track record maybe he'd be better off not knowing—'

His children both chipped in then, contradicting him, telling him he was a good father, the best...

'What about "My way or the highway"?' he quoted back at them from one of their recent conversations. 'What about all the morals I stuffed down your throats?'

'Well, at least you had principles, even if you weren't always strong enough to stick to them,' Jack said reasonably.

'And you've always loved us, even if you were a bit tough and uncompromising, and we've always known that,' Lucy said, reaching out and squeezing his hand. 'Don't worry. Just give him time. And we'll be there, too. Once he's better I'll take the kids in to visit. They love him, and he's their uncle, of course. I think he may find that a bit of a shock when he works it out.'

'I hadn't even thought of that,' Nick said, and picked his fork up again, suddenly hungry. 'This is good chilli, Ben. Thanks.'

'My pleasure,' Ben said, giving him a wry smile. 'There's plenty more.'

'D'you know, I don't mind if I do,' he said with a grin, and handed Ben his plate.

Kate waited for him, lying awake on the top of the bed they'd given her at the hospital, and when he called her, shortly before midnight, she told him to come up. He tapped on the door and came in and perched beside her, and she reached for his hand and held it.

'How was it?'

'Oh, pretty much as expected. They were angry at first,

worried about Jem, about the impact this would have on
him—you were right about them, they've taken him to their
hearts, he's part of the family now whether he likes it or
not. Curiously it wasn't that much about the fact that I was
unfaithful to their mother, although that didn't thrill them.
They seemed more concerned for him—about my provision
for him in my will, about his education and what I intend to
do to take care of him, and about you.'

He hesitated, then went on, 'I told them about us, about
how we met, and a bit about that night—not all of it, but
enough. I know you didn't want me to, but they didn't understand, and how could they, without being there, without understanding how devastated we were that night, how bonded
together by our grief we were. So I tried to explain.'

'And did they understand, in the end?'

He gave a low laugh. 'I think so. I was pretty graphic. Not
about us, but the rest. They apologised for making me dredge
it all up—they were pretty shocked. They hadn't realised
what it had been like that day, and I didn't pull any punches.
I even told them about their Uncle Phil and how he died.'

'Oh, Nick,' she said, squeezing his hand tighter. 'I'm sorry
you had to go through it all again.'

'It's all right. It was important that they understood, and
I think they do now. I also thought they should know that
Annabel sent me to make sure you were all right.'

She stared at him. 'Annabel sent you?'

'Yes. I thought you knew that?'

'How would I know, Nick? We've never talked about it—
never discussed the night of the storm. I'm not sure I even
know fully what happened. Will you tell me?'

'Really?'

'If you can bear to go over it all again.'

He shrugged. 'Sure. If you really want to know.'

'I do,' she said, and then, because he was still clearly running it over in his head, still chock-full of emotion, she patted the bed and shuffled over. 'Come here. You need a hug.'

For a moment he did nothing, but then with a tired sigh he lay down beside her and drew her into his arms. She put her head on his shoulder, and wrapped her arms round him and held him.

'So tell me,' she urged softly. 'Tell me how it happened.'

'Well, you know the school kids were stranded down on the rocks at the foot of the headland—that's where James was, of course, and my father was on the top of the headland, helping with the children that had been brought up the cliff while my brother was abseiling down the face and rescuing the ones still stranded. The last child's helmet had fallen off on the way up, and so Phil took his off and gave it to her, and then a huge wave—the same wave that swept James off the rocks—picked them up and threw them against the cliff and shattered his skull. My father helped pull them up, and failed to tell anyone he'd had a heart attack three weeks earlier.

'I hadn't been there at first, I was in my surgery over in Wadebridge, but I was called to help and I arrived to find my father collapsing with another heart attack, and my brother lying on the grass in the lashing rain with the back of his skull caved in. There was nothing I could do for Phil, he'd died instantly. My mother was at home, unaware of what was going on, but Annabel was in the church hall, making tea for everyone, so I told her to pick my mother up and meet us at the hospital, and I went in the ambulance with my father, trying to keep him alive when he arrested. And by the time we set off, we knew that James had been washed off the rocks by the same wave.

'I managed to keep my father going until we got to the hospital, and my mother was with him when he died, although he never recovered consciousness, and after she'd said good-bye to her husband, I had to take her down to the chapel of rest to say goodbye to her son.'

He broke off for a moment, reliving it, and beside him he heard Kate suck in a shaky breath. 'Nick, you don't have to do this.'

'It's OK,' he said softly, taking her hand and squeezing it. 'It's time we talked about it, because otherwise it's too damned easy to say we should have known better. Anyway, I took them back to the house, Annabel and my mother, and we had tea.' He gave a shaky laugh. 'It's funny how tea always seems to come into this equation. I can't tell you how much tea and coffee I've drunk in the last couple of days. Anyway, after a while Mum started to cry—that terrible sound of grief.'

'Oh, Nick. Poor, poor woman. How on earth did she cope, losing both of them on the same day?'

'She didn't. It broke her. And on that night of course we couldn't leave her, but I couldn't stop thinking about James, and neither could Annabel. She told me to go and find you and see if there was any news of him. I think we both knew he was dead, and afterwards I wondered if she knew what she was doing when she sent me. I suspect she did. She wasn't stupid.'

It had been a bizarre conversation, most of the words unsaid, he remembered. And he could remember, too, the look in her eyes. The understanding, the quiet resignation. The blessing. He gave a quiet sigh and went on.

'The rest you know. I found you on the headland, with the wind and rain lashing your clothes, and you were so cold—chilled to the bone.'

'I was waiting for you. I knew you'd come.'

'I don't know how. I just knew I had to.'

He'd undressed her and put her in the shower, and put the kettle on, just like the other day. And just like the other day, he'd heard her crying, like his mother, with inconsolable grief, and he'd gone to her. The woman he loved, the girl he'd fallen for. The woman, he realised, he still loved with all his heart. He closed his eyes and swallowed.

He paused, remembering that he'd already stripped off his saturated, blood-stained shirt, and he'd taken off the rest and gone into the shower and put his arms around her and held her, and she'd clung to him, just as she'd clung to him that morning, and they'd cried together. He had no idea how long for. Ten minutes? An hour?

He wasn't really sure what had happened then. He hadn't understood it at the time and he still didn't understand it now, but they'd needed each other in a way so deep, so elemental that there had been no denying it. They were both angry, furious that something so crazy had happened to kill two young, healthy men with years ahead of them and an old man who should have lived to enjoy his retirement and instead had been snuffed out like a candle.

Maybe it was just defiance, and the fact that people they'd loved had died so senselessly, and it was almost as if they'd had to prove to themselves that they were still alive, but there had been no stopping it, no reasoning, just a soul-deep need that had driven them half-crazed into each other's arms.

Afterwards he'd turned off the water and dried her and put her to bed and then he'd gone home and showered and changed and gone back to his wife. They'd never spoken of it again, but after that, nothing had been quite the same...

'Nick?'

He started a little and stared at Kate, then shook his head to clear it of the unwanted, haunting images.

'I'm sorry that night was so awful for you all,' she whispered. 'Thank you for telling me. And I'm sorry the kids were hard on you.'

'It's OK. It's over now, and I'm glad it's out in the open. I think they realise now that it wasn't a premeditated decision to betray their mother, or that Jem was conceived as a drunken result of some sordid little date, just two people, who had always cared about each other, on the edge of despair and reaching out to each other that night.'

'We weren't ourselves. No wonder we didn't think about contraception, not then and not afterwards.'

'I did, but not till weeks later, when you told me you were pregnant, and I asked you if it was my child, and you said no. And I accepted it without question, with relief, even, because I didn't ever want to have to think of that night again. But you knew, didn't you? You knew he was mine because of the fertility problems.'

'Yes. Yes, I knew. James's notes had gone back to the PCT when he died, so I'd had to ring the clinic and ask them for the results, and they'd told me that James was sterile. But I couldn't tell you. Not then. It wouldn't have achieved anything and so many more people would have been hurt. But maybe now we can move on.'

'Maybe.'

He turned his head, and she lifted her face and their lips met in a gentle, tender kiss that made her heart skip a beat. He shifted, turning towards her, and their legs tangled, their bodies hard against each other.

'Nick, we can't,' she whispered, and he sighed, his breath soft against her cheek.

'I know. I just need to hold you.'

But he kept on kissing her, his lips tracing soft circles over her cheeks, her eyes, her throat.

'Nick…'

'Shh. It's all right,' he murmured, drawing her closer again and settling her head on his shoulder once more. 'I'm going in a minute.'

Except he didn't. He was asleep in seconds, emotionally exhausted, and although her arm had gone to sleep, she didn't have the heart to wake him. So she lay there for an hour, until he stirred and gave a sleepy grunt, and she murmured his name.

'Sorry—I didn't mean to doze off. Are you all right?' he asked, sitting up and shifting out of her way.

'I'm fine. My arm's dead, though.'

He tutted and took it in his hands, rubbing it briskly until the pins and needles had gone and she sighed with relief, and then he stood up. 'I ought to go home. How's Jem been? Did he go to sleep all right?'

'Yes, he's fine. And Sam and Gemma have a baby boy. They're calling him Archie—Archie Nicholas, for you.'

She heard him suck in his breath, and then let it out again, obviously touched by the gesture. 'That's great. How are they?'

'Well. Fine. The baby's beautiful, and Gemma's OK, it was a nice, straightforward delivery. It was lovely to see them. A bit of normality, really. They send their love.'

'I'll pop up tomorrow, take them something. And I ought to bring Jem in something, but I have no idea what. I don't want to look as if I'm trying to buy him,' he said with a wry grin, and she laughed.

'So bring him grapes. He adores grapes, and he needs fruit on all these opiates.'

'Grapes? Lucy gives him a games console that probably cost well over a hundred pounds, and you suggest I bring him grapes?' he said, laughing softly.

'Or you could look as if you're trying to buy him,' she said reasonably, and he sighed.

'OK. Grapes it is. And I suppose the games console's only on loan.'

It was, although of course he could always buy him his own, she thought, but she didn't suggest it. Time enough later for extravagant gestures, and she'd rather he didn't get into the habit of playing on a games machine as a regular thing.

He bent and kissed her cheek, then lifted his head slightly, stared into her eyes and slowly lowered his head again, touching his lips to hers once more. Just briefly, very lightly, but it was like being stroked with fire.

'Sleep tight. I'll see you in the morning,' he murmured, and he went out and closed the door softly behind him, leaving her lying there with her fingers on her lips, and her body tingling with anticipation.

CHAPTER SEVEN

NICK didn't arrive until ten the next day, to her surprise.

By the time he came in, Martin Bradley had been round, and as Jem seemed comfortable, the surgeon said he could try sitting up a little in bed, instead of just having his head and shoulders being propped up.

It ached a bit, Jem said, but Kate could tell he was happier. He was getting so bored lying down, and sitting up properly he was able to play with the games console to his heart's content while she sat beside him with a magazine and let it all go on around her.

Her presence was less essential now than it had been. He was no longer in danger, and he was used to the staff, familiar with his surroundings and happier about being left.

She'd already decided the night before that it would be the last time she stayed, and she was getting desperate for her own bed.

Or at least one that didn't have a plastic mattress.

If Nick would only arrive, she thought, she could talk to him about the barn. She hadn't told Jem yet what their plans were, she wanted to do that with Nick, preferably before he signed on the dotted line at the letting agent's, but when he arrived he dangled a bunch of keys in front of her with a smug grin, like a magician pulling a rabbit out of a hat.

'Your keys, ma'am,' he said, dropping them into her hand. 'You can move in whenever you like.'

She was at the nurses' station, out in the ward, talking to the ward sister and Megan Phillips about what was to happen next, and she stared at the keys in slight consternation.

'What's the matter?' he said, his voice dropping. 'I thought that was what you wanted?'

'It is,' she said. 'But—I thought we were going to talk to Jem first? What if he says no?'

'What if he does? He's ten years old, Kate. There are some decisions that aren't his to make. This is a temporary fix, for a few weeks initially, to cover his convalescence. His friends can come and visit, he can treat it as a holiday—and if it doesn't work out, if he doesn't want me around, then I can go home. It doesn't change anything. It's just for now.'

He was right, of course—he was always right, she thought, except when he was wrong, and then it tended to be on an epic scale. But this—this was just common sense, and she let her breath out on a little huff of laughter and tried to smile.

'You're right. I'm sorry, it's not as if it's a permanent thing. I'm being silly.'

And she'd been letting herself get carried away with all the possibilities. A temporary fix, she reminded herself. Just that, nothing more, for a few weeks, and it might be a total disaster on several counts.

'This might be more long term,' he said then, pulling another set of keys from his pocket, and dropping them in her hand too.

She glanced down, and blinked. 'Car keys?'

'Mmm. I wasn't sure what you wanted, so I asked Chloe if you'd said anything. She mentioned a model you liked.'

She stared at the keys, confused. 'You've got me a car on the PCT contract this quickly?' she said. Surely she had to sign something…

'No. I've bought you a Golf—a nice economical little diesel. They're delivering it to the barn this afternoon.'

She stared at him as if he'd gone mad. 'You bought me a new car?'

'No. It's not new. It's two years old. I thought you'd shout at me if I got you a new one.'

She opened her mouth to shout at him anyway, and to her horror a little sob came out instead.

'Kate?'

'Sorry,' she said, flapping her hand and blinking hard. 'I— It's just— Oh, Nick, you didn't have to do that. I could have got myself another car. Renting the house is one thing, this is quite another. You're doing too much, going too fast.'

'No, I'm not.' This one's got a much better NCAP crash rating. I'm not trying to bribe you,' he said grimly, 'I'm try-ing—too late—to make sure my son stays safe.'

She swallowed, unable to argue, filled with guilt that her car had contributed to his injuries, but he misunderstood her silence and sighed.

'I'm sorry. I know I interfere. It doesn't matter, you can use it for the moment and once you get yourself the car you want, I'll give it to Lucy or something, make it a pool car for the practice maybe.'

'No!' She closed her hand around the keys, reached up and kissed his cheek. 'Thank you. I was just stunned, that's all. I've had to rely on myself for so long, and— Oh, damn.'

Her eyes were welling up, and she rummaged for a tissue in her pocket. He got there first, plucking one off the top of the nurses' station and handing it to her, and she blew her nose and sniffed hard. 'Sorry. It's been a bit of a roller-coaster.'

'I know. How is he?'

She filled him in on the day's events, and he went in to see Jem while she packed her things in the little room she'd been using and gave herself a thorough talking to. She handed the key back to the staff nurse and thanked her, and went into Jem's room to find Nick perched beside him on the bed, leaning up against the backrest and watching him with the games console while he ate grapes.

'You could put that down for five minutes, you know,' she pointed out, but Jem just grinned.

'Uncle Nick wanted to see how I was doing. I was just showing him. I've been teaching him how to use it.'

She stared at him, realising how easily these two had slipped into an easy relationship, almost as if Jem knew Nick was his father. He must have been so desperate for a father all these years, she thought, and he'd never said a word about it; perhaps he didn't realise it, even now. She'd thought he was all right, that they were fine on their own, but maybe she'd been deluding herself and all the time there'd been a void.

A void that should have been filled by Nick.

'We've got something to talk to you about,' she said, determined to get the barn out into the open. 'Could you put that down and listen, please?'

He looked up at her, his eyes wary, and then looked down again. 'Oh, no, it killed me!' he wailed, and put the console down on the locker, then looked up at her again a little worriedly. 'What did you want to talk about?'

'You. When you come out of here, you might not be able to walk up and down stairs for a while, and we've got no bathroom downstairs.'

'Oh. Does that mean I'll have to stay in here longer, till I can go upstairs?' he asked miserably. 'I don't want to. I want to go home as soon as I can. It's not the same here.'

'I know. And, no, it doesn't mean that. It means we'll have to stay somewhere else for a little while. Uncle N—' She broke off, met Nick's eyes ruefully and went on, 'Uncle Nick's found somewhere for us, somewhere he can stay, too, just outside Penhally, near Ben and Lucy. It's a barn, and it's got a downstairs bedroom with doors out to the garden, and an en suite wetroom—'

'What's a non-sweet wetroom?'

'En suite—it's French. It means it's a bathroom attached just to one bedroom. And a wetroom means it's got a tiled floor and you just walk into it and shower, so you wouldn't even have to step up to a shower tray.'

'Wow. And we can stay there?'

'Yes.'

'And you're coming?' he asked, swivelling his head round to look at Nick, and he nodded.

'Yes—so I can help out, and I can do stuff for you that you might not want your mum doing, like help you shower and so on, if you need help at first.'

He nodded. 'Can the dog come?'

'Yes.'

'OK. So was that all you want to talk about?'

She met Nick's eyes and they were full of relief and wry humour. She smiled. 'Nothing else. Just that.'

'Oh. Well, can I try and get to the next level, then? I was nearly there and then it killed me.'

'Kids.'

'Don't. I can't believe he took it so well.'

'Of course he did,' Nick said as if it was obvious, and put the tray down on the table. 'He trusts you to take care of him. You've done it—made it possible for him to be discharged as soon as it's practicable. Why should he take it any other way?'

'Because we always talk everything through. Before I do anything, we talk it through. We're not impulsive like you.'

He looked at her as if she had two heads, and she thought of Lucy and Jack pointing out to him that he interfered, and stifled a smile.

'Don't laugh at me. I'm not impulsive, I'm decisive. It's different,' he protested.

'Actually, you're both,' she pointed out gently, reaching for her coffee. 'Nick, you're going to have to get used to him. Jem likes to see all sides of a thing before he'll commit to it. If I say jump, he doesn't ask how high, he asks why. And I know it's an alien concept to you, but it's the way I've brought him up.'

'It's not an alien concept,' he disagreed, stirring his coffee with huge concentration. 'It's just that some things are as they are. He has to know that there isn't always an answer, that sometimes you have to take some things and some people on trust.'

'And you know what he'd say to that?'

'"Why?"' they said together, and then laughed, reaching out and linking their fingers on the table.

'Did you get anything for Gemma's baby?' she asked, and he nodded.

'Yes. I found a lovely pop-up book of farm animals. It's not for now, obviously, but I thought he might like it later.'

'That's a lovely idea, and it goes really well with my present. I've knitted him a little jumper with fluffy sheep on the front.'

He frowned quizzically. 'Really? You can knit?'

She laughed. 'Of course I can knit! All women can knit.'

'Annabel couldn't knit.'

She felt her smile die. 'Nick, I'm not Annabel,' she reminded him gently. 'And that's not a criticism of her, it's just a fact.'

He closed his eyes for a second and sighed. 'I know you're not Annabel. I'm only too aware of who you are. I just didn't know you could knit. It's one of the very many things I don't know about you, that I've never had the chance to find out. I didn't mean to offend you by comparing you to Annabel.'

'I'm not offended,' she said quickly. 'Not at all. But we are—were—different. You need to realise that if we're going to live together.'

'Well, then, isn't it a good job that I've already noticed?' he said softly, and, draining his coffee, he got to his feet. 'There's Lucy—she said she'd try and pop in. Come on, we'll go up with her.'

He held out his hand to help Kate up, and then tucked her hand in the crook of his arm. 'Hello, darling,' he said, kissing his daughter's cheek, and she took his other arm and walked with them to the ward.

'I've got something for you, from Ben. His chilli recipe. He says you can look after Kate, spoil her a little. Here.'

He grinned and tucked it in his pocket, and vowed to make it for her soon.

They left Jem with Lucy, telling him they were going to see the barn and would be back later, and twenty minutes later they'd pulled up outside and unlocked the door.

'Welcome home,' he said softly, pushing the door open, and she stepped inside, a little bit of her disappointed that he hadn't carried her over the threshold. But how stupid was that? They weren't married—far from it, and they might never be. This was just about Jem, and if she'd expected more because of his tenderness with her last night, she was deluded.

The entrance was in the single-story section on the left-hand side, between the living space and the bedrooms, and they walked through to the sitting room with its low beamed ceiling and comfortable furniture grouped around the log burner, and into the central section where a battered old oak refectory table sat in pride of place.

It would be the perfect setting for family get-togethers, she thought—all Nick's children with their spouses and families gathered around, the air filled with their laughter. She could hear it now, as she looked around her at the great vaulted space of the dining hall. Its huge, soaring window faced the courtyard, with its flat, winding paths and low shrubs giving structure to the sheltered little garden, the wings of the house wrapped round it like arms, protecting it from the elements, and then beyond it were the fields and then the sea.

And like Nick had the first time he'd stepped inside, she felt the house welcome her, as if those arms had folded round her and gathered her to its heart.

Romantic nonsense, she thought, and yet...

'You were right, it is calm and tranquil here,' she said softly, feeling the tension drain out of her. 'It'll be so good for him. Thank you, Nick.'

And going up on tiptoe, she kissed his cheek.

For a long moment he stared at her, their eyes locked, and then he seemed to pull himself together and looked away, and they walked around the rest of the house slowly and had their first real, proper look.

'It's amazing,' she said, standing on the galleried walkway above the dining hall and looking out over the courtyard to the sea in the distance. 'Beautiful. I could stand here all day and look at that view.'

'There are plenty of chairs you could sit on,' Nick pointed out with a smile, and she laughed softly and turned away from the window, looking up at the vaulted ceiling with its heavy beams. The gallery spanned the space, leading to a bedroom at each end, and they were both amazing.

'Which bedroom do you want?'

She glanced at him. 'I don't know. Maybe I should be downstairs with Jem. He could call me then, if he needed me in the night.'

And she'd be further from temptation.

'It doesn't have its own shower.'

'There's a bathroom almost next to it. I'm sure I'll manage.' She went back downstairs and round the corner to the wing with the two bedrooms and the study in it, on the other side of the entrance hall. The bedroom there which she would take was a small room in comparison to the ones upstairs, but big enough for her, and most importantly it was close to Jem's.

'It'll be fine,' she said firmly, and he nodded. She wasn't sure, but she thought he looked a tiny bit relieved. 'What about you?'

He gave a wry smile. 'If there's no competition, I'll have the one with the sea view from the window by the bed.'

It also had a view of her bedroom window, she realised, glancing out of it and looking up at the taller section of the barn. 'We ought to get some food in,' she said, trying to be practical and not think about his bedroom.

'I've done it. I ordered it on line last night. It's being delivered in the morning between seven and nine.'

'Will you be here?'

'Yes. I thought I'd stay here tonight, start moving some things in. I ought to go into the practice tomorrow, too, and catch up on some admin. I can't just bail on them, and Jem seems to be improving steadily. I'll take you over there whenever you like so you can be with him, if you don't feel ready to drive yet. Just tell me when you want to be picked up.'

'After the shopping arrives?'

He nodded. 'Sure. I'll come and get you from your place once it's here.'

'Or I could stay here, too,' she said rashly, and his eyes locked with hers.

'You could.'

But their eyes remained locked, both of them trapped, like rabbits in headlights, transfixed by the prospect of being alone together in this house.

Nick dragged his eyes away. 'Of course you could move in, start getting settled, and I could stay at home. And you could get the dog back from Chloe and Oliver. He must miss you.'

'But I can't really leave him alone here, he's not used to it. He'd be better in our puppy crèche until Jem's out of hospital, at least for the days. And I'm not sure how safe the garden is. I don't want him getting out.'

'There's a fenced area—I had a look at it this morning on my way to the agents. I couldn't get into the house, but I walked all round the garden, and the back of it's entirely enclosed to about four feet in height with sheep netting. He'd be quite safe. He could just run around and let off steam when you're here, and he could go to the puppy crèche when neither of us is around. And I can come over and help you walk him.'

'But you've ordered food. It should be you here, not me.'

'I can eat with you. You have to eat, too, Kate. As Ben said, I can wait on you,' he said with a wry smile, and she chuckled.

'I can just see that.'

'Let me try. You never know, I might be good at it. One of my hidden talents.'

She gave a splutter of laughter. 'Very successfully hidden. You've kept it from me for thirty-four years,' she said drily, and went back to the kitchen to acquaint herself with it.

She heard a quiet sigh behind her, and turned back to him, shocked by the sadness in his eyes. 'Oh, Nick...'

'I'm sorry,' he said, his voice bleak. 'It wasn't the way it was meant to be, was it?'

'What?'

'Life. Our plans.'

'We don't always get what we're expecting in life,' she said gently. 'I always thought you'd come back from university and marry me and I'd have your children. Instead you married Annabel, and I married James, and we couldn't have any, and you ended up with loads.'

'Was that why you gave up midwifery? Because it hurt too much not being able to have your own?'

She smiled. 'That and watching you and Annabel bring the children down here on holiday year after year when they were little. All the children I might have had if I'd been with you, and yet there I was with James, banging our heads against a brick wall. And then you moved back down here close to your family and got a job in Wadebridge and bought the house on Harbour Road, and I was falling over you all the time, a constant reminder of what I'd lost.'

He sighed heavily. 'Kate, don't. We can't turn the clock back.'

'No. But even if we haven't gone home together every night, I've worked with you for years now in the practice. I've seen you every day, spent time with you, so it hasn't all been bad,' she pointed out gently. 'You've still been part of my life. And I have Jem. You can have no idea what that's meant to me, over the years.'

'I can imagine. My children are infinitely precious to me, even though I haven't always seen eye to eye with them, so you don't have to try and explain.'

She smiled sadly, wishing that Jem had been one of those precious children, that she'd been their mother, but, as he said, they couldn't turn the clock back and if they did, it would all be very different. And so she couldn't wish it undone, no matter how hard it had been at times.

He came over to her, standing just inches away, and with the tip of a long forefinger he tilted her head up so she met his eyes. 'Don't be sad, Kate. We've got a chance now, if we choose to take it. Let's not waste it.'

A chance? For them? So maybe she hadn't misunderstood. 'I still don't know how good you could be at waiting on me,' she said lightly, and he laughed.

'Oh, I'm good,' he said, his eyes twinkling with mischief, and she sucked in a tiny little breath and turned away, before she did something silly, like kiss him. He'd kissed her last night, but that had been in the safety of the hospital, where anyone could have come in. They were alone here, and awareness of that and of him made her tingle with nerves.

'I'm looking forward to finding out,' she said lightly. 'So, are you moving in here tonight, or am I?'

'Do you want to?'

'Not alone. It makes me feel a bit nervous,' she admitted. She held her breath for a second, then said, 'We could always be grown up about it and share.'

His mouth twisted into something that could have been a smile if it hadn't been so touched with sadness.

'Grown-ups sleep together, Kate,' he said softly. 'And I'm not sure you're ready for that yet.'

Her heart hammered against her ribcage. 'Can't we have a little restraint?'

'Oh, yes. We can have a little. I just think it might take rather more than that.'

She looked away, his eyes too revealing suddenly, full of feelings that had been locked away for very many years. Her tongue flicked out and moistened her lips, and he groaned.

'Kate, don't,' he whispered, his voice almost inaudible.

The air was vibrating with tension, almost solid, as if she could cut it with a knife, and it seemed to have set all around them, holding them in place, their eyes locked again.

The sound of the doorbell was shocking, dissolving the air so they could move again, and Nick walked to the door as if he was in a trance.

He opened it and looked past the man standing on the broad flagstone path. There were three cars outside. His, and two others.

Of course. Kate's new car.

'Delivery for Mrs Althorp?' the man said, brandishing a clipboard and some keys, and he gave himself a mental shake and breathed in.

'Yes—thank you. Kate?'

'I'm here,' she said, coming to stand beside him. 'Is that it?'

'The metallic grey one,' he said, his voice sounding strained. 'You have to sign for it.'

'You'd better check it over,' the man said.

It could have had square wheels, for all the attention they gave it. Kate could see nothing but the look in Nick's eyes, he could see nothing but her tongue flicking out to lick her lips.

'It's fine,' he said, and she signed the sheet with trembling fingers and the delivery driver handed her the keys.

'Enjoy your car, then,' he said, and drove away in the other vehicle, leaving them standing there.

'So, will it be all right? The car?' he asked, trying desperately for normality, and she nodded.

Not that she was really able to concentrate on it, but it was exactly what she'd wanted, top of her wish list, and she was thrilled with it. She would be thrilled with it, just the moment she could get that look in his eyes out of her head.

'It's wonderful. Thank you, Nick. I'll look after it, I promise.'

'No. I'll look after it. I've bought a service package with it. It's got the next three years of servicing paid for. All you have to do is book it in.'

Her eyes filled. He seemed to have thought of everything, and she ought to pay a bit more attention to it after all his trouble and expense. She sat in the driver's seat, and rested her head back with a sigh.

'All right?'

'Lovely. Really good seat. Gosh, it's nice to rest my head. My neck's still a bit achy.'

He gave a short sigh and held the door for her. 'Come on, you need to lie down, and I'm going to massage it for you,' he said firmly, and, locking the car, he ushered her back inside and down the corridor to her bedroom.

'We'll need to bring bed linen,' she said, clutching at normality.

'Yes. What have you got on under that top?' he asked, and she swallowed.

'A vest top and a bra.'

'Right. Take the top off, leave the vest top on and lie down on your back with your head at the foot of the bed,' he instructed in a businesslike doctor's voice, and then he covered her with her top so only her shoulders were exposed, put a pillow under her knees, knelt down on the floor by her head and slid his warm, hard hands under her shoulders, running his fingers gently but firmly up the columns of muscle each side of her spine and up into her neck.

'Oh, that's amazing,' she groaned, and he said nothing, just kept on with the gentle, rhythmic movement until the tension had eased out of her neck and shoulders and she was utterly relaxed. Then he got to his feet and stood looking down at her, an odd expression in his eyes.

'Stay there for a while, have a rest. I won't be long.'

'What are you going to do?'

'Get us some milk from the Trevellyans' farm shop, and something for supper. I'll only be a few minutes, it's just up the road. Try and have a sleep.'

She heard the front door close behind him, and then the sound of a car driving away, crunching on the gravel. Odd, how they hadn't heard the other two arrive, but, then, she'd not been able to hear anything over the pounding of her heart.

She got up and pulled her top back on, lay down the right way up with a pillow under her head, and curled on her side, staring unseeingly out of the French doors at the courtyard beyond.

There. They'd managed it—been in a bedroom, had their hands on each other, even, and survived it.

They could do this. Behave like grown-ups.

Grown-ups sleep together, Kate.

'Not if they choose not to,' she said out loud, and closed her eyes determinedly. Before she knew it, she'd drifted off to sleep.

He wasn't long—just long enough to give himself some much-needed sea air and take Kate's new car out for a spin. He drove to the Trevellyans' with the windows open and the wind in his hair, and by the time he'd returned with the shopping, he was almost back under control.

He pottered round the kitchen, putting everything away while the kettle boiled and investigating the contents of the cupboards. It was such a blessing that the place was furnished as a holiday cottage and equipped with everything. It meant they only had to bring clothes and bedding, and they could pick them up later. Or whoever was staying would. He still wasn't sure who it would be.

The kettle boiled, and he made a pot of tea, left it to brew and tapped on her door.

There was no reply, and when he opened the door he saw she was fast asleep on her side, her hand lying open, relaxed, the fingers loosely curled. He stood there for a few moments, watching the slow rise and fall of her chest, and as if she'd become aware of him she opened her eyes and looked up.

'Oh. You're back,' she said softly.

'I've made tea. It's in the kitchen. And Mike Trevellyan sends his love.'

'Oh, you saw him.'

'Yes. And he'd heard a rumour about me and Jem. I told him it was true. He won't spread it further, but I thought he ought to know. And, anyway, they're Ben and Lucy's neighbours.'

'Yes, of course. So it's out, is it?'

She sat up on the edge of the bed and ran her hands through her hair, lifting it away from her neck and letting it fall, and he felt heat slam through him.

'It seems that way.' He walked away, heading back to the kitchen before he did something he'd regret. 'I've poured the tea,' he called over his shoulder, 'and I bought one of Fran's lemon drizzle cakes.'

She followed him, tugging her top straight and reminding him of what was underneath it. Not that he needed reminding, after kneeling by her head and staring down her cleavage for ten minutes. 'That's my favourite,' she said with a smile.

'I know. That's why I bought it.'

He slid a plate towards her with a generous slice on it, and followed it with a cup of tea, and she sat down at the table overlooking the courtyard and the sea and smiled again.

'I could learn to love it here,' she said.

He sat down beside her, propped his elbows on the table and looked out at the view while he bit into the cake.

'Good. Me, too. So, who's moving in when?'

'Both of us. Tonight,' she said firmly, and he nearly choked. He couldn't blow it, he reminded himself. It was too important, there was far too much at stake.

He could do this. He could.

Even if it killed him.

CHAPTER EIGHT

WATCHING Jem slowly recover his strength was both a joy and a relief, but unbelievably draining.

Every hour brought further progress—sitting up in bed, then sitting out, then standing for a moment on his right leg as he swivelled onto the chair for himself. It was like watching a time-lapse sequence of a baby turning into a toddler, but Kate was more than happy to sit through it. She was looking forward to seeing him walk again, to seeing him run, but for now, she was just glad he was alive and making progress.

And to know she'd be going home to the barn every night with Nick. She felt that if she pinched herself, she'd wake up and find it was all a dream, and the thought was frightening.

They'd moved in last night, collecting just enough clothes and linen to see them over the next few days, and then he'd cooked for her—not Ben's chilli, but a cold chicken and ham pie from the farm shop, with a lovely fresh salad and boiled new potatoes, followed by some utterly delectable honey and ginger ice cream made on the farm.

And they'd talked about telling Jem. Today. Later, after Nick arrived. He was at the surgery now, doing a clinic and seeing a few patients, and then he was coming over and they were going to tell him.

Somehow. She still had no idea how.

She went for a walk up the corridor to see Gemma and her baby while they took out Jem's catheter, to his relief, and then they moved him to the ward downstairs, which was for the children who were on the mend; it had access on one side to a courtyard with seats and toys and lots of things to look at, and on the other side, right near his bed, was the courtyard with the ducklings.

Five of them, they finally concluded, watching them peck about amongst the moss and bark chips, brown and yellow and fluffy and very cute. They watched them for ages, until at last the mother tucked them back under her wings for a rest, and he went back to his games console.

He was allowed other visitors now, and the first people to come in the afternoon were Rob and Matthew.

The boys had plenty to talk about and they left them to it. Rob took her hand and squeezed it fleetingly. 'How are you? It must have been hell—have you coped OK?'

She nodded. 'Yes. It's been pretty awful, but Nick's been great. Rob—there's something you need to know.'

He shook his head and smiled. 'I know already—I can see it in your eyes, and I'm really pleased for you. You go for it. I know how you feel. Your heart will never really belong to anybody else, just as mine won't, but at least you've now got that chance, and you have to take it.' He glanced at Jem, his head close to Matt's, bent over the games console. 'Does Jem know yet?' he asked softly.

'The paternity thing?' she murmured. 'No. Or about Nick and me. That's so new I'm not sure I know about it, really.'

He smiled. 'I think Jem will be fine with it once he's used to the idea. Is there anything I can do, anything I can get you?'

She shook her head. 'No. Just bring Matt to see him sometimes. He's going to be horribly bored. Oh, and we've taken a rented barn up near the Trevellyans' farm, with some bedrooms and a shower room on the ground floor, in case he can't manage stairs for a while. I'll give you the directions. Matt can come and stay later on, if you like. It'll give Jem something to look forward to when he comes out.'

'That would be really nice. Look, is Nick all right about this? He does realise I'm just bringing Matt to see Jem?'

'Yes, he does. And he's fine with it. He likes you.'

Rob laughed softly. 'That's good of him. I'm not sure I'd be so generous in his shoes. I hope you can make this work.'

So did she, but they still had the hurdle of the great reveal, as she was beginning to call it in her head, and she couldn't really think past that.

They didn't stay long, and Nick appeared soon afterwards. She wondered if he'd been lurking somewhere, waiting until the coast was clear, giving them space.

She didn't know. He'd been a little odd with her that morning, maybe because of the barn and being there alone together. She'd gone to bed early, closing her door quite firmly, and he'd gone up a short while later. She'd seen his light come on, seen it go off shortly afterwards, and she wondered if he'd slept as well as her. They were both tired, both drained, and he'd looked better at breakfast, but he'd been quiet, a little distracted.

'So, how's it going?' he asked Jem. 'Worked your way up another level yet?'

'My battery's flat again,' he said. 'I had to ask the nurses upstairs to charge it, but I don't know any of the nurses down here so I don't know who to ask.'

'I can charge it for you,' he said. 'We've got to go soon— we're going to pick Bruno up from Chloe and take him back to the barn and settle him in, so it can be charging while we do that and we can bring it back this evening.'

'Great—and then can we do the face thing on it, Uncle Nick?'

'Yes, I'm sure we can,' he said, and there was a flicker of

emotion in his eyes, just as there always was when Jem called him that. And Kate got a stupid lump in her throat, just as she always did. But maybe not for much longer. She felt a shiver of dread, and stifled it. It would be fine. It would.

He found the charger in the locker, and packed it up with the console and put it in her bag, and they went back to the barn, put it on charge and collected Bruno. He was so excited to see her, she thought the young dog was going to wag his tail right off, and her eyes filled with tears.

'Oh, sweetheart, have you missed me? I'm so sorry,' she said, getting down on the floor with him and hugging him, but he was too excited, and bounced around barking, and Chloe laughed and let him out into the garden so he could race round like a lunatic and have a mad five minutes with Chloe and Oliver's little bitch from the same litter of flat-coated retriever puppies.

'It's been a bit hectic on the puppy-sitting front this last week,' Chloe admitted when Kate thanked her yet again for her kindness. 'I haven't even had time to see Gemma yet—how's the baby?'

Kate smiled. 'Gorgeous. He's absolutely gorgeous. I had the nicest cuddle yesterday morning. One of the advantages of being a midwife—I can pull rank and sneak in outside visiting hours! But they were coming home today, so you should be able to pop over there anytime over the weekend.'

'Oh, I will, don't worry!' Chloe laughed. 'I'll give her ten minutes to settle in, and I'll be there. Right, young man, back inside and settle down, and then I think you're going to go to your new home. That'll be a bit exciting, won't it?'

Bruno wagged and leant up against her leg, tongue lolling and a big smile on his face, and Kate clipped his lead on.

'Come on, you big hussy. That's enough flirting,' Nick said, and put him in his crate in the back of his estate car—much, much easier to transport him in—and they drove back to the barn and introduced him to the house.

'It's a good job they don't mind pets here,' she said, wondering how much damage he would do, but he hadn't wrecked anything at home yet, and she hoped if he settled here quickly, there wouldn't be a problem.

'Can you put him in the crate, if necessary?' Nick asked, reading her mind, and she nodded.

'Yes, but I hardly ever use it, he's been so good. And I've got him a new rope toy to play with. That might keep him occupied.'

They took him out and let him run around in the garden, and he christened a few of the bushes and came back inside, flopping down in a patch of sunshine on the wooden floor of the dining room and watching them from under his eyebrows as they made a pot of tea.

'We mustn't forget to take this back,' Kate said, checking the charge on the games console while Nick poured the tea, and while she waited for it to cool and stared at the view, he cut them thick slices of the lemon drizzle cake and put one down in front of her.

'I'll be like a house,' she protested, but he just smiled.

'You haven't put an ounce on in years,' he told her. 'You work too hard.'

'Well, I'm not working now.'

'No, but you haven't been eating in the hospital.'

'That's rubbish, I've been eating junk food! Except for the pie last night, and that was hardly low calorie.'

'It was good, though, and let's face it, a little weight on you won't hurt. You'll just get curvier, and there's nothing wrong with that. You've got a beautiful body, Kate. Be proud of it.'

She met his eyes and saw the heat flicker in them before he banked it, and she felt tears clog her throat. He didn't know what he was talking about. Maybe once, but not any more. Not since her surgery.

She looked away. 'I'd rather not gain if I can avoid it,' she said, 'so I hope you're planning something low calorie for supper.'

'Not tonight,' he said with a wry laugh. 'Tonight is Ben's chilli, but I'll cut down on the oil and it's extra-lean steak mince. And kidney beans are good for you. Anyway, you'll love it, it's a great recipe—assuming I can pull it off.'

She raised an eyebrow. 'Isn't it a bit ambitious for you?' she asked, glad to get off the topic of her body. 'I mean, I know you're trying to spoil me, but we all know you're the king of the ready meals aisle.'

He laughed and picked up his cake. 'I don't know. We'll see, won't we?' He took a bite of the cake and put it down, then stared back out of the window, his smile fading. A quiet sigh eased from his body, and he turned to her, his eyes troubled.

'How are we going to tell him, Kate?' he asked softly.

She gave a helpless little shrug. 'I have absolutely no idea.'

In the end, it was easy.

Jem was sitting up in his bed when they arrived, waiting for them. They gave him the games console and settled themselves down, Kate on the armchair by the bed where he sat during the day when he was allowed out, and Nick on a hard plastic chair facing them, so they could both see him.

There was a child in a bed near Jem who was having a blood transfusion, and he looked around, his eyes tracking to his drip and up to the bag of blood running slowly into him. He watched it drip for a moment, then said thoughtfully, 'I wonder who my blood came from?'

She saw Nick stiffen slightly, and their eyes met. Was this it? The time? She felt her heart thump against her ribs, and he gave her an imperceptible nod.

'It could have been Uncle Nick,' she said quietly. 'Or Jack. They took some from both of them. You're B-negative—it's a fairly rare blood group and they'd run out, and you have to have the same otherwise it makes you very ill.'

'And you're the same as me?' he asked, looking straight at Nick.

She saw his jaw clench. 'Yes.'

'That was lucky. Are you the same, Mum?'

She shook her head. 'No.' His head swivelled back to Nick. 'So how did they know we were the same?'

'They tested you. I know mine, because I give blood regularly. So does Jack.' He hesitated, then said carefully, 'You inherit the genes that determine your blood group from one or other of your parents,' he said, and then waited.

Jem frowned. 'So—my dad must have been B-negative, too, then?'

'Yes.'

It wasn't strictly true. His father could have been AB, but they both knew he wasn't, and thankfully Nick didn't complicate it any more than it already was. Because the essence of it was already registering, Kate could see.

'And it's rare?' Jem was saying, a little frown pleating his brow, and she saw the muscle in Nick's jaw flicker again.

'Yes. Yes, it's rare. Less than three in a hundred people.'

The frown deepened, and his eyes swivelled to Kate's. 'That's weird.'

'Not really.' She could feel her heart pounding, and she swallowed before continuing, 'Jem, there's something you need to know, something I should have told you before.'

She saw the light dawn in his eyes, and he turned his head slowly back to Nick and stared at him hard. 'Are you my father?' he asked, his voice flat.

She saw Nick's throat work, and he nodded slightly. 'Yes,' he said, his voice gruff. 'Yes, I am.'

For an endless moment he just stared at Nick in silence, and Kate could see the pulse beating in his throat.

'But—how? I thought— Why didn't you tell me? Why

did you tell me my dad was dead?' he asked, turning back to Kate and spearing her with accusing eyes. 'I thought I didn't have a father, but if Uncle Nick's my father, I could have had a dad all my life! Why didn't you tell me?'

Her stomach knotted into a ball at the look in his eyes. 'I couldn't. Nick was married, he had a family, and I didn't think making them all sad would make us any happier, and it wouldn't have helped us. We had each other, Jem. We were all right—'

'No, we weren't! I didn't have a dad. I wanted a dad—I've always wanted a dad. But I thought he was dead, and all the time he was alive and you didn't tell me! If I hadn't had the accident, if I hadn't needed his blood, would you have told me? Ever?'

She swallowed down the tears. 'Of course I would. I always knew I'd have to tell you one day when the time was right, I just didn't know when that would be. We've been trying to work out how to do it without hurting you.'

He stared reproachfully at her, then at Nick again, and asked him a question she'd asked herself over and over. 'Why don't you want to be my dad?'

Nick flinched as if he'd been kicked in the gut. 'I do.'

'You don't,' Jem said firmly. 'When we were on the beach flying the kite, ages ago, after Christmas last year, that American lady said I was like my father, and I laughed, and you said you couldn't do this and stormed off. I didn't understand, but that was it, wasn't it? She realised you were my dad, and you didn't want me to know, so you walked away, because you don't want to be my father.'

'I do.'

'No, you don't!' he said, his voice rising, a catch in it. 'If you did want to, you would have stayed, you would have told me then. But you didn't want me.'

'I did want you, Jeremiah,' Nick said hoarsely. 'I do want you—more than you can ever imagine. But I didn't think you'd want me. The man you've always thought was your father was a hero, a brave man. How could I be as good as that?'

He stopped abruptly, turning to the window and propping his hand on the frame, staring out into the courtyard. Kate could see the muscles working in his jaw, see the tears tracking down his cheek, and she reached out a hand and laid it against his side in comfort. He closed his eyes and swallowed, and she dropped her hand and turned back to her son.

'Don't blame him, Jem,' she said softly. 'It was me who lied to you, me who let you believe my husband was your father. And Nick didn't know. I didn't tell him for ages, because of Auntie Annabel. It wouldn't have been fair to her. He's only known for two years.'

'So why didn't you tell me before? After Auntie Annabel died, why didn't you tell him then? You could have told him then,' he said, his voice accusing.

'I didn't know how,' she said softly. 'He was very sad and angry when she died, and he was very busy at work sorting out the practice. It wouldn't have been a good time. There was never a good time. I thought there would be, I kept waiting, but then—when he did know—'

'I tried,' Nick said, turning back from the window again, his face taut. 'It may not seem like it, but I did try. But James was a hard act to follow. I thought maybe you'd be happier with things as they were, with me just as Uncle Nick, just as I've always been. And I tried to spend more time with you, quality time, to get to know you and let you get to know me, and I thought we might be getting somewhere, but then that woman commented on us looking alike, and I panicked. I wasn't sure the time was right, and I was so worried I'd make it worse. And just when I thought we ought to try again, your mother met Rob, and they seemed to be getting on so well. He's a good man, and I thought he'd make you a good father, a much better father than I would. You all seemed to be so happy together, and I didn't feel I had the right to destroy that. What good would it have done, Jem? I could have ruined it for you, for all of you. I didn't want to do that. I didn't have the right—'

'But you're my real father,' Jem sobbed, his bruised face anguished. 'You should have told me! I should have known.' I don't care if you're complete rubbish. It's better than being dead!' And he turned his face into the pillow and sobbed brokenly.

Kate leant forwards, resting a hand on his shoulder, but he shrugged her off, and she bit her lip and tried to stop the tears, but they fell anyway, coursing down her cheeks and dripping off her chin, and then she felt Nick's arms round her, cradling her gently against his side as he perched on the arm of the chair.

'Shh. Come on, he'll be all right,' he murmured, his voice ragged. 'He'll come round.'

'No, I won't,' Jem sobbed from the depths of the pillow. 'I won't be all right. Leave me alone! I hate you both! Go away!'

And then she felt Nick shudder, felt the pain tearing through him, and she slid her arms around his waist and hung on.

'Come on, let's give him some space,' he muttered after a few seconds, but she wouldn't leave him.

'I can't go. Not now. You go, leave me with him. I'll talk to him.'

'Will you be all right?'

She lifted her tear-stained face to him and tried to smile. 'I'll have to be, won't I? I have to do this, Nick. He's my son.'

A tremor ran through him, and he stood up. 'I'll see you later—I'll give you an hour. Call me if you need me to come back,' he said, and, closing the curtains around the bed, he walked swiftly away.

* * *

She watched him go, listened to the sound of his footsteps retreating, and then she turned back to Jem, biting her lip and wondering how on earth she could unravel this sorry mess of hurt and lies and broken trust that they'd created.

She had no idea. She just knew she had to find a way.

Tentatively, with nothing but love on her side, she reached out her hand and touched him.

'I'm sorry. I'm so, so sorry,' she said unsteadily, and after a moment he opened his eyes and turned his head to look at her.

'Why?' he asked, his voice breaking. 'Why didn't you tell me? I could have kept a secret. All these years, I thought I didn't have a dad, that I'd never have a dad. And then you met Rob, and I thought maybe he could be my stepdad, but all the time I had a real father, and I didn't know!'

'I know. But you do at least know him, even if you didn't realise he was your father. I've made sure you see him regularly, and he knows you, and all about you. I did everything I could under the circumstances. Don't blame him, Jem. It was my fault, too, and he didn't have any choice. I kept it from him too. And I'm so sorry we've hurt you.'

He sniffed, but the tears still welled, and, unable to bear it, she got up and leant over, taking him gently into her arms, and he burrowed his face into the side of her neck.

Nick held it together just long enough to get out of St Piran, and then he pulled over on the coast road into a parking area, got out of the car and sucked in a lungful of the fresh, salt air.

If he'd been that sort of man, he could have wept bitter, anguished tears for the son he'd let down and all the years that had been lost. Years he couldn't give him back, years that were gone for ever. But he wasn't, and so he shoved it all aside and concentrated his efforts on the future.

If it took him till the end of his life, he vowed, he'd do his best to build a relationship with this child.

He got back in the car and drove to his house. There were some things he needed to pick up, and he could be alone there, think things through.

Except he wasn't alone. Sam Cavendish was there, just coming out of his mother's house next door, and he propped himself against the fence and frowned at Nick.

'You look like hell. Fancy a drink?'

'No, I'm going back to the hospital. We just told him.'

Sam winced sympathetically. 'Ouch. How did it go?'

'Pretty much as expected. Why don't you come in? I don't really want to talk about it here.'

So Sam followed him into the house and propped himself up on the worktop while Nick put the kettle on, for something to do as much as anything.

'So—what happened?' Sam prompted.

Nick sighed and rammed a hand through his hair. 'There was a kid in there having a blood transfusion, and Jem was asking about where his own blood transfusion had come from, and it sort of followed from there. He's the same blood group as me.'

'Yeah, Jack told me,' Sam said. 'And how did he take it?'

'Badly. He's angry. He said he'd spent nearly eleven years thinking he didn't have a father, and all the time he did, and he said...' His voice cracked, and he coughed again and flexed his fingers. 'He said he didn't care if I was complete rubbish, it was better than being dead.'

Sam snorted. 'Well, I'd agree with him if my own wasn't so useless he might as well be dead, but what made him think you'd be rubbish?'

'I did. I told him James was a hard act to follow, that he might have preferred a hero. Apparently not. I didn't realise Jack had told you about the blood group thing.'

'Mmm. He was angry, but he's not really surprised.'

Nick's head snapped up and he stared at Sam, stunned. 'What makes you say that?'

Sam laughed softly. 'Oh, come on, Nick, everyone knows you've always loved Kate.'

They did? Well, why the hell hadn't they all reminded him of that in Freshers' Week when he'd been busy drinking himself senseless and making love to the first pretty girl who'd had enough alcohol to make her forget her common sense and sleep with him—the pretty girl who'd told him four weeks later that she was pregnant, and nine months later had presented him with twins, and then a year later with another son, while he'd worked his way through university supported by their parents and tried not to think about the girl he'd left behind. Had Annabel known she wasn't his first choice? Had she known he'd only done the decent thing and made the best marriage he could with the hand fate had dealt him? He sincerely hoped not, but if his feelings had been so obvious to everyone else, then why not to her?

And she'd sent him into Kate's arms, the night of the storm, almost as if she'd known that only Kate could comfort him.

'I tried to love her,' he murmured, as much to himself as to Sam, then he lifted his head and met Sam's eyes. 'I did love her, and I tried to be a good husband, and I think we had a good marriage, but maybe I was deluding myself.'

'I don't think so. I remember her—I grew up next door, don't forget. I spent a lot of time in this house. It was like a second home to me at one point. And she always seemed very happy, contented. At peace. She had a good life with you and a lovely family. I don't think you let her down, Nick. And she's been gone five years now. I think if anything you let yourself down, cheated yourself, and Kate, for too long. And maybe now it's time to do something positive about that.'

Sam shrugged away from the worktop, clapped Nick on the

shoulder and headed for the front door. 'I'm going home to my wife and child. And tomorrow we're going house-hunting.'

Nick followed him through to the hall.

'Why?'

Sam laughed. 'Because my ankle doesn't like the hill and Gemma can't lift the buggy up the steps into the house. And we need to be nearer my mother.'

'How much nearer?' he asked, an idea dawning. 'Like—next door?'

Sam's eyes narrowed and he tilted his head on one side. 'Next door? As in, here?'

He nodded. 'There's a barn. I've just moved into it with Kate, so that when Jem comes out of the hospital in a few days he can live on the flat for a bit until he's got his mobility back—assuming he's speaking to us by then. And it's for sale. We're renting it at the moment, but I think it's time to move on, time to lay Annabel's ghost to rest, whatever happens with me and Kate and Jeremiah. So I'm going to sell this house, and buy the barn, and then if it works out…'

Sam's jaw sagged slightly, and then he laughed. 'Really? You're selling? How much?'

He shrugged. 'I have no idea. It's the least of my worries. I won't cheat you, Sam.'

Sam grinned. 'I'll make sure of it. Talk to the agents—let me know. And I'll go and sound Gemma out, but I know what she'll say. She loves this house, and so do I.'

Nick felt himself smile as the weight lifted a little. 'I know you do,' he said. 'And it needs another family.'

And if Sam and Gemma bought it from him, it would bring his dream a little closer…

CHAPTER NINE

HE FOUND Kate in the deserted café, sitting nursing a stale cup of coffee and looking like death.

He sat down opposite her and took the cup out of her hands. It was stone cold, and he tutted softly and wrapped her hands in his to warm them. 'How is he?'

She shrugged. 'They had to give him some more morphine and something to help him sleep. I think it was all the upset...'

She trailed off, and he sighed, stroking his thumb over the back of her hand. 'What did he say? After I left.'

She shrugged again, a helpless little gesture that made his heart ache for her. 'He's just really shocked, I think. It's a lot for him to take in. I explained to the staff—the night sister and Megan Phillips. They were really nice to him. Megan, especially, was really lovely. She's such a nice girl. And I rang Jess Carmichael, and she came up and talked to me for a minute while he was asleep, and she makes so much sense. She's going to come and see him when he's feeling a little better and let him talk it through with her.'

'Do you think he will?' Nick asked, not sure about the idea of unburdening to a counsellor, but Kate nodded.

'I think so. He likes her. He talked to her before, when I was ill.' She sighed. 'Nick, I'm really tired, can you take me home?' she asked, and his heart contracted.

'Sure,' he said softly, and, helping her to her feet, he wrapped an arm round her shoulders and led her out to the car.

'So much for Ben's chilli,' she said as they went into the house, and he just pulled her into his arms and held her while the dog sniffed and wagged around their feet. She was exhausted, and she had to be hungry. He was—or his body was. His heart wasn't in the least bit interested in anything as trivial as food, but for her sake, he'd fix them something to eat and make sure she ate it.

'I'll cook us something quick,' he said, giving her a last little hug and letting her go. 'We can have more of the cold pie, or toast, or anything you want.'

'Toast,' she said. 'Toast and a nice, hot cup of tea. And it's cold—I know it's April, but do you think it would be possible to put the heating on?'

'Want me to light the fire?'

She glanced at the big woodburner and sighed longingly. 'Oh, that would be lovely. Is there any wood?'

He nodded. 'There's a pile out in the cart lodge, I'll get some while I'm taking the dog out. I'll put the kettle on, you go and sit down. You look done in.'

'Do you think we could have done things any differently?' she asked later, as they lay side by side with their legs stretched out towards the fire and its living hearthrug.

Nick stared at the dog and wondered what it must be like to have no responsibilities. 'In what way?' he asked. 'Do you mean the way we told him now, or if we should have told him years ago? Either way, I don't know. I don't think there was a right way, under the circumstances, but I wish you'd told me sooner, Kate. I wish I'd known, right back at the beginning. I would have made sure I saw more of him.'

'How?' she asked, turning her head to face him, searching his eyes and finding only confusion that mirrored her own.

'You were working in Wadebridge, living in Penhally, and I can see your house from mine—I could look across sometimes and see Annabel hanging the washing out! How were you going to spend time with him, under those circumstances, without arousing suspicion? And I didn't want to do that to you, to put you under that sort of pressure for something that hadn't been your fault.'

'Of course it was my fault!' he said. 'I heard you crying and I walked in when I knew you were naked, when I'd seen you, I'd undressed you—dammit, Kate, I knew what was going to happen if I opened that door.'

'Nick, I was falling apart, and so were you.' She lifted her hand and cradled his jaw, feeling the muscles clench beneath her palm. 'You needed me, every bit as much as I needed you. We were on autopilot—we didn't set out to make love, and if I hadn't got pregnant, nobody would ever have known.'

'I would have known. I never forgot, Kate. It haunted me—it still haunts me. And things with Annabel were never quite the same after that. I don't really know why, if it was because I'd changed, or because she sensed what happened between us that night. Maybe she even knew Jem was mine. I'll never know. But I knew when I walked through that door how dangerous it was, and I should have stopped myself.'

'And left me there alone, in that state? How was that right?' She leant over, closing the gap and touching her lips lightly to his cheek, then rested her head on his shoulder. 'I needed you, Nick, and you needed me, more than we'd ever needed anyone before. It wasn't your fault, it was just one of those things—part of being human. And you can't take all the responsibility for the fact that I got pregnant.'

'Why not? I know how the system works, Kate, and God knows I'd had enough object lessons in it!'

She eased back so she could look at him. 'Was Annabel on the Pill?'

'Yes.'

'So it wasn't unreasonable that you didn't think about contraception, because it wasn't a normal part of your sex life at the time. Nor was it mine. I didn't even think about it. James and I had been trying for three years, and we'd finally admitted that there might be something wrong and gone for tests, just a week before. We were still waiting for the results when he died, and maybe I should have told you, but how? Who would have gained?'

He sighed, and his arm around her back tightened a fraction and eased her closer.

'You're right,' he murmured as she rested her head back on his shoulder. 'It was an impossible decision, a no-win situation. There was no right way to deal with it, we've just got to make sure we do it right now. Maybe you'd better give me a script.'

'You don't need a script. Just rely on your instincts, Nick.'

'My instincts are fatally flawed,' he said drily. 'If we rely on them, it's a sure-fire recipe for disaster. And talking of my instincts, before I do anything else I'll regret, I'm going to take the dog out, and then I'm going to bed.'

She tilted her head and stared up into his eyes, held motionless by the sensual message in their rich chocolate depths, and with a ragged sigh he eased her closer and touched his mouth to hers.

She parted her lips, and he growled low in his throat and took instant advantage, the hot, silken sweep of his tongue plundering her mouth, sliding one hand around the back of her neck and threading his fingers through her hair to steady her as the other hand curled around her bottom and hauled her closer. Her legs parted at the pressure from his knee, and one hard thigh lodged between them, sending need shooting through her, turning her body to fire.

'Nick,' she moaned, but the sound of her voice seemed to

stop him in his tracks, and he pulled back, lifting his head and staring down at her, his chest rising and falling rapidly. She could see the hammer of his heartbeat in the hollow of his throat, and after an endless moment he got to his feet and walked away, calling the dog.

'Nick?'

'Leave it, Kate. For the love of God, just leave it,' he said rawly, and she heard the door shut behind him, the lights coming on automatically as he walked out of the back door from the utility room into the garden, the dog at his heels.

For an age she sat there, staring after him, her eyes fixed blindly on the closed door, and then with a fractured little sigh she got to her feet, put their glasses in the kitchen and went to bed.

They were supposed to be being grown up about this, she reminded herself, and so far it was only Nick who was sticking to the plot. How long that would last, she had no idea, but as she lay down in her bed, her mind went back to Jem.

How on earth had she forgotten about him? He was lying there in hospital, distressed and heartbroken, and all she could think about was making love with Nick, which was what had got them all in this mess in the first place!

It was a long, long time before she went to sleep.

The next day was very hard.

Jem refused to talk to Kate at first, and he refused to let Nick visit. After he'd got over his crying spell the night before, he'd withdrawn into himself, and the only thing he showed any interest in was Lucy's games console. It took him out of himself, she thought, gave him something to concentrate on, something to hide behind while his subconscious sorted out the wood from the trees.

So she just sat beside him, reading a magazine and waiting, and finally he cracked.

'Why did you lie to me?' he asked suddenly, and she put her magazine down and made herself meet his hurt, accusing eyes.

'I didn't—well, not really. I tried very hard not to, and I never actually told you that James was your father, because I knew it was a lie, and it was more a case of letting you believe something than telling you something wrong. So when you asked about your father, I told you that if he'd known he had a son, he would have been very proud of you, and that, at least, is true. He is proud of you, and he loves you. He always has.'

'But you let me think that James was my father. That was a sort of lie.'

It was. A lie of omission, and she nodded. 'Yes, it was. But it seemed like the best of some not very good choices, and I wanted to do the best I could for everyone. I didn't really know what else to do without hurting innocent people.'

'I'm innocent,' he said, and her eyes filled.

'I know. I'm sorry. It's a mess, and it's my fault, not your father's. You shouldn't blame him, he had no say in it.'

'Where is Uncle N—?' he asked, and then frowned. 'Mum, what do I call him now?' he asked fretfully.

She stroked his hair. 'I don't know. You'll have to ask him that. Whatever feels right. What do you want to call him?'

He shrugged. 'Dunno. I mean, he's my dad, isn't he?'

She nodded, blinking back the ever-ready tears. 'Yes. Yes, he is, but you must do what feels right for you both. I can't tell you that, darling, it's up to you. And he's here—I expect he's in the café. Why? Do you want to see him now?'

He shrugged his skinny shoulders again. 'Just wondered if he'd gone. He went home yesterday.'

'Because you told him to.'

'But I didn't think he'd go,' he said perversely. 'Not if he really cared.'

'Oh, he cares, Jem,' she said softly. 'He was really upset. He went because you asked him to, not because he wanted to, and that's why he's not here now, but he is in the hospital, in case you want to see him. And he'll be here, waiting, until you're ready.'

'Really?'

She nodded. 'Really. However long it takes. He wants to see you,' she told him, and she watched that sink in, watched the realisation that Nick did care, that he wanted Jem. Was here for him, any time he asked.

He didn't ask, not then, but later, when he'd obviously been thinking about it for a while, he lifted his head and said, 'This face-merging thing. Do you think it would work with him and me?'

She took a second to realise he was talking about the games console, and lifted her shoulders. 'I don't know. Probably. Do you want to try?'

'Maybe. If he's still here.'

She felt a great weight lift off her chest, and smiled. 'I'll find him.'

He was in the café, in a litter of torn sugar and salt packets, pushing a pile of white crystals around on the tabletop.

She sat down next to him, and he lifted his head and gave her a weary smile. 'Hi. How is he?'

'He's OK. He wants to see you.'

His eyes widened, and she could see hope flickering in them. 'Really?'

'Really. He was talking about the photo-merging thing. I think he wants to try with your faces.'

'Ah. That might need Jack or Lucy.'

'It might not. You might be able to work it out. You've got the instructions.'

He nodded slowly. 'I could try. Any tips or hints? For him, not the game.'

'Give him time. He's still angry with us, but more than that, he's confused and he needs time to adjust to the new reality of having a father. We all need time to adjust to it, but we'll get there.'

'Will we?' he asked doubtfully, as they left the café and walked along to the ward. 'I hope you're right.'

She sent him in on his own, and Jem looked up and gave him a wary smile.

He smiled back just as warily and sat down on the chair. 'Hiya. Your mum says you want to try the face-merging thing.'

'Mmm.' Jem fiddled with the games console for a moment, then mumbled, 'Uncle Nick? Can I call you Dad? 'Cos that's what you are, really, and it's what Jack and Lucy call you. But I'm still mad with you, though, for walking off and not explaining,' he added hastily, just in case he wasn't aware of it.

No chance of that. Nick's throat closed, and he swallowed hard. 'That's fine, I deserve it. You can call me whatever you want. And if you want to call me Dad—well, that would be awesome.'

His son rolled his eyes and grinned, looking so like Jack that Nick couldn't believe he'd never seen it. 'You can't say that, Dad, you're too old, you sound silly. And I am still mad with you.'

He gave him a wry smile. 'That's OK. We can talk about that,' he agreed, and blinked hard. He'd called him Dad—as if he'd been practising it in his head all day, and finally felt brave enough to try it out. Brave enough, and trusting enough.

He sucked in a deep breath, and picked up the games console. 'Right. Instructions?'

'They're here. Where's Mum?'

'I think she's having a drink and a bit of fresh air. Why?'

He shrugged. 'Just wondered. I thought she'd like to see this.'

'We can show her later when she comes back, if we can work it out. Or I can go outside and phone her,' Nick suggested, realising Jem was still scared. Still scared, and still needing his mother, but the man who'd been Uncle Nick all his life didn't have the power to fill that gap, and maybe never would. He realised that he was jealous of her relationship with him. So stupid. Of course he needed his mother, he was a little boy, still not quite eleven years old, for all his courage.

'Want me to call her? She could come now, I'm sure. She's not far away.'

Jem shook his head. 'No, it's OK. We can show her later, like you said,' he agreed, and Nick felt himself relax a little. One step at a time...

'We did it, Mum, it was amazing,' their son said by way of greeting, and she felt the tension ease out of her.

'Did you make it work, then?' she asked him, and he nodded.

'Yeah—come here, let me show you. And I'm going to look so like him when I'm older. It's awesome, isn't it, Dad?' he said, and Kate's eyes widened slightly and then filled with tears.

'Yes, you will be like him,' she said, looking at the games console as Jem switched from one face to another, the similarities striking. Her voice wobbled slightly, and she swallowed hard and avoided Nick's eyes. But he'd seen, and his hand came out and squeezed hers in support.

'Lucy sent me a text. She's invited us for supper. Want to go?'

She shook her head. 'No. I ought to let the dog out and I could do with putting some washing on before I come back here this evening, but you can go, if you like.'

'No. That's fine. I'll drop in and have a cup of tea with her after I take you home, and I could go and pick up my post—yours, too.'

'You can go now, Dad, if you like,' Jem said. 'Mum and me'll be all right.'

'Mum and I,' she corrected automatically, and turned in time to see the flicker of pain on Nick's face.

'Sure. I'll do the dog and the post and have tea with Lucy, and I'll come back this evening and take you home after visiting, then, if you're both sure?' Nick said gruffly, and then, after a fractional hesitation, he bent over the bed and dropped a kiss on his son's bruised forehead. Just a fleeting one, the sort of kiss he'd given his other boys in their youth, but he wasn't sure of his reception and when Jem slid his arms round him and gave him a quick hug, he felt the love swell in his chest and threaten to choke him.

'You take care,' he said gruffly, ruffling his hair with a gentle hand, and because he didn't want to leave her out, he stooped and kissed Kate's cheek, as well, in passing, and he was rewarded by her smile.

At least supper was sorted out, he thought as he headed back to Lucy's—fresh sea bass from one of the fishermen in the harbour. He'd been spotted turning into his drive when he'd collected his post, and Toby Penhaligan had pulled in behind him and given him two beautiful, plump fish straight from the sea.

'How's the lad?' he'd asked, and Nick wondered if he'd heard the rumour, too.

'Doing well, thanks,' he'd told him. 'He should be out of hospital by the end of next week.'

'I hear you've taken the barn for the summer.'

So the jungle drums were working overtime. No surprises there, then. 'For a while, anyway. I'm giving Kate a hand to look after Jem—he can't manage the stairs, so it seemed to make sense.'

He'd felt Toby's eyes track to the more-than-adequate family house behind him, and was hugely grateful that the barn was out of the way and might afford them a little much-needed privacy.

He'd gone straight there, put the fish in the fridge and walked the dog, then gone to Lucy's.

'So, how is he?' she asked.

'OK,' he told them. 'Good. He called me Dad today...'

His voice cracked a bit, and he cleared his throat and gave them a wry smile. They were gathered round the kitchen table, his two eldest children and Ben, drinking tea and talking through Jem's progress, and Lucy reached out a hand and squeezed his shoulder. 'Sorry,' he muttered, patting her hand. 'It got to me. But he says he's still mad with me. He thinks I don't want to be his father.'

'Do you?' Jack asked. 'Because I could understand if you didn't. I was appalled when India died and I was told Freddie was mine—talk about hurled in at the deep end. It really wasn't easy, but you've got to give it a go, Dad, because— well, he's the best thing that's ever happened to me, him and Alison and our growing family. But it was Freddie that turned me around, and he's given me so much.'

'I'm sure you're the best thing that's ever happened to him, as well. And I do want to be his father. I just hope I can do him justice.'

'Of course you can! It's not about being perfect, it's about being there,' Lucy told him. 'And listening. You could maybe do a bit more of that. But we were never short of love, and that's what he needs most of all. To know you love him.'

'I do.' He swallowed and tried to smile. 'He hugged me. When I said goodbye. He's never hugged me before.'

Lucy tutted again, and got up and came round and snuggled onto his lap. 'You soft old thing,' she said kindly, and he laughed and tapped her on the bottom.

'Less of the old,' he told her, and hugged her back, then frowned and looked down at her slightly rounded abdomen. 'Are you pregnant again?'

She blushed. 'Um—I might be.'

'I think you might. Congratulations. I take it this is planned?'

Ben's lips twitched. 'Sort of. She caught me in a weak moment. I think it's a ploy to be on permanent maternity leave.'

Nick laughed again. 'Come on, let me up. I have to go and see your little brother.'

Jem was tired—exhausted, really, after a busy day with two lots of visitors and all the upset of the previous day—and he was still getting used to being out in an open ward with six-bed bays, rather than his own quiet little side room, so Kate and Nick didn't stay late, and were home by quarter to eight.

Home, he thought, turning into the drive, and wondered how, in just a little over forty-eight hours, it could possibly feel like home.

Because Kate was there.

There was no other possible reason, and he ushered her in, poured her a glass of wine while she let the dog out and fussed over him, then scrubbed the new potatoes while she sat and sipped the wine and watched the last pink streaks of the sunset fade over the sea.

'Anything I can do?' she asked him, feeling guilty for sitting there, but he just smiled at her and carried on scraping and scrubbing.

'No. You stay there and enjoy being waited on. You heard the doctor—I have to spoil you.'

She chuckled. 'If you insist. So how was Lucy?'

'Ah, Lucy. Pregnant again.'

Kate smiled indulgently. 'Have you only just realised?' she said.

He rolled his eyes. 'Of course, you're a midwife. You notice these things.'

'That's right,' she said smugly. 'So, what are you feeding me for supper?' she asked, and he grinned.

'Sea bass, courtesy of Toby Penhaligan.'

'Sea bass? Really? Are you going to make the house smell of fish?' she queried, and he laughed.

'I shouldn't think so, the extractor fan's like a jet engine, I'll be surprised if it doesn't suck the fish out of the pan. I tell you what, while I do this, why don't you go and have a shower?'

'Do you mind?'

'Not at all. Consider it all part of your pampering,' he said, and his eyes raked slowly over her and he smiled. 'You could even wear something pretty.'

Pretty? Her heart thudded, and she felt a sudden flutter of nerves. He was looking at her as if...

Oh, lord. She wasn't ready for this. Last night she had been, but tonight, just like that, without the benefit of cuddling up to him and getting in the mood, she felt a shiver of ice slide down her spine. Nick wasn't coy, and he wouldn't be a shy lover. He'd want the lights on and access to every part of her, and she wasn't sure she could do this. Not now, and maybe not ever.

'I'll see what I've got. It might just be jumper and jeans,' she said, and headed for her bedroom, panic clawing at her throat.

He put the potatoes in the pan and glanced at his watch. She might be half an hour in the shower and then getting ready, so he had time to light the fire to give it time to warm up the room.

He brought some wood in, and while he was laying the fire, he heard a noise coming from the area of her bedroom.

'Kate?'

He walked down the corridor towards her room, and heard the shower running, and then a muffled sob.

He rested his head against the door. Not again. He couldn't do this again.

So he went into her room and stood by the window, staring out into the courtyard and listening in agony as she wept just feet away from him. There was nothing he could do—nothing he would let himself do—but wait until the crying stopped, and a minute later she turned off the water, then he heard the door open and she walked into the room, closing the door and then dropping her towel.

And then she saw him, and gasped, scrabbling for the towel, her eyes red-rimmed and wild with some unfathomable emotion.

He reached for her, shocked at the ravaged look on her face, the pain in her eyes, desperate to comfort her, but she wouldn't let him.

'Nick, no,' she said, pushing him away and trying to turn her back to him, the towel twisted somehow round her now. 'Please!'

'Don't be silly, I've seen you cry umpteen times in the last few days,' he said gently, his hands cupping her shoulders, but she shook her head.

'No—it's not that. Please, Nick, just go—'

She broke off, the smothered sobs returning, and he felt swamped by her pain, the light slowly dawning as he realised belatedly why she'd turned away.

'Oh, my love, my darling girl, come here,' he said tenderly, turning her back into his arms and folding her against his chest once more, his hands stroking her back rhythmically through the damp towel. 'After all we've been through, do you really think a few scars are going to make any difference to me?'

'They make a difference to me,' she sobbed, pushing him away again, but he wouldn't let her go this time, he couldn't, because the pain and fear for her, suppressed for nearly a year now, were rising up and choking him, and he cradled her tenderly against his heart and rocked her. Rocked them both.

'I thought you were going to die,' he said unevenly. 'I thought I was going to lose you, lose everything that kept me sane. You're my best friend, Kate, the one person who really understands me; the only thing that's kept me going is working with you, having you there near me, even if you weren't with me. I prayed so hard that you'd make it, even if you ended up with Rob—that didn't matter, just so long as you were alive, just so long as I knew you were somewhere in the world. Why the hell should I care about a scar?'

'Oh, Nick,' she whispered tearfully, and, resting her head against his shoulder, she slid her arms round him and held him. 'I'm sorry. I didn't even think about how you might have felt, just that you hadn't been there for me, but nobody was there for you. I'm so, so sorry.'

She breathed deeply, then looked at him again. 'It's just— Nobody's seen it, and when you said wear something pretty, I felt ridiculously shy all of a sudden, and I thought, what if it turned you off?'

'Kate!' he chided softly, gutted that she thought so little of him. 'How shallow do you think I am?'

'I don't. It's how shallow I am.'

He gave a ragged sigh and cradled her head against his shoulder. 'Can we start again? Wear something that makes you feel good. Something that makes you feel all woman, because you are, Kate. You're a beautiful woman, and I want to show you that, but only when you're ready. There's no pressure. I don't care if it takes months. Years. I want you, and I'll wait for you.'

She sucked in a breath and took a little step back. 'I'll see what I can find. Why don't you go and start cooking?'

CHAPTER TEN

'ANYTHING I can do?'

He lifted his head and smiled at her, but he didn't comment on her clothes, and she felt perversely irritated. 'You could top and tail the mangetout, if you're bored. And you look lovely, by the way. Beautiful.'

The irritation dissolved in an instant, replaced by a rush of heat and affection for this complicated and loveable man. He brought her the packet of peas, a pan and a small knife, dropped a tender, lingering kiss on her lips, and she sat at the table with a silly smile and trimmed the peas and sipped another glass of wine while he put the fish on to cook and prodded the potatoes. Music was playing in the background, something soft and smoky and sensual, and between that and the wine and the last streaks of the sunset fading into the night, it was the perfect romantic setting.

All she needed was her son back home, safe and sound, and her happiness would be complete. Once she'd found the courage to make love to Nick, at least.

Did he feel the same way about it? She glanced across at him, and saw he was humming softly as he worked. He looked happy enough. It was lovely to be able to sit there and enjoy all of the house without moving, she thought, and told herself it could be permanent, that they could stay there and make it their home.

'Right, let's have those peas. How's your wine?'

'It's fine. I don't need any more. I'm still on the occasional anti-inflammatory and I don't like to mix drugs and alcohol.'

'I thought that was what the modern youth did.'

'It is. I'm not the modern youth.'

'I'm thankful for that.'

They shared a smile, and then with a shake of his head, as if he was collecting himself, he turned back to his cooking and the moment was gone.

'That was gorgeous, Nick. Thank you.'

'My pleasure. It was worth being grilled by Toby Penhaligan to get those sea bass. They were gorgeous.'

'Did he give you a very hard time?'

Nick shrugged. 'The jungle drums are obviously working, but I suppose we should expect that. I think we need to present a united front, for Jem's sake, and if the gossip gets too much—well, who knows what the future might hold?'

His words hung in the air, and Kate met his eyes and saw a hope in them that must surely be reflected in her own. She wanted him. She wanted to be with him, to spend her life with him, and their son did, too.

And to do that, she had to find the courage to do what she had to do next.

'Nick? Will you do something for me?'

'Sure. What is it?'

'Will you make love to me?'

He froze, his glass suspended above the table, and after what seemed like for ever he set it back down very, very carefully and uncurled his fingers from the stem.

'Are you sure?' he asked hoarsely.

'Yes. Yes, I'm sure, but I'm scared.'

'Oh, Kate…'

He stood up and came round to her side, taking her hands

in his. 'You don't have to be scared. This is me. Why on earth are you scared?'

'Because—I just am. It's been a long time, Nick. And—well, I don't look the same.'

'You know what I feel about that,' he said.

'But it's not only about what you feel, it's about what I feel, and I feel—I know it's stupid, I know it's irrational, I've seen lots of women who've had breast surgery, but they weren't me. This is me, my body, and that makes it different. And illogical,' she explained, and he frowned slightly and squeezed her hand.

'I can understand that, but, Kate, I could have lost you, but I didn't. You're here with me, now, and that, at the end, is the only thing that matters. That you're alive and well.'

'And then there's the competition,' she went on, ignoring him. 'I'm not Annabel,' she said, pointing out the obvious. 'Or any one of the other glamorous women you've been seen with.'

He sighed and shifted to the chair beside her, lifting her hand and pressing it to his cheek. 'I know you're not Annabel,' he said gently. 'You don't have to live up to her, Kate. I loved her, just not the way I've always loved you. You were always my soul mate. You were the one I should have been with all this time. She was a lovely girl, and she turned into a kind, sensitive and generous woman; as a mother, I couldn't fault her. As a wife, she was perfect. We were good friends in many ways, but there was no great passion there, no desperate yearning. And as for the other women—there's only really been one since Annabel, and she has no expectations. I've seen her from time to time. Her name's Louise. We've had dinner, gone to the cinema.'

'Made love?'

'I'm not a monk, Kate. Neither am I promiscuous. The others have just been passing distractions, but I haven't slept with them. And I'm not going to beat you up about Rob.'

'What makes you think I slept with him?'

He shook his head and gave a wry smile. 'I saw you. I came to see you, last summer. I wanted to talk to you, and I pulled up outside. And Rob was kissing you, in the kitchen, right in front of the window. And then you walked away, and a light came on upstairs, and you shut the bedroom curtains. It wasn't rocket science, Kate.'

She felt sick. 'Nick, you weren't meant to see that.'

'Of course not. But you're adults, so why not? After all, we weren't going anywhere, were we, at the time, and he's a good guy. So—why not? It's what people do. I know that. And I can understand it, but it's all very well in theory, but in practice, I realised I was jealous.'

'Because even though you didn't want me, you didn't want anyone else to?'

'But I did want you. I just didn't know how to ask. I went to see Louise, after I drove away that night. I thought—what was sauce for the goose, I suppose. But, well, let's just say I think I was a bit of a disappointment to her. I couldn't get you out of my head, couldn't stop seeing you kissing him, and I didn't want to be with her. I didn't want to be with anyone if I couldn't be with you, and obviously I couldn't. So I went home, picked up a bottle of Scotch from the kitchen, walked down to the beach and drank half of it. I haven't seen her since.'

'So who was the woman at Ben and Lucy's barbecue last summer?' she asked.

'An old friend from London. She's divorced, she was down here on holiday, and she was lonely.'

Kate smiled indulgently. 'I think she was probably more than lonely, the way she was looking at you.'

He shrugged. 'I'm a good-looking guy—what can I say?' he murmured, and she laughed, as he'd meant her to. But then his smile faded, and he lifted his hand and touched her cheek. 'She was nothing, Kate. Nothing happened with her,

I promise. I can't dismiss Annabel, she was my wife, the mother of three of my children, a very important person in our lives, and I loved her. But there truly has been no one else who matters at all, no one who's ever claimed my heart or made me want to behave like an irrational teenager or a romantic fool. No one else who's been such a good friend to me no matter how badly I've behaved. No one else that I've loved the way I love you. The way I've always loved you.'

'Oh, Nick. What happened to us?' she asked softly, and he stood up slowly and drew her to her feet.

'I don't know. I just know that now we seem to have a chance, and I want to take that chance with you, Kate. Let me try again,' he murmured softly. 'I know I don't deserve it, but give me a chance to prove that I can be a good husband and father. We're stuck with each other for good now, anyway, as Jem's parents—why not do it properly? There's so much at stake here now—so much that's infinitely precious that I really don't think I can bear to lose.'

Her mouth dropped open slightly, and she stared at him in confusion. 'Are you—? Did I imagine it, or did you just ask me to marry you?'

He felt emotion choke him, and swallowed. 'I'm not sure. I think I might have done, but not just because of Jem. I can be a father to him whatever, if I get the chance, and that's down to him. And if he hates me, if he wants me out of his life...'

'He doesn't. He won't.'

'Then give me a chance, Kate. Let's wind back the clock and start again, only as adults with hopefully a bit more judgement and common sense and compassion. See if we can make it work this time.'

She studied him doubtfully. 'Do you think we can do that?'

'I think we can try.'

'Maybe.'

'Is that a maybe maybe, or a definite maybe?' he asked, sure his smile didn't reach his eyes because her answer was so important to him.

'I think that's a definite maybe,' she said, her smile slow, and he felt the tension drain out of him. And then ratchet up again another gear. He lifted his hand and grazed his knuckles gently against her cheek.

'I want to make love to you,' he murmured, 'but I want you to be sure that you're ready for this, because if you're going to change your mind, I'd rather you did it now.'

She gave a quiet sigh. 'The only thing that would change my mind is Jem, and he seems to love you. He's always been very fond of you, and now, knowing you're his father just seems to be strengthening that bond. So, no, I'm not going to change my mind, Nick. But I am still scared.'

He drew her into his arms and cradled her against his heart. 'Don't be scared, my love. I'll take care of you. I'll always take care of you.'

He let her go, then took her hand and led her slowly and carefully up the stairs to his room, closing the door behind them just in case Bruno decided to follow them, but he was lying on a rug chasing rabbits in his sleep, and she didn't think he'd worry.

'Do you want the lights off?' he asked, and she swallowed.

She had to do this. She had to be brave enough to show herself to him, to open up all her physical and emotional scars to him and trust him to heal them. But the lights...

'How about the bathroom light? We could leave the door open,' he suggested, and she nodded, ridiculously nervous now.

He turned back the bed, stripped off his clothes down to his boxers—jersey boxers that fitted snugly over his firm, muscular buttocks and thighs and did heart-stopping things in other areas—and then held out his hand to her.

She went to his side, and he stared down at her, his eyes sombre. 'Are you sure, Kate?' he said softly. 'We've had years to talk this up in our heads, and I don't want to disappoint you.'

'You won't disappoint me.' She knew he wouldn't. She didn't know how, she just knew. She went up on tiptoe and brushed her lips against his, then dropped back onto her heels and waited.

He unbuttoned the silky blouse she'd put on, the sheer fabric sliding against her skin as he loosened it and slipped it over her shoulders. He laid it carefully on the chair, then his fingers found the zip on her trousers and slid it down, the faint noise loud in the breathless silence. The button was next, and then they joined the blouse on the chair and he stood back and looked at her, standing there in her underwear.

'You're still a really beautiful woman, Kate,' he said softly. 'Come here. I need you.'

He held out his hand, and she put hers in it and went into his arms, closing the gap between them slowly, so that when their bodies touched, it was like coming home.

She rested her head on his shoulder, and he slid his arms round her waist and held her gently against his body, so she could feel the beating of his heart, the rise and fall of his chest as he breathed, the warmth of his skin, and as she lifted her head, his came down and his lips found hers, meshing and melding in a gentle dance that was filled with promise.

She knew he wanted her. She also knew he'd wait for her, give her time for her fears to fade, and it gave her the confidence to step back out of his arms and take off the last of her clothes, so she was standing in front of him naked.

And then she waited.

Her trust was unbearably touching.

He felt his eyes fill with tears, and because he knew she wanted him to, he made himself look down, to study the scar on her left breast, the fine line that ran round underneath it in the crease, the hollow left by the surgery that had saved her life. The skin was a little discoloured from the radiotherapy, but that would fade with time. And it was very neat. The doctor in him admired the surgery. The man wanted her, more than he'd ever wanted any other woman in his life, and if it killed him, he was going to do her justice now.

Her courage humbled him, and he gave her an unsteady smile. 'I feel a little overdressed,' he said gruffly, and skimmed off his boxers, tossing them aside and standing in front of her, wondering how he measured up to Rob and hating himself for caring about something so trivial. Well, at least she could see that he wasn't in the least put off by her appearance. In fact, if she kept him waiting much longer…

'Nick?'

He met her eyes.

'Make love to me.'

He lifted her carefully onto the bed, tutting at the faint bruising on her right foot, touching his lips gently to the little stain. He could imagine her feet trapped in the footwell, knew that if the fuel tank had blown, she would have died.

Don't think about that, he told himself, and moved up, skimming past her thighs, not allowing himself to linger till he reached her waist, then trailing his tongue slowly around her navel, dipping into it, teasing her till she trembled.

Then he moved higher, his hand cupping her left breast, pressing a gentle, healing kiss to the scar. She shuddered a little, and he moved on, his lips sipping and tasting the other breast, reluctant to miss a single inch of her. She moaned and arched up, her body image issues forgotten now, need taking over, the need that had haunted them both for so very many years. The purely sensual need that their one tragic night had never addressed.

He moved up until his face was level with hers, and kissed her as he'd always wanted to kiss her, long and slow and deep—heavy, drugging kisses that cranked up the heat and made his body burn for her.

And hers for him. She plucked at him, her fingers restless, her breathing light and rapid, almost hyperventilating. 'Nick, please…now,' she begged, and doing what he'd failed to do before, taking the time to protect her, he moved over her and thrust slowly, lingeringly home.

She gasped, her body bucking beneath his, and he locked his mouth to hers, plundering it as he drove into her again and again and again, until at last he could hold it no more and he let himself go, joining her in the long freefall into ecstasy.

The next few days were blissful.

The weather was gorgeous, and when they weren't in the hospital visiting Jem, they were at the barn, sitting under a little ornamental tree in the courtyard garden with the dog at their feet and drinking coffee or sipping wine, and every now and then he'd cook them something wonderful.

And his hidden talent for waiting on her was turning into an art form. He ran errands for her, spoiled her rotten, massaged her neck when it ached and then, when she was boneless and utterly relaxed, he'd make love to her.

They were slow, lazy days, days in which they all recovered from what had been a gruelling ordeal, and gradually they relaxed into a quiet, orderly routine.

He went back to work in the mornings, coming home to cook them lunch before driving to the hospital to visit Jem. He'd settled really well in the new ward, made friends, watched the ducklings grow and gradually, bit by bit, he was getting back on his feet.

Jess Carmichael had been to see him, and he was less angry with his parents, more accepting now that there had been valid reasons why his parentage had been kept from him. 'She's a wonderful person,' Kate said. 'I don't know how I would have coped last year without her. She's a miracle.'

She wasn't the only miracle. Lucy had formed a wonderfully close attachment to Jem, and on a day when Nick was there alone because he'd treated Kate to a pamper break, she brought the children in to see him.

'Hey, you've got the monsters,' Jem said with a grin, and Lucy chuckled.

'Annabel, say hello to Uncle Jem,' she said, letting go of her daughter's hand, and his eyes widened.

'Wow—I really am an uncle, aren't I? That's weird—awesome! Hi, Annabel.'

'We bringed you grapes,' Annabel said, handing him the bag shyly.

'That's because Grandad ate the last lot,' Lucy pointed out with a firm look at her father, and he rolled his eyes.

'Naughty G'andad!' Annabel said, and stared at them longingly.

Jem gave her some, and she settled down on the floor by the window and ate the grapes and counted the ducklings, while Lucy hung onto the baby and tried to keep him out of mischief.

'I can't believe he's a year old,' she said.

'I can't believe I'm a grandfather,' Nick said drily.

Lucy grinned. 'Oh, I can. Look at the grey hairs, Dad! But I can't believe Annabel's nearly two and a half. It seems like five minutes. Joshy, no! You can't have the grapes.'

'Gape!' he yelled, his little fist working, and lunged for them, slipping out of Lucy's grasp and cracking his head on the edge of the clipboard hanging on the end of the bed.

'Oh, I don't believe it!' Lucy wailed, lifting him up and hugging him while Nick looked at the little gash on the screaming toddler's temple.

'He'll live, but it needs gluing,' Nick said, pressing a clean tissue to the cut and holding it there.

'Oh, well, at least it's into the hairline,' she said with a sigh. 'Come on, Annabel, we're going to have to take him to see Daddy. Joshy's got a little cut.'

'Leave her here, she'll be fine with me,' Nick said, and she smiled gratefully and hurried along the corridor and out of the ward, Josh's screams fading as she took him further away.

'Joshy's screaming,' Annabel said matter-of-factly. 'He always screams.'

'He's a little boy. They get in trouble a lot, but he'll be fine,' Nick said with a reassuring smile, and sat down on the floor with his granddaughter and watched the ducklings.

'Oh, Megan, brilliant—are you busy?'

She wasn't, but she didn't want to hang around in A and E any longer than she had to. She'd managed to avoid Josh O'Hara so far, but she could hardly refuse to help Ben Carter. She stepped into the cubicle and smiled at the woman. Lucy. She'd seen her on Paeds, visiting Jem, and knew she was Ben's wife. 'Well—no, not really. What's the matter?'

'This is our son,' he said. 'He's managed to cut his head, and we could do with a hand to hold onto him while I glue it, but he's like an eel and the nurses are all busy.'

'I can do eels,' she said, conjuring up a smile, and she took him from Lucy, steeling herself against the warm, sturdy little body writhing against her.

'Shh, shh,' his mother said, holding his hands and kissing them and blowing raspberries on them, and Megan sat down and held the child's head firmly against her shoulder while Ben glued the little laceration.

'Did you make that kid scream loud enough?' a lazy, sexy voice asked as he finished, and Megan felt her blood run hot and cold.

Ben lifted his head and laughed. 'Yes, thank you for your concern. This is my son—Josh, say hello to mini-Josh. We even gave him your name, so don't be too rude about him. I take it you've met Megan Phillips, our paeds registrar?'

Met her? Oh, yes, he'd met her. And seeing her there, comforting the wriggling, unhappy baby, sent a shaft of pain right through him, stealing his breath away.

Megan looked up at him, a desperate pleading in her eyes, but she needn't have bothered. He was in no hurry to have the past dragged out for public consumption.

'We met the other day up on Paeds,' he said, being deliberately noncommittal, and to his relief his pager went off and he was able to walk away.

Away from Megan and the child, but not his memories...

Nick got back to the barn to find Kate there, home after her spa day relaxed, sleepy and looking utterly irresistible.

So he didn't even try. 'Good day?' he asked, snuggling up to her on the sofa, and she turned into his arms and kissed him.

'Lovely. I've been spoiled to bits. Thank you.'

'My pleasure.' He nuzzled her neck. 'You smell nice. Do you smell nice all over?'

'I don't know. You probably ought to check.'

She did, he discovered, although he got blissfully distracted and forgot what he was supposed to be looking for, and it was almost an hour later before he remembered about little Josh's accident.

He told Kate, lying lazily beside her on the big bed with the view of the sea in the distance and wondering when he was going to wake up and find it was all a dream.

'Poor little mite. You ought to ring and find out how he is.' She trailed her hand over his chest and propped herself up, looking down at him with a slightly bemused smile.

'What?'

'I find it really hard to believe I'm sleeping with a grandfather,' she teased, and he closed his eyes and groaned as she slid her hand down his ribs and kept going.

'I was a very early starter,' he reminded her, and caught her hand. 'Stop. I have to phone Lucy.'

'Mmm. You do. And then we need to go to the hospital. I haven't seen Jem all day, and I miss him.'

She handed him his mobile, and he rang Lucy.

'So how's the little hooligan?' he asked, and she chuckled.

'OK. He's running around as if nothing's happened. There's something funny going on with Josh O'Hara and Megan Phillips, though,' she told him. 'Ben doesn't remember him ever talking about a Megan, but she was helping with holding him and Josh came in and Ben introduced them, and there was a definite atmosphere. He said he'd met her on Paeds, but I'm sure there was more to it. Something in his eyes.'

'Don't go there, Lucy,' he warned. 'Lots of people have a past. Sometimes it's best left where it belongs. Just remember Pandora's box.'

'Oh, don't worry, I'm not going to say anything, but at least Ben's alerted so he can keep an ear open in case of trouble. You never know when Josh might need a friend.'

'You're a good girl,' he told her with quiet pride. 'You've got your mother's kindness. Give the kids a hug from me, and we'll see you tomorrow.'

Kate met his eyes. 'What was that about?' she asked as he put the phone down.

'Nothing, really. They think Josh and Megan might have a past, and not a happy one, judging by the sound of it.'

She frowned. 'Do you know, I was thinking the other day she looked sad and a little lost. Poor girl. Poor both of them, whatever it is.'

She glanced at her watch. 'Come on, Grandad. We need to get a move on.'

'You realise if you marry me they'll be calling you Grannie,' he said slyly, and her eyes widened.

'Well, that's a good reason not to,' she said, but he just laughed and got out of bed, hauling her up into his arms and kissing her soundly.

'Coming in the shower with me?' he asked, and she chuckled.

'Now, there's an offer I can't refuse,' she said.

They took Bruno in to see Jem the next day, after arranging access to the courtyard off the ward with the help and permission of the ward sister and Sid Evans, the ancient and very co-operative handyman, who was only too happy to let them into the garden through the locked outer gate.

Jem was delighted to see him, and Bruno, far from being over-excitable and boisterous, sniffed him cautiously, licked his hand and, when he leant forwards and brought it in range, his face, and then sat beside him, his head on his knee, gazing adoringly at him and moving not a muscle.

'Do you think Bruno realises he's not well?' Kate murmured to Nick.

'I have no idea, but if you told me that, I'd believe it. He's much livelier with me than he is with you, so maybe he knows I'm stronger. He knows I can take it, so he jumps all over me.'

'Yes, and you shouldn't let him! And am I imagining it or did I see dog hair on the sofa yesterday?'

He looked guilty, and she laughed and told him off.

'He's not allowed on the furniture! Especially when it's not ours!'

'He just wanted a cuddle,' Nick said, revealing more of the sentimental side of him she'd hardly known existed.

But there was lots about him she hadn't known. She'd expected him to be a skilful lover, for instance, but he was far more than that, he was patient, humorous and teasing and then, when the chips were down, shockingly passionate. She discovered highs she hadn't known existed, and she just hoped she'd never have to discover the lows to balance them.

Or maybe they'd already had their lows. Maybe now it was time for their highs, their time served, and this was their time.

She hoped so, because to walk away from this was going to be far harder than walking away from him before, and she'd thought that would break her.

But Jem wasn't home yet, and that was the acid test, whether he'd accept Nick being part of their lives, whether he'd accept his authority, learn to take his say-so without question instead of debating every issue to death. And Nick might have to learn to compromise, not something that was second nature to him.

Jem came 'home' three days later, to the barn, and Bruno was overjoyed.

He followed him everywhere, sat beside him, and had to be dragged off to go for walks. Long, energetic walks along the cliffs that helped Nick work off some of the unforeseen frustration. Because since Jem had been home, there had been no long, lazy love-making, no romantic dinners, no casual touches, random kisses in the kitchen, unscheduled hugs that had gone on to become something much, much more.

And he was climbing the walls.

Not that he was any stranger to sexual frustration, but having her so close, wanting her so much, needing her for so very, very long and finally having her there—it was eating him alive.

So he walked the dog, and he went to work to try and forget about her, and every time he came home she'd look up and smile, and the need would slam through him and he'd be back to square one.

But Jem was flourishing, growing stronger every day, and with the help of Lauren, the physio, he was doing strengthening exercises that helped to keep his body balanced. Kate was still not working, but she was driving Jem here, there and everywhere, loving her new car, and she brought him down to the surgery to see Lauren three times a week, and sometimes, if they were lucky, they could catch a few minutes alone together.

But even though that time alone was short, Nick had no complaints. The crooked little slab pot Jem had made her on the day of his accident always sat in pride of place in the middle of the dining table, and today she was arranging yellow tulips in it, a troubled look on her face, and he left the cooking and went and hugged her.

'He's all right,' he murmured, knowing the pot served as a reminder of how close she'd come to losing him.

'I know.' And she turned in his arms and kissed him, then rested her head against his shoulder for a moment before easing away. Just in case Jem came in. Just in case he saw them and it upset him.

They were very wary about that. Jem had forgiven his mother, her reasons for not telling him the truth had been understandable, but Nick's initial reluctance to accept Jem as his son had left deep scars, and although he called him Dad and seemed to love him, there was still a certain wariness.

But Nick couldn't wait any more—couldn't go on like this, living in the barn and playing happy families and hiding his head in the sand. Jem was now strong enough to go up steps, and soon would be able to climb the stairs. Which meant if necessary they could go home to their house, and he could go home to his, and life could carry on as it had been, with a few adjustments.

It would be down to Jem to make that decision, and it was time to ask him to make it.

So when he got home from work that afternoon, he went

and found him. It wasn't hard. He just patted the dog when he came to greet him, and then followed him when he ran off again.

They were in the garden, sitting in the courtyard under a tree, Kate reading a book, Jem doing a maths puzzle—in a book, this time, the games console having been returned to Lucy—and he looked up and grinned. 'Hi, Dad,' he said, and carried on.

'Oh, you're back early! I'll go and put the kettle on,' Kate said with a welcoming smile, getting to her feet and squeezing his hand in passing. 'In fact, I need to ring Chloe. Want to keep Jem company?'

'Sure.' It was, after all, why he was there, and this just made it easier. He smiled reassuringly, and she smiled back and went in, and he sat down beside his son and turned towards him, his arm along the back of the bench.

'Jeremiah, can we talk?'

He put the puzzle book down and looked at Nick warily. 'Why do I always get the feeling that when you call me Jeremiah I'm in trouble?' he asked, and Nick chuckled.

'You're not in trouble, son. Far from it. I want to ask you something—well, several things, really. First of all, and probably most important, are you happy?'

'What, here?'

'Here, with me here, with us as a family—all of it, really.'

'Oh. Well—yeah. The house is great, but I know it's only for now, but us—yeah, it's good. You're a bit stuffy sometimes, and you tell me what to do, but I guess that's just being a dad, and I want a dad, so it's cool.'

Hurdle one, he thought with a sigh of relief. 'What about your mother? Do you think she's happy?'

'Oh, yeah. She's much smilier. She's like she used to be, before she was ill, but more than that, too. Like she's really happy, all the time.'

'And do you think that's anything to do with me?' he asked tentatively, and Jem nodded.

'I guess. She watches you sometimes, and gets a soppy look on her face, a bit like when she looks at Bruno, but sort of more. And I think she likes it that we're all together.'

Nick felt a huge weight lift off his chest, but a sudden attack of nerves took him by surprise and he rubbed his hand over his leg, surreptitiously wiping his palm, flexing the fingers of the other hand.

'Um—there's something else, too. It's sort of a tradition that when a man wants to marry a woman, he asks her father for permission, so he has his blessing first. And your mum hasn't got a father, and her mother lives a long way away, and I was thinking, you're the man in her life, really. So I was wondering, if I wanted to ask your mother to marry me, would you be happy with that?'

Jem stared at him. 'You want to marry Mum?'

He nodded, and Jem frowned thoughtfully. 'So we'll live together always? Like a proper family?'

He nodded. 'If that's what you want, and what your mum wants. But it won't make any difference to you and me, really, because I love you, and you'll always be very precious to me. And I want to be a part of your life, whatever happens, so don't think that if I don't marry your mother, you won't see me whenever you want to, because you will. But we don't want to make you unhappy. We've done enough of that, for one reason or another, and we want to do the right thing now, which for me means spending as much time with you as you feel you'd like, and being with your mother if I can, because I love her, and I always have. I just couldn't be with her before. But if you have a problem with that, then we can talk about it, maybe find another way that I can spend time with her. It's up to you, really.'

'Wow. So if I say yes, we can all be together? For ever? Like a real family?'

He opened his mouth to say yes, but couldn't speak, so he just nodded, and Jem grinned even wider.

'Excellent! Wow, that would be epic! But no yucky stuff when I'm around,' he added firmly, and Nick had to stifle a smile.

Actually, no, he didn't. He grinned back, and said, 'Absolutely no yucky stuff at all. No PDAs whatsoever.'

Jem frowned in confusion. 'They're funny diary things, aren't they? Like phones and stuff all in one?'

'That's personal digital assistants. This PDA means public displays of affection.'

'Oh. Right. That's OK, then. No PDAs.'

'Except at the wedding. I'll be expected to kiss her at the wedding.'

His son's eyes widened. 'Wow—are you going to have a real wedding?'

'I don't know. I haven't asked her yet—not properly.'

'Are you going to go down on one knee? 'Cos she might like that. It was on a film, and she went all pink and blew her nose.'

'I haven't got that far,' he said laughing, 'but I'll bear it in mind.'

'And she'll want a ring.'

'And a house. Yours isn't big enough, mine's—well, it's in a very busy place, and there isn't much garden for the dog. But—how would you feel about living here? If we could buy it?'

His eyes grew even wider. 'Here? For ever?'

He nodded, and to his surprise Jem's eyes filled. 'Mum would love that,' he said unsteadily. 'And so would the dog.'

'And you?'

'And me,' he said, and Nick forgot everything about PDAs and yucky stuff, and, putting his arms round his son, he hugged him firmly to his chest.

'That's settled, then,' he said, releasing him, and cleared his throat. 'I'd better ask her.'

'I'll go and tell her you want to talk to her,' Jem said, getting up and limping hurriedly towards the house.

'Hey, Jem, I wasn't going to do it now—'

He turned. 'What? You want to wait? Why?'

Why, indeed. He smiled. 'OK. Tell her I'd like to speak to her. I'll be down the garden.'

He walked slowly down across the lawn to the fence, and leant on the top rail staring out over the sea in the distance, twisting a blade of grass into a little circle around his finger and plaiting the ends in.

'Nick? What's going on? Jem said you want me.'

He turned and smiled, and held out his hands, taking hers and drawing her closer. 'Clever boy. I do.'

She blushed slightly and laughed. 'Don't be silly. What did you want?'

'You. In my life. For ever.' He glanced towards the house, and saw Jem standing outlined in the window, the dog at his side. He'd had his orders. With a wry smile, he went down on one knee in front of her, looked up into her slightly shocked, welling eyes and, his son forgotten, he said, 'Kate, I love you. I've always loved you, through everything. You've been the one constant in my life, the rock that's always been there. I need you, but more than that, I need you to need me, to want me, to smile every time you see me, to open your arms to me because you want to hold me, to make me feel whole again. I don't want you unless you want to be with me. This isn't for Jem. He's another thing altogether, and I'll always be part of his life. This is about us, you and me, and how we feel.

'I know I'm not much of a catch—and you probably never thought when you fell in love with me that I'd be a grandfather when I got round to doing this—but will you do me the honour of sharing the rest of your life with me? Will you marry me, Kate?'

'Oh, Nick,' she said, biting her lip and pressing her fingers to her lips as the tears cascaded down her cheeks. 'Oh, my darling, of course I'll marry you! I've waited years for you—I'd given up hope. Oh, Nick, of course I'll marry you,' she said again, so he took her hand and slipped the little twisted circle of grass onto her ring finger.

'This is just for now, because Jem said you should have a ring, but we'll go and get you a proper one,' he said, and as he got to his feet and she fell sobbing into his arms, he turned his head and gave Jem a thumbs-up.

There was a cheer from the house, and she lifted her head and looked up at him. 'What are you doing?'

'He's watching us.'

She turned and looked at him, and held out her arms, and he limped down the path to them, meeting them at the edge of the lawn, and their arms wrapped around each other, the three of them together, laughing and crying and holding on, because finally—finally!—it was all going to be all right...

EPILOGUE

HE GAVE Kate away, their son, so proud, so serious, walking her down the aisle of the crowded church and standing straight and tall beside her, and, when the time came, he placed her hand in his father's with the greatest solemnity and then gave him the biggest grin she'd ever seen.

And Nick grinned back, and winked at him, and then they turned back to Jeff Saunders and made their vows, long overdue but so very heartfelt, and when Jeff said, 'You may kiss the bride,' she saw Nick wink at their son as he bent his head to kiss her, and a great cheer went up from the congregation.

Family, friends, patients—there wasn't a soul there who wasn't cheering this long overdue couple on their way, and Kate felt her eyes fill as Nick touched his lips to hers and sealed their vows with a tender, lingering kiss.

While the choir sang, they signed the register, Jack and Lucy their witnesses, and then turned and walked back down the aisle between all the people who'd come to see them do what should have been done so many years ago.

Her mother was there, mopping her eyes and smiling, and Nick's children, of course—Lucy, Kate's very pregnant matron of honour, with Ben and their children; Jack, his best man, with his growing family and of course Jem, fully recovered and fizzing with excitement and pride at his role in the proceedings.

Nick's niece Charlotte was there with her husband James, and Jess Carmichael, the counsellor who'd helped them all so much, with her 'plus one'. And of course the practice was closed, their on-call covered by an agency because everyone was there with an assortment of babies and children.

Showered with love and good wishes, they walked down between the pews, packed so tightly that Health and Safety would have had a fit, dozens more standing outside or crowded into the doorway, listening over a PA link, and as they came out into the glorious September sunshine, everyone cheered and showered them with rose petals.

Cameras were clicking, everyone was hugging them, and Kate thought she'd never been kissed by so many people in her life. All sorts of people. Friends, family, colleagues, but others, patients, neighbours, people she'd known all her life, people who'd taken this little broken family to their hearts and made them whole again with their kindness and acceptance.

Nick stopped and looked around. 'Thank you so much for coming. I'm sorry we can't fit everybody for the reception,' he said, 'but if you go up to the Smugglers' and see Tony, there's a drink there for all of you on the house.'

That raised a cheer, and in a blizzard of rose petals Nick and Kate walked down the path, through the lychgate and to the waiting car.

'You're coming with us,' Kate heard Lucy say to Jem, and they entered the car alone, Jem standing with his sister and brothers. The chauffeur handed them glasses of champagne, and as they linked arms and drank and the cameras were popping, the car pulled slowly away.

'All right?' Nick said softly, and Kate smiled back at him.

'Very all right,' she said, and kissed him again.

* * *

'Good party?'

'Fantastic party. It's a good party house.'

He chuckled and slid his arms round her from behind, nuzzling her neck. 'No doubt we'll regret that when he's seventeen,' he said wryly, and she laughed.

'We'll get over it.' She turned in his arms, lifting her face up and kissing him softly in the moonlight. 'I want to be alone with you. It's been utterly fabulous, but I just want them to go now. Is that really selfish of me?'

He laughed quietly. 'No, not at all. I feel just the same. I love them all to bits, but I want them to go now.'

'So how do we get rid of them all?'

'We don't, Jack does. I've bribed him. We're having the kids for them next weekend when they go away. And when the coach turns into a pumpkin, he's kicking them all out. He said we should have gone away, but why would we, when we live here, in this beautiful place? We've waited all our lives for this. I don't want to run away from it.'

'Nor do I, but I wish they would.'

There was a quiet cough, and she looked up to see Jack standing a few feet away, an indulgent smile on his face. 'You need to come for the last dance, and say goodbye,' he told them, and so they went into the marquee on the lawn, swirling round the dance floor one last time before they saw their guests off, closed the front door behind them and turned.

'It's a mess!' Kate wailed, but Nick just scooped her up in his arms and carried her up the stairs.

'It's fine,' he said firmly. 'We're going to Ben and Lucy's for lunch tomorrow with Jack and Alison and all the children, and the catering team's coming back to sort it. You don't have to do a thing. And besides, you're busy.'

'I am?'

'Oh, yes.'

She gave a slow smile.

'I do love it when you're masterful, Dr T.,' she said, and kissed him…

LET'S TALK
Romance

For exclusive extracts, competitions
and special offers, find us online:

f facebook.com/millsandboon

◎ @millsandboonuk

𝕏 @millsandboon

Or get in touch on 0844 844 1351*

For all the latest titles coming soon, visit
millsandboon.co.uk/nextmonth